ONE
TOUGH
COOKIE

ONE TOUGH COOKIE

A Novel

DELISE TORRES

alcove
press

Published in the United States by Alcove Press, an imprint of The Quick Brown Fox & Company LLC.

Alcove Press and its logo are trademarks of The Quick Brown Fox & Company LLC.

Library of Congress Catalog-in-Publication data available upon request.

ISBN (paperback): 978-1-63910-378-2
ISBN (ebook): 978-1-63910-379-9

Cover design by Sarah Brody

Printed in the United States.

www.alcovepress.com

Alcove Press
34 West 27th St., 10th Floor
New York, NY 10001

First Edition: July 2023

10 9 8 7 6 5 4 3 2 1

To Michael
for accepting me as I am

SINGULAR COOKIES, INC.®

Where every cookie has a personality of its own

Breakfast cookies with functional ingredients
Ready-to-eat . . . All natural . . . No refined sugars

PERKY COOKIE

The energetic one, with coffee and dark chocolate

BRIGHT COOKIE

The smart one, with antioxidant-rich carrots, dates, and walnuts

MELLOW COOKIE

The laid-back one, with chamomile, lemon, and honey

FLIRTY COOKIE

The sexy one, with dark chocolate nibs, dried cherries,
and maca root powder

ACTIVE COOKIE

The sporty one, with high-protein whey powder, quinoa,
and peanut butter

What's your cookie personality?
Take the quiz today at www.singularcookies.com

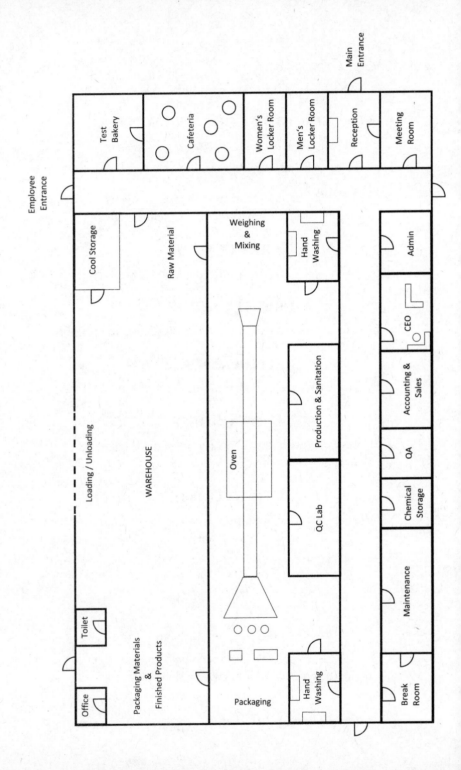

CHAPTER ONE

At Singular Cookies, Inc., cookies are like people, each with their own personality.

Karina's stomach grumbled for Perky Cookies. The coffee-chocolate breakfast cookie was energetic, ready to take on the day, much like Karina herself. It had saved her earlier after she'd overslept and couldn't make it to the drive-through for breakfast, but one was never enough. Now in her hangry state, she needed more before she punched somebody in the face.

Karina placed the packaged Perky on the scale and recorded its weight. A few more checks and she could leave for her midmorning break and gobble up the stash in her locker. She returned the cookie to the twelve-pack of singles and took it to the stainless-steel table beside her, where Cordelia stuffed it inside a carton.

The other three packers at the end of the wrapping machine were steadily collecting the individually wrapped cookies into twelve-packs. Marisa should be back from her break soon, and Cordelia was filling up boxes. Gloves in place. No hair sticking out of the hairnet. Smocks buttoned up. Check. Check. Check. Now on to her last checks and then *food*.

Cordelia gasped so loudly Karina could hear her over the clatter of the wrapping machine. "Look at him." She slapped Karina's arm and pointed to their left at the plastic strip curtains covering the warehouse entrance.

"Who?" An inspector? Why had nobody warned her? She craned her neck for a better look.

"The new mechanic," Cordelia said in a dreamy voice. "Ay, Dios mío, está buenísimo. Super-hot. Just your type."

Karina slumped in relief and glared at her. Cordelia was fanning herself, eyes closed, a big smile on her face.

Ugh. "Don't start." How many times had Karina told her she didn't want to date anyone from work? Cordelia was so consumed by the idea of "soul mates," she couldn't understand Karina was happy on her own. Besides, knowing Cordelia, the new guy was probably average looking with—at most—a nice ass. If Cordelia had a cookie named after her, it'd be Drama-Queen Cookie, with lots of sprinkles and colors to call attention to itself.

Cordelia slapped her arm again. "¿Sabes qué? You should pretend there's something wrong with the equipment so they send him in and you can check him out."

"You're crazy, you know that?" Karina stuffed the pen into the clipboard, ready to get away. "I'll see him when I see him. The company's not that big." Which was exactly why she couldn't date anyone here. With only thirty-three employees in the place, she'd never be able to escape him. She preferred her men far away once they reached their expiration date. And after what happened with their old quality assurance manager—

The sound of Cordelia's tape gun sealing the carton snapped Karina back to the present.

"Oh, you'll change your mind once you see him." Cordelia waved dismissively. "And don't worry. I'll have all the deets on him by lunchtime."

"Whatever."

Karina's safety shoes echoed through the cavernous space as she began her trek back to the mixing room, the noise of the wrapping machine fading in the distance. To her right stood the cooling tunnel, the conveyor belt inside transporting the cookies from the oven to the packaging room. To her left, the mechanics were installing the new production line—with their crap all over the place! A wrench, a dirty cloth, and a bottle of lubricant blocked her path.

"You guys, keep your chemicals away from my production area. How many times?" She picked up the lubricant and shoved it into one guy's chest as he approached. "This better not be here when I come back." She kept walking. Damn contract. Their CEO had big dreams for the company, and Karina needed to be supportive, but just because Lacey wanted to sell to every Whole-Mart in the country shouldn't mean Karina had to babysit a bunch of mechanics who couldn't pick up after themselves. She had more than enough added to her workload with the extra checks, thanks to the new quality assurance manager and his "improvements." Everyone was fed up with the additional documentation they had to do, all in the name of passing the food safety inspection Whole-Mart required for their suppliers.

The coffee-sweet smell of the fresh-baked Perkys from the tunnel oven made her stomach groan. *Soon, belly, soon.* If it weren't against the rules to eat in the production area, she'd grab a bunch from the conveyor belt and stuff them in her mouth.

She checked on the guys in the mixing room. One was weighing the espresso powder, two were adding oatmeal and flour into the mixer to start a new batch, and another was rolling the mixing bowl with prepared dough to the dough feeder. Uniforms clean. Hairnets. Gloves. No spills. Check—

The guy rolling the bowl tripped, pushing it away. Karina ran and caught it before it bumped against the dough feeder.

"Tyler, what the hell? Don't tell me you're hungover again." She spun toward him, ready for a rant, but then stopped at the sight of him pressing a hand against his head.

"I'm sorry," he said. "I'm kinda dizzy."

He *had* looked pale the last couple of days, but he was always so cheerful, so she'd assumed it was due to a lack of sleep. He was twenty-six, a party boy if there ever was one. But this seemed more serious than a simple hangover.

"Come sit." She led him to one of the stools by the scales. "Did you have breakfast?"

"Yeah. I don't know what's going on with me. I've been feeling weak lately."

"Maybe you should take the rest of the day off and go to the doctor."

"That's way overboard, don't you think?" He stood. "Look, I'm fine." He wobbled and held on to Karina to keep steady.

"You don't look fine to me." She helped him to sit. "I better see a doctor's note tomorrow, or don't even bother showing up. Got that?"

He nodded.

"And you"—she pointed at the guys who'd gathered around them—"make sure he goes home."

Karina rolled the mixing bowl to the feed unit, where it was lifted into position, then tipped, allowing the cookie dough to fall into the funnel-shape feeder. As the fresh-cut cookies dropped onto the conveyor, she scooped one up and placed it on the scale. Ninety grams. Perfect. Only the oven left to check, and then she could eat. She entered the oven room and peeked at the temperature display.

It read 348°F.

According to the Perky recipe, it should never dip below 350°F.

"Are you fucking kidding me?" Karina looked through the data recorded over the last hour. About forty-five minutes ago, the temperature had dropped to 349°F. Fuck. Why hadn't the alarm rung? She reset the oven to the correct temperature and waited. Her stomach growled. "Hurry, you stupid oven." A few minutes later, the temperature rose to 352°F. At least the oven still worked. But that probably wasn't the end, with all the procedures they had to follow.

This better not take too long.

She picked up the binder with the HACCP plan from the table in the corner and found the section for corrective actions. The hazard analysis and critical control points plan was their go-to guide for cases like these, although Karina hardly ever used it. The last time the oven malfunctioned, the alarm had rung at 350°F and they'd been able to salvage the cookies before any real harm took place. Now, according to the plan, she needed to stop the line and separate out the baked cookies so they couldn't get sold.

Sighing, Karina called the mixing room.

"Don't put anything in the dough feeder," she told the guy who answered. "There's something wrong with the oven. And stop the line. Where's Roy?"

"In the warehouse, I think," he said.

Karina pressed a trembling hand to her forehead. Roy Cooper could never stand still or stay in his office like a production manager should. No, he needed to supervise every other area of the plant, especially the warehouse. Karina always had to run around after him. But not today.

"If you see him, tell him to come to the oven room right away."

Next, she called maintenance and asked them to send a mechanic. Then the quality control lab, where she told Natalie, one of the technicians and her housemate, to put a hold on the lot.

What else? She scanned the plan. That seemed to cover all the steps, but now she had to fill out the corrective actions section of her checklist, listing everything she'd done. Fuck, why couldn't this happen after her break?

The oven temperature remained steady at 352°F. No sign of any malfunction. *Stupid oven. You're just messing with me, aren't you?*

Roy stomped into the room. "Karina, I can't hear about the oven from one of the guys. You must come find me." He smoothed down the wrinkles on his face with his hand.

"I was busy writing this." She handed him her notes.

He cursed under his breath as he read. Roy was a Grumpy Cookie, made with raisins that would put you in a bad mood when you confused them with chocolate chips.

"Wait just one minute," he said, looking up. "What do you mean I can't sell these cookies? I'm counting on them for an order."

Karina raised both hands. "Don't look at me. I only followed the procedure."

"Over two degrees?" Roy scoffed. "We'll see about that. Did you tell the doc?"

He meant their new quality assurance manager, Dwight Johnson, who had a PhD in food science. "No."

"Good, good. I'll go get him. Stay here and wait for the mechanic."

Looked like Dwight was in store for another confrontation with Roy. The two had been at each other's throats since Dwight started working at the company three months ago. And with good cause. Roy should call Dwight out for the extra work he was making them do.

Karina glanced at the display. Already ten. She should've gone on break fifteen minutes ago. *That mechanic better be here soon.* Since Roy was the one in charge, she could leave once he came back.

A cool breeze whooshed in as the door opened. Karina turned, and her breath caught in her throat. The mechanic strolled in, but he wasn't any mechanic. This was the new guy. For once, Cordelia hadn't been exaggerating. He was as smoking hot as a rack of barbecue ribs. Mouthwatering. The overalls he wore fit him to perfection. Even the hairnet looked good on him.

He smiled at her. "Karina, right? I'm Ian. What's the problem?"

Wow. Those dimples. And the way he said *Ian*, with emphasis on the *a*, not the *i*, was so sexy. Not to mention the slight Spanish accent and his gruffy voice. Definitely a Sexy Cookie, with decadent, smooth chocolate and cayenne pepper for extra heat. She could almost taste it—

"Karina?" Ian waved his hand in front of her eyes. "I can't fix it if I don't know what's wrong."

"Oh. Right." She actually wiped her mouth with the back of her sleeve. *Get a grip, Karina. It's not like you've never seen a hot guy before.* "The oven . . ." His intense gaze made her stomach flutter. And not from hunger. She cleared her throat. "The temperature's not supposed to dip below three hundred fifty degrees." She handed him her notes.

He frowned as he looked through them. "Hmm, well, there must be something wrong with the programming." He reached into his bag for the oven manual and leafed through it, stopping to read.

Karina wiped the sweat off her forehead with her sleeve. Was it always this hot inside the oven room? Ian's brow furrowed in concentration as he read. Karina licked her lips.

"Shouldn't an alarm have gone off?" he asked.

"Um, yeah. But it didn't." Could she sound any dumber?

He put the manual aside and accessed the control panel. After a few clicks he said, "It smells delicious in here. What's the name of this cookie?"

"The Perky."

He turned toward her, crossing his arms and leaning against the oven. "The names here are so cute. 'What's your cookie personality?'" He echoed the company's slogan with a laugh, and the dimples came out in full force.

Wow. Those dimples made him look both sexy and adorable. How was that possible?

"You know," he continued, "I thought working here would be more of a bakery. I imagined people making cookies by hand and all that, but this is similar to the supplement producer where I worked before. Sterile and industrial."

"And is that a bad thing?"

"No. But I was looking forward to a change . . ." He shrugged. "At least it smells good. And I like that we can buy the product at a discount. Not that I eat much cookies." He slapped his abdomen. "Have to stay in shape."

"I bet." She gazed at his abs and bit her lip. They must be rock hard. His whole body probably was.

"How long have you worked here?" he asked.

"Me?" *Of course he means you. Snap out of it.* "Since it started. Nine years ago. I'm one of the originals: me, Roy, and Lacey."

"You must love it."

"It's a job, keeps food on the table, you know."

"But don't you like being a part of something like this, watching it grow?"

She shrugged. "I guess." There had been a time when Karina felt like she was part of something special, something important. Back when Lacey had recruited her to work for her newly founded company, when Karina would assist with coming up with new cookie recipes. But then the company had grown and they'd moved to this plant and the magic was over. Karina was relegated to production, because how could a high school dropout with only a GED consult on the product anymore?

Ian had a curious look on his face, as if he were reading her mind, so she straightened and added, "When we started, we sold the cookies to neighbors and friends, then we moved to a commercial kitchen and sold to supermarkets, and it was like you said, more of a bakery. Lacey and I would make the cookies and bake them. And then we moved here, and we added all of this equipment and people. Now, if we pass the upcoming inspection, we'll be selling Singular Cookies all over the country."

"Wow, that's great. Sounds like you made a lot of progress in a short amount of time."

"I guess." She shrugged. "I liked it more before. It was . . . cozier. More intimate. And now, we're bigger, but not too big. For me, that's enough growth, but Lacey wants more, so . . ."

"You must share her passion," he said. "To stick with her all this time, I mean."

"Nah, not really. Lacey's the one with the dreams. I just do whatever she needs me to."

"Well, then she's lucky to have you on her side."

Karina nodded, even though she wasn't so sure. Lacey didn't rely on her as much anymore, except to follow orders. That was the cost of progress, she guessed. Karina had just been the first employee, nothing more. And she shouldn't complain. If she hadn't worked as a maid for Roy and met his niece, Lacey, where would she be? Still scrubbing other people's toilets for a living, probably. That had been an okay job, but this was more respectable. And even if she wasn't smart enough to be part of the inner circle anymore, she had a steady paycheck and a good salary, working for a company she believed in. Plus cookies.

Ian's intense gaze brought her back to the present. One more step and they'd be close enough to kiss. His lips were tempting. She craved a bite of Sexy Cookie.

Roy barged in, followed closely by Dwight and Lacey. Karina jumped. Ian spun to face the control panel. What the hell was she doing, flirting with a guy at work? Hunger must've been making her delirious.

"You know what's wrong with the oven yet, kid?" Roy asked.

"Working on it." Ian stood stiffly, eyes on the oven, no sign of the laid-back guy he'd been a few seconds ago. What she'd give to be that control panel . . .

"May I have this?" Dwight pointed at the clipboard in Karina's hands, and she gave it to him. He looked ridiculous with not only the hairnet but a beard net around his mouth to cover his goatee and mustache. "Let's see what we got here." He adjusted his glasses. "Forty-five minutes? That's quite the deviation." He handed the checklist to Lacey.

This was Karina's chance to leave. Roy could handle this. Ian glanced sideways at Karina, giving her another flash of those dimples.

Mmm.

Why did she want to leave again?

CHAPTER TWO

Roy and Dwight argued back and forth about whether the cookies were safe to sell.

"I don't give a rat's ass if it's written in the HACCP plan!" Roy yelled. "I'm not gonna throw away two pallets of cookies that are perfectly fine. I need to fulfill my orders."

"The cookies didn't bake at the correct temperature and may be contaminated," Dwight snapped. "The HACCP plan is designed to assess these types of risks and reduce them. If you had a problem with it, you shouldn't have signed it."

Whoa. Karina forced her gaze away from Ian. No way would she miss her first Dwight-Roy blowout fight.

Dwight was gritting his teeth and scowling at Roy, who scowled back, towering over him. Karina had to admit—Dwight had balls. Roy might be an old guy in his seventies, but he was ex-Navy, intimidating even when in a good mood. Still, that didn't mean Dwight was right. He sounded as if Roy were some dumb employee who couldn't read, when it was Roy who'd developed their whole process. Dwight was an Arrogant Cookie—a chocolate-chip caramel nut extravaganza that didn't taste as good as it looked.

"Why don't we calm down?" Lacey stepped between them, her face flushed pink. She was always the Mellow Cookie, a chamomile-lemon one, pleasant and soothing. "What does the HACCP plan say we do with the cookies?" she asked Dwight.

"We can sell them for processing into animal feed."

"That's not so bad, Uncle." She raised a hopeful eyebrow at Roy. "We'll get some revenue through that."

"Not as much as we'd make if we sell them to our customers. And also the overtime we'll have to pay to make them again." Roy pulled at his hairnet. "We're already stretched thin as it is. We may be late on our other orders as well."

Lacey gave Dwight a questioning look.

Dwight shook his head. "It's too much of a risk."

Lacey put a hand on Roy's arm. "Dwight is more familiar with the HACCP plan than we are, so let's trust him on this."

Roy's jaw slackened. He had every right to be shocked. Frankly, so was Karina. Lacey had always trusted her uncle's judgment and his years of experience in the food industry, but all of a sudden she was pro-Dwight, who'd landed here right out of his PhD program?

Roy pulled at the collar of his smock. "Well, not all of us have time to memorize every little detail of these procedures." He glared at Dwight. "But that's what your fancy degree is for. Isn't that right, Doc?"

Another stare-down. So far, this confrontation was epic. So worth staying for. If only there were popcorn. Ian tapped the control panel, but he too was spying on the action.

"There is no need to memorize it." Dwight grabbed the binder with the HACCP plan from the table in the corner. "That's why we keep it accessible." He turned to Karina. "I take it you read this to know what steps to follow?"

Karina gave a slow nod.

"You documented it beautifully." He gave her a reassuring smile. "Well done."

Even though he was complimenting her, Karina didn't want to give him any points, so she remained impassive. Roy grunted.

"Ian," Lacey said. "Do we know what's wrong with the oven?"

"Actually . . ." Ian clicked on the control panel. "Think I found the problem. Somebody changed the program parameters."

"What?" Karina shoved him aside so she could see. He was right. Someone had set the oven to drop two degrees after operating for ninety minutes.

"Who has access to the control panel?" Dwight asked.

"Only Karina and me," Roy said. "But she's the one who operates it."

They stared at her. Did they think this was her fault? Her body went cold. The nerve of them. As if she didn't go above and beyond all the time. She crossed her arms. "I never change the parameters. I choose the program and press start."

Lacey placed a hand on Karina's shoulder. "Anyone can make mistakes. We know you wouldn't do this on purpose."

Karina pulled back. "I don't make mistakes. And if I did, I wouldn't lie about it." Didn't Lacey know that about her? She was the one who'd always told Karina she was capable of more, who'd convinced her to take the GED so she could work at Singular, but now Karina was dumb enough to make such a stupid mistake and not even know it?

"It's not that we don't trust you, Karina," Roy said.

It's exactly like you don't trust me.

"But if it wasn't either of us," he continued, "who was it?"

"Beats me."

So much for being like family. That's what Roy and Lacey were always telling her, inviting her over for holidays and special occasions, trying to fill the void left after Karina's mom threw her out at seventeen when she became too much of a hassle.

Her chin trembled, and she turned her head to gaze out into the production area. It shouldn't surprise her. Families betrayed you when you least expected it. Though Karina had never bought their act. They were only doing it out of pity. Why else would they? This was just more proof. They didn't believe her when it counted.

She shouldn't care so much what they thought of her anyway. They were her bosses, nothing more. Lacey would never fire her, either.

She was too loyal to her employees and believed in second chances. Plus, Karina had earned pity points for being the girl nobody wanted.

Unless she did mess up and the pity ran out.

Karina wiped her hands on her smock. Had her hunger this morning made her change the program?

Ten thousand cookies.

Her eyes locked with Ian's. He seemed worried for her, concerned lines all over his forehead. Karina's breath evened and she straightened. Not even hangry would she do something so stupid. Her routine was locked into her brain.

"What about the mechanics?" she asked, glancing at Ian. "They have access."

"I can check the maintenance records," Ian said. "I have them here." He reached into his bag for his clipboard and leafed through the papers. "According to this, the last preventive maintenance was on December thirteenth." He removed a sheet and handed it to Roy.

"And we haven't done the Perkys since." Karina bounced with excitement. "That's gotta be it."

She and Ian grinned at each other. Those dimples again. And his lips . . .

Roy stepped between her and Ian to access the control panel. "Let's see if they changed any other programs."

Lacey examined the PM record and shook her head. "They're probably overworked, trying to balance everything. I'll have a talk with them. Now that Ian's here, it should help lighten the load."

Why had Karina been so worried before? Lacey was taking the blame, like she should. If it hadn't been for her Whole-Mart contract, none of this would've happened.

While Lacey and Dwight looked over Roy's shoulder, Karina stared at Ian as he made notes on his clipboard. She had the urge to throw herself at him, kiss him for his help. But that would be unprofessional. And so unlike her. She didn't drool over guys; guys drooled over *her*. What made this guy so special?

"Everything else is in order," Roy said. "I changed the program back to the correct settings."

"Good," Lacey said. "Now that we've resolved this issue, why don't we head over to the lab to look at the cookies and continue our discussion civilly?" She directed a pointed look at Roy, then turned to Karina. "I'm sorry if I doubted you before. I know you'd never lie about something like that." She winked at her before she and the men stepped out.

Karina beamed and sighed in relief. Crisis averted.

"Diablo," Ian said. "Is it always like this?"

Karina laughed. "It's this damned contract. It has everyone on edge."

"Not you. You were able to think fast and come up with an alternative." His eyes lingered on her, as if he were checking her out, which was impossible with her body indistinguishable underneath the smock. "You saved the day."

Her heart thumped fast against her chest. Was she having a heart attack? Probably too much time spent in the heat. "I should get back to work. I have to tell the guys to turn the line back on."

He frowned, looking confused. "Sure, just sign here."

Her hand shook as she scribbled her name. He was standing too close. As she gave him back the clipboard, her stomach let out a huge growl that echoed in the small room.

They both laughed.

"I missed my break," Karina explained.

"Ay, bendito. Go and eat. You deserve a break after all your hard work today."

She couldn't help smiling. Why was he being so nice?

"Maybe I can join you?" he asked. "I haven't had my break either."

Karina straightened. This was getting out of hand. "Uh, I still have to write down what happened. I'll probably wait until lunch."

"Aw, too bad. Maybe some other time?" He raised an eyebrow.

Karina smiled like an idiot. Instead of saying no and putting a stop to this charade, she only managed a weak shrug.

"Great. See you around, Karina."

He waved good-bye. She stared at his ass as he left.

What a man.

Too bad he was off-limits.

CHAPTER THREE

Karina was famished by lunchtime. She rushed into the cafeteria and rummaged through the refrigerator for Cordelia's cool bag. Most days Cordelia brought Karina leftovers, since she loved people eating her food and the praise that came with it. And since Karina didn't cook but loved to eat, it was the perfect arrangement.

Karina opened the bowl. Her mouth watered at the sight of lasagna. Cordelia made the best lasagna in the world.

As she waited for it to warm up in the microwave, Marisa came in and ran to her. "Is it true you changed the programming of the oven so you could meet the new guy?" she asked, flustered. "Cordelia meant for you to pretend, not to actually damage the equipment."

"What? Where did you hear that?" They were still blaming her?

"Rosa told us. Cordelia's out in the hallway with her. So, is it true? Will you get in trouble?"

"Ugh, no. It wasn't me."

Marisa sighed in relief. "Oh, good. I knew you wouldn't do something like that." She removed her bag from the refrigerator.

Knowing Rosa, she'd probably overheard Lacey and Roy talking about what had happened while performing her custodian duties and given it her own malicious spin. That fucking crone. Always in her business ever since Karina had hooked up with her nephew and supposedly "broken his heart." Rosa should focus on keeping the plant clean and her mouth shut. But she was Popular Cookie—a macaron that ended up everywhere and that everybody liked so much they couldn't control themselves around it.

The microwave beeped. As Karina grabbed the steaming bowl with a napkin, her housemate, Natalie, came in, followed by Nicholas, one of the dough preparers, who also ate lunch at this hour. Karina was glad Tyler, his usual partner in crime, had listened to her and was nowhere to be seen.

Karina and Natalie sat with Marisa at their usual table by the window, while Nicholas ate silently at a table closer to the entrance, under the framed photo of a Perky Cookie, part of the set of five that decorated the cafeteria walls. They were the only ones from production having lunch at this hour. Since the process was continuous, employees had to take breaks in small shifts. Karina had used her perks as a supervisor so she and the girls could eat together. They'd gravitated toward each other due to being around the same age and the only Puerto Ricans in the company.

Karina moaned at the first bite of lasagna. "You guys need to taste this."

"I'm good." Natalie munched on her salad. Everything she ate was raw. She was more a rabbit than a person.

"You know I can't do just one bite," Marisa said.

"Try it." Karina offered her a forkful. "You won't gain weight from one piece."

"I can't. I'm starting a low-carb diet today." She gestured at her meal of tuna, eggs, and tomatoes. "I need to get rid of these saddlebags once and for all." She pouted and pinched her hips. Insecure Cookie, a plain thing hiding the yummiest chocolate filling inside. Karina would kill for those curves, but no matter how much she ate, her french-fry body wouldn't budge.

Anyway, she shouldn't complain. If it hadn't been for Marisa's eternal dieting, Karina wouldn't be eating this lasagna now. It was Marisa who Cordelia used to bring leftovers for, but when the food turned out to be too rich for her weight-loss plans, Marisa had suggested Cordelia give them to Karina, so she would eat something substantial instead of the "junk" she usually ate.

"What you need is a workout regimen to go with it," Natalie told Marisa. "Eating low-carb is a lifestyle, not short term. You have to stick with it if you want to see results."

"I know, but it's so hard." Marisa took a sip of Diet Coke. "How do you do it?"

Karina stuffed herself with lasagna while Natalie gave Marisa tips on eating like a farm animal. Although, with her toned arms and abs, it was hard not to take her seriously. She was their own Bright Cookie, wholesome and hearty, full of carrots, dates, and nuts.

Natalie gulped down half the water in her reusable bottle. "Did you hear Dennis changed the programming of the oven?"

"It was Dennis?" Of course Karina would miss this tidbit, what with staring at Ian the whole time.

"Roy and Lacey were talking about it in the lab."

"Oh no, poor guy." Marisa palmed her cheeks. "Are they going to fire him? He's so close to retirement."

"Lacey was more concerned than angry," Natalie said. "I doubt it goes much further than a friendly chat. They'll probably have him on work-order duty from now on."

Cordelia strolled in straight toward them. Once she reached their table, she crossed her arms against her full figure. "You started without me?"

"We only have half an hour, and you know I can't resist your amazing, orgasm-inducing lasagna." Karina stuck another piece in her mouth and gestured a chef's kiss. It always helped to lay it on as thick as possible so that Cordelia would keep bringing her food.

As expected, Cordelia beamed and, without another word, got her bowl from the refrigerator and took it to the microwave, her long ponytail swaying behind her. She pulled her dress pants up and straightened her flowery blouse. Karina had told her on her first day not to bother dressing so fancy, since she'd have to wear a smock the whole day, but Cordelia had responded, "Perdona, sae, but I have a duty to look fabulous no matter what."

Marisa twisted in her chair to face Cordelia. "Rosa was wrong. It wasn't Karina, it was Dennis."

"Who cares about that anymore? I have the lowdown on the new guy," Cordelia said in a singsong voice as she salsa danced in place.

"Not this shit again." Karina rested her head on her hands. They'd had this same conversation about their old QA manager, Leonard, plus Dwight, and every other single guy who'd started working there.

"His name's Ian. He's Puerto Rican, twenty-eight years old—perfect for you, Karina, just one year older—and most importantly, very, very *single!*" She shrieked and waved her arms in the air before sitting next to Karina. "He asked about you."

"Ooh." Natalie elbowed Karina on the side. "He already has a crush on you?"

Karina's face burned. "Who did he ask? Rosa?"

"Who else?"

"Great." So by now, even Lacey knew Ian was interested in her.

"What did he ask?" Natalie asked.

"He wanted to find out more about her."

"And what did Rosa tell him?" Karina asked.

"Well, you know she doesn't have hairs on her tongue." Cordelia made a face. "She told him you like to play."

"She really told him that?" Karina asked. It was the truth, but it made her sound so slutty. And although she wasn't ashamed of her casual lifestyle, it bothered her that Ian already thought of her that way.

"Don't worry," Cordelia said. "She said he still seemed interested despite her warnings, so he'll probably make a move soon."

"What are you going to do if he asks you out?" Marisa asked. "You'll say yes, right?"

"Wrong," Karina said.

"Why?" Marisa asked.

"Because we work together, duh."

"Just because you blew it with Leonard," Cordelia said, "doesn't mean it can't work with Ian."

Why bring Leonard into this? For all anybody knew, Leonard had had a crush on Karina that had gone unrequited, since she'd never given him a chance. If they knew the truth—that she'd hooked up with him once out of pity—they'd never stop hounding her. *He told you he loved you, but you didn't want a relationship, so he quit?* they'd say. *What's wrong with you?* they'd be really asking, looking at her with pity in their eyes. And with Cordelia's gossiping, it would get back to Lacey, and how would *she* react? Would knowing Leonard left because of Karina be enough grounds to fire her?

She shook those thoughts aside. "You only want to set me up to have gossip material."

Cordelia gasped and pressed her hand to her chest. "How dare you accuse me of something that is only partially true?" She grinned and waved dismissively. "Believe it or not, I care about your happiness, Karina. I want you to find your soul mate, like I did."

"Soul mates don't exist. You found someone you liked enough to settle down with, but I don't want to settle down. You all know this." She looked at each in turn. "Anyway, I don't know what you're so excited about. With what Rosa told him, he probably only wants to hook up."

"Or maybe it's love at first sight."

Karina rolled her eyes. "Spare me."

"Are you really going to say no to *that*?" Marisa asked. "I saw him on my way back from break this morning, and he's so dreamy."

"There are more hot men out there. I'll survive."

"Hot men like that?" Marisa asked. "I mean, my Jaime's pretty hot, but he's not that hot."

Ugh, in what universe is Jaime hot? Karina scraped the last bits of lasagna from the bowl to keep from blurting it out. Marisa's boyfriend was a drunk, unemployed loser who lived off of her and took advantage of her good heart, but after Karina said as much during Cordelia's destination wedding weekend in Puerto Rico, Marisa had asked her to butt out. That had been a month and a half ago, and Karina was trying her best, but whenever she heard Marisa acting all googly eyed and making excuses for him, it made Karina's blood boil.

"Is he really *that* hot?" Natalie asked. "I need to see this guy."

"If she doesn't want him," Cordelia said, "maybe you should make a move."

"No, he already has the hots for Karina. I wouldn't want to get in the way. For all I know, he'll be *the* one to finally rid her of that fear of intimacy she has going on."

"Ugh, please. You and your psychobabble, always trying to analyze me. I'm not a case for you to solve."

"But you show the signs. You can't discuss anything emotional, you go from one guy to the other, you can't show any weaknesses. And then there's all this anger. Where is it stemming from?"

"Will you just stop?" Karina burst out of her chair. "I'm not afraid of anything." She stomped to the sink and threw the bowl inside.

"You should listen to her, Karina," Marisa said in a small voice. "Natalie knows what she's talking about."

"Just because she has a psychology degree doesn't make her an expert, especially not on me." As she washed the bowl, the feeling of the suds between her fingers helped keep her breathing even. Why did she have to hang out with these girls so much? All they did was try to change her. Karina dried the bowl and lid and returned them to Cordelia's lunch box. "You know what, Nat, you can have him. I don't care."

Leaving them to their gossiping, Karina headed back to the production area. As she rounded a corner, she almost bumped into Dwight.

"Sorry." He adjusted his glasses. "I was about to come find you and say thank you for everything you did. If you hadn't followed the procedure or dismissed it as only two degrees, we would've been in much bigger trouble, not to mention the possibility of a recall or worse—a food outbreak with people getting sick."

Karina shrugged. "I was just doing my job."

"But you kept your cool and did everything as written. That's worth gold to me." He smiled. Karina had to admit he had an awesome smile, with perfectly even, white teeth. He was around Karina's age, but with dress pants and his shirt buttoned all the way up, he looked like a high school principal twice his age.

"Listen," he continued, "I'm fixing to put together a new HACCP team, and I think you'd be a fantastic addition. We meet for an hour once a month to discuss food safety topics and improvements to the plan. Would you be interested?"

A boring meeting and more work? Her decision was an obvious choice, like eating when hungry. "Not really."

"Oh."

"You can ask Natalie; maybe she's interested." Natalie was the smart one; what could Karina contribute? She started to walk past him but stopped when she remembered his fight with Roy. "Hey, what are you going to do about the cookies? Are you going to sell them for animal feed, like you said?"

"That's what's written in the plan."

"But you can change it, right? Isn't that what the meetings are for?"

"We can discuss it, sure, but I think that's part of the problem. I'm assuming the former QA wrote the plan on his own, and Roy and Lacey signed it without discussing the details. He probably did that with most procedures, and that's why nobody's clear about what they have to do."

Karina stiffened. "Leonard was good at his job." He hadn't acted all superior or tried to undermine Roy every chance he got.

"I don't doubt it. But his approach . . ." He leaned closer to Karina and lowered his voice. "I've noticed the procedures are outdated, even though they should be revised yearly. He changed the style and reprinted them, but they're not accurate. Do you know anything about this? Lacey told me you worked closely with him."

Too closely. But that was probably not what Lacey meant. There was no way she could know. "I just answered his questions. He was always asking me about the procedures so he could revise them, so maybe you're the one who's not familiar with them yet."

He jerked his head back. "Oh, I apologize. I meant nothing by it. It was something I noticed." He cleared his throat. "Are you certain about not joining the team?"

"Positive." She stared at him, waiting for him to let her pass. When he still stood there, she added, "I have to go back inside now. Bye." She walked past him into the dressing area.

Arrogant asshole. She put on her smock and hairnet. He didn't know how hard Leonard had worked—how hard all of them had worked—to get this far. She wet her hands at the sink and scrubbed them roughly with soap. Leonard had created those procedures from nothing while Dwight got everything handed to him. She dried her hands and entered the processing area.

It was as if Dwight was trying to change everything just to prove he could do it better. Why had Leonard had to leave? If he hadn't, they could have been focusing on what needed to be done instead of trying to rewrite the past.

CHAPTER FOUR

When four PM hit, Karina couldn't get out fast enough. Since Roy always did the last checks, she could leave with the rest of the production employees.

"You guys want to go to a bar?" Karina took out her black leather jacket and turquoise fanny pack from her locker in the women's bathroom.

"On a Tuesday?" Cordelia was already rummaging through her cosmetics bag.

"We haven't gone out all this month. Let's be spontaneous."

"I can't." Marisa combed through her wavy hair. "I promised Jaime I'd pick him up."

"Did he finally get a job?"

"No," she mumbled. "He's at a friend's house today." Marisa returned the comb to her floral handmade tote.

"Oh, right, how silly of me." Karina stepped aside to let another woman pass.

"And I have to go home to my hubby, you know that." Cordelia stood close to the mirror taped to the back of her locker, carefully applying foundation. Every day before they left, she had to do a full makeup routine. The personnel hygiene rules forbade employees from wearing makeup, perfume, jewelry, or nail polish inside the production area, but that didn't stop Cordelia from being Cordelia.

"Natalie, come on," Karina said. "Skip the gym and come with me."

"What if I meet the man of my dreams today?" She put on a headband, flattening her tight curls.

"Maybe you'll meet him in the bar."

"I don't want a guy who hangs out at a bar on a Tuesday."

"You guys are so lame." Karina dropped onto the long bench between the two rows of lockers, shoulders slumped, and waited for Natalie to exchange her work yoga pants for her gym yoga pants, as if they looked any different. Her car was at the shop this week, and Karina was on chauffeur duty. The noise from toilets flushing, running water, and slamming locker doors eased as the other packers left.

Karina sighed, and powered up Candy Crush on her phone. Ever since Cordelia's wedding, their friendship—if that's what it even was—had changed for the worse. Cordelia couldn't step away from her new "hubby" for one second. Natalie had become obsessed with finding "the one," turning her into a serial dater who spent hours creating visual boards to inspire her for when the day finally arrived. And Marisa had distanced herself from Karina for speaking up against Jaime. He was still in the picture and seemed like he always would be. He'd proven time and time again what a loser he was, preferring to spend his days lying on the couch playing video games instead of looking for another job to help pay the rent. And when he got extra cash, he spent it on beers for himself and his buddies. But Marisa "loved him" and believed he was "trying his best." Ugh.

She'd go to the bar alone. Who needed them anyway? Karina only relied on Natalie for rent for the small house they shared and on Cordelia for food, but that should be it. It had been a mistake to hang out with them so much. Time to return to how it used to be.

A text from her mom flashed across the screen.

We're celebrating Lily's 10th birthday at home on Saturday. Want to come? It'd be nice to see you.

Karina clicked dismiss and continued playing her game. Some nerve Debbie had, inviting her to a party for a sister she didn't know, in a house she hadn't grown up in, after throwing her out onto the street when she was seventeen. Did her mom really want to see her, or did she just want to show off the life she'd built without Karina? Debbie was another person she didn't need in her life. She was better off alone.

*   *   *

The parking lot was empty except for the cars belonging to the office employees who worked until five. Ian stood next to a white pickup truck. He smiled and waved at her when he noticed her.

"Karina," he said. "Can I ask you something?"

Cordelia gasped. "Guy works fast," she mumbled under her breath.

Karina veered in Ian's direction. "What's up?" It was hard not to stare at him. He was a vision in a brown leather jacket, jeans, and T-shirt.

"You want to get something to eat?" he asked.

"Now?" He really did work fast.

"You're not hungry? I'm starving." He wiped his hand across his flat stomach.

Oh, she could eat. And not just food. But he was off-limits. "I can't go now, looking like this, all sweaty from hanging around the oven."

"You look nice to me." He stared at her chest and laughed. "I like your T-shirt."

Karina glanced down at the slogan, which read *There's nothing a good curse word won't fix.* She arched her back and messed up her black hair. Ian perked up and took notice. Now he could see what she looked like without that ugly smock. French fry or not, she always brought it.

Remember Leonard.

She straightened. Ian was still checking her out.

"Look, I like you, Ian—"

"So you do like me," he said with a grin.

"But we can't go out."

He frowned, then laughed. "I don't get that. If you like me, we should definitely go out."

"I mean, it's not a good idea. We work together."

"You think the bosses won't approve?"

"It's not that. I don't want to mix work life with private life. I-I've done it before," she stammered. "Anyway, it could get messy."

"I don't mind messy." He grinned and gazed into her eyes.

Karina stopped breathing. She glanced at the cloudless sky to compose herself. "I don't mind messy either, but not at work. You get it now?"

"No. Let's get a bite to eat. I'm not asking you to marry me. I only want to feed you. Do I have to curse to get you to say yes?"

She tried not to grin, but it was impossible. He was adorable. One night with him wouldn't hurt. And who was she kidding? She wasn't the kind to play hard to get or say no to a guy she was attracted to. She couldn't let what happened with Leonard ruin her chances. This wouldn't be a repeat. Ian hadn't known her long enough to be secretly in love with her. Plus he already knew from Rosa the type of girl she was.

"Why did you ask Rosa about me? She hates me, you know."

"Oh." He winced and rubbed the back of his neck. "Sorry. I only wanted to know if you were single."

"And you're okay with casual, right?"

"Me? Oh, sure. I can do casual. I just got out of a serious relationship, and casual is exactly what I'm looking for."

Karina relaxed. What more assurances did she need? They were both on the same page. She could ask him to join her at the bar, but that would make her seem too eager. Better play it cool. "Okay. I'll go out with you. But not today. How about Friday Fest? I was thinking of going anyway. You can tag along." Friday Fest was a monthly celebration in Fort Pierce with food and music. Karina never missed it.

He seemed confused by this but then shook his head and grinned. "Sounds like fun." He pushed himself off the truck and stepped closer, his hands on the back pockets of his jeans. For a moment, Karina thought he was going to kiss her, and she held her breath. "See you Friday, Karina, if I don't see you before." He held her gaze for a moment before turning to leave. Karina let out her breath slowly as he hopped into his truck, admiring his tight ass.

The girls were waiting next to her car, far enough away they couldn't possibly have overheard. They were probably itching to tease her about Ian and romanticize the whole encounter. She couldn't prove them right.

"I'll save you the trouble," Karina said as she approached them. "He asked me out, but I said no."

"Then what was with all the posing?" Cordelia asked.

"Hey, it's me. I had to give him something. Now go home and stop bothering me."

Marisa looked at Karina with pity before heading to her car. Cordelia stayed put, her eyebrow raised. "Liar."

Karina crossed her arms. "What's it to you? Go home to your hubby. Weren't you in a big hurry to get back to him?"

"Ugh, why do you have to suck the fun out of everything? Is it so bad we want you to go out with the hot new guy?"

"It's my life. I decide who I date. You're jealous because you're married and can't date whoever you want."

"I'm not jealous. If anything, you should be jealous of me. I found my soul mate, while you'll probably end up alone."

She made it sound as if being alone were the worst thing in the world, as if marriage were the ultimate goal and a woman couldn't be happy staying single.

"I'd rather be alone than tied to someone for the rest of my life."

Her life was perfect, and she had no intention of changing it. No way would she end up like her mother. Throughout Karina's childhood, her mom had hammered into her that "you don't need anyone but yourself," "being alone is better," and "love makes you weak," but at the first sight of Bob, she'd abandoned her paralegal studies and become his Stepford wife.

"You're impossible." Cordelia turned her back on her.

"Whatever. Let's go, Nat."

They both got into Karina's car.

Karina put the key into the ignition. Why couldn't Cordelia accept Karina wasn't like her, that she didn't want to give up her life for a man, that she was happy not having to answer to anyone but herself?

Natalie put on her seat belt. "Why did you say no? By the way you two were looking at each other, I could tell there was a spark."

Karina usually tuned Natalie out when she started talking about "the spark"—that elusive feeling she needed for her to know if a guy had potential to be "the one"—but this time she perked up. There *had* been something there, a deep feeling of attraction, a sort of breathlessness. But it was probably because she was due to get laid, nothing more.

"You've been watching too many rom-coms."

"No, there was definitely something there." Natalie took out her phone and fired up her favorite social media site. "If you weren't so jaded, you would've seen it." She scrolled through photos of wedding dresses to pin to her boards.

Karina rolled her eyes and exited the lot.

CHAPTER FIVE

The next day, Cordelia the Drama Queen Cookie didn't bring extra leftovers. It seemed Karina couldn't speak her truth without being punished.

Luckily, Lacey invited her for lunch in her office, something they rarely did anymore. They hadn't had lunch together since the early days of the move to this plant, what with Lacey's hectic schedule and Karina being relegated to production.

They sat on the light-pink sofa Lacey kept to make visitors feel welcomed, fast-food bags on the coffee table in front of them. Karina ripped open the bag and dug into her burger, while Lacey slowly unwrapped hers. She and Karina shared the same complexion, dark-brown hair and eyes. Back when they worked at the commercial kitchen, a deliveryman had confused them for sisters, which Karina had laughed off. Besides their looks and their commitment to Singular Cookies, they had nothing in common. Lacey was seven years older, more conservative, and from a wealthier background.

Lacey ate a dainty bite from her burger. "I invited you to lunch today because I need your help. Dwight told me you rejected his offer to join the HACCP team?"

So this wasn't a friendly lunch to catch up but more of a business meeting. Karina bit her lip. *What am I so upset about? Lacey's my boss, not my sister.*

"I didn't think it was a big deal."

"He thinks you're the perfect choice, and frankly, so do I."

"I don't want the hassle."

"The hassle or the challenge?" Lacey took a sip of water and turned to face her. "Why is it always so hard for you to believe in yourself? Didn't you pass the GED when you didn't think you could? Haven't you been a wonderful floor supervisor for the last seven years?"

And yet, you doubted me just yesterday. Karina stuffed three french fries into her mouth. There'd been a time when Karina had believed in Lacey, when she'd striven to better herself and make Lacey proud, like she had back in high school when her mom was studying to become a paralegal. But her mom had set her aside after Bob came along and it got too complicated, and so had Lacey.

"That was then and this is now. I've reached the end of my capabilities. Maybe you want more for me, but I don't."

Lacey put down her burger. "I'll tell you what—if you won't do it for yourself, do it for me. The inspection is only five months away, and to pass, Dwight needs to have this HACCP team, and it can only be you. We can't spare anyone else from production, and you're the most qualified after my uncle. He doesn't want to be on the team anymore."

"Why would he, with Dwight leading it? They'd be at each other's throats all the time."

"So, will you do it?"

Karina took a huge bite of her burger and focused on chewing. Crap. She couldn't say no to a direct order or to Lacey, period, and Lacey knew it.

Karina glanced at the photos on the wall across from them, an assortment of family moments and company milestones. There were Lacey and Karina with the first batch of Perkys prepared in the commercial kitchen Lacey had rented when she got serious about the company. To its right was a photo of the two of them and Roy at the ribbon-cutting ceremony for moving into this plant two years later. That was the beginning of the end of their tight-knit team. Now with the contract, another expansion was on its way. A new line, more people to supervise, more distance from the top.

"Fine." Karina wiped her mouth and crumpled the paper wrapper, throwing it back into the bag. "I don't understand why you're giving yourself so much stress over this inspection. Isn't it voluntary?"

"Whole-Mart requires it for their suppliers."

"But why do we need this contract at all? We're okay like we are now. We don't need to grow more." She ate the last fry and flattened the empty carton.

"You sound like my uncle. He wanted me to wait with the contract; he doesn't think we're ready for such a rigorous inspection. Dwight doesn't think so either."

"If *he* doesn't even think we're ready, why not cancel it?"

"There are penalties involved, and frankly, I don't want to. It's now or never." Lacey dabbed her mouth with a napkin. "In business, you grab every opportunity that comes along, and that's exactly what I did. Dwight thinks we should've had everything ready before we scheduled the inspection, but I didn't count on Leonard leaving so soon after we signed. I wasn't going to tell Whole-Mart, 'No thanks. Maybe in a few years.' That's not how it works. I know Dwight still has to adjust to how we work around here, but if he'd stop questioning everything, I'm sure he could handle it."

Karina slurped the last of her soda, turning her attention back to the photos. There was Leonard with the rest of the group at the last company picnic. He was standing close to Karina, grinning at her instead of the camera. Stupid boy. Of all the times to leave, it had to be right as they were preparing for the inspection. And for what? Because it supposedly broke his heart to see her every day and know he couldn't have her? That was the reason she'd slept with him in the first place—to give him a treat. He was her friend, and she liked him. But she'd never suspected he was in love with her. If she had, she never would've taken it that far. Even though she hadn't wanted him to leave, she couldn't give him what he wanted. Not only because it would've been a huge mistake—she could never love him the way he loved her—but because love had no place in her life. It made a mess of everything, and Karina wanted to keep her life as uncomplicated as possible.

Lacey bit off a piece of burger. She was only halfway done, her fries untouched. Still hungry, Karina grabbed a packaged Perky from the tray on the coffee table, ready for visitors to sample. She bit into it, and the combination of coffee and chocolate worked its magic, easing her tension.

"I also need you to help Dwight work well with my uncle," Lacey said. "You know how he is."

Karina almost choked and coughed. "Dwight's the one changing everything we worked so hard to establish. Just because he has a doctorate doesn't mean he knows better than us. He wasn't here from the beginning like we were. He doesn't know."

"He knows other things. And he has good intentions. He wants us to pass the inspection, and that's all that matters to me."

Karina gaped. "How can you defend him when he's making Roy's life so difficult? Maybe it's time to find someone else, someone like Leonard who can get along with Roy and is not so disruptive."

"Or we can give Dwight a chance. He has good ideas. My uncle needs to listen more to him."

"What's going on with you, Lacey? We're supposed to be on Roy's side."

"I'm on the company's side." Lacey put the last burger bite aside and turned to face Karina. "That's why I want you to help them work together. We need all hands on deck."

"And what happens if we don't pass the inspection?"

"We have to. If we don't . . . not only will we have to pay the penalties, but I don't think Whole-Mart would be interested anymore. We'd appear incompetent, unable to deliver."

"How big are the penalties?"

Lacey pinched her eyebrow. "You don't want to know."

"Enough for the company to go under?"

"I hope not."

Karina's eyes bulged, and she chewed some more Perky. What had Lacey gotten them into? Karina had supported her through it all, but now Lacey's dreams could turn into a nightmare that would affect everyone. What would Karina do if Singular closed? Who would hire her? Would she even find another job as good as this one? She wiped her clammy hands on her jeans.

"Don't worry. I'm handling it." Lacey latched on to Karina's hand and squeezed. "But in order to succeed, we need to work as a team. Will you do that?"

Karina gazed at Lacey's smiling face. In the past, even the smallest reassurance from her would've been enough. But with the distance between them and now her siding with Dwight over Roy, Karina wasn't sure she should. In the end, Lacey was her boss, and Karina had to do what she said.

"I'll try," Karina grumbled.

"I'll take that as a yes." Lacey stood and walked over to her desk. "I'll let Dwight know you changed your mind."

Karina pointed at the table. "Are you going to eat your fries?"

"Go ahead."

Karina gobbled them up while Lacey called Dwight. After she told him the news, Dwight replied over the speaker, "Thank you, Karina. You'll do great, you'll see. The meeting's next week. I'll keep you posted."

"She can't wait to get started." Lacey made a face at Karina. "I'll see you later?"

Dwight cleared his throat. "Yes. Of course."

Lacey came back to the sofa, her face flushed, a small smile on her lips. She finally finished her burger, then said, "We still have a few minutes before you have to go back in. How are things going with you? I hear there's romance in the air between you and our new mechanic."

What was this now, gossip time? Lacey knew Karina wasn't the romantic type, that she was happy being single. Sure, they used to talk about sex and relationships, but in general terms. What was Lacey so interested about? Maybe there was a rule about dating coworkers? "He asked me out. That's okay, right? It doesn't break company policy?"

"No. We have nothing against dating. At least, I don't think we do. I'll check." She leaned over the side of the sofa to grab a Post-it from her desk, and jotted a reminder. "I need to hire an HR person. I don't have time to keep these rules straight." She grinned at Karina. "And? Do you like him?"

Karina shifted in her seat. "I just met him."

Lacey leaned back, supporting her head on her fist, a wistful look on her face. "Those early days are the best. There's so much potential and anything is possible." She sat up and took Karina's hands. "Oh, Karina, I have to tell someone or I'll burst. I actually met someone too. I don't know if it's right or if it will work out, but I'm so excited for what could be."

Alarm bells rang inside Karina's head. Lacey was stepping over the boundaries. The times when they would gossip like this were long gone. And Lacey was never this gushy. If there was one thing Karina admired about Lacey, it was her focus on the company and its success and not on men. She was the sort of independent woman Karina's mom had raised Karina to be, the ideal her mom had then turned her back on.

After Lacey's husband left her for another woman, she'd sworn off men and developed the Perky Cookie, paving the way to a booming business. Proof of what women could accomplish when they weren't preoccupied with men.

"You should focus on the inspection and keeping us afloat, Lacey." Karina stood. "I should get back to work."

Lacey visibly deflated. "Of course. Go ahead." She wiped the bangs away from her eyes.

Karina stumbled out of the office. The fries threatened to come out, and she pushed down the guilt she shouldn't be feeling. Lacey was her boss, not her sister. She never was and never would be.

First her mom, then the girls, and now this. What was wrong with every woman in her orbit?

CHAPTER SIX

Friday Fest was *the* monthly event in Fort Pierce, at least for Karina. Marina Square was overflowing with food trucks carrying all sorts of deliciousness: Greek, Latin, American, but above all else—barbecue.

Karina headed toward her favorite truck, munching on Flirty Cookie. The tanginess of the dried cherries complemented the smooth, dark chocolate chips. There was only a hint of the nuttiness of maca root powder, which was supposed to induce libido. Not that Karina needed any help in that department, but it couldn't hurt to increase her stamina for the night ahead.

The weather was amazing for a Florida February with clear, sunny skies and cool fresh air. Karina was the first in line at her favorite truck. Her mouth watered as Joe handed her a large carton full of his signature fall-off-the-bone, spicy-sweet-barbecue-sauce ribs. If only she could have these every day instead of once a month. Then her life would be truly perfect.

She settled on a bench overlooking the Indian River and dug in, turning to look over her shoulder now and then for Ian. The memory of their brief interaction on Tuesday had her revved up, and she couldn't wait to munch on Sexy Cookie for dessert.

Almost done with the ribs, she turned to find Ian's dimpled smile a few feet away. A piece of meat stuck in her throat, and she coughed.

"You okay?" He tapped on her back.

"I'm fine." She straightened and wiped her mouth with the back of her hand.

"I see you already started." He pointed at the carton in her hand.

"Oh, yeah. I was hungry. You want one?"

"Sure." He took one and chewed into it. "Mmm. Delicious." He licked the excess sauce on his lips.

Mmm, indeed. "You want the last one?"

"Eat it. I'll go get my own."

"No, let me. The guy knows me. He'll give us a discount." Karina chewed off the last bone, threw the carton in a nearby trash can, and led Ian to the barbecue food truck. She ordered one batch for Ian and another for herself, along with a corn on the cob. If it upset him that she paid, he didn't show it. Sometimes guys got weird about that.

They returned to the bench, Karina stealing glances at him as they ate in silence. He chewed each rib carefully, sucking it down to the bone, then licking his fingers before going on to the next. Would he lick her that thoroughly later? She shivered.

Once they finished, Ian bought sodas, and they wandered through the square. It was slow going with people crowded in front of the booths, checking out the self-made purses and candles, watching their kids at the bounce house, or waiting in line for food.

"I haven't been here in a while," Ian said.

"Really? I come every month."

"You always come alone? What about your friends, the girls I saw you with the other day?"

"They're not really my friends; we're just coworkers. Besides, they prefer to spend their free time with their men." She moved to the side to avoid bumping into a woman yelling at her kid. "I prefer to fly solo."

"Well, I'm glad you made an exception for me tonight." He smiled.

Trying not to slobber at those dimples, Karina walked ahead of him to buy churros. She offered to buy a pack for Ian, but he refused.

As she gobbled the first one, he said, "I was wrong about wanting to feed you. Where do you pack it all in, woman?"

Karina laughed. "I'm one of those freaks who stays thin no matter how much I eat. You hate me?"

"A little. I guess what you need is nourishment. I need to nourish you."

Karina's skin flushed. She knew he was talking about food, but he made it sound so much sexier.

They stopped in front of the stage, where a local band was playing "Super Freak." The sun had set, and the lampposts around the square emitted a soft glow. Karina threw away the empty pack and wiped her hands on her jeans. Time to get physical.

"Let's dance." She dragged him closer to the stage, joining the other dancing couples.

His hands circled her waist. Much better. But there was still too much space between them. And he was so stiff.

"I heard you're Puerto Rican," Ian said.

Karina nodded. "My mom moved us to Orlando when I was two."

"And you've never been back?"

"I went in December for a wedding but only for a weekend." She shrugged. "The beach was nice."

"Ah, but there's so much more to see." His eyes brightened. "I miss my island so much. There's no other place like it in the world."

Cordelia always said the same thing. To Karina, it hadn't been so special. Of course, Jaime and his constant complaining—instead of being grateful his girlfriend had paid for him to go—had soured the whole experience.

"What about your dad? He still there?" Ian asked.

What was with all the questions? Ian didn't need to know she'd never met her father, that he'd never tried to contact her, even though he knew she existed. "I don't have one. Let's leave it at that."

"Sorry, didn't mean—"

"It's okay. Can't miss what you've never known, right?" And if her father didn't care, neither would she.

39

"Can't imagine my life without my dad," he said. "He's my best friend. I talk to him every day."

Good for you. Why was he telling her this? Guys didn't get so personal when they only wanted to hook up.

Oh. Her stomach clenched. Of course. He was a Relationship Guy. He'd warned her when he mentioned his past relationship, but she hadn't been paying attention. Karina glanced toward the stage to hide her annoyance. Relationship Guys were the worst to get rid of. Leonard was proof of that. Normally, she'd cut the date short, but Ian had told her he wanted casual, and she'd been looking forward to having sex with him all week. She couldn't give up when she was so close.

"You have any other family here, besides your mom?" he asked.

More questions? *Relax, Karina. This is probably his normal MO.* "I don't need family. I can take care of myself."

"Everyone needs family."

"Not me." The only family she'd ever known was her mom, and Karina was better off without her. Only good things had happened since she'd left home. Having the freedom to make her own decisions had led her to become part of Singular Cookies, and she wouldn't trade that for anything in the world.

Ian pointed behind her. "Look, there's Rosa." He waved.

Karina pulled his arm down, but it was too late. Already, Rosa was leading her husband toward them. Damn it. Karina had never seen Rosa here before, but of course they had to run into each other when she was with Ian. She moved to Ian's side.

"Ian, so nice to see you again." Rosa stood on her toes to kiss him on the cheek, and Ian bent forward so she could reach him. While the men shook hands, Rosa wrinkled her nose at Karina, as if she were a cobweb in her freshly cleaned space. "Are you two on a date?"

"What? No." Karina glanced sideways at Ian. "We ran into each other, right, Ian?"

He frowned at Karina's insistent expression but said, "Right."

Rosa eyed each of them and scratched her short salt-and-pepper hair. "Mm-hmm." She pursed her lips. "Well, have fun. See you Monday." She smirked as she waved good-bye.

Crap. Now the whole plant would know about her and Ian. Might as well go on as planned and make the night worth it. She grabbed Ian and resumed dancing, now to the beat of "It's Your Thing."

"Why didn't you want her to know we're here together?" he asked.

"Because I want to keep work and personal separate, remember? But enough about her." She stroked his hair, and her fingers got stuck on the surface. "Wow, how much gel do you put on?"

He chuckled. "Enough to keep my hair from running wild."

"You don't like being wild?" She pressed closer to him, rubbing her leather jacket against his.

He glanced up at the band. If he'd had lighter skin, it'd be obvious he was blushing. How could a guy this hot be a boring, uptight Relationship Guy?

"Uh . . ." A nervous laugh now. "I've never been the wild type."

"Maybe we can change that." She wrapped her arms around his neck and rested her head on his chest. Kissing him would probably scare him off. It was a tight balance with these guys. If she came on too strong, they got intimidated and couldn't deliver, but if she was too timid, they'd never make the first move, and she'd have to go home to her vibrator.

"I'd like that." He grabbed her hips and swayed her to the music.

She looked up at him. Okay, this was more like it.

He spun her around, and she fell back into his chest. Their mouths were inches away and she was about to kiss him when he pushed her back and twirled her around. He held on to one hand, his other at her waist, and began some intricate steps that she recognized as salsa from having seen Cordelia dance so much. She followed him as best she could with no idea what she was doing, but his steady hand on her back guided her through the moves. By the time the song ended, she was out of breath.

"Wow," she said. "What was that?"

"I guess I can be wild sometimes." He gave her a shy smile.

"Looks like it." His chest rose against his jacket as he caught his breath. Karina wanted to rip it off right then and there.

She was about to suggest they go back to his place when he asked, "Why don't we go to Crabby's and get a drink? Freshen up?"

Karina stared longingly at his body. She yearned to touch him so much, to feel his lips on hers. But if he needed more time, she was game. The last thing she wanted was to ruin the momentum. She agreed.

* * *

Crabby's Dockside was located down the pier next to Marina Square.

The restaurant filled up quickly. With no alcohol sold at the fest and it ending so early, the festive mood needed to continue somewhere. They grabbed a table overlooking the marina and ordered two beers.

She unzipped her jacket, exposing her T-shirt with the slogan *Ride me to the finish line.*

He stared at her chest. "I see you have some expectations for tonight."

"I do. Can you deliver?"

"I'm confident I can give you the ride of your life."

Holy shit.

"But," he continued, "we have all night. For now, let's enjoy our beers and this view."

"I don't like to wait."

"Do you want that ride or not?"

Damn him. She sipped from her beer. It was like he was keeping her hostage. But she so wanted that ride.

"So, what else do you like to do for fun?" he asked. "Besides coming to the Friday Fest every month?"

Karina shrugged. "I like going to the beach. The sound of the ocean relaxes me."

"I love jogging along the beach and being in nature. I have a home gym, but sometimes I just need to be outside."

"I'm the opposite. I love being in bed under the covers."

"So you're a lazy girl, huh?"

"A Lazy Cookie. One that melts in your mouth so you don't have to chew."

He laughed.

"Which cookie are you?" she asked.

"Sorry?"

"From Singular. Every cookie has a personality of its own."

"I've only tried the Active one."

Of course that would be the only one he'd tried. It had whey powder, and with his body, he probably mostly ate protein crap. "So, is that you? We all have a type. Cordelia's Perky, Marisa's Mellow, and Natalie's Bright, 'cause she's the smartest."

He leaned forward, resting his elbows on the table. "And what are you?"

"Haven't you figured it out?" She stroked his thigh.

He smiled, his dimples teasing her. "Flirty."

"I actually inspired it; did you know that?" She winked. Lacey had wanted a cookie to match Karina's boldness and sensuality, so she'd sought the perfect ingredients to match.

"You don't say." He didn't look at all surprised.

"And of course, the quiz says that's my type, but my favorite is the Perky. I can't live without coffee."

"There's a quiz?"

"On the website. Haven't you read our ad? Why don't we go to your place and fill it out?" She gulped down her beer and stood. "Come. I want to see where you live."

He narrowed his eyes and slowly finished his beer. "Sure, let's go."

*   *   *

Karina followed Ian in her car down South Indian River Drive to a small beige wooden house with white trim in a well-kept neighborhood about a fifteen-minute drive away. Inside, the walls were also beige, with dark wooden floors and an open space plan. A Puerto Rican flag hung on the wall, and the built-in shelves were full of photos of Ian with what she assumed was his family.

"You live here alone?" Karina asked.

"Yes. I bought the house cheap and fixed it up myself."

"Wow, really?" This was her cue to get the hell out of there. A guy with a house of his own was ready to start a family. *He told you he wants casual. Chill.* But it was a risk to be involved with this type of guy. The sooner they got started, the sooner she could leave.

"Want something to drink?" he asked.

"No, I'm okay." She sat on his brown leather couch and patted the space next to her. "Why don't you take off your jacket and sit here next to me?"

When he shrugged off his jacket and she could finally see some skin, the wait was totally worth it. His arms looked like they could rip through his T-shirt with only one bicep curl.

He sat next to her. She straddled him.

He brushed his hand down her arms, causing tingles down her spine. "We don't have to do anything. We can just talk."

Such a Relationship Guy thing to say. "I don't want to 'just talk.' I want to fuck."

"Whoa, okay." He laughed. "Direct and to the point." He threaded his fingers through her hair. "I like that."

"That's me."

She reached for his belt.

"You don't waste time, do you?"

"Why wait? I'm ready to go, and"—she palmed his crotch and smiled—"so are you."

He removed her hand and moved her higher on his hips so that his erection pressed between her legs. He rocked her against him, making her moan. "I like going slow."

"Why?"

He chuckled. "Humor me. Or do you have other plans?" He cupped her face and kissed her.

His lips were soft and strong. Warm. Inviting. She sighed and leaned into him. Karina had always considered kissing a step to starting the action, nothing more. But the way he teased her with his tongue and his teeth, demanding but withholding, made her both alert to his every move and foggy, like in a dream. Who knew kissing could be so exciting?

He lowered her to the couch and ran his hands all over her body, alternating between soft caresses and rough grabs, tugging at her hair, making her crazy. She tried to push against him so she could take control, but he pressed his whole body weight against her, pinning her to the sofa.

"Come on," she said. "I'm burning up."

"Not yet."

"When?"

"The anticipation's the best part."

"What kind of bullshit is that?"

"You'll see." He bit her ear, and she moaned. Since when was a bite on the ear so erotic?

Karina had never been a fan of foreplay. She was always ready, and it seemed like an unnecessarily long wait to get to the good stuff. But the way Ian kissed her, the way he touched her, could almost convince her of its merits. Almost.

"Ian, I need you to fuck me right now."

He chuckled. "Come on." He stood and extended his hand to her. If it weren't for the bulge in his pants, she wouldn't know he was aroused. How could this guy be so relaxed when she was dying?

They fell onto his bed. This time he explored her body with his mouth instead of his hands, stopping only to remove items of clothing. By the time he licked between her thighs, she was trembling all over. When he stopped right before she came, she screamed in frustration.

"You're killing me."

"Not much longer now." He stood beside the bed.

Her anger evaporated at the sight of him undressing. *Wow.* His body was more amazing than she'd imagined—smooth, lean, and sculpted to perfection. He sat next to her and tore open a condom wrapper.

"Wait, let me look at you." She got him to lie down and ran her hands across his ripped chest and abs. "I need to do things to this gorgeous body before we do anything else."

She took him inside her mouth and it was glorious—how he clenched his legs as she sucked, his hands on her head, his moans. Karina could've done that for hours, but her ache for him couldn't wait much longer. She rolled on the condom and slid him inside.

"Holy shit," she said.

"See?"

It was as if she were a dead cell phone being charged back to life, her body vibrating and pulsing everywhere. Every fiber of her being felt raw, exposed. She rode him hard, unable to contain the surging need inside her.

"Fuck, I'm coming."

"Slow down." He rolled on top of her and slowed the pace.

"But—" Her back arched and she moaned. The sensation grew stronger, more intense, but there was no release in sight. It was torture. "I hate you." But how could she hate him when she loved everything he was doing to her?

She moaned and screamed and writhed under him until finally, *finally*, she orgasmed. If him sliding inside her was a charge, this was an electric shock. Her body convulsed. It was the strongest orgasm of her life.

After their breath evened, he moved the hair out of her face. "You okay?"

"Are you kidding? I'm amazing." Her body shivered with aftershocks.

He laughed. "I meant, you thirsty, hungry, want anything?"

"No, I'm good."

He stroked her face and traced her body with his fingertips.

"That feels good," she said.

He continued tracing circles around her belly. "You can spend the night, if you want."

"I don't do sleepovers."

"But you can stay a little while?"

"Hmm."

He shifted her so he could spoon her, his hand continuing its tracing motion.

Oh no, not a cuddler. She should've known. Karina needed to make her escape; she couldn't encourage him. But she was too weak to move. And his sheets were so soft.

She yawned. "Your bed is really comfy."

"Then go to sleep." He kissed her shoulder.

"I can't. I have things to do tomorrow."

She closed her eyes. The faint smell of an ocean breeze filled her nostrils. When had she gotten to the beach? No, not the beach—somewhere else, somewhere safe. Maybe she was floating atop a cloud, protected from view, warm and cozy inside.

CHAPTER SEVEN

Karina woke up alone in a strange bed.

Fuck. She'd slept over. *No, no, no.* She shot up and dressed. Damn bed. It was all its fault. According to the clock on the nightstand, it was already ten. Hopefully Natalie thought she was asleep in her room and she could sneak in, pretend everything was normal.

Karina used the master bathroom, and when she came out, she jumped at the sight of Ian entering the bedroom with a tray full of food.

"You leaving already? I made you breakfast."

"I can see that." Breakfast in bed; was he kidding? Once a Relationship Guy, always a Relationship Guy, no matter what he'd told her.

"Come. Eat."

She never let food go to waste, but damn it, she should get the hell out of here. The smell of bacon filled her nostrils, and her stomach grumbled. There was no other choice but to sit on the bed.

He placed the tray on her lap. Scrambled eggs, toast with butter, strips of bacon, and a steaming cup of hot coffee. Her mouth watered, and she dug in. Ian lay next to her wearing only his tight boxer shorts.

48

His body was truly amazing. She took in every rippled muscle and let her eyes linger on his crotch. She forked in a huge lump of eggs. "Did you eat already?"

"Yes. I'm used to having a protein shake for breakfast."

"Ah. You're one of those."

"One of those what?"

"I was with a guy like you once. He lived in the gym and only ate protein crap. Do you even eat bread, or did you go out and buy it for me?"

"For your information, I'm nothing like that guy, whoever he is. I told you; I have a weight room here at home, I enjoy jogging at the beach, and I do eat bread." He paused. "Once in a while. I freeze it so it doesn't go bad."

"Oh, okay. You're nothing like him. Except that you're a complete muscle body. I mean, look at you. It's ridiculous."

"You don't like my body?" He rubbed his hand across his six-pack.

"Oh, I didn't say that." Her fingers itched from the memory of the feel of his muscles. *Get your mind out of the gutter before you stay for round two.* She sipped her coffee and kept her gaze focused on the tray. It was white wood with small foldable legs, the type they showed in those lame romantic movies Natalie loved to watch.

"Why do you have this tray?"

"What do you mean? I bought it in Whole-Mart."

"I mean, do you eat in bed a lot? Or is it to be all romantic and make breakfast in bed for the girls who spend the night?"

He grinned. "Maybe a little of both."

"And what is up with this bed?" She spread her hand across the white sheets. "Do you spray it with something to get girls to sleep over so you can use your tray?"

He looked down at the sheets. "I . . . bueno, the sheets are made of bamboo. They're softer than cotton. And, uh, I actually use a linen spray." He dug a spray bottle out of the drawer of his nightstand and handed it to her. "It helps me sleep."

The label on the bottle read *Sea Salt Oil*. She sniffed it. It smelled like a warm summer day near the ocean. "I knew it." She stuck out the fork at him. "You're a sneaky bastard, Ian."

He laughed. "And you're something else." He kissed her hand.

"What does that mean?"

"Nothing. You're different from the women I usually date."

Date. She'd turned a one-night stand into a date by lingering. Why was she still here, chatting so much? She stuffed the last of the food into her mouth.

"Still hungry? I can make more."

"No, this is good." She moved the tray to the floor. "I need to go. I have to take Natalie to pick up her car from the shop."

"Oh. I thought . . ." He pulled her back into the bed. "Last night was phenomenal." He climbed on top of her. "You have to go right this minute? I won't go as slow this time." He kissed her.

You have to go, Karina. Don't let a man ruin your plans. She pulled him closer.

* * *

She woke up in his arms to the faint ringing of her cell phone.

"Shit. What the fuck? What time is it?" She got out of the bed and tripped over the tray, its contents banging loudly as they hit the floor.

"Diablo. What's going on?" Ian rubbed his face and sat up.

Karina put on her underwear and ran to the living room. She dug her phone out of her purse. One missed call and a couple of texts from Natalie.

Where are you? Are you okay?

I'm worried. Please call me.

Fuck. It was already one. She'd wasted half the day. Karina texted back—*On my way*—and returned to the bedroom. "I need to go." She stopped walking at the sight of Ian standing at the foot of the bed, completely naked with a full-on erection.

"Everything okay? Was that Natalie?" He walked toward her.

She put her hands up. "No, stay away."

"What? Why?"

"You . . ." She gestured down at his body. "I can't waste a perfectly good hard-on."

He grinned. "Then don't." He kissed her neck.

"Fuck." She moved her hand along his length. What was it about this guy that she couldn't let go? Why were his lips so enticing she had to kiss him? What was it about his taste that she couldn't have enough of it? She'd been with plenty of hot guys, but this guy's body hypnotized her.

She dropped to her knees, slid him into her mouth, and moaned. The pressure of his hands against her head and the tension of his legs as she sucked him drove her wild. When she released him, he dropped to the bed.

"Wow." He let out a huge breath. "That was incredible."

Karina wiped her mouth and smirked. "There's more where that came from." What was she saying? She couldn't let this last more than one night.

He gave her a sleepy smile. With his satisfied face and rumpled hair, wild curls over his forehead, he looked adorable. Her heart skipped a beat.

"When will I see you again?" he asked.

"At work sometime." She pulled on her jeans and T-shirt.

"No, I mean . . . like this."

"I don't know." She stuffed her feet into her shoes. "Let's be spontaneous. I gotta go." She ran out of the house, got in her car, and drove away.

Why did she have to say that? Now he'd think she wanted to see him again. But she did want to see him again; that was the problem. She should've lain down next to him and had sex all day instead of driving away like a bank robber. What was going on with her? Did she like him? Her heart beat faster.

What the fuck? Was her heart trying to sabotage her?

No, Heart. I can't like him. Not him, not a Relationship Guy, not the guy I work with, the one I won't be able to avoid when I grow tired of him.

If she grew tired of him.

Would she grow tired of him?

She was shaking from head to toe when she got to her house. Natalie was watering the plants she insisted they keep all over the house, because "green was life," although it made Karina feel like they were living in a jungle.

"There you are." Natalie stepped off the ladder. "Where were you?"

Karina made a beeline to her room. "Let me take a quick shower, and we'll get out of here."

Natalie followed. "The shop closes at five. We have time." She crossed her arms and leaned against the doorframe. "So, did you meet someone at the fest?"

"I don't want to talk about it."

As she rummaged through her dresser for something to wear, she could see Natalie's grin from the corner of her eye. Karina wished for the hundredth time she lived alone, but a roommate was the only way she could afford a place this nice.

"Come on, Karina, spill. Don't make me beg."

"There's nothing to tell. I hooked up with a guy and fell asleep at his place." She headed to the bathroom.

"And you've been asleep all this time? Come on, tell me. This guy must be special if he got you to spend the night. Was it, like, the best sex of your life? So great you couldn't get enough?"

Karina stopped and turned around. "Fine. It was amazing. An incredible one-night stand."

"Why one night? If there was a spark—"

"It was Ian." The secret would be out on Monday; it was useless to hide it. She could still taste him, feel his touch over every inch of her body.

Natalie's jaw dropped. "So Cordelia was right? You lied to us?"

"I wanted you guys off my case. Anyway, he's a Relationship Guy, and I don't want a relationship. End of story."

"But—"

"It's already decided. I don't want to hear one more word about Ian." Karina tried to close the door on her, but Natalie pushed and came in.

She wagged her finger at Karina. "You like him."

"No, I don't."

"Look at me."

Karina shut her eyes.

"Ha, I knew it."

"It's not funny. I don't want to feel things for him." For any man. It was a weakness, a disease.

"Oh, I think it's too late."

Karina tipped her head to the ceiling. It couldn't be too late. It was only one night. She couldn't let a man she hardly knew wreak havoc on her mind and body like this.

Natalie took her by the shoulders. "Hey, this is normal. You're allowed to have feelings for a guy."

"But why him? We work together. What do I do when I see him again?"

"You say hi, and if he asks you out again, you say yes."

"If I say yes, he'll expect a relationship," Karina said.

"Would that be the end of the world?"

"Yes." After what happened with her first, Jason, back in high school, she'd sworn a man would never hold so much power over her. And she'd kept her promise all these years. Seeing her mom become a different person after she fell in love with Bob had only solidified that she needed to be vigilant.

Natalie frowned and let go of her. "You really believe that, don't you? Something traumatic must've happened to you as a child."

Karina curled her fists and stomped her foot. "Don't start with your psycho bull—"

"Okay. Sorry." Natalie took a deep breath. "Maybe it'll fizzle out. Sometimes that happens."

"But what if it doesn't?"

"Then you deal with it when the time comes. In the meantime, you can enjoy being with him. Don't think about it."

"I can't not think about it. I thought about it on the drive here."

"Relax and let your emotions settle. With time—"

Karina groaned. "Forget it. I don't even know why I'm talking to you. Now, can you get the fuck out so I can take a shower?"

Natalie sighed and left. Karina shut the door and locked it. Why was she exposing her feelings to Natalie? If Natalie were in Karina's place, she'd be picking out a wedding date. Her dream was to find a man to lose herself in, to drown in. She'd never understand that was Karina's worst nightmare.

The hot shower washed away all traces of Ian and cleared her head. Natalie was waiting in the hallway, and before she could say one word, Karina announced, "I left it very casual with him, so he's not expecting anything. When I see him, I'll act like nothing happened. I can't let some guy affect me like this. I'm stronger than that."

Natalie shook her head. "Cordelia is so wise. You do suck the fun out of everything."

CHAPTER EIGHT

"How was it, Karina?" Cordelia asked on Monday, as soon as Karina sat for lunch.

"How was what?" Karina kept her gaze on the other side of the room, through one of the Plexiglas windows that divided the cafeteria from the test bakery. Lacey was in there, alone, making cookies. That could only mean she was developing a new one.

Karina's chest ached. She'd worked at this plant for seven years and had never stepped foot in there.

"Don't play dumb," Cordelia said. "I know you lied to us. Rosa saw you with Ian at Friday Fest, and knowing you, you didn't waste the chance. So how was the sex?"

Oh. That. So the rumor had already spread. Karina turned her attention to the leftovers Cordelia had brought her—rice, beans, and fried chicken—and mixed them together. "I don't know what you're talking about. We ran into each other at the fest." She took a forkful into her mouth.

"Sí, ajá," Cordelia said, looking not at all convinced. "Please. A otro perro con ese hueso. You don't have to tell us any details. On a scale of one to ten, how was it?"

Fifteen? Twenty? They'd probably broken the scale. Karina hadn't been able to think about anything else all weekend. Her face burned.

"Ooh, she's blushing." Marisa pointed.

"I am not."

"It was fabulous, wasn't it?" Cordelia said.

"And not only the sex, but him too, right?" Marisa said.

"Leave the poor girl alone." Natalie wrapped her arm around Karina's shoulder. "She has it bad, and she hates herself for it."

"No, I don't." Karina glared at Natalie.

"Aw," Marisa said. "When will you see him again?"

"She's not," Natalie said, "which is why we have to convince her to give him another chance."

"Por Dios, Karina, don't be stupid," Cordelia said. "He's gorgeous, you like him, you had tremendous sex—why would you ruin it?"

"Enough." Karina dropped the fork onto the table. "I'm done explaining this. No matter how many times I say, 'I don't want a relationship,' you keep trying to fix me up. Life doesn't revolve around all that bullshit. When was the last time we talked about something real? Like you, Cordelia, are you finally quitting here to open your own restaurant? Or you"—she pointed at Marisa—"when are you going to stop supporting that asshole you call a boyfriend and use that money for something you want, like sewing classes? And don't get me started on you, Nat."

They stared at her with wide eyes. Shit. Karina gazed at her half-eaten food. Tyler and Nicholas were raving about last night's Super Bowl game, oblivious to the dead silence that had fallen over the table across the room.

A lump formed in her throat; she wouldn't be able to eat one more bite. So much for keeping her mouth shut.

Screw them. What she said was the truth, and if they couldn't handle it, they couldn't handle her, and then what was the point of being friends, if that's what they even were?

"We just want you to be happy," Marisa whispered.

"I am happy. Are you?" Karina looked up at her.

Marisa's jaw slackened.

Shit, shit, shit.

"Maybe I'm not always happy, but I know what it's like to love someone—sometimes so much it hurts—but I get it. You don't want to open yourself up like that, and that's okay. But don't attack us when we're trying to help."

"You're not trying to help," Karina said. "You were teasing me."

"You always tease us," Cordelia said. "Look, it's your life. You can mess it up as much as you want."

"If by mess up, you mean be free to do what I want and not answer to anyone? Gladly."

Cordelia rolled her eyes. "You're impossible."

Karina was about to retort when she noticed a small smile at the edge of Cordelia's lips. The tension in Karina's shoulders eased. She picked up her fork and moved the food around the bowl. "But you still like hanging out with me, right?"

"Not when you're in one of your moods."

"Isn't she always?" Natalie asked.

"Sometimes she's worse." Marisa pressed her lips together, suppressing a smile.

"There you go again." Karina threw her hands up, then grinned. Maybe they *could* handle her. She resumed eating, then stopped. But hadn't she believed that once about Leonard? And yet as soon as she'd shown him she wasn't who he wanted her to be, he'd abandoned her. It would only be a matter of time before these so-called friends of hers abandoned her too, just like everyone else had before.

The door that led to the test bakery opened, and Lacey walked in, carrying a tray of cookies. "Hello, girls, would you like to try my newest creation? It's made with licorice root powder."

"Licorice? Yuck." The first time Karina had tasted licorice, the sickening medicine taste had turned her off for good.

Judging by the others' expressions of disgust, they shared her apprehension.

"It's a hot new flavor right now. Not to mention its wonderful functional properties, such as soothing gastrointestinal problems and acting as an antioxidant and anti-inflammatory. The root doesn't taste as intense as the candy. Try them."

They each took a cookie and bit into it. It was sweet. Too sweet. And somehow also bitter. Karina forced it down and drank from her soda to wash out the taste. "That's so gross."

Natalie glared at Karina. "I think what Karina means to say is . . . there's no balance between the flavors. I only taste licorice."

The others nodded.

Lacey's shoulders drooped. "My mom and I loved them, but we're fans of licorice. I'll see what the guys think." She walked over to Tyler and Nicholas. From their reactions, they were not impressed either.

Lacey returned to the test bakery, shutting the door behind her.

"What was she thinking?" Karina asked. "Licorice, of all things." Lacey was losing her touch. But Karina wasn't part of the development side anymore, so what did she know?

Cordelia finished the water in her glass. "This was a miss. That's for sure. But I've always wished I could be Lacey and try all sorts of cookie recipes and have people taste them. When I tell people I work at a cookie plant, that's what they picture. The sexy side. When I describe the reality—how the machines do most of the work and the noise they make all day—they're turned off pretty quickly."

"Well, that's the reality of making a food product on such a large scale," Natalie said. "Can you imagine how long it would take us to fulfill our orders if we did the cookies by hand? I think Lacey was smart to go this route rather than opening a bakery. It's less trouble. You don't have to make fresh cookies every day or worry they'll go bad before you can sell them."

"That was basically Roy's reasoning when he convinced Lacey to start a company," Karina said.

Cordelia sighed. "I wish I had a Roy by my side. I don't know anything about the business side of cooking. That's why me opening a restaurant is more of a dream than an actual plan."

"You could ask him for tips," Karina said. "Or Lacey. Not that she's the portrait of a brilliant CEO these days."

"What do you mean?" Natalie asked.

"Um . . ." She cleared her throat. "Well, look at her new experiment. And she did make a questionable choice by signing that contract with Whole-Mart."

"True," Natalie said. "She should've waited with that. The fact that we have to redo the procedures and create new ones says we're ill prepared."

"But the risk will pay off, right?" Marisa asked. "It's not like the company will go under if we don't pass the inspection."

"I hope not," Cordelia said.

"Me too," Karina said. "Just in case . . . it's not a bad idea to have a plan B. I'd go back to being a maid, and you"—she gestured toward Cordelia—"could open a restaurant."

Cordelia waved her hand dismissively. "I don't need to work. My hubby earns enough to sustain me."

"So you'd rather live off a man than live your dream?"

Cordelia raised her eyebrows and shrugged. "What do you want me to say?"

"If it came to that," Marisa said, "I guess I'd go back to stocking shelves at Whole-Mart." Her shoulders slumped. "My sewing is a hobby. I wouldn't be able to make much money off it."

"But you're so talented," Karina told her. "People would pay good money for your stuff—the dresses, custom curtains, tablecloths—all of it."

Marisa snorted. "Doubtful."

Why couldn't she believe in herself? That asshole Jaime must've done a number on her. "What about you, Nat?"

Natalie sighed. "I'd have to dust off my psychology degree and look for jobs again. But I doubt I'd find anything."

"What happened to saving money for grad school?" Karina asked.

Natalie gazed at her salad and mumbled, "I'm thinking of using the money for a wedding instead." She stuck a piece of radish in her mouth.

"But you don't even have a boyfriend!" Karina gaped at them. What was wrong with these girls?

"This is silly," Marisa said. "We'll pass the inspection. And if we don't, we'll always have each other's backs, right?"

"Right," Cordelia and Natalie agreed.

But Karina knew their relationship would never last without Singular Cookies.

*　*　*

When she entered Dwight's office later for the HACCP team meeting, there were already two people there, seated in front of Dwight's L-shaped desk: Scott, the warehouse manager, his blond head dipped as he tapped on his phone, and Ian.

He grinned when he saw her. What the hell was he doing here? She hadn't expected to see him so soon. Or to feel like she was melting under his gaze. There were two free seats: one at the far end next to Scott and one next to Ian. If she sat there, it meant she was interested in more, but if she sat far away, he'd think she was mad at him.

She sat beside him. "They dragged you here too, huh?"

"Don't know why. Must be my good looks."

"Must be." She smiled. Why was she smiling? She was supposed to cut him out of her life, not invite him back in.

"Sorry I'm late." Lacey hurried in and sat. "I was talking to a potential customer. Is everyone here?"

"Yes." Dwight handed out an agenda for the meeting. "Thank y'all for being here. I hope to be as brief as possible, since I know we have other things to do. I'd like to first discuss the issue we had with the oven last week." After summarizing what had happened, he continued, "The tests for the cookies came back, and they're safe, but we must sell them for animal feed according to our HACCP plan. I've retrained the mechanics so they don't change any of the programming. I've also added a step to the procedure requiring that a supervisor—that would be you, Karina, or Roy—should stay with the mechanic while he does the preventive maintenance."

"Does Roy know about this?" Karina asked. He hated to stay in one place, and the PM usually happened during start-up when she wasn't there to cover for him. How did they expect him to manage? Would she have to come earlier for this?

"He will." Dwight glanced at the agenda. "Next up—"

"When?"

Lacey peered around Scott. "I already approved the procedure. We will let him know when it's appropriate. Dwight, please continue."

So, discussion over? Lacey had asked Karina to help Roy and Dwight work together, but it seemed her actual plan was for Roy to follow Dwight's orders.

Dwight started talking about the inspection while Lacey leaned forward in her seat, as if to soak in his every word.

"According to the food safety certification program, we need to abide—"

"Sorry," Ian said. "What's that?"

"Ah, yes, Ian, you're new. Of course this should've been in your training, but we seem to have forgotten about it." He glanced at Lacey, who wrote something down. "Whole-Mart requires all of their suppliers to become certified by this program through an inspection. We already have the basics in place, but in order for us to pass, we need to meet all of the program's requirements, which are outlined here, in this code." He held up a thick stack of papers. "In my view, there are two major issues we should address. One is our training program, which I find lacking, as we've discussed, and the other is implementing an internal auditing program. Performing regular audits will help us identify issues we may be missing and try to fix them before they become a problem."

Blah, blah, blah. Dwight kept on listing other changes he wanted to make, then blabbered on about revisions to the HACCP plan. Karina glanced sideways at Ian, who was taking notes. He looked so yummy. Her hand itched to run through his hair, stroke his arm, his thigh . . . *Don't go there.*

Her gaze wandered around the room. Hanging on the wall behind Dwight were his diplomas, framed and lined up one on top of the other. The one for his doctorate was larger than the others, as if to say, *Hey, look at me, I'm a doctor.* What a pompous ass. Leonard had a master's degree, and yet no one would've known it. He'd preferred to display his training certificates. His desk had always been a mess, not so neat like Dwight had it. If Leonard hadn't left, she wouldn't be here bored out of her mind.

"Finally, Lacey has some news that will affect our HACCP plan." Dwight gestured at Lacey. "Why don't you talk to us about your plans?"

Lacey stood and faced them. "In order to keep up with new trends and our competitors, I've decided to develop a new cookie with licorice root powder—"

Scott groaned.

Lacey glanced at him. "The recipe still needs some improvements, I agree, but I have a lot of faith in it. I want our cookies to live up to their name and be truly unique. Which is why I've decided to remove the Flirty from the line. You can't taste the maca root powder, which results in a chocolate chip and cherry cookie, nothing more."

Karina felt as if she'd been punched in the gut. Lacey was going to replace the Flirty with that abomination? How could she? First, she'd relegated Karina to production, where she couldn't contribute to new product development, and now she was eliminating the cookie Karina had inspired?

Nine years ago, back when they had worked at the commercial kitchen, Karina had come in late one day.

"I slept through my alarm, but I'm here now." She put on a hairnet and smock and washed her hands. "You won't believe what happened. I was at the supermarket buying frozen pizza when this guy came up behind me and told me it was bad for my health."

"And you ended up sleeping with him."

"Don't spoil it! Let me get there." Karina joined Lacey at the counter, grabbed a scoopful of Perky dough, and deposited a ball onto a pregreased baking sheet, pressing the bottom of the scoop against the top side to flatten it. "So, I was ready to snap at him, but when I turned around, I got a good look at him, and he was so hot. And he had this teasing smile on his face as if daring me to tell him off. So I fussed up my hair and said, 'I eat these all the time. Maybe you can give me a full checkup to make sure I'm okay?'"

"Oh my God." Lacey laughed. "You are shameless." She took a full tray to the oven rack nearby.

"No risk, no glory. I would've missed out big-time, believe me."

Lacey continued scooping out dough onto a new tray. "I wish I were like you and could enjoy sex with a stranger. I need the romance."

"Romance is overrated."

Lacey dropped the scoop into the bowl. "You know what?" She took off her gloves. "I need to design a cookie for women like you. The ones unafraid of their sexuality." She grabbed a notepad.

"You want to make a cookie about me?"

"You inspire me." She smiled and began to write.

Lacey researched a functional ingredient that would fit and found maca root powder, which was said to improve mood and increase sexual libido. Karina wanted to add chocolate chips, and Lacey rounded it out with dried cherries. A perfect cookie for a perfect moment.

One that Lacey wanted to completely erase now.

"But why?" Karina asked Lacey. "Flirty is part of our history."

"It is. But it's not selling as well as the others. I need to focus on the products that people want."

"And you think a licorice cookie is going to outsell the Flirty? Are you kidding me?"

Dwight cleared his throat. "I think we've gotten off topic. The important thing to keep in mind is that we have to remove Flirty from the plan and add the new cookie once the recipe is fine-tuned."

"Yes," Lacey said. "Thank you, Dwight." She smiled at him.

He returned the smile. "If there aren't any questions, we'll leave it here for today."

They all stood. Lacey walked over to Dwight and told him something. He grinned. They stood way too close to each other.

Karina swayed in place and held on to the back of her chair for support. It couldn't be. Was Dwight the "someone" Lacey had met? Was this why she didn't want to get rid of him? First Flirty and now this.

Ian stood in front of her, blocking her view. "I'm sorry about your cookie."

Karina shrugged.

"How was your weekend? Was Natalie mad you were late?"

"Hmm?" Lacey laughed at something Dwight said.

"Want to come over after work?"

"Sure." The word tumbled out of her mouth before she could stop it. *It was supposed to be no, you stupid mouth.* She stared at him. What had she done?

His dimples made an appearance. "Great. I'll think of something nourishing to cook for you." He walked away, leaving her breathless and staring at his ass.

CHAPTER NINE

Karina shook herself out of her trance when she caught sight of Lacey leaving the office.

"Lacey, can we talk?"

Lacey spun around. "If this is about the Flirty—" Her tone said, *Don't mess with me.*

Karina jerked back. With Dwight she'd been all smiles, but with Karina she was mad? "Are you and Dwight seeing each other?"

Lacey's eyes widened, and she dragged Karina by the arm until they were shut inside her office. "I tried to tell you the other day, but . . ."

No, no, no. Karina's legs trembled, and she fell onto the sofa.

"I know you don't like him, and that I'm his boss—"

Karina shot up. "Is that why you want me to help him so bad? He clearly doesn't fit in here, but you want to force him down our throats because you like him? Why would you put the company at risk like this?"

Lacey's eyes grew even bigger. "My personal feelings have no bearing on this. I think Dwight is the perfect person for the job. All he needs is time and for you and my uncle to give him a chance."

Karina dug her hands into her hair and paced around the room. She wanted so much to believe Lacey, to be infected by her optimism once more, but she'd never imagined Lacey would fall into the same trap as her mom. Once Bob came into the picture, it hadn't taken Debbie long to turn her back on everything she believed in. Karina had thought Lacey was different, but here she was, romantically involved with an employee, wasting her energy on him when she should've been focusing on keeping the company afloat.

It was like Karina was back in the small apartment she'd grown up in, on that afternoon when her mom dropped the bomb, the news that would change everything.

Her mom had looked radiant when she said, "I need to talk to you about something."

Sixteen-year-old Karina bounced on the sofa as her mom sat beside her. "Did you get a job?" Her mom still had a year and a half left in her paralegal studies, but maybe she'd impressed that professor she was always talking about and he'd offered her an internship at his law firm.

Her mom looked at her hands. "Not exactly." She raised her head and grinned. "But it's great news." She took a deep breath. "I'm getting married."

Karina gaped. Her mom had never wanted to get married. Karina hadn't even known she was seeing someone. "I don't understand. To who?"

"Professor Smith." She paused. "Bob."

"You're dating your professor?" No wonder she always talked about him. But Karina had never suspected her mom would be so unprofessional as to bang her teacher. "How long?"

"About a month." She laughed. "It happened so fast; I didn't see it coming. But . . . there's something else." Another deep breath. "I'm pregnant."

Karina felt faint. "So you're telling me you're marrying some guy I never met because you're pregnant?"

Mom took her hands. "I know it's a shock. I'm shocked too. But it happened, and I'm really happy."

Her mom was beaming. Karina had never seen like this. "Do you love him?"

"Of course. Why wouldn't I?"

"But doesn't that make you weak?"

"I know that's what I've always said—"

"What about school?"

Mom sighed. "That's the other thing I wanted to talk to you about. Bob doesn't want me to work. He makes enough money, and he wants me to stay at home with the baby."

"So . . . you're going to depend on him? What about everything you say about us not needing anyone else?"

"This is different. A baby needs a father, and Bob wants to be there."

"*I* didn't need a father. And you didn't need a husband. You managed fine on your own."

"I was younger then. And it was hard. Why would I put myself through that again when Bob is offering to take care of us?"

Karina couldn't believe what she was hearing. Was this the same woman who'd called other women lazy for living off their husbands, who was always bragging about how she'd raised Karina on her own? There must be some mistake.

"But you'll still get your degree, right?"

Mom hung her head. "I don't think being a paralegal is for me."

"Wait, what? You're quitting? What about our plans?"

"Our plans don't have to change. I'll be at home more, with you and the baby. No more nights alone for you, like we talked about. Bob wants us to move in with him, so we'll have a nice house—"

"Bob's house." Her mom had promised they'd move out of the projects and buy a house once she started making money as a paralegal. But it was supposed to be theirs, for the two of them. Now there'd be a man and a baby. It was all wrong.

Mom stroked her hair. "Bob is willing to adopt you. You'll have a father."

"I thought I didn't need a father."

"No, but . . . it would be nice, wouldn't it? Bob's a good man."

Bob sounded like a chauvinistic pig. Couldn't her mom see that? He just wanted a woman to serve him. He didn't want to take care of her mom; he wanted to control her. And her strong, independent mom had fallen for it. How could that be? Love was truly dangerous.

Back then, Karina had been powerless to stop her mom. Debbie had married Bob, and it had quickly become all about him and the baby, while Karina was left with nothing. But now she still had time to prevent Lacey from destroying everything they'd built together.

"What does Roy say about this?" Surely he couldn't approve.

Lacey twisted her lips. "He doesn't know. And I would appreciate it if you don't say anything to him. Or to Dwight. He's somewhat uncomfortable with us dating and prefers to keep it private, as do I."

Roy didn't know? But Lacey told him everything. She probably knew deep down it was wrong and didn't want him bursting her out of the romance novel she'd written in her head.

The phone rang.

Lacey wavered a moment before heading to her desk. "I have to get this. But rest assured that Dwight and I are perfectly capable of staying professional. We both want the company to succeed. And please, Karina, be happy for me. I have a good feeling about this."

Karina didn't know whether to run away or shake Lacey to rid her of these stupid romantic fantasies.

She stumbled into the production area, searching for Roy. If anyone could straighten Lacey out, it would be him.

In the mixing room, the guys were joking with each other as they weighed and mixed the ingredients for Mellow Cookie, having no idea the company was at risk of going under if Lacey continued down this path. Everyone who worked here counted on this company to put food on the table. What would become of them if Singular ceased to exist?

Karina spotted Roy at the exit of the oven room, where the freshly baked Mellows were being stacked onto conveyor belts and directed toward the cooling tunnel. The smell of lemon and honey filled the air.

Was she really going to betray Lacey's trust? Karina hadn't made any promises, and this was Roy, Lacey's uncle, the one who'd encouraged her to start this business. He'd know what to do.

As soon as she reached him, she blurted, "Lacey and Dwight are dating."

The smell of Mellow Cookies was usually relaxing, but Roy suddenly looked like he was suffering a stroke. "How do you know this?"

"Lacey told me."

Roy narrowed his eyes. "I knew it." He wagged his finger. "I knew there was something going on between them. That explains it."

"What?"

He sighed. "I think they're trying to push me out." When he turned his face toward her, Karina noticed the dark circles under his eyes.

The first time she'd seen him, ten years ago, she'd been interviewing for a job as a live-in maid. Roy's wife, Anne, was getting chemotherapy for her liver cancer and was too weak to do the chores. They had no children, and Roy was taking care of her by himself. Even after her death, he didn't look as worn out as he did right now.

"Lacey's been telling me I'm working too much and that I should take it easy." He shook his head. "After everything I've done to turn this place into what it is."

This was not happening. Lacey couldn't be planning to push Roy out. She wouldn't have gotten this far if it wasn't for his years of experience in the food industry. Karina had witnessed countless moments when Lacey had threatened to quit and Roy had figured out a way to find the right piece of equipment, tweak the process so the cookies wouldn't fall apart after baking, get their label approved by the FDA . . . and who would be there to tell Karina what to do, to take over the stress of it all? Roy not being part of Singular Cookies was unimaginable. He *was* Singular Cookies. One could not exist without the other.

"She can't get rid of you," she said. "Who else could run things around here like you?"

He scoffed. "What about the doc? He's already taking over. Might as well let him."

No, no, no. Karina hugged her stomach. Was Lacey that far gone already?

"Let's face it, kiddo. Lacey's lost confidence in me. She signed this contract against my wishes. She's never done that. This inspection's only creating chaos, especially with the doc wanting all these changes. I keep telling him, don't fix what ain't broken. But he wants everything to be perfect, and it'll never be perfect. He only knows what he was taught in school. He doesn't know what it's like in real life, like I do. And now he's turning Lacey against me. If she and the doc are involved and she listens to him more than me—how can I compete with that?"

"You're family. Blood is thicker than water and all that." But that was a bunch of bullshit, wasn't it? If a mom betrayed her own daughter because of a man, why wouldn't Lacey do the same to an uncle?

Roy set his jaw. "I don't know, kiddo. We'll see." He patted her on the shoulder and walked away.

This was worse than Karina had imagined. Lacey had said her personal feelings wouldn't get in the way, but this was proof that her judgment was now clouded by hormones and feelings. Just like Karina's mom's had been. There was only one thing left to do.

Karina needed to break them up.

CHAPTER TEN

Karina stood at Ian's front door.

She shouldn't be here. It was a bad idea. But Natalie had said, "Don't think about it," and for once she was following Natalie's advice. Karina wouldn't deprive herself of the amazing sex she could have with Ian over the potential of falling for him. She'd never fallen for a guy, so why would she fall for him?

Well, that wasn't exactly true. She'd fallen for Jason, but she'd been a naïve fifteen-year-old then. She was stronger now.

Okay, Karina. Eat, have sex, and leave. No sleeping over, no matter how comfy his bed is. She rang the bell.

He greeted her with a smile, and her knees went weak. *It's just a smile. Get a grip.* The delicious smells emerging from inside carried her in.

"Yum. What did you cook?" She shrugged off her jacket, and he laughed at the slogan on her T-shirt: *Do not make me hangry.*

Her heart fluttered. *Stop it, Heart. Just because I picked it out for him doesn't mean you're in charge. You're trying to make me weak for him, but it won't work. I'm stronger than you.*

"Where do you get those?" He pointed at her T-shirt.

"Online."

"Well, sit." He gestured at his dining table, which was already set. "Let me feed you. I don't want to find out what happens when you're hangry. Want some wine?"

"I'm not a big wine drinker, but I'll try it."

He poured. "You like beer better?"

"Yeah."

"I'll keep that in mind for next time."

Next time. She rubbed her palms on her jeans.

He set a plate of pork chops in a brown sauce with mixed vegetables and white rice in front of her. His plate had only meat and vegetables.

"You don't like rice?" she asked.

"I don't eat carbs for dinner."

She rolled her eyes.

"What?"

"Nothing. Eat what you want." She mixed the rice with the vegetables and ate a forkful. "Mmm."

"Okay, okay. I will have a little." He walked to the stove, served himself one spoonful, and came back to the table. "Mmm, you're right. You need the rice to soak up the sauce."

"Duh." She smiled.

"Oh, um, I forgot. I want to make a toast." He raised his glass. "To our first home-cooked dinner."

First. As in the first of many. Her hand shook as she clinked her glass with his.

"You like the food?"

"Yeah. It's awesome. I think Cordelia made this once."

"We call it chuletas a la jardinera. Gardening pork chops."

"Because of the vegetables? That's funny."

"You don't speak Spanish?"

"My mom never taught me." More like Debbie had wanted to cut away everything that tied her to her Puerto Rican family, who'd thrown her out when they found out she was pregnant with Karina, out of wedlock and only sixteen.

"You visit her often?"

"No."

"Why not?"

Why did he have to ask so many questions? Would it alarm him to know she hadn't seen her mom in ten years? "We don't get along. Can we talk about something else? I don't like talking about personal stuff."

"What do you want to talk about?"

"I don't know." She raised an eyebrow. "What I'm going to do to you later?"

He laughed. "Oh, hey, I took the quiz. Turns out I'm a Mellow, but like you, I like the Active better."

He'd rather talk about cookies than sex? That was new. "I guess we're rebels."

"I've never been a rebel," he said.

"Really?"

"Guess I never wanted to upset my parents. And I wanted to be a role model for my two sisters. One is older, but she always looked up to me."

"I've been nothing but rebellious. I dropped out of school, ran away from home, the works."

He stared at her wide-eyed. "It was that bad with your mom?"

Karina looked at her plate and forced herself to continue eating. What was it to him? From the sounds of it, he had the perfect family. What would he know about a mother who'd forgotten she had a daughter the minute she found a man to settle down with, who'd thrown her out and never apologized for it?

"Any siblings?" Ian asked.

Karina glared at him.

"What? *That* is too personal?"

She sighed. "One sister. She just turned ten." Her mom had bombarded her with photos of the party, rubbing in what a happy family they made. "We don't have the same father. Can I have some more?"

He took her plate to the stove. Couldn't he stop with the questions? And why was she volunteering so much information?

73

They ate in silence for a few minutes until Ian asked, "What about your work friends? Can I ask about them?"

This she could handle. "Yeah. I met Natalie first. She's one of the QC techs. We live together."

"Oh, I didn't know you were in a relationship already." He smiled.

"You better watch your step. She does a lot of yoga, so she's super flexible and strong. She can probably take you."

He laughed.

"Cordelia came later. She's married and, like, the mom of the group, 'cause she's the oldest. She likes to cook, and she brings me leftovers."

"You don't cook?"

"Why cook when I can get a perfectly good meal out of the freezer or from a fast-food restaurant?" That had been her mom's philosophy—until, of course, she'd married Bob and learned to cook so she could prepare his favorite meals.

"See, I was right," Ian said. "I need to nourish you. You can take leftovers for lunch tomorrow if you want."

If she took Ian's food to work, she'd never live it down. "No, keep it for your dinner. I'm set. And no offense—you're an all-right cook—but you can't beat Cordelia. Her food's amazing."

"Guess I must try her food sometime. Maybe she'll teach me her secrets. And your other friend? There are three, right?"

"Marisa. She's the kindest person you'll ever meet. Sometimes so kind people take advantage of her. Like her boyfriend. He lives at her place but doesn't pay one cent of rent or help pay for her new car, which he also uses. Can you believe that?"

"Doesn't he work?"

"He lost his job a year ago, but he says he wants to open his own garage, needs to make more connections, that sort of bullshit."

"Diablo. I mean, how do you say?" He thought about it. "The hell?"

Karina laughed. "Exactly. But she defends him. They've been together two years, and she doesn't seem to tire of him. The sex must be out of this world."

74

"Maybe she loves him."

"Why would she love an asshole who only mooches off of her? I would've kicked him out a long time ago. No, wait, I would've never let him move in."

"Some people like the drama. My younger sister, Gabi, dated a guy who kept cheating on her. But she always said, 'I love him. I can't live without him.'"

"See, women buy into this theory that there's only one person for them, and they'll put up with all kinds of shit if they think it's love." Karina shook her head. "What happened to your sister? Did she finally dump his ass?"

"She gave him one last chance, and he's behaving."

Karina shook her head again. "Women can be so stupid. I bet he's still screwing around."

Ian took a long sip of wine, staring at her over the glass. "So, you're not the romantic type?"

"How'd you guess?"

He chuckled. "And you've never been in love?"

Only once, but she'd been stupid. "No. Have you?" Why had she asked that? She didn't want to know. It was getting way too personal.

"Yes. Many times, but the last one was the hardest. We were engaged, but then my feelings changed, and I broke it off. It was the hardest thing I ever did." He stared off into the distance.

Enough of all this talk. Time to get to the good stuff. She scraped her plate clean, walked over to him, and straddled him. "Want another blow job? I've been craving your dick in my mouth all weekend."

His eyes widened. "Uh . . ." A nervous laugh. "You don't want any more food?"

"No. I'm starving for something else." She kissed him. The feel of his lips and his taste ignited every part of her.

He pulled back. "Why don't we save it for later? I thought we could watch a movie or something."

"You're kidding me. I offer you a blow job and you want to watch TV?"

75

"Waiting won't kill you. I told you, the anticipation's the best part." He pecked her lips. "I will think about that blow job while we watch." He shifted her so he could stand. "Help me with the dishes, please. Sure you don't want leftovers?"

What had just happened? "Yeah, I'm okay."

They cleared the table and stored the food. Karina poured herself more wine. "So, you prefer to torture yourself?"

He laughed and sat on the couch, gesturing for her to join him. "What do you like to watch?"

They were seriously going to watch TV? "I like comedies."

"There's a show I want to watch. I heard it's hilarious. Want to watch it with me?"

A show meant she'd be obligated to continue watching it with him. It meant a time commitment. A future. She rubbed her hands on her jeans and sat next to him. "I think I'd rather watch a movie."

"Okay." He searched the menu. "Seen this one?" It was *Swiss Army Man.*

"Yeah, but we can watch it again. It's weird but good."

He started the movie and put his arm around her. Karina gulped down the wine, which wasn't half bad. Was he really going to wait until the movie was over? About ten minutes in, he trailed his fingertips up and down the back of her neck. Ah. He was going to tease her the whole time. She couldn't let him call the shots again. Karina got on her knees in front of him.

He sighed in annoyance. "Karina . . ."

"You can keep watching. I'll be busy down here for, I don't know, the next hour? Depends on how much you can take."

Ian ended up not watching the movie.

* * *

Karina awoke the next morning to the sound of Ian's alarm. "Son of a bitch."

"And good morning to you too." Ian kissed her neck and pressed her back to his chest.

76

He'd rewarded her for the amazing blow job by going down on her and making her come three times. After that, she'd lost consciousness. Sex with him was more effective than a sleeping pill.

"What time is it?" she asked.

"Five."

"You get in today at six?" Karina went in at seven since Roy took care of the start-up.

"I have to do the PM on the oven. Roy didn't tell you?"

"He never tells me anything. At least I have time to go home and shower." She tried to sit up, but Ian pulled her down again.

"I think we have time for something else too." He rolled on top of her and pressed his erection against her belly. "You don't want to waste this, do you?"

She groaned and grabbed his butt.

"Didn't think so." He bit her ear.

"What if I fall asleep again?"

"I think it'll help you wake up."

With Karina's sex life of late-night hookups and no sleepovers, she'd never experimented with morning sex, but wow, having an orgasm right after waking up was a better pick-me-up than coffee. It had the opposite effect of doing it at night, like Ian said. She was alert, energized, and blissfully relaxed.

*　*　*

Natalie grinned as Karina walked into the house. "Good morning, roomie. You look all glowy. Did you sleep well?" She sat at the table, with plates of fruits, oatmeal, and a cup of tea in front of her.

"Don't start." Karina's stomach grumbled, and she walked into the kitchen. She should've let Ian make her breakfast like he offered, but she needed to have some space from him, especially when she'd have to see him again as soon as she got to work. She grabbed a Perky Cookie from her stash on the counter and bit off a huge mouthful. As she turned to exit, Natalie blocked the way.

"Just tell me one thing," Natalie said. "How do you feel? Are you still freaked out?"

Karina shrugged. "I don't know if I can do this. He kept hinting at future dates, and then he wanted to watch a movie instead of having sex—who does that, by the way? And I have to see him at work, like, right at start-up today."

"But?"

"But . . . I had fun. He cooked for me, and . . . as you can see, the sex was so amazing I stayed over."

"Focus on that, on the good. Don't worry about the rest."

If only it were that easy. Karina's casual dating life hadn't prepared her for a man who wanted to pamper her and make her feel special. And the scariest thing was, she looked forward to being with him again.

CHAPTER ELEVEN

When Karina entered the oven room, the sight of Ian in his overalls with a tool belt around his waist took her breath away.

"Don't look at me like that. We're at work." He winked at her.

Great, was she that obvious? She was already becoming pathetic. "I'm going to do my rounds."

"Wait. I need someone to stay here until I'm done."

"Oh, right, the new procedure. Roy didn't stay with you?"

"He said something about not having time to babysit me." He grimaced. "You should've seen the look on his face when I told him he was supposed to stay. I thought he'd punch me."

"So Roy didn't know about the change?"

"Didn't seem like it."

Karina's knees wobbled, and she held on to the door frame for support. Dwight's job was to train employees on all changes to procedure. Did he and Lacey not think it was appropriate yet to let Roy know of a change, even though the PM was this morning? They were already leaving him out of the loop. How could Lacey do this?

"Are you okay?"

"Huh? I mean, yeah." She took a deep breath. "Are you almost done?"

"Give me just a few minutes. Then you can check if I did everything right."

He gazed at her like he wanted to tear her apart. Karina's face flushed, and she forced herself to focus on the production schedule in her hand. More Actives today—they were becoming their most popular—and Perkys later. She stole a glance at Ian, who was leaning into the oven to reach the right spot. He always strove to find the right spot . . .

Stop it. If she didn't watch her step, she'd be just as bad as Lacey.

But how was she supposed to stay professional when an hour ago he'd been inside her? Most men she dated disappeared after one night. That's how she liked it—no complications. The ones who lingered were the hardest to get rid of, but she always managed. How would she manage with Ian?

Don't think about it.

"Done," Ian said.

Karina made sure every program was unchanged while Ian stood beside her, his body radiating more heat than the oven. He'd better leave before she ripped those overalls off him. She signed the work order to approve the maintenance and returned it to him.

"See you tonight?" he asked.

Yes! She clenched her jaw to keep the word in. "Don't you think we've seen a lot of each other?"

He frowned. "What's a lot?"

"I'm just saying maybe we should ease on the brakes. I thought you liked taking it slow."

He laughed, and his dimples almost made her chew back her words. "True, true. What about this weekend? Any plans?"

"I was going to hang out at the beach. It's supposed to be warm on Saturday."

"By yourself? What about your friends?"

"If I waited on them, I'd never go. I told you I prefer to fly solo."

His eyebrows lifted. "Right. Well . . . mind if I join you? You can watch me while I jog."

She smirked. That would be the ultimate view. And Saturday meant a much-needed break from him and all these stupid thoughts circling in her head. But the beach was sacred, and she was already sharing too much of herself with him.

Karina opened her mouth to say no, but his puppy-dog eyes made her say, "I'll pick you up at nine."

A few minutes after Ian left, Roy barged into the room. "Where's that mechanic?"

"Don't worry," she told him. "I checked his work and signed the work order."

"Oh, good." He ran his palm over his face. "Can you believe they're making us do this? Did you know about the change?"

"Dwight mentioned it yesterday at the HACCP meeting. Lacey said they would tell you."

"Well, they didn't. I can't believe she would leave me in the dark like this. As soon as they arrive, I'm gonna chew him and Lacey out about this joke of a procedure. I need you to back me up."

Oh, this was going to be epic. No way would she miss this. Dwight deserved everything coming his way after all his meddling with their procedures.

*   *   *

An hour later, in the mixing room, Tyler told her he'd been diagnosed with anemia.

"That's why I tripped last week, yo. I started going vegan, but I wasn't getting enough iron. Now I got supplements and I'm feeling much better, so don't worry; you won't get more accidents from me."

Karina smiled. "That's good to know. But veganism? Really, Tyler? What gives?"

Tyler laughed. Before he could answer, the mixer beeped the end of its run, beckoning him back to work. Across from him, Roy was barreling toward her. Grumpy was not the word to describe him today. More like Rabid Cookie, with some whipped cream on top to symbolize the foam she could almost spot on his mouth.

"The doc is finally here," he said. "Let's go."

He left Tyler in charge, then stomped away so fast Karina had to run to keep up with him. She didn't have time to remove her smock or hairnet, since Roy continued walking with his on.

Lacey was not in her office, and Roy marched on to Dwight's, throwing the door open without knocking. Both Dwight and Lacey jumped to attention, a guilty look in their eyes. If not for the desk that separated them, Karina would've assumed they'd been making out.

"What's this about us supervising the mechanics?" Roy barked at Lacey. "You didn't consult me on this."

"Oh, Uncle." Lacey pleaded with her hands. "I was going to tell you, but it slipped my mind. It's only a precaution."

Wasn't Dwight supposed to tell Roy? Lacey was already acting like the good little girlfriend, covering for him.

"Didn't you train the mechanics not to change the programming of the oven?" Roy turned his wrath on Dwight.

Dwight pressed his lips and sat. "A verification step is always necessary, to ensure everything's in order."

"You want us to babysit while there's a million other things we have to do?" Roy slammed his fists on Dwight's desk. "Why can't the maintenance manager take care of that?"

Lacey tugged on Roy's arm. "Don't yell at him."

Dwight pulled at his collar, remaining seated, and glanced at Lacey briefly before turning his attention back to Roy. "It should be up to the production management to check the programming."

Roy broke free from Lacey's grasp. "How could you approve this stupid procedure without my permission, Lacey?"

Lacey pulled her shoulders back. "It's my prerogative to approve any procedure I find suitable, which in this case I did."

Roy frowned while Karina gaped at Lacey. How could she keep taking Dwight's side? Out in the hallway, hurried footsteps neared and stopped, followed by the sound of murmured chatter.

"You should've consulted me." Roy rubbed his face as if clearing his mind. "I can't be at two places at once during start-up." He let out a breath. "Tell them how we did it, Karina."

Karina jumped at the mention of her name. Everyone stared at her. More shuffling behind her.

"Ian was almost done when I got there," she said. "I checked that everything was in order when he finished."

Dwight swiveled in his chair. "And do you think we should change the procedure?"

"I don't think we should stay there the *whole* time," Karina said. "Maybe just check at the end, like I did today."

Roy grunted in agreement.

Now all eyes were on Dwight. He shuffled the papers on his desk. "That makes sense. Thank you for the suggestion. I'll change the procedure. Anything else?"

"In the future"—Roy pointed between Dwight and Lacey—"I expect you to notify me immediately of any change to a procedure that affects production. I'm the one who's in charge of it. Is that clear?"

Lacey and Dwight nodded.

"Good." Roy brushed his hands together. "Karina, stay here with Dr. Dwight and make sure he makes those changes." He stormed out, then barked, "Get back to work." She heard the sound of footsteps as the eavesdroppers scattered.

Lacey went around Dwight's desk and put her hand on his shoulder. "Are you okay?"

He spun his chair away from her. "I'm fine. I should've notified him. I'll work on the changes and leave the procedure on your desk."

Lacey pulled her hand back, remaining still for a moment, staring at the back of Dwight's head as he pounded the keyboard with his fingers.

Roy had done it! This could be the beginning of the end. Dwight hadn't looked too happy when Lacey spoke for him. It could turn out he'd succumb to the pressure and break things up first.

Lacey gestured at Karina to join her out in the hallway.

"I can't believe my uncle yelled at Dwight like that," Lacey said in a low voice. "It was humiliating."

"Why were you covering for him? Isn't it his job to notify Roy of any procedure change?"

"Yes, but I said I'd do it, and here we are." Lacey put her hand on Karina's shoulder. "Look, I know you don't approve of our relationship, but I need you to help Dwight work with my uncle. Could you please talk to him?"

Karina struggled to keep her face neutral. *Sure, let's keep worrying about Dwight and his problems instead of everyone else's,* she wanted to yell. But she had to stay professional. If Karina earned Dwight's trust, she could maybe find a weakness she could exploit to get him to back off and break up with Lacey so she could stay focused on the company.

"I'll see what I can do."

Lacey smiled. "Thank you. I appreciate it."

Karina waited until Lacey was out of view before going back inside. Dwight was glaring at his monitor.

She sat across from him. She should try to be nice. "Don't feel bad. Roy's like that with everyone. You saw how he screamed at Lacey. He was the same with Leonard. I think he hates having other people tell him what to do, especially people who don't have as much work experience as he does."

He considered it. "Perhaps that's the reason for the disorganization here. Lacey agrees we should make changes to the procedures, but she has no spine when it comes to her uncle, and I don't know what to do. If I do everything Roy's way, we'll never pass the inspection." He closed his eyes and rested his head on his hand.

He was being overdramatic, acting as if Roy were an idiot. "He has to do everything your way, then?"

"No, that's not what I'm saying. I mean . . ." He shook his head. "I wish he would at least consider my suggestions and not dismiss them immediately."

"What do you expect? Roy quit his job at Tropicana, where he worked most of his life, to help Lacey. He set all this up, worked hard to make it what it is today, and you show up one day, waving your degree, and tell him everything he's done until now is wrong."

He jerked his head back. "Not wrong, but quality assurance is about continuous improvement. Roy believes that since we've never had to issue a recall or had any problems with the FDA, we're set. But regulations change, and we have to keep up with them. That's the basis of my job, and I can't sit quietly when there's so much in need of change."

"But does *everything* have to change?"

He sighed. "You're right. I should make a priority list and focus on the most important items."

"Good, do that. And if you want to be on Roy's good side, ask for his opinion. Show him some respect."

"I need to kiss his hand, like the Godfather?"

"Not so extreme, no, but you have to be humbler if you want to get him to work with you."

"Well, I . . ." He reshuffled the papers on his desk. "I meant no offense. Lacey says I come on too strong. But see it from my point of view. They scheduled this inspection without being ready, then expect me to prepare in only eight months. I'm new here, and I'm a perfectionist, and nobody cares about this but me, and I'm this close to having a nervous breakdown." He rested his head on his hands.

"Whoa, okay, take a deep breath."

He complied. Maybe she shouldn't worry so much about him and Lacey. With this amount of stress, he'd probably quit before the inspection.

Dwight opened his eyes and smiled at her, looking a lot calmer.

"Start with your priority list and take it from there," she said.

"You know what?" He smiled. "You're right. I'll do that, thank you. And thank you for listening. I don't have many allies here. Perhaps I should vent to you more often."

Karina grinned. This was too easy.

*　　*　　*

"I still can't believe you got to witness Roy's fight with Dwight," Cordelia said during lunch. "Locked inside production, we never know what's going on. I should've gone out to the bathroom."

"So, Karina," Natalie said. "Aren't you gonna tell them your big news?"

Karina frowned.

"Does it have to do with Ian?" Marisa asked. "Are you still seeing him? Tell us."

"Oh, Nat, thanks so much for reminding me," Karina said in a sarcastic tone. "Okay. Don't make a big deal out of it, but yes."

There was a gasp from Cordelia and a squeal from Marisa.

"What did I just say?"

"So, are we talking just sex or more couple-y stuff?" Marisa asked.

"He cooked for her last night and she slept over," Natalie said.

"You just can't keep your mouth shut, can you?" Karina said.

Natalie shrugged.

"Oh my God, this is huge," Cordelia said.

"No, it's not. It's just me liking a guy enough to want to see him again. That's it."

"Yeah, right," Cordelia said. "You're already in, girl. He already got you."

"Whatever."

Karina's phone beeped, and she grabbed it. There was a text from Ian: *Heard everything. You handled it like a champ. Proud of you.*

So he'd been one of the eavesdroppers on the Roy-Dwight show-down. Karina's heart thumped in her chest. He was proud of her. For what? Speaking her mind? That's how she always was. Maybe he liked that about her.

Did he like her? The thumping of her heart got louder. Her face burned.

"Ooh, is that a text from Ian?" Cordelia asked. "You're blushing, mamita."

"What did he write?" Natalie asked.

"Is it something romantic?" Marisa asked.

Damn it. Karina pressed the phone to her chest. "None of your business."

"Oooh," her friends said in unison.

"I need to go to the bathroom." Karina walked out to the hall-way. Cordelia's words from earlier followed her out.

You're already in, girl. He already got you.

Fuck.

CHAPTER TWELVE

Karina turned to lie on her stomach, resting her cheek on her folded arm. She dug one hand into the sand, rubbing it against her skin. A warm breeze enveloped her with the salty scent of the ocean, and she sighed. Paradise.

Finally, it was warm enough for lying on a blanket in a bikini, absorbing the sun's rays. She glanced to the horizon. A figure jogged leisurely in her direction. Ian, his skin glistening, his curly hair flowing wildly. The past days without him had calmed her, had even made her wonder what she was so scared of. But when she'd picked him up earlier this morning, her heart had caught in her chest at the sight of him, exactly like it did now.

A group of girls next to Karina were checking him out. Ian waved to her, and Karina's stomach fluttered. She waved back, then smirked at the girls. *Suck it, bitches. He's with me.* She'd never been possessive over a man before, but it felt good to be a source of envy.

Ian plopped next to her, and Karina slithered on top of him, running her hands over his torso and arms. He was sweaty, rough with sand. She kissed his neck. *Mmm.*

"You looked amazing out there," she said. "Those girls were checking you out."

"I know."

"Is that why you jog on the beach? So you can have women ogling you?"

"I jog on the beach because I like to hear the waves and feel the sand between my toes."

"Mm-hmm. Are you hungry? I brought a few snacks."

"Me too." He sat up and took out two bananas and two apples from his backpack.

"I think I'll stick with mine." She took out two Perky Cookies. "I brought you Active Cookies." She handed them to him.

His dimples made her skin flush. His smile was her reward for the embarrassment of bringing him cookies.

"That's so nice." He stroked her cheek. "Thanks for thinking of me."

Karina shrugged and bit into her cookie. This need to please him was getting out of control. Soon she'd be learning to cook so she could prepare his favorite meals or start shopping for him, like her mother did for Bob.

Don't think about it.

"Can I try?" He pointed at her half-eaten Perky. She handed it to him, and he took a bite. "Mmm. Maybe too much coffee for me. Want some of mine?"

"I don't know." She made a face. "Quinoa?"

"You've never tried it? Thought you helped develop them."

"Not this one. I helped with the Flirty and the Mellow. Back when we worked at the commercial kitchen, before moving to the plant where we are now."

She gazed at the ocean. Karina had not only inspired the Flirty, she'd also come up with the idea for the Mellow. It was basically the chamomile tea–honey–lemon combination Lacey drank nonstop to release stress. But after the expansion, it had all become about regulations and procedures and a more scientific approach to product development. Lacey relied more on Leonard, who had the education Karina lacked.

"Then you have to try it. Here." Ian placed the cookie in front of her mouth.

The need to please took over again, and she bit into it. As she chewed, the taste of peanut butter filled her mouth. There was also a hint of something earthy. Probably the quinoa. It wasn't too overpowering.

"And?" He looked at her expectantly.

She swallowed and nodded. "Not bad."

He grinned. "See? It's good to try new things."

"I think I'll stick with the Perky. If Lacey doesn't get the idea to stop making that one too."

He took her hand. "I'm sorry about the Flirty."

She removed her hand from his. "It's just a stupid cookie." She continued munching on the Perky. If Lacey didn't care about their history, then neither should she.

Ian wiped the crumbs from his mouth, stood, and tugged on her arm. "Come, let's get in the water."

"No way. The water's freezing this time of year."

"No, it's not. Come on." He dragged her to the edge of the ocean. When her feet met the icy coldness, she yelled and tried to free herself from his grasp, but Ian pulled her in deeper. As the water enveloped her, her body acclimated, and she relaxed. But when the water reached her chin and Ian dove further, Karina yelled, "Stop. I can't swim."

"Hold on to me." He wrapped her arms around his neck and swam with her on his back.

She clamped her legs around his waist. "Don't you fucking let go of me."

"I got you, don't worry."

Karina shut her eyes and clung tighter. What if he got tired and she fell? She'd drown. "Go back."

He turned around but stopped farther out than she'd ever been. He moved her to his front, his arms wrapped tightly around her waist.

Her toes couldn't touch the bottom. "Take me back right now."

"I got you." He kissed her, and every muscle relaxed. He had her. It was safe. She wrapped her legs around his waist. Nothing bad would happen.

The water lapped around them, a few distant shouts the only sign they weren't alone. Out here they might as well be.

Now her body was too warm. She slid her hand into the front of his swimsuit.

"What . . ." He laughed. "What are you doing?"

"What does it feel like?" She rubbed along his length.

"We're in a public place."

"Oh, Ian, be a rebel. No one's going to know." She kissed his jaw. "They'll think we're making out."

After a few minutes, his hand reached into her bikini bottom.

* * *

"I can't believe I had sex on the beach," Ian said on the drive back to his place.

"I can't believe you lived on an island and never had sex on the beach." She glanced at him sideways. "And with that body."

"What does my body have to do with anything?"

"Oh, come on. Why look like that if it's not to get laid?"

"I like to exercise. It relaxes me."

"Then why eat all that protein stuff? Admit it, you *want* to look like that."

"Okay, yes, I do. I like how I look."

"And you must like having women throw themselves at you all the time."

"I'm not made of stone, so yes, but I don't want to be only about sex."

"Oh, please, that's what all men want. If you don't want women like me to throw themselves at you, then get fatter."

He laughed. "You would still like me if I was fat?"

"I don't know. Maybe." Why hadn't she said no? Now he'd think she liked him for more than his body. Which was true, but he didn't need to know that.

"I wouldn't mind if you had a few more pounds on you." He squeezed her thigh.

Karina laughed. "I wouldn't mind either." She drove into his driveway and put the car in park. "It was fun today." When he made no move to leave, she added, "See you around."

"You're not coming in?"

"I need to go home and shower." She'd already had an orgasm; she shouldn't be greedy. Going into his place meant cuddling and falling asleep in his arms. She was already spending too much time with him. It was too risky.

"You can shower here."

"I don't have any bath stuff or clothes."

"You don't need clothes. And you can use my stuff. We could shower together."

"Why?"

He laughed. "Some people think it's romantic."

"You know I'm not the romantic type."

"You never showered with anyone before?"

"Nope."

"Then let's try it. I bet you'll like it. I'll make it special for your first time. Come." He got out of the car without waiting for a response, already sure she'd say yes.

Karina stared after him. *Leave. Don't let him manipulate you. You already said no.* But those puppy-dog eyes of his were hard to resist. She turned off the car and stepped out.

"You won't regret it." He took her hand and led her into his house, down the hall to his master bath. "Let's take this off." He removed her bikini and his shorts, started the shower, then placed her underneath the stream of warm water. "I'm going to wash your hair now." He poured shampoo on her head and massaged her scalp.

Karina closed her eyes. The warm water, the feel of his fingers, and the citrusy scent of his shower gel were intoxicating. Her muscles relaxed, like before, when he'd kissed her in the ocean, and she sighed. He rinsed her hair and moved on to her body, massaging her slowly, not sexually but efficiently. He turned her around to face him and massaged her breasts, stomach, hips. When he went on his knees to do her legs and feet, she expected him to go down on her, but he didn't. He lingered a bit between her legs, but that was it.

After she rinsed, he said, "Now do me."

She put shampoo on her hands and washed his hair. He closed his eyes and smiled. She could do anything she wanted to him, but he seemed content to just be.

"Hmm, that feels good," he said. "I love head massages."

She massaged every area of his head. His smile and contented sigh made her heart skip a beat. Why was making him happy so important?

Karina turned her attention to his body, caressing every inch as he'd done for her. But when she got to his dick, she couldn't help putting it in her mouth.

"Why don't we wait with that?" He pulled her up to stand. "We're taking a shower."

"Don't people have sex in their showers?"

He shook his head. "Why is it so hard for you to wait? You're the horniest woman I've ever met."

"You should be thrilled instead of making me stop."

"I'm trying to make it special."

"I don't need special. I need to be fucked."

"And I don't need a porn star. I want a normal woman to pleasure."

She swallowed. "I guess I'm not normal, then."

"That's not—"

"Most guys would die to be in your place."

"Guess I'm not most guys."

They stared at each other. Karina's lower lip trembled. Was this it, was it over? So soon?

"What more do you want from me?" she whispered.

"I want you, K. The real you. Not the porn star, not the tough girl, but the sweet girl who got me cookies and clung to me in the ocean because she was afraid." He cupped her face and kissed her, softly, gently. Karina's body went limp. He turned off the shower and held on to her, kissing her some more. He tasted like the ocean.

Ian cooked lunch for them, and Karina tried to stay in the moment and just enjoy the food and the company, without any worries about what had happened before in the shower or what would happen later or what it all meant. She wanted her worries to be carried away just like Ian had carried her effortlessly into the deep end of the ocean.

They watched a movie, and after it ended, Karina kissed him, unable to contain her desire for him any longer. He carried her to his bed, and what followed was not normal sex. It was a body take-over, an invasion. He filled all her senses: his taut skin beneath her fingers, his hands entangled in her hair, his breath against the top of her head, his grunts as he thrust, his citrusy smell, the taste of his lips, his gaze penetrating straight to her heart. She shouldn't let him possess her like this. Her body belonged only to her. But oh, it was freeing to let go, to let someone else take control.

*   *   *

When she woke, it was dark, her body flush to his back, spooning him, her arm around his chest.

Damn it. Not again. "I have to go."

He groaned. "What time is it?"

"I don't know, but it's late." She went into the bathroom to collect her things. Her hair was a tangled mess. She put on her shorts and T-shirt, picked up her swimsuit from the floor, and walked out.

Ian was already dressed. "You don't have to leave. Why don't we order out and watch another movie?"

"Because that'll lead to more sex, and then I'll sleep over."

"Is that a bad thing?"

"Let me go, okay? We had a fun day together. That should count, right?"

He stared at her for a moment, probably not liking that the tough girl was back, but he'd have to get used to it. "I'll walk you to the car."

As he led the way, her chest tightened. Why did she feel bad about leaving? She could go whenever she wanted.

Karina walked ahead of him and reached the car first, hoping for a clean getaway, but he grabbed her arm before she could open the driver's door. He turned her around and kissed her, pinning her against the car. That feeling of relaxation overtook her again, and she sighed.

"Your hair's a mess." He ran his fingers through it, getting stuck on the knots.

"Ow."

"Sorry." He kept fussing with her hair, moving loose strands around, avoiding eye contact.

"What is it?"

He smiled and took a deep breath, finally looking at her. "Valentine's Day is next week."

"Ugh."

"I know you're not a romantic, but what if I make you dinner?"

Say no. Don't fall into his trap. "Do we have to exchange presents?"

"Up to you."

Say no. "I'll think about it."

"To the presents or dinner?"

"Both."

"It won't be corny," he said. "I promise. It would be like last time. You had fun, right? And not only the sex part."

Karina sighed. "It was nice."

He grinned, and her heart soared. "What's your favorite food?"

"Pizza."

"Not the most romantic food in the world."

"It's not supposed to be romantic." She made a face. "Oh, but it has carbs. Lots and lots of carbs."

He narrowed his eyes at her. "I'll make an exception. So is that a yes?"

"You're going to make pizza from scratch?"

"I never have, but I can try." He kissed her. "You can help me with the toppings."

How could she say no to that? "Okay, but no flowers or romantic movies or anything like that, got it?"

He nodded.

"And I'll . . . consider getting you something." Who was she turning into?

"Great. Looking forward to it." He kissed her harder this time. Suddenly, she didn't feel like leaving anymore, but when he broke the kiss and stepped back, she got into the car.

He waited by his garage door, hands in pockets, looking adorable with his hair tousled. *What are you doing, Karina? Stay. You can cuddle on the couch, watch a movie, make out, have sex again. So what if you end up sleeping in? It was nice waking up in his arms and having sex in the morning.*

Karina stared at Ian a few seconds more, then turned the ignition, backed out of the driveway, and drove away.

* * *

"I expected you to sleep over at Ian's," Natalie said when Karina got back. She was sitting cross-legged on the couch, looking at her phone.

"I can't sleep over every time. It will give him the wrong idea." She walked behind Natalie to see what she was so engrossed with. Wedding photos, as expected. "Didn't you have a date tonight?"

"He was nice, but there was no spark."

"You talk about me, but you're no better." Karina sat next to her. "Why don't you give a guy longer than a minute before you let him go? Did you at least get some?"

"Yuck. Why would I have sex with someone when there's no spark?"

"Were you attracted to him?"

"A little."

"Then why not have sex? You get something out of it, at least. Dating's not all butterflies and rainbows. You expect too much."

"And you only want sex. That's why you like Ian so much. It isn't all about sex with him."

Karina's face burned as she remembered the way Ian had taken over her body. Luckily, Natalie was searching for photos and didn't notice. "Mostly, it is. If it wasn't, I wouldn't keep seeing him."

"Then you do it your way, and I'll do it mine." She gasped. "Ooh, look at this dress." She showed Karina a photo of a mermaid wedding dress covered in lace. "Wouldn't this look divine on me?"

Karina had learned a long time ago not to criticize this stupid obsession. It only led to them not talking for days until Natalie got over it. "Yeah, it's nice."

"This one goes to the top choices."

Karina rubbed her face to keep herself from gagging. "Did you eat already?"

"I made myself a salad. You could have some if you cared at all about your health."

"I care more about my taste buds." She opened the freezer. Jackpot. Frozen pizza. She turned on the oven. As she unwrapped it, she smiled, looking forward to Ian's homemade pizza next week. Why would he go to all that trouble for her? Maybe he had that same need to please.

After putting the pizza in the oven, Karina asked, "You want to watch a movie or something?"

"I was about to go to bed. I'm going on an early hike tomorrow so I can be back by lunch and spend the afternoon journaling and reading."

Karina twisted her lips. Natalie was always too busy to hang out. She would've probably picked another rom-com anyway. Ian would've watched whatever Karina wanted. Why couldn't she have stayed with him?

"What are your plans for tomorrow?" Natalie asked.

"Oh, um, I thought maybe I'd go to the mall. I need to buy a gift."

"A gift?" Natalie gave her a curious look. "What's the occasion?"

"Uh . . ." Karina's face flushed.

"Wait, is this about Valentine's Day?" Natalie dropped the phone next to her. "Do you want to buy something for Ian?"

Karina shrugged. "Yes?"

Natalie laughed and clapped. "Can I come with? I'll help you buy the perfect gift. Is he getting you something too?"

Karina shouldn't have said anything, but she needed help with this. It was unfamiliar territory. "He's making me dinner."

"That is *so* romantic." Natalie pressed her hands together in prayer and closed her eyes. "Please, universe, send me a boyfriend like that."

"First of all, he's not my boyfriend. And second, you eat only raw food, so what would the poor guy cook?"

"Yeah, yeah. So what do you want to get him?"

Karina leaned against the doorframe. "I don't know," she lied. She'd figured it out during the drive. "Maybe some lingerie?"

"Oh my gosh, you're such a girly girl. I knew your toughness was only a facade."

"Ha-ha."

"What about a nice, sexy dress too?"

"I have some nice dresses. Somewhere."

"But this would be something you pick out for him. Imagine the look on his face when he sees you."

Karina pictured his huge dimpled grin, and her heart melted.

Natalie squealed. "You should see your face. You're falling for him."

"No, don't say that. It's just shopping." She crossed her arms. "But if you want to come with me, you can't breathe a word to the others."

"That's not fair."

"I won't let you come unless you swear."

"Fine. I'll start looking for some ideas." She scrolled through her phone.

Karina returned to the kitchen to wait for the pizza. Tomorrow she would buy a present for a guy. Spend actual money on him. Her heart rate sped up. The need to please him had officially taken over.

CHAPTER THIRTEEN

Karina tripped on the step to Ian's front door and twisted her foot. Damn heels. How did women wear these on a regular basis? And stockings. They were itchy as hell. She ran her sweaty palms down her strapless black minidress for the umpteenth time.

Why had she let Natalie convince her to buy all this stuff? It had been expensive, and for what? To impress a guy? To please him?

You can still back out. He doesn't know you're here. Get in the car and go.

But he'd gone to all that trouble, had already texted a photo of the dough he'd made. Plus she was hungry. She shut her eyes, took a deep breath, and rang the doorbell.

His mouth dropped open when he saw her. "Wow." He grabbed her hand and pulled her inside, closing the door behind her. "You look incredible." He took off her jacket and twirled her around. "Absolutely beautiful." He kissed her.

Karina sighed. Okay, maybe Natalie had the right idea.

"You look nice too." He wore a long-sleeved burgundy shirt rolled up to the elbows and beige slacks under his apron.

"Not as nice as you." He gazed up and down her body. "Is this my present? Because I love it." He kissed her again.

"There's something else underneath."

"Oh?" He hooked his index finger into the top of her dress and pulled. "Red lace. Nice."

She slapped his hand away. "No peeking."

"Mmm. I can't wait to unwrap you." More kissing. This was turning out to be the best investment ever. "Wow, okay, I need to cool off." He ran his hands up and down her body, admiring her. "I wasn't expecting this." He glanced behind her and pointed at the backpack she'd dropped by the door. "What's that?"

"Oh, some clothes for tomorrow. And my toothbrush and stuff." She shrugged. "In case I spend the night."

His grin lit up the whole room. "So, no waking up to your cursing?"

She laughed. "No."

"This present keeps getting better and better." He kissed her but immediately pulled back. "Okay, time to stop. You must be hungry."

He pulled her toward the kitchen, where bowls full of different pizza toppings sat on the counter: pepperoni, black olives, onions, bacon, tomatoes, and shredded cheese. "I still need to chop the mushrooms and bell pepper. Want to help me with that?"

"You want to put me to work dressed like this?"

"I have an extra apron." He rummaged through a drawer.

"Of course you do."

Before he could hand her the apron, Karina said, "Wait," and kicked off her shoes. "That's better. They were killing me."

He laughed. "Not used to high heels, huh?" He tied the apron around her, folding it at the waist so it wouldn't fall to the floor.

"I'm sure a man came up with that form of torture. And of course, stupid women obeyed to make them happy." She glanced at the cutting board and the vegetables beside it. "So what do you need me to do? You should know, I've never done this."

He kissed the back of her neck, making her skin tingle. "I'll teach you." He took a mushroom, cut off the stem, then sliced it. "Easy, right?" He handed the knife to Karina.

Karina followed his steps, but her slices were uneven. "They're not as nice as yours."

"They're perfect, don't worry." He next showed her how to cut the bell pepper, then started rolling out the dough.

Karina stole glances at him while she tried not to cut off a finger. Roy had tried to teach her to cook once, back when she was his maid and he was taking care of his sick wife. Karina had made a mess and burned the stew. She smiled at the memory. Roy could have fired her, but he took charge and prepared the meals from then on, while she cleaned afterward. He'd probably done it because he felt sorry for her, after everything she'd gone through, but it had still felt nice to belong, to not be thrown away at the first sign of trouble. Being here with Ian brought back those feelings of belonging and family, even if they had been temporary and make-believe. Roy wasn't her family, but her boss. And Ian was . . . she didn't know what Ian was yet.

"There, that should be good enough." He pointed at the formed dough. "I'm not even going to try rolling it like the Italians."

"Oh, come on, put those biceps to work."

He laughed, picking up the dough and placing it carefully on top of the pizza pan. He expertly spread tomato sauce on it.

"Did you make the sauce from scratch too?"

"Mm-hmm."

"Wow. You went all out."

"Hope you like it." He turned to smile at her.

Karina's heart skipped a beat. "I love it already." She kissed his cheek.

He grinned. "What toppings do you want?"

"What if I only want meat and cheese? Would you still eat it?"

"We can do half and half and then we share. Deal?"

"Deal."

Karina put pepperoni, bacon, tomatoes, and mushrooms on her half while Ian used only the vegetables. While the pizza baked, Ian rolled out more dough.

"How much do you think you'll eat?" he asked.

"How much do you have?"

He laughed. "Enough, I hope." He paused. "Forgot to tell you. I got you beer. It's in the fridge."

She peeked inside. There was a six-pack of Corona between cartons of milk and eggs. She grabbed two and popped them open. That he'd remembered to get her beer made her heart flutter. The need to please worked both ways.

She handed one to him. "Beer and pizza, the perfect combination." She clinked her bottle against his.

"Not so sure about that, but if it makes you happy . . ." He took a sip and smiled.

Her heart beat faster. *Oh, Heart, what is he doing to us?* She couldn't help kissing him.

By the time the pizza was ready, Karina's stomach was grumbling so hard, Ian could hear it.

"Come, sit, I need to feed you." He cut off a slice from her half and handed it to her.

She burned the top of her mouth taking a bite. "Mmm, Ian, this is amazing. Not even Cordelia has made pizza from scratch. Way to go." She raised her beer at him and took a sip.

He chewed off a piece. "Not bad for my first try. And it only took three hours to make."

"That long?"

"It was worth it to see you so happy, like a little girl at Christmas." He leaned his head on his hand. "Has no one ever made you feel special before?"

Karina's heart sank, and she looked away. The last time she'd felt special was with Lacey back at the commercial kitchen, the first time she'd tasted Flirty, the cookie Lacey had created in her honor. Had Karina really been an inspiration, or had Lacey just used her personality to make a profit?

What did it matter? She shouldn't let memories of Lacey ruin her night. Karina smiled at Ian. "You shouldn't have gone to all this trouble to make me feel special. I told you I don't need that."

He took her hand. "Well, maybe *I* do."

Her insides turned to mush.

It took them a couple of hours to finish eating, what with preparing the rest of the pizzas and waiting for them to bake. By the end, they ate three pizzas between them, with two left over.

Karina flopped into the couch. She'd never eaten so much.

"Stay there and close your eyes," Ian said. "Have a little surprise for you."

"What is it?"

"I said close your eyes."

She did. A few moments later, she felt Ian sit beside her, then heard the crinkle of plastic and some fumbling. His thumb rubbed against her lips. "Open your mouth."

Karina smiled and complied. He placed something on her lower lip and instructed her to bite into it. Chocolate.

"Hmm."

"Keep your eyes closed. Really savor it."

She took her time, tasting every singular flavor—the silky chocolate, sweet caramel, and crunchy nuts. When she opened her mouth for another piece, she got his mouth instead. He tasted just as rich, and she savored him just as thoroughly.

Karina opened her eyes. He was holding a box of Whitman's Sampler. "I haven't eaten these in a long time."

"They were my favorite as a kid. My mom always got me a box for my birthday."

She smiled. "Okay. My turn. Which do you like?"

"Surprise me." He closed his eyes and opened his mouth.

She chose a toffee and placed it inside. "Mmm, I love those. Eat one." He fed her one, and when she finished, he kissed her. "I like them even better when they taste like you."

They ate through the whole box this way, taking turns savoring the chocolates and each other.

"Hey, Ian, I know you like taking it slow, but can we skip to your present? I need all this stuff off me." She tugged at the dress and stockings. "They're super uncomfy."

He laughed and took her hand.

She made him sit at the edge of the bed and turned her back to him so he could unzip her, revealing the red lace teddy she'd bought. When she turned to face him, the look he gave her made her breath catch in her throat. Karina had never bought fancy lingerie. Her underwear didn't match. She never stayed with a guy long enough to "spice things up," and she didn't need any help seducing one—she had her hands, mouth, and body to do that for her. But now she knew why women bothered. The need to please—to give him a treat, to surprise him, to make him happy—made her happy in return.

"You're so beautiful, K." He stroked her face and kissed her.

Leonard had called her beautiful. He'd also had that same dreamy look in his eyes. Could Ian be in love with her too? She stiffened. No, it couldn't be. What had she gotten herself into?

"What's wrong?"

"I . . ."

"K?"

"This was a bad idea." She walked backward, away from him.

"No, no, no. Wait." He pulled her onto his lap. "You look so sexy." He bit her earlobe. "What are you going to do to me?"

This she could handle. She let out a breath and straddled him. "You're in for a treat."

CHAPTER FOURTEEN

Karina awoke to Ian's alarm, but this time she knew exactly where she was. She turned to face him. "Good morning."

"Ah, so you don't always wake up cursing."

She smiled and tentatively stroked his face and massaged his head, threading her fingers through his hair. Last night had been wild enough to get her out of her head and loosen the tightness in her chest, allowing her to fall asleep in his arms with no concern of what it might mean. Now all she felt was a sense of peace, of being in the right place. Karina was reluctant to let that feeling go, at least for the moment.

They had sex, then showered together. Ian made her a breakfast of scrambled eggs, bacon, and toast and even sat to eat with her. He took her hand and she gazed at him. He smiled. She smiled back. This wasn't so bad. She was still the same person, only slightly more . . . relaxed. Happy. Happier than she'd ever been. Was this why everyone made so much fuss about relationships?

"K." He smiled. "There you are."

Her face flushed, and she looked away before she freaked out again.

"Want to take pizza for lunch?" he asked. "You can have it all."

"Nah. We can eat it for dinner tonight." She paused. "And maybe we can watch that show you mentioned."

He grinned and kissed her hand. "I'd love that."

On the way to work, she kept catching herself smiling and tried to stop, but it was useless. As soon as she stepped into the mixing room, Roy greeted her with a "Not you too."

Stop smiling. "What?"

"Everybody caught the love bug last night. This one got engaged." Roy pointed at Tyler over at the scales.

"But you're so young," Karina said.

"I'm twenty-six, yo." Tyler finished weighing the chopped walnuts for the Bright Cookies and dumped them into the mixing bowl beside him. "I'm ready for the next step."

Karina wasn't sure whether to congratulate him or pity him. So young and already settling down. She was only one year older and couldn't deal with two weeks of dating.

"What about you?" Tyler asked her. "Did Ian splurge on you last night?"

Did he ever. Karina blushed. Tyler whooped, and the other three guys laughed.

"Cut it out, boys," Roy said. "I want your heads out of the clouds while you're here at work. Once you leave, you can go back to your lovesickness."

Everyone sobered and continued weighing. Tyler rolled the mixing bowl to the mixer and lowered the beater to start making the dough. Roy busied himself reading the orders for the day, acting all Grumpy Cookie when inside he must be hurting. Karina had witnessed how he'd brought his wife, Anne, flowers every week, how he'd read her favorite books aloud to her, how sometimes he'd sung her their song, "Wouldn't it Be Nice." He was a bigger romantic than Ian, even if he hid it well.

Karina tried to focus as she went through her checklists, but every five seconds Ian's face popped up or she remembered something he'd said, and her lips would spread into a goofy smile. What was going on with her? She fought to keep her face neutral as she continued her tasks. Thankfully, no one made any teasing comments.

Until she joined the girls for lunch.

"Rosa said Ian made you pizza last night," Cordelia said. "Why did you say yesterday you'd order out? Did you also lie about exchanging presents?"

Damn Rosa. And Ian. Why did he have to blab to her? After Natalie had sworn she wouldn't say anything, Karina figured she'd be safe, but she hadn't counted on Ian telling.

Karina glanced sideways at Natalie as a warning to keep quiet. "No."

"Come on, Karina," Natalie said. "It's no use now." She turned to the others. "She bought him lingerie."

Cordelia pressed her hand to her chest and coughed. "¿Qué, qué?"

"You guys should've seen her," Natalie continued. "It was so cute. She tried it on and everything, trying to find the right one."

"Aw," Marisa said.

"Stop it," Karina said.

"You know I'm only teasing you," Natalie said. "It's exciting to see you crushing like this."

"I'm not crushing. I just wanted to give my guy a hot, sexy night. There's nothing cute about it."

They gaped at her.

"What?" Karina asked.

"You called him your guy," Natalie said.

"I did not." *Oh my God, did I?*

"You did." Natalie laughed and pulled Karina to her. "You should see the look on your face. We have officially lost you."

"I'm not lost; I'm right here."

"Hey, K."

Everyone turned to look at Ian as he walked into the cafeteria, including the dough preparers, Tyler and Nicholas.

"You forgot your phone." Ian handed it to her, then turned to the girls. "We haven't officially met, but Karina told me all about you. Cordelia, the expert chef; Marisa, the kindest person in the world; and Natalie, the roomie."

"Aw, you said that about me?" Marisa asked.

Karina looked away to hide the emotion of being back on Marisa's good side.

Ian put his hand on Karina's shoulder. "She speaks highly of all of you. Like how I should get some pointers from you, Cordelia, since you make the most amazing food."

Cordelia glowed. "I'd be happy to show you some tricks."

"She tell you I made pizza for her last night?"

"No, she didn't. I had to find out from Rosa," Cordelia said, glaring at Karina. "And was it hard to make? I've never done it."

"Wasn't that hard. Karina loved it. Right, K?"

Karina didn't move or make any sign of acknowledgment. Why was he embarrassing her like this?

"And what else did you do last night?" Marisa asked Ian, in a too-flirty tone.

"Uh . . ." He rubbed the back of his neck and laughed. "We hung out."

Karina cleared her throat. "Ian, let's go outside a moment."

"Yeah, sure. Nice meeting you." He waved at them, and they waved back, all smiles.

When they were out of earshot, Karina said between gritted teeth, "Don't do that again."

"Do what?"

"Be all lovey-dovey in front of everyone."

He frowned. "I only said K."

She crossed her arms. "That was already too much."

"Everyone knows we're together. What's the big deal?"

"I told you I wanted to keep my private life separate from my work life. Everyone talks about us too much." She dropped her arms. "Let's not give them more fuel for the fire."

"But they're your friends. Didn't think they counted."

"We still work together. And they're not the only ones in there."

"Okay, you're right. I won't bother you at work."

Karina let out a breath. "Good."

"Or stand close to you like this." He pressed her against the wall.

She pushed him back. "Stop it."

He laughed.

"Hello," Dwight said from behind Ian.

Ian started and sobered. Karina pressed her hand to her forehead. "Hi, Dwight." Where had he come from?

Dwight cleared his throat. "I was on my way to the test bakery to run some samples, but I'm glad I caught you two. I'm thinking of creating an internal auditing team. Would you be interested in joining?"

"Another team?" Karina asked. "What's that about?"

"As I mentioned in the last HACCP meeting, I want to implement an internal auditing program, and for that, I need a team. I think the two of you would be excellent. What do you say?"

Karina pointed between her and Ian. "You want both of us?"

"Yes. Is there a problem?" Dwight's eyes widened. "Oh, or maybe only you, Karina? I wouldn't want it to interfere with your . . . relationship."

Karina's mouth fell open. So he and Lacey could work together fine, but Karina would have problems? Sure, another work team with Ian meant seeing him more often when she was already seeing him too much, but Dwight didn't need to know that. And she had offered to help him, so there was no getting out of it.

"It's not a problem," Ian said. "We'd love to join."

"Splendid," Dwight said. "I'll set up a training for next week. Oh, and Karina, please clear it with Roy? I want no more problems."

Karina nodded. Maybe having Dwight steal her away would make Roy explode and create more conflict between them, which could lead to Dwight quitting or Lacey having to choose between her uncle and her boyfriend. It was worth a shot.

"My apologies for, uh, interrupting." He walked past them into the test bakery down the hall.

"Why did you answer for me?" Karina asked Ian. "I can answer for myself."

"Sorry. I thought—"

"I need to pee."

Did he think he owned her now because she'd spent the night at his place? She pushed open the door to the bathroom, passed the lockers on her way to the toilets, and there was Rosa, cleaning the sinks.

"Hello, Karina. Ian told us about your romantic night." She rinsed the sponge she'd been using. "They don't make men like that anymore."

"Uh-huh." Damn it. Couldn't people leave her alone? She couldn't even pee in peace. Karina entered a free stall, slamming the door shut, signaling she was done talking. It seemed to work. All she heard from Rosa was her humming and the sound of a spray bottle.

But as soon as Karina stepped out to wash her hands, Rosa continued. "You know, I told him to stay away from you, but he didn't listen. Frankly, I don't know what all these boys see in you."

"Is there a point you want to make?"

"Ian's a nice boy, not like the lowlifes you usually surround yourself with."

"What about Marcos?" Karina grabbed a paper towel from the dispenser and dried her hands. "Is he a lowlife too?"

"My nephew's a pendejo, still asking about you after you spit him out like gum. But if you plan to do the same to Ian, do it now, before he goes in too deep."

"Oh, it's too late for that." She smirked. "He's gone *way* deep already."

Rosa's lip curled, and with one last look of disdain, she rolled her cleaning cart out.

Karina threw the paper towel in the trash and faced the mirror, fluffing up her hair with her hand. Who the hell was Rosa to tell her anything? She wasn't her mother. Then again, Debbie had also cleaned for a living and knew nothing about Karina's personal life, so they both had that in common. Rosa should learn from her mom and stay the fuck away.

As Karina turned to exit, she bumped into Lacey coming in.

"How are you, Karina? Isn't this a beautiful day?" She sighed. "How was your Valentine's Day? Did you celebrate it with Ian?"

Karina clenched her jaw to keep from yelling out, *Not you too!* She had to act friendly, find out more about Lacey's relationship with Dwight. She forced herself to smile. "Yeah. Did you do anything with Dwight?"

Lacey's eyes lit up. "We went out to dinner. It was so romantic, and at the end of the night . . . he kissed me. Oh, Karina, I haven't felt like this about a man in such a long time."

Why wasn't Rosa here to hear this so she could hassle Lacey? Maybe Karina should tell Rosa and spread the rumor. Dwight would break up with her for sure. But if Karina told, Lacey would know it was her, and they needed to stay on friendly terms.

"Roy told me you'd be working late on some projections for the expansion," Karina said. "How are we doing with the contract? Are we on track?"

Lacey seemed to come back to Earth. "What? Sure, we are. But oh, I need your opinion on something. Dwight wants me to come to his church on Sunday. I know it's a gigantic step, but what do you think? Should I go?"

Karina gaped. Lacey was already falling for Dwight. The disease was spreading too fast. Was she already too late to save Lacey—and the company?

"Karina, did you hear me? I know you don't approve, but you're the only one who knows about me and Dwight. Please, I need your insight on this."

"You know I have no idea about this kind of thing."

"But you're dating Ian now. How long has it been, two weeks? You've never been with the same guy that long. It appears someone has changed her mind about being in a serious relationship."

"Whoa, whoa, whoa. Two weeks is not that long. And do you see me gushing like a teenage girl asking for advice? You and me are not the same."

Lacey pressed her palm against her chest, eyes wide. "What—"

"You're losing it! This"—Karina gestured toward Lacey—"is not the woman I met, the one who, after her divorce, said she'd never let a man mess up her life again. What happened to her?"

Lacey's jaw slackened. So much for being friendly, but what had Lacey expected? For Karina to act sisterly and supportive all of a sudden?

"Never mind." Lacey straightened. "I'll follow my instinct, as I always have." She ducked into a stall.

Karina stormed out. Fucking Valentine's Day.

CHAPTER FIFTEEN

The rest of the afternoon went something like this:

"You must've been very distracted this morning to forget your phone," Natalie said with a wink.

"Aw, you two looked so cute together," Marisa gushed. "And he calls you K! Do you have a nickname for him too?"

"Already in love, Karina?" Tyler asked with a straight face. "I can tell Ian where I bought the ring."

And to think the day had started so well.

By the end of the shift, Karina was dying for an escape. In the women's locker room, she checked her messages. A text from her mom asking, *How was your Valentine's Day? Did you spend it with someone special?* What was everyone's obsession with this fucking holiday? Yesterday, her mom had wished her a happy day, sharing a pic quote about unconditional love. Ugh.

"Karina," Cordelia said from her locker.

"What?" No message from Ian. She was supposed to go over to his place, but after the day she'd had, she just wanted to be alone.

"Have you talked to Ian about your relationship?"

Karina snapped her head back at Cordelia, who was applying eyeshadow. "What relationship?"

"I know you've never had a boyfriend, but Ian—"

"He's not my boyfriend."

"Maybe not officially, but the way he was acting—"

"Why do you have to read so much into everything?" Karina stuffed the phone back into her fanny pack. "We're just having fun."

Cordelia swiped her finger against her eyelid. "After you left, I talked to him and asked him some questions."

Karina slammed her locker door shut. "You did what?" The chatter around them died as everyone's eyes turned to her.

Cordelia continued her blending. "Did you know he's had four steady girlfriends and that he was engaged to the last one?"

Karina wrapped her fanny pack around her waist.

"You can't have fun with a man like that," Cordelia said. "He's the serious type."

"He knows we're casual."

"Does he?" Cordelia put her eyeshadow case back in her cosmetics bag and finally had the guts to look her in the eye. "Maybe he thinks you changed your mind."

"Oh, have you?" Marisa asked from her spot near the entrance to the stalls. "Because we think he's great."

Natalie sat on the bench. "Isn't it too soon for a talk like that?" she asked Cordelia.

"Usually, yes, but this isn't the typical situation. He won't get scared if she brings it up." Cordelia turned back to Karina. "That man—he's out to conquer you. How he looks at you, making you dinner, calling you K . . . he wants more."

Karina crossed her arms. "Why don't you work on your own relationship and leave me alone?"

Some "oohs" from the other packers.

Cordelia rolled her eyes. "What are you talking about? My relationship's solid. There's nothing to fix."

"Right." Karina gazed around. The small crowd was enthralled. "I thought Charlie was cool, but he's turned into the old-fashioned husband who expects the wife to have dinner cooked by the time he arrives. I'm surprised he even lets you work."

Cordelia frowned. "Charlie doesn't expect that of me."

"Then let's go grab a bite to eat now."

"I have to go home and cook dinner for him."

Karina threw up her hands. "You just said he doesn't expect you to."

"He doesn't. I want to."

"Didn't you cook for him last night?"

"You finished the leftovers."

"Can't he cook something for himself?"

"Can *you*?"

"Then why don't we meet afterward, grab a drink?"

"I'd have to ask him."

"See. There it is." Karina pointed at her. "Are you capable of doing anything without his permission?"

Cordelia gripped the makeup bag in her hand. "He's my husband. I can't run off."

"You can meet up with me, then tell him when you're at home."

"What if he wants to do something else with me?"

"And what? What you want doesn't count?"

"Of course it does. But we're married—"

"Face it. You have no life separate from your husband. And you weren't like this before. But ever since you got married, it's like no one else exists. You and Mari. At least she escapes that asshole now and then—"

Cordelia pointed her index finger at Karina's face. "Don't compare my dear husband to Jaime. They're not the same. Charlie loves me for real, and that's why I enjoy spending my free time with him. Because I love him. But you wouldn't understand."

"Why wouldn't I understand?" Karina asked. "Because I've never loved a man? I love . . . other things. It should all be the same."

"Jaime loves me for real," Marisa mumbled and escaped into a stall.

"Mari," Cordelia called after her, "we didn't mean it." She shook her head at Karina, as if to say, *Look what you did.*

Karina shrugged.

Cordelia returned to her makeup routine, applying mascara this time. The tension around the room broke, and the other women left, one of them whispering, "I was waiting for Cordelia to yank her hair out," before the door shut behind them.

Cordelia blotted at her lips with a tissue. "You say I live only for my husband, but you know what?" She glanced at the entrance to the stalls and whispered, "I'm throwing Marisa a surprise birthday party."

"Ha," Karina said. "I'll believe it when I see it."

Cordelia gasped and placed a hand to her chest, looking hurt. "I love throwing parties."

"When you were single. You haven't even invited us to your new house, and it's been two months since your wedding."

"Nobody's keeping you from visiting. Marisa brought us a wonderful housewarming gift, and we gave her a tour. If you weren't so selfish, you could've done the same."

Karina felt as if she'd been slapped. Next to kind, thoughtful Marisa, they all looked bad in comparison. No wonder Cordelia would throw a party for her and not for Karina.

"Guys, stop," Natalie said in a high whisper. "She's coming."

Marisa returned, eyes to the ground, and busied herself with her locker. Natalie finished packing her gym bag. Karina and Cordelia stared each other down until Cordelia turned back to the mirror.

"It's no use talking to you when you're grumpy like this." Cordelia smacked her lips together, then dabbed at the corner of her mouth. "I only wanted to give you some advice. Take it, don't take it, it's up to you."

"If Ian wants something serious, he can bring it up himself." Karina picked up her jacket from the bench and threw it over her shoulder. "You act like he's a naïve little boy, but he knows the kind of girl I am, thanks to Rosa. If he wants to be with me, it's his own problem. I'm out of here." She threw the door open. "I've had enough bullshit for one day."

* * *

At home, Karina opened a can of beer and popped a bag of microwave popcorn. Then she settled into her velvet couch to watch *Gone Girl*, wrapping her favorite blanket around her, a plush cocoon against romance, love, and the dupes who fell for both.

Ten minutes in, she got a text from Ian. *You on your way?*
She texted back. *Staying in. Headache.*
Her phone rang. She paused the movie and answered. "What?"
"Still in a bad mood?"
"I told you not to talk to my friends."
"Cordelia asked me questions, and I felt obligated to answer."
"You're too much of a gentleman." She munched on popcorn.
"And a gossip, it turns out. Stop talking to Rosa. She's the reason
everyone knows about us."
"I'll try not to mention you."
She slurped the last of the beer. "Why do you call me K?"
"You don't like it? I thought it was a cute nickname."
"My friends think so too."
"Ah, ya veo. Your friends teased you because of me. I'm sorry.
I won't talk to them without your permission. I promise. Now, will
you please come over? You must be hungry. There's a pizza with your
name on it."
"I'm eating popcorn." She stuffed her mouth and chewed loudly.
"You know that won't keep you full."
Damn it, he already knew her too well.

* * *

As soon as Ian opened his front door and kissed her, the bad mood
faded away. While they shared the leftover pizza, Cordelia's so-called
advice banged in her head. Should she make it clear she still wanted
casual? But if she did and he said he'd changed his mind, she'd have
to stop seeing him, and she was nowhere near ready for that yet.
"You okay?" Ian asked. "You're too quiet."
"I'm just tired."
"Hey, um, I know it's been only two weeks . . ."
Not now.
"But I want to make sure we agree."
Karina gulped. "About what?"
"You're not . . . you're not seeing other guys, are you?"
"What? No. I don't like to mix." Juggling more than one guy was
too much of a hassle.

He laughed. "Good. Good. I'm not seeing anyone else either."

Wait, was this his way of telling her they were serious now? Why couldn't he come out and say it?

He kissed her, and she relaxed, repeating Natalie's words in her head: *Don't think about it.*

CHAPTER SIXTEEN

Ian surprised her with breakfast in bed. "Happy monthiversary."

"What?" Karina was still groggy from sleep. Was she having a nightmare?

He opened the blinds. "Today marks one month since our first date, and I wanted to do something special."

"One month? Wow. So fast." The time since Valentine's Day was a blur, but it *was* possible two weeks had passed. She checked her phone for the date. Friday, March the second. Exactly one month. Shit, how could that be?

He sat next to her. "Not hungry? That would be a first for you."

Karina eyed the tray on her lap. It had a plate stacked with pancakes, a mug of coffee, and maple syrup. She took a sip of coffee—caffeine was necessary to help her fully wake up and decipher what the hell had happened. "Pancakes? Isn't that too many carbs in the morning?"

"They're made with cottage cheese, so they're high in protein. Try them."

That didn't sound very appetizing, but even with the tightness in her chest, her body needed food in order to flee as soon as possible. She added maple syrup and tried a piece. "Mmm. Not bad."

"Right?" He opened his mouth wide.

It took her a few seconds to understand what he wanted. She cut off a piece and fed it to him. They'd gotten used to feeding each other. When had this become her life?

"My dad thinks you're a good influence on me."

She choked and drank coffee to stop the coughing. "You talked to your dad about me?"

"I tell him everything. And I told him you make fun of me for eating protein bars and shakes—he does too—and that since I met you, I'm eating more proper food, and he approves."

"Uh-huh." What the fuck? She'd run away right now if there weren't food left to eat. But as soon as she swallowed the last bite, she put the tray on the floor. "I should get ready for work. It's getting late."

"Wait." He took her hand. "I also got you something." He leaned over the edge of the bed, rummaged through his nightstand drawer, and took out a small gift-wrapped box. "Here."

"What is it?"

"Open it."

Karina eyed the package apprehensively. What if it was something cheesy like a photo of them in a heart-shaped frame?

What if it was a ring?

She wiped her hands on the sheets.

"It won't bite you. Here, I'll open it."

She sighed in relief when she saw it was a small box of Whitman's Sampler.

"Close your eyes."

"No." She jumped from the bed. No way was she going to engage in another disgustingly romantic session of feeding each other chocolate.

"You don't want chocolate?"

"Isn't it too early for chocolate? And I'm going to be late for work." She ran into the bathroom and locked herself in, leaning back on the door for support. Her breath came out in quick gasps.

One month.

The door rattled. "K? You all right? Why did you lock the door? I also need to shower."

They were used to showering together. In fact, they'd been doing everything together these past two weeks. She glanced around the room. There was her deodorant and the body lotion Ian loved next to the sink. Her comb and blow dryer. And inside the hamper, her dirty clothes—even her underwear—jumbled with Ian's, ready for his washing machine.

Oh my God.

She was living with him.

"Karina?"

"Hold on. I'm doing number two." She sat on the toilet and rested her head on her hands. How could this have happened without her noticing? She was supposed to be in control.

Oh, she knew why. Because she'd programmed herself to "not think about it."

This was all Natalie's fault.

Karina texted her. *On my way home. Don't leave until I get there. It's an emergency.*

She showered super fast and unlocked the door. "I need to go. Natalie just texted me. She wants to talk to me." Karina went to the dresser—she had her own drawer, for God's sake—and threw on a pair of jeans and a T-shirt that said *I'm awake for this?*

"Hold it." Ian blocked her way before she could escape. "You okay?"

"Yeah. Why wouldn't I be?"

He stroked her cheek. "Is this the first time you've been with a guy this long?"

"What?" She scoffed. "No."

"It's okay to be afraid." He wrapped his arms around her and pulled her close. "I shouldn't have made a big deal of it. Sorry. I'm just so happy to know you this long." He kissed her.

She relaxed into him. How could everything be wrong but still feel right?

It was him. He was the problem.

"We won't mention it again." He smoothed down her hair. "We'll keep going like we have been. Deal?"

She was about to say *Yeah*, but the answer should've been *No, I can't keep going on like this or I'll be lost.* She settled for "Uh-huh."

"I really have to go." She kissed him one more time and left.

Once in her car, she started hyperventilating again. Her hands shook as she put the car in motion. It was time she put distance between them, maybe even break up.

A wave of nausea overcame her, and she gripped the steering wheel. *What am I supposed to do, Heart? I can't keep doing this.* Her chest ached. *Okay. Maybe I won't break up completely, but I need some space from him.*

* * *

Karina ran inside the house and found Natalie putting her breakfast dishes into the dishwasher.

"Did you know I've been with Ian for a month?"

Natalie froze. "That's your big emergency?"

"You told me not to think about it, and I didn't, and now a month has passed, and . . ." She dropped to the floor, covering her face.

Natalie shut the dishwasher door and crouched beside Karina, stroking her back. "Deep breaths."

Karina obeyed, and her breathing slowed.

"This is not the end of the world."

"He gave me a gift. And he's been talking to his parents about me."

"These are good things. Things all women want."

"Spare me."

"I've been so excited for you, and here you are, getting hysterical over nothing."

Karina dropped her hands. "Excited about what?"

"You and Ian. You've been so happy and relaxed since Valentine's Day. I thought you finally gave in. You're practically living with him."

Karina sat up straight. "So you noticed? Why didn't you warn me?"

"Warn you?" She laughed. "Karina, this is good. It means you're getting serious about him."

"But I don't want to get serious." She jumped to her feet. "You know I never wanted to get serious, and now I'm fucking living with him."

Natalie stood and held on to Karina's shoulders. "Look, it's getting late, and we both need to get going. Why don't you take the rest of the morning to process everything? We'll talk more at lunch."

"No. The others cannot know. I don't want another lecture from Cordelia or more pity from Marisa. Promise me you won't tell them. And this time really mean it, Natalie, or I swear . . ."

"Okay, okay, I won't tell them. We'll talk after work. Don't do anything stupid until then."

* * *

On her way to work, Karina took more deep breaths. She could avoid Ian until later. No equipment was on schedule for maintenance. Unless something broke down, she'd be safe. But no . . . She groaned. Dwight had scheduled a meeting for the internal auditing team that afternoon. Ian would be there.

Deep breath in, deep breath out. No biggie. They didn't talk about anything personal at work. It would be okay.

As she parked, her stomach growled. So much stress had left her depleted. She entered through reception, heading to the small display of Singular Cookies for sale to visitors. Employees got a twenty-five percent discount. Karina grabbed a bunch of Perkys, and then her eye landed on the Mellow Cookie. It had chamomile. Maybe it would help her relax. She hadn't eaten it since the days of the commercial kitchen, when she'd helped Lacey develop it. It hadn't had an effect on her then, but it was worth a shot. After paying Sofia, the receptionist, she walked toward the cafeteria.

Karina sat and ripped open the package. The smell immediately took her back. Lacey had been under so much stress that she was always drinking chamomile tea with lemon and honey. Karina joked about it being Lacey's signature drink. "Why don't you make a cookie after it?"

And Lacey had done it, proving once again she could do anything she set her mind to. Of course, that was in the past. Present Lacey couldn't even get a new cookie recipe right.

Karina bit into the cookie. She'd taken sips of Lacey's tea, and the cookie tasted just like it: lemony sweet. Her muscles loosened.

Though Karina was happy for their current success, she'd give anything to go back to those early days. At least these cookies were tangible proof of their partnership, the only consolation she had left.

* * *

Karina's hectic morning left no room for worries. Lunch was uneventful—for once Natalie kept her mouth shut. When Karina arrived at the meeting, Ian smiled at her. So he wasn't mad at her for running off or suspicious she'd lied to him about Natalie needing to talk.

So far, so good.

During training last week, Dwight had explained the process for conducting internal audits and different techniques to use, like focus area auditing (observing for ten minutes to focus on one item of the checklist at a time) and asking open questions (who, what, when, where, how, and why) rather than closed questions that required only a yes or no answer. It hadn't been as boring as Karina had imagined, but she wasn't sure she could manage one on her own. The team was small—only Dwight, Karina, and Ian.

"I finished the auditing schedule." Dwight handed them a chart, listing the audits they needed to do. "We have twelve programs, so we can do one per month. However, since no one has done such an in-depth audit of the plant before, I thought we could do more so we're better prepared for the inspection in four months."

He assigned an area to each of them: production for Ian and the warehouse for Karina.

"In order to perform the audit," Dwight said, "you must become familiar with the procedures for each area." He handed each of them a binder.

Karina looked through hers. It contained all the procedures related to the warehouse—receiving, storage, shipping—and the audit checklist with the items she needed to look out for. Great, homework. Hadn't she dropped out of high school so she wouldn't have to deal with that again? All the extra work she was doing to try to break up Lacey and Dwight hadn't resulted in anything useful. No new insights and no extra pressure from Roy. He had agreed to let her join the team without a word. Karina hoped he wasn't giving up the fight. Singular Cookies needed him.

"What happens if we find something that's not right?" Ian asked.

"If it's nothing too critical, we can change the procedure to fit the process. Otherwise, we must retrain. You must also do a record audit. They're all filed here, so you can look through them after you finish the physical audit. I'll help you with that. Do you think you can handle this?"

No. Karina shrugged. Ian nodded.

"You'll do fine," Dwight said. "This is new to us all. We'll learn from each other."

"How long do we have?" Ian asked. "Until the end of the month?"

"Yes, including the record audit. You have to document the corrective actions for every nonconformity you find, communicate them to the person responsible, and verify that they fix it."

Karina let out a breath. "Is that all?" Dwight had told them they wouldn't have to invest more than a couple of hours a month for this team, and they'd already had a training plus this stupid meeting. This warehouse audit would probably take her a whole day, if she could even manage it. Dwight and his changes and the stupid inspection.

After the meeting adjourned, Ian called out to her in the hallway.

"We're not supposed to talk at work," she whispered through gritted teeth, glancing around for eavesdroppers.

"I know, I know," he whispered back. "You left so fast this morning, I forgot to ask you. Want to go to Friday Fest later? It could become our tradition."

"Tradition?" Her voice sounded like a balloon letting air out.

"Or not. Forget I said *tradition*. Want to go? You said you looked forward to it every month."

"Yeah, that's true, but . . ." She wiped her hands on her jeans. "I already made plans with Natalie."

"You did?"

He looked so disappointed, she added, "We made the plans before I met you. That's why she texted me, to remind me. I'd completely forgotten about them." *Why are you giving him so many explanations? You should be able to make plans whenever you want.*

"What will you do?" he asked.

"You mean with Natalie? Oh, we're going down to Miami for a girl's weekend. There's a show we want to see. I don't really know. Natalie made all the arrangements."

"Oh, okay. Cool." He scratched his head. "Wish you'd told me."

"Why? I can't have a girl's weekend?" Now she was definitely going.

"Of course you can. Es solo . . . it's not how I imagined the weekend."

"Look, I have to go, but I'll see you on Monday, okay?" Her chest ached. Three whole nights without him?

"That long? I'll miss you."

"You'll survive." She left before his sad face made her kiss him and confess everything.

But . . . if she could convince Natalie, it wouldn't be a complete lie. Miami was only a two-hour drive away. They'd be there by nightfall, ready for an Ian-free weekend to decide what to do about him.

Once inside the production area, Karina went straight to the QC lab. Natalie was studying an Active Cookie and chatting with her lab mate, Maya. They laughed at something Maya said.

"Natalie, can you come out here?" Karina asked from the doorway. "I need to talk to you."

Natalie nodded, jotted something down, then joined Karina in front of the cooling tunnel. "How are you doing?"

"You can't go to the gym today. We're going to Miami."

"I'm sorry, what?"

"Ian wanted us to start the tradition of going to Friday Fest every month. I needed a way out. This is it."

"You lied to him?"

"It's not a lie if we go through with it."

"I have a date tomorrow."

"Cancel it. I'll help you hook up with a guy over there. And I'll pay for everything. It shouldn't be much of a sacrifice. But we have to leave tonight."

Natalie tipped her head to the ceiling and sighed. "Fine. But you owe me so much for this."

"Owe you more than a free trip to Miami? Give me a fucking break, Nat. Besides, didn't you say you owed me for Benjamin?"

Natalie pressed her lips and returned to the lab. When Karina had helped her with that stalker, she hadn't been expecting a payback, but if this is what it took for Natalie to get on board, so be it.

* * *

Karina booked a hotel, and by six that night, they were in her car driving south on the turnpike.

"Don't you feel guilty for lying to Ian?" Natalie asked. "You're literally running away from him. Are you going to stop seeing him?"

"I don't know." She switched lanes to pass a truck.

"Do you like being with him?"

"Yeah, but maybe that's the problem. I like being with him too much. Maybe I should ask him for a break."

"People don't take breaks because they like someone too much. He'll think you're breaking up with him."

"Maybe I should." Another wave of nausea. She gripped the steering wheel until it passed.

"But he's perfect for you."

"He's not the only man in the world."

"Oh, Karina, if that were true, I'd be married already. You don't know how hard it is to have that kind of spark with someone."

Her heart ached. There were sparks, tons of sparks, too many. But maybe it was time to snuff them out before a fire consumed her and she wasn't able to save herself.

"I have to stop spending so much time at his place," Karina said. "I'm getting too comfortable there anyway. He needs to see that I will not change my whole lifestyle because he's around."

"Are you sure about that? You could end up alienating him."

"It has to end, eventually. Maybe this is it."

"I can't believe you're still so afraid of intimacy. I thought he'd changed you."

She set her jaw. "No man can change me."

CHAPTER SEVENTEEN

"You coming over?" Ian asked Karina over the phone Sunday night.

Karina threw her bag into the closet and collapsed on the bed, piling her cushions around her and cuddling up to them. Only a few seconds had passed since she'd texted him she was back home. Couldn't he give her time to breathe? He hadn't stopped texting all weekend. She'd sent him photos of the hotel and the places they visited so he wouldn't think she'd lied, but so what if she had? It shouldn't matter so much, but it did. She hated that it did.

Sure, she'd missed him. Way too much, and her body craved his touch. But the fog in her brain—obscuring everything except him and his needs—had lifted, and going over to his place was too much of a risk. "I'm exhausted from the drive."

"Oh." He paused. "But I'll definitely see you tomorrow, verdad? I went to the farmers' market and found plantains on sale. Thought I'd make my mom's mofongo recipe. You'll love it."

Already tempting her back with food. "Actually . . . Natalie confessed on our trip she's being stalked by some guy she dated." Benjamin was serving all sorts of purposes these days.

"She call the police?"

"No, it hasn't gotten that bad yet. But she doesn't want to be alone in the house, especially at night. She didn't want to tell me because of you, but now that she has, I can't leave her."

"No, of course not." He paused. "Then how about I bring everything there and cook for the two of you?"

What could she say now? *No, don't be so wonderful and cook for my roommate and me because I need to stay away from you?* It sounded ludicrous even to Karina. "Yeah, but we hardly use our kitchen. We don't have any cooking utensils like you do. And you know Natalie only eats raw food."

"She won't be able to resist my mom's mofongo, you'll see. I'll cook everything here and bring it there, how about that?"

Could he stop being such a saint? "Sounds like a plan." She hung up and put a cushion over her head.

Natalie shook her head when Karina told her what she'd told Ian. "This is what you're afraid of? A man who wants to cook for you?" She reached for a plant on the shelf above her desk and watered it.

"And you can't eat with us. It would be too friendly. I want to tell him you don't approve of him sleeping over."

"Now I'm a nun?" Some of the water spilled onto the floor. "Karina, this is wrong. Tell him you need space."

"What if he's offended and . . ." *Breaks up with me?*

She wiped the floor with a sock. "He should be able to understand if you're straight with him."

"I think this is better."

"By making me out to be the bad guy?"

"It's just until I figure out something else."

"But I love mofongo." She pouted.

"Remember Benjamin," Karina said in a singsong voice.

Natalie let out an exasperated sigh. "Fine, I'll go along with it. For now." She reached for another plant. "You can only hang Benjamin over me for so long. I hope you realize soon how stupid you're being."

* * *

When Karina entered the cafeteria for work the next day, Lacey was again inside the test bakery.

"Ugh," she told Natalie. "Not that stupid cookie again. I'm not trying one bite this time."

"Maybe it will be better today," Natalie said, though she didn't look convinced.

They prepped their food and were about to eat when Cordelia marched in with Marisa close behind her.

"You went to Miami without us?" Cordelia asked. "How nice."

"Who told you?" Karina glared at Natalie, who raised her hands in defense.

"Rosa overheard Ian telling Brody how much he missed you this weekend because you were away with your friend Natalie." She grabbed her bowl from the refrigerator and placed it in the microwave. "I guess she's your only friend."

Why was Ian still talking about her at work? "You wouldn't have gone even if we'd asked."

"It was something spontaneous," Natalie said.

"We can do spontaneous," Cordelia said.

"And by we, you mean you and your dear hubby, don't you?" Karina said. "It was a girls' weekend away. No men allowed."

"Ah, bueno. In that case . . ."

"What about me?" Marisa asked as she sat. "I would've come. Jaime was busy with his friends, so I was at home by myself."

"I'm sorry, Mari," Natalie said. "We'll plan another one."

"How about for my birthday?" She dropped her sandwich back into her bowl and clapped. "Oh, that would be so fun."

"We can't go that weekend," Cordelia said in a rush. She was still going on about a surprise birthday party for Marisa.

"Why not? You can bring Charlie if you want. We won't mind, right, guys?"

Natalie and Karina stared at Cordelia. Cordelia raised her eyebrows at them as if to ask, *What do I say now?*

Marisa eyed them. "What is it? Do you all . . . have plans already?" There was a hint of pain in her voice. "It's okay if you do. If you forgot . . ."

"Of course we didn't forget," Cordelia said, a bit offended. "I'm throwing you a party at my house."

"What? Really?" Marisa half laughed, half cried. "Why haven't you said anything?"

Cordelia removed her bowl from the microwave and joined them. "I wanted it to be a surprise."

Marisa spread her hands to her cheeks. "Oh no, I ruined my own surprise?"

"Don't worry." Cordelia patted her on the back. "At least you won't get mad at me for not wanting to go to Miami."

"Aw, that's so nice, you guys."

"You can invite anyone you want."

"Oh, just you guys. And your men, of course. Natalie, you can bring a date. And, uh . . ." She picked at her cuticles. "I know you guys don't like Jaime, but he'll be on his best behavior, I promise."

Yeah, right. Karina chewed her rice and beans to keep quiet. At Cordelia's wedding reception, he'd drunk so much he couldn't stop groping poor Marisa on the dance floor, to her total embarrassment. But when Karina went to pull him off her, instead of standing up for herself, Marisa had gotten mad at Karina for interfering. It had all deteriorated from there, to a final confrontation the next morning where Karina called Jaime a moocher and they almost came to blows.

That asshole better not look at her twice at this party. If it even took place. Single Cordelia had hosted parties for every occasion, even inviting them over for dinner sometimes "just because." But that Cordelia was gone. Same as Karina's mom. Marriage had made them obsessed with pleasing their husbands to the point of ignoring everyone else. At least Cordelia hadn't completely forsaken Karina and still brought her food. Karina couldn't say the same thing about her mom.

"Karina," Cordelia said, "give me Ian's email address so I can send him an invitation."

"I'll let him know; don't worry." No way would Ian step one foot into this party.

Lacey walked in carrying a tray of fresh-baked cookies. "Hi, ladies. This time I reduced the amount of licorice root powder. Could you try and let me know what you think?"

Karina continued eating, but the others reached tentatively into the tray, picked up a cookie, and took a bite.

"Karina, don't you want one?" Lacey asked.

"Nope."

Lacey stared at her but said nothing. Ever since their fight in the bathroom, the only words they'd exchanged had been related to work, all traces of their friendly rapport gone. But not even guilt would make her try that Traitor Cookie.

"The flavor's not as strong this time," Natalie said. "Try one."

Everyone was staring at her, and she sighed. "Fine." She grabbed a cookie and took a tiny little bite. Natalie was right; it wasn't as bad as last time. Karina took a slightly bigger bite. But it was also nothing special. *Good.*

"It's too plain," Natalie said.

"I agree," Cordelia said. She took another bite and smacked her lips. "There's something missing."

"Yes," Marisa said. "I think so too."

"But the licorice is tolerable?" Lacey asked.

Natalie nodded. "But you also can't tell it's licorice. So you'll have to add more. Or something else."

Lacey sighed. "Back to the drawing board again. Thanks, ladies." She walked over to the guys.

Karina dropped the rest of the cookie on the table. "Why doesn't she give it up?" she whispered. "This shit's never gonna work."

"It worked with the others," Cordelia said. "She'll find the right balance soon."

*　*　*

When Karina saw Ian in Dwight's office as she came in for the HACCP team meeting, all she wanted was to straddle him and kiss him, but she settled for sitting next to him.

His smile made her heart flutter and her whole body tingle. She lay her palm on his knee.

"I want to kiss you so bad," he whispered into her ear.

Karina giggled, then coughed to cover it up. No one seemed to notice. Scott typed into his phone, and Dwight wrote on the white-board next to his desk.

When Lacey walked in, Dwight smiled at her and cleared his throat to start the meeting. "I want to update you on what we've been doing to prepare for the inspection. Karina, Ian, and I are ready to audit internally. Karina needs to schedule with you, Scott, so she can audit the warehouse and your processes, preferably for this week or next."

Scott nodded.

"I've also been able to write a procedure for our new training program. I want to implement a monthly training for everyone at the plant, something more in depth than what we have now. For that, we must interrupt production for an hour."

"Ha! Good luck with that," Karina blurted.

"Don't you think it's a good idea?" Dwight asked.

"We can't even have lunch together. You think Roy is going to allow that?"

"Then we'll do it early in the morning before production starts," Dwight said. "Or after."

Lacey peeked over Scott at her. "Do you have any other suggestions, Karina?"

"No."

"Then let us handle it," Lacey said. "Dwight will give a presentation tomorrow at the management meeting, and my uncle will have to see how this new training strategy is for the good of the company."

"I don't think you ganging up on Roy is going to work."

"We're not 'ganging up' on him," Lacey said, with air quotes. "Why would you say that?"

"It's just . . . you and Dwight are . . ."

Lacey glared at her, gesturing with her eyes toward Dwight.

"Roy might feel left out," Karina finished.

"I think I know how to handle my uncle better than you."

"Then why did you ask me to help him work better with Dwight?"

"I was wrong. I should've taken care of that myself."

"Right. He's not my family. Funny how you used to say he was."

"He thought of you as family. I did too. But you were right, we're not your family, so stay out of it."

Karina's stomach ached as if Lacey had punched her. They'd been the perfect team, and now . . . Lacey had never looked at her with so much disdain. Karina had been right to have clear boundaries, to find her own place after Roy's wife died, to never go back to that house, to reject all invitations, to discuss only work topics. Roy and Lacey were not her family and never would be.

Back when Karina was still Roy's maid, before Lacey had established Singular Cookies, Inc., Karina had helped Lacey make Perky Cookies in Roy's kitchen one day. A friend of a friend of the family had ordered one hundred of them for a party she was hosting.

One batch was already in the oven, and Karina and Lacey were each mixing one batch.

"You should definitely listen to your uncle and start a company. He knows what he's talking about. And I'm sure he'll support you."

"Yes, I know. He's like a second dad. Sometimes he's been more of a dad than my own. I can always count on him."

"Must be nice to have someone like that in your life."

"He could be a dad for you, too, if you let him."

Karina scoffed. "He's my boss."

"Does he treat you like a boss?"

"He gives me orders."

Lacey laughed. "He gives everyone orders."

"But he doesn't pay you to have dinner with him."

"He pays you to clean the house. He has dinner with you because he likes you."

"He has dinner with me because he's lonely."

"And what about when I come over for dinner? He's not lonely then, and he still asks you to join us. Someone who's only a boss wouldn't do that."

It was true. He did always want to include her, sometimes even when she didn't want to be included. But Karina knew it was mostly out of pity. He knew her mom had thrown her out. The owner of the cleaning company, her mom's old boss, had told him. That was the only reason he'd given her this job and put up with her. It didn't mean he actually cared.

"Once your aunt gets better or . . ." Karina couldn't bring herself to say it. Anne was getting worse, and it was clear she wouldn't last long. "I'll have to leave."

"You can stay working as a maid. I'm sure he won't mind."

"And live alone here with an old man? I don't think so."

"Then maybe you can work for me."

"With the cookies?"

"Yes, with the cookies." She slapped the counter. "I'm doing it. I'm going to find out about renting a commercial kitchen to start with. What do you say, do you want to be my assistant?"

Working with cookies rather than a sick person? "Yes."

"Then it's a deal." Lacey held out her hand to Karina.

And Karina had taken her hand and shaken it, sealing them together all these years.

"Are you okay?" Ian whispered in her ear, bringing her back to the present.

Karina nodded. She glanced at Dwight, who was staring at her with concern. So was Scott, who wasn't looking at his phone for once.

"Please continue, Dwight," Lacey said.

Dwight cleared his throat. "Let's move on to another topic." He started in about the HACCP plan again. Scott's gaze moved back to his phone.

Karina tuned him out, Lacey's voice still ringing in her ears. Just because they weren't family didn't mean Lacey knew Roy better than her. He'd confided in Karina about his fears of being pushed out. It was Karina who was closer to Roy now, and Lacey had no idea.

CHAPTER EIGHTEEN

"Am I in the right house?" Natalie asked when she arrived home from the gym.

Karina was mopping, having already picked up the clutter, vacuumed, and cleaned the bathroom. It wasn't like she never cleaned—she used to be a maid, after all. But they divided the tasks between them, and Karina was doing more than she should. Since both had spent the weekend in Miami, no one had cleaned.

"Ha-ha, hilarious. Ian's coming over with dinner, remember?"

"And you want to make a good impression?" Natalie laughed. "You say you want nothing serious, but I think it already is if you're cleaning for him."

"Shut up. I just don't want him to think I'm a pig."

Ian was the first guy to see where she lived. Maybe mopping when it wasn't her turn was a bit overboard, but what else was she supposed to do—tell him not to come? Then she'd have to admit the truth, and it was too late for that.

Natalie tiptoed across the floor. "Do you want me to hide out in my room?"

"You can stay until he gets here and then ignore him or something."

"This is so stupid." Natalie disappeared down the hallway.

* * *

By the time Ian came over an hour later, the house was spotless and Karina had showered and put on a T-shirt that said *My everyday mood: hungry with a side of horny.*

He laughed when he read it. "Don't I know it." He grabbed her neck and kissed her.

Karina sighed and pushed her hands into his hair. Why had she deprived herself of this for three days?

"Hmm, I looked forward to that all day," he said. "But we should eat this before it gets cold." He held up two bags he was holding in one hand.

"Right." She let him in. Natalie sat cross-legged on the couch, her eyes fixed on her phone.

"So many plants." He maneuvered around them. Karina could've sworn they were multiplying, although Natalie denied buying any new ones.

"That's Natalie's doing," Karina said. "You can unload here." She pointed to the dining table behind the sofa. "I'll go get the plates."

"Get some deep ones. I made beef broth." There was the crinkle of plastic bags. "Hi, Natalie. Hope you're hungry."

"Oh, um, don't serve any for me."

Karina came back with the plates. "Are you sure you don't want to try? Ian went to all this trouble."

Natalie stared at her, her lips a tight line. "No, I'll make myself a salad and eat it in my room." She went into the kitchen.

Karina helped Ian serve. He'd made balls of mofongo—mashed plantains with garlic and bacon—beef broth, and fried pork chunks. Yum. When she went back to the kitchen for silverware, Natalie whispered, "It smells divine. I can't believe I let you talk me into this."

"You'll be happier with your salad," Karina whispered back and returned to Ian.

Karina had eaten mofongo before—you couldn't be friends with a Puerto Rican without having tried it; it was their signature dish—but she still let Ian teach her how to soak the ball of mofongo into the broth before eating it.

"Wow," Karina said when she took a bite. The mofongo melted into her tongue, a garlicky masterpiece. "This is amazing. I can't believe you made this."

"Me neither. I never made it before, but it tastes just like my mom's." His gaze took on a faraway look. "Like home."

Natalie passed by with her bowl of salad.

"You sure you don't want any, Natalie?" Ian asked. "It's delicious."

Natalie stared at the mofongo. She looked angry as she shook her head, walking away and shutting herself in her room.

"Diablo," Ian said. "Guess I was wrong. She looked like she can't even stand looking at carbs. She okay?"

Karina responded with a dismissive wave. "She's just upset over the whole stalker thing." She bit into the pork. Perfectly seasoned and crispy.

"Or is it me? Maybe she doesn't like me?"

"I don't know. She wasn't thrilled when I said you were coming over. I've never had a guy over before, so maybe that's it."

"And she's never brought guys here?"

"Not really. I think she's a virgin. You know, the religious type."

"Really?"

"Yeah, so you better leave soon after we eat, so she doesn't get upset."

"And no sex?"

"Not *right* after we eat, but we have to be quiet, and you can't sleep over."

He frowned, mashing the mofongo into the broth, taking his time with each bite. "It's funny you two are roommates. I didn't expect her to be so . . . conservative."

"Why, because I'm a slut?"

His eyes widened. "No. That's not—"

"'Cause there's more to me than meets the eye. And life's not all about sex and men. There are other things, like our jobs—"

"I know, I know. I didn't mean it like that. Only . . . does she approve of your cursing? And your T-shirts?"

Why was she angry at him? She was the one lying, though not completely: Natalie had been a virgin when they'd met, and they *had* bonded over working at Singular. And those sex tips Karina had given her. "I don't care if she approves. I always do what I want, even if I lived with the pope."

He laughed, then shook his head. "Dios, I missed you so much this weekend."

"You missed my snarky remarks?"

"And your cursing, your grumpiness, everything."

Her heart skipped a beat.

"But," he said, "if everything you said was true, you wouldn't care that the sex was loud or that I slept over."

He had her there. "I should still be considerate."

"I don't like sneaking around," he said. "Natalie should go to the police station and get a restraining order. Or just explain to her that, in case the guy shows up, it's better if I'm here."

"You don't think I can defend her? Women can take care of each other." It was Karina who'd gotten Benjamin to stop lurking around after she'd gotten in his face and threatened him. The poor guy had gone so pale, Karina had thought he'd faint.

"Karina . . ." He rubbed his brow. "You know I don't mean it like that."

Karina lowered her head and filled her mouth with mofongo. "Don't you think it's nice to have a break from each other now and then? Aren't you sick of me being at your place all the time?"

"Of course not. I love having you at my place. And I sleep so much better with you. I've slept terrible these past few nights."

Tell me about it. Not even her own bed had helped her sleep as soundly as she did with Ian. She hoped it was the lack of sex and not that she depended on him or something.

"And you can call me machista or . . . sexist or whatever," he continued, "but you girls shouldn't be alone if there's a crazy man outside your house."

He seemed really worried. This was getting out of hand. "He's not a psycho killer, just a guy obsessed with Natalie. I'll tell her to get the restraining order if he doesn't stop."

They cleaned the dishes, and then Karina led Ian to her room. She shifted from one foot to the other as he looked around at the beachy-themed prints on her wall, her turquoise plush chair, the dozens of cushions mounted on her bed and scattered on the floor. He picked one up and plopped onto the bed. It was the *Toy Story* one with Woody and Jessie that Marisa had sewn for her birthday.

"Why didn't you tell me you like cushions so much? I could've bought some for my place, so you feel more comfortable."

How could she tell him he made her feel cozier than all her cushions combined? She settled next to him.

"Or you could bring some to my house," he said. "I wouldn't mind."

Then she would really move in. Enough of that. She threw the cushion away and shoved him flat to the bed, straddling him.

He slithered to the top of the bed. "What's this?" He dug underneath the cushions near the headboard and held up her old Woody rag doll.

Karina's face burned. *Good job hiding it.* Now he'd think she was a silly little girl who kept dolls to cuddle with.

"He's the one that accompanies you when I'm not here?" he asked.

"It's just a silly toy Marisa gave me."

"Really?" He examined it. "It looks so old."

She grabbed the doll from him and threw it to the floor. "It's vintage." No need for him to know she'd had it since childhood, a gift from her mom, the only thing she'd kept that connected them.

"Bendito." He pulled her to his chest. "You were right before. There's more to you than meets the eye. I'm happy I can see a little more tonight." He stroked her head. "The guys at work find you intimidating, but you're just misunderstood, aren't you?"

She kissed him to shut him up.

During the quiet sex that followed, Karina tried to "not think about it" like before, but it was useless. In her search for more space, she'd ended up giving him more territory to invade. She shouldn't have let him in here. Now he knew more about her than any other guy she'd ever slept with.

"Stop." Karina pushed him away.

"What's wrong?" He sat up.

"I'm not feeling it. Maybe it's being here. Or the thing with Natalie. I don't know."

"It's okay." He stroked her face. "We can cuddle." He shifted her so he could spoon her.

How could he be okay with no sex after so long? There must be something wrong with him. Or maybe there was something wrong with her. She'd never stopped sex halfway. "Are you sure?"

"Yes, don't worry. We don't have to have sex. I'm just happy to be with you." He stroked her belly.

Normally this soothed her, but tonight it was annoying, probably because of the lack of an orgasm. "It's getting late. You should go."

He groaned. "What about I stay and then sneak out early in the morning before she wakes up?"

"My bed's not as big as yours. It won't be as comfy."

"We sleep tangled with each other anyway." He pulled her closer. "Don't make me go to my empty bed without you."

Why couldn't he just go? "Ian. I don't want Natalie to get mad at me."

He huffed, jumped out of bed, and got dressed. "Make sure she gets a restraining order. If not, I'm definitely staying here tomorrow."

"No, it has to be how we say." She shot from the bed. "You can't boss us around. Natalie and I are the ones who live here, not you. If she doesn't want me to have guys over, then you have to respect that."

"Okay, okay, you're right. Only . . ." His shoulders slumped. "Tonight didn't go how I imagined."

She crossed her arms. "It didn't for me either."

"I want things back how they were." He held her and kissed the top of her head.

Karina circled his waist. Why was she being so mean to him? She needed time alone to think. If the only way to get him to do what she wanted was to be mean, then so be it.

"Can I come over tomorrow?" he asked. "We can eat the leftovers, watch our show, stop fighting, and maybe have sex. I promise I won't complain so much."

Thank God. "Okay. I'm up for all of that, especially the sex."
He laughed and kissed her.

When he left, Karina put on her sleep shirt and lay on the bed, expelling a huge breath. That had been much more difficult than she'd expected. Maybe it was time to end it. Why go to all this trouble? Any other guy would have stopped hearing from her already. They hadn't even had sex tonight.

He cooks for you; you enjoy being with him; he makes you happy.

She could say the same about her friends. She didn't need a man for those things. Why not end it once and for all? Her heart ached.

It's your fault, you stupid heart. But I can't let you win. I can't. And I won't.

CHAPTER NINETEEN

Karina twisted her neck, trying to release the tightness that wouldn't budge as she watched the guys working in the mixing room with Roy beside her. Nicholas was weighing the chocolate chips for a new batch of Flirtys while Tyler rolled the mixing bowl with the previous batch off to the side of the room to let the dough rest before taking it to the dough feeder.

Last night, Ian had come over, and it had all turned out like he'd said: dinner, TV, and amazing sex. But afterward, she'd fallen asleep in his arms—apparently, his bed had nothing to do with that—and then he'd woken her up early for more sex, and the fog in her brain had returned. So now, either she broke it off for good or she figured out how to keep him away until she could tame her heart into behaving.

Scott poked his uncovered blond head through the plastic strip curtains at the entrance to the warehouse, waving at Karina.

She groaned. "I have to go do my stupid warehouse audit now."

"How long will that take?" Roy asked. "I leave by two today."

"Well, I have to inspect the warehouse and watch Scott loading a truck after lunch, but that shouldn't take long."

"Karina," Scott hollered, pointing at his wristwatch. "The truck's waiting."

Before Karina could leave, Roy said, "Make sure he enters the load into the inventory system. He forgets sometimes and then I don't have the correct count." He shook his head. "Lacey should've fired that imbecile years ago, but he always comes up with a good excuse, and she takes pity on him."

Scott led her to the back, where the truck waited. The driver was chatting with Josh, the warehouse assistant. Scott broke off the seal that kept the doors shut, and then Josh started unloading the pallets of oatmeal with the forklift.

"Don't you have to check all this?" Karina pointed at the receiving checklist Scott had to fill out, marking that the truck was clean inside, that there were no signs of rodents, that there were no off odors.

He shot her a dismissive wave. "I fill that out later. It's always good."

Karina wrote *Unloads without checking* on her audit checklist. She peered inside the truck. It looked clean. Scott at least inspected the load, walking around the pallet, making sure the bags were intact. But he didn't seem to care if the lot matched what was in the driver's papers. Karina made another note. She took the papers from the driver and verified that everything was in order.

"Where's the certificate of analysis?" she asked the driver. Every load was supposed to arrive with a certification from the supplier that the product was safe. If not, they had to reject the load. It should've been the first thing checked.

The driver flipped through the papers.

"It's not there?" Karina asked.

"Did you leave something with the receptionist?" Scott asked him. After a head shake, Scott turned to Karina. "Sometimes Sofia keeps it, since she checks the paperwork before sending the trucks back here."

"Then she shouldn't have allowed the truck to come in."

"It's okay," Scott said with another dismissive wave. "It happens. Someone will email the supplier, and they'll send it."

"Who?"

"I don't know. Dwight?"

The level of incompetence. Karina made more notes.

"Look," Scott said, "if I don't accept this, Roy will be pissed, and I don't want to be on his bad side. Do you?"

"I'm only observing, Scott." Karina used her most authoritative voice. Dwight had trained them to only ask questions and write down what was wrong. He'd be the one in charge of retraining the poor bastard, in any case. *Good luck with that.*

Josh finished unloading, Scott signed the papers, and the driver went on his way. Then Scott mounted his own forklift.

"Aren't you going to enter the load into the system?" Karina asked him.

Scott slapped his head and nodded, dismounting and heading to the computer. More notes. Roy was right to be pissed at him all the time. How was Scott still working here?

Karina left him to continue her audit of the warehouse, making sure it was clean and that items were properly stored. Nothing seemed out of order. Scott wasn't completely useless. She checked off the last item right as her stomach grumbled. Lunchtime. That hadn't been so difficult after all. *Go, Karina!*

Only the loading audit was left. But no, wait, she still needed to do the record audit, and Roy was leaving early. There was no way she could do it before her shift ended. Maybe she could do it after?

The tension in her neck and shoulders vanished. Yes, that was it! She'd work overtime, and then she'd have a great excuse to avoid Ian.

* * *

"Don't worry about it," Dwight said when Karina asked to finish the audit after her shift. "You did most of the work. I can look at the records."

Now he didn't need her help? "But I'd like to finish it, get a view of the whole process. And I wouldn't mind getting paid overtime. Plus you have lots to do. Let me help you."

He gazed around his office, which wasn't as tidy as it used to be, with papers and binders everywhere. "If you don't mind staying extra hours, I can assign you a multitude of tasks."

Even more overtime? Jackpot.

When Dwight explained his plan to Lacey, she frowned. "And this was your idea, Karina?"

Uh-oh. Maybe this was a mistake. Lacey always had to convince her to take extra work; it was never volunteered. "Well, Dwight asked me to help. Right, Dwight?" Karina glanced at him.

Dwight nodded. "You know how overwhelmed I am."

Lacey's frown stayed put. In a stroke of genius, Karina added, "And so did you, Lacey, remember? This is me helping."

"Of course." Lacey didn't seem convinced. She walked around her desk. "Would you mind giving us a moment, Dwight? I need to speak to Karina."

Karina gazed at her shoes. Lacey meant business. The door shut.

"Did you tell anyone about me and Dwight?"

Karina raised her head but kept her gaze away from Lacey. "What? No."

"Maybe you let something slip to my uncle?"

"Did he say something?"

"He said nothing outright, but he accused Dwight of influencing me."

Okay, she doesn't know. Relax. Karina crossed her arms and looked at Lacey. "Maybe he came to it on his own. There's enough evidence to make him suspect."

Lacey crossed her arms as well, her jaw set. "Like what?"

"Like you always siding with Dwight?"

Lacey fidgeted with her watch. "Well, Dwight has been explaining what we need to pass the inspection, and I see all the holes we need to patch up. Leonard neglected many things."

"Or maybe Dwight is exaggerating."

"I don't believe he is."

"It's obvious you'd think that. He can do no wrong, right?"

Lacey stared at her. Karina stared back. Why were they still talking about Dwight? This was supposed to be about Karina.

"Look, Lacey, whatever's going on between you and Roy, that's your thing. I need to know if I can stay after my shift—and help

Dwight like you asked me to—so I can get back to work. Roy is leaving early today, as you know."

Lacey tilted her head, studying Karina. "Tell me the truth. Did you tell him about me and Dwight?"

"Yeah, okay?" Karina threw up her hands. "I'm worried about you. You're focusing on the wrong things, letting Dwight manipulate you into believing he's right, when he's not."

Lacey pressed a hand to her chest. "I can't believe this. I told you explicitly not to tell him. Now he'll get involved, say something to Dwight, and then . . ." Lacey's eyes widened. "Are you trying to break us up?"

Karina let her mouth hang open, feigning shock.

"Is that why you want to work late with him, to steal him away?"

How could Lacey think that? Karina might sleep around, but she never slept with two guys at the same time or stole boyfriends. Love was definitely clouding Lacey's judgment.

"You think he'll go for me?"

"Please don't do this." Lacey grabbed Karina by the arms. "He's mine, all right? You have Ian. Keep Ian and let me have Dwight."

Who was this groveling woman? Karina freed herself from her grasp. "I don't care about Dwight; keep him. But do you think he'll stay with you if the whole company found out you're dating your subordinate?"

"Are you threatening me?"

"I'm saving you."

"From what?"

"From love."

"I don't need saving. I'm finally opening my heart to someone. You know how hard my divorce was. My therapist has been helping me see how I've used work to keep myself safe."

Lacey, in therapy? The Lacey Karina knew was smart, strong, and level-headed, not crazy. What had love done to her?

"But now," Lacey continued, "I found a man who I can see a future with. And no one is going to mess that up for me. Not you, not my uncle, no one. You were right about one thing—we're not the same. I'm not afraid to love and be loved."

"Who says I'm afraid?"

"You're nothing but afraid. My uncle and I could've been a family for you, and you rejected us. You still reject us. As for the company, I've taken it this far, and I will continue to take it further, with or without your help." She returned to her desk and sat. "And if you tell anyone else about me and Dwight, you're fired."

This time, Karina's mouth fell open on its own. "You won't fire Scott or Dwight, but you'd fire me? After all these years of being committed to you and this company?"

"What do you expect? I confided in you, and you betrayed me. You're putting the future of this company at risk with your insubordination."

"No, you're the one putting it at risk by trying to push out Roy."

Lacey's eyes widened. "What? I'm not trying to push him out."

"That's what he thinks. And so do I. You do nothing but undermine him and side with Dwight. How do you think that makes him feel?"

Lacey looked shocked into silence.

"But he's your uncle, not mine, right?"

"Right." Lacey straightened. "And I will talk to him. As for you, I gave you a direct order as your boss and the owner of this company, and I expect you to follow it. I don't want you anywhere near Dwight. You're relieved of your duties with him."

"But—"

"Are we clear?"

Karina swallowed. "I, uh, I really do want to keep working with Dwight. I want to help."

"Save it. I'm not falling for it."

Karina wiped her hands on her legs. "Look, here's the truth, okay?" She sighed. "I need some time away from Ian. I won't say anything to Dwight, I swear."

Lacey tapped her fingers on her desk, studying her. "You have a chance at love and you're trying to avoid Ian? And you say you're not afraid." Lacey stared at her like her friends did sometimes, trying to figure out the puzzle that was her. She threw up her hands. "It's your life. I don't care. You can work late with Dwight. But I'm allowing it only because he desperately needs the help. But make no mistake: if you do anything inappropriate, you're fired." She moved her mouse and tapped on the keyboard. "You're dismissed."

Karina gaped at her. The old Lacey would've never treated her like this. And for what, for a man? Lacey was officially a goner, and there was nothing Karina could do about it, not if she wanted to keep the best job she'd ever had. Now she could only try to save herself if she didn't want to be a goner too.

CHAPTER TWENTY

"Where's Ian?" Cordelia asked when Karina arrived for Marisa's birthday party.

"I'm fine. How are you?" Karina stepped past Cordelia into the house.

Cordelia shut the door. "You didn't invite him, did you? I knew I should've done it personally."

"I did tell him, but he wasn't feeling well. Jeez, don't make such a big deal about it." Karina had told Ian the party was "girls only," and though he was disappointed, he'd been okay with it.

Working late with Dwight for the last week and a half had given her the space she needed, though Ian kept nagging to see her every day, making her feel guilty for neglecting him. But she shouldn't feel guilty. She had the right to earn extra bucks working overtime and go alone to a party without him hanging around her.

"We'll give out the presents after dinner." Cordelia took Karina's gift and placed it on the red-and-white polka-dot armchair by the door. In fact, everything in the small living room was red and white. Figured. Cordelia always needed to match.

Cordelia looked up and down at Karina's outfit, her lips pressed in disapproval. "Couldn't you step away from your uniform for one night? You know every event at my house is formal." She gestured down at her long red dress, which coordinated perfectly with the red-and-white polka-dot apron around her waist.

Karina had worn her usual jeans and T-shirt to every party, but she replied in a fake-apologetic tone, "It's been so long since you've invited me over, I forgot."

Cordelia pursed her lips. "And you thought it wouldn't happen, but here we are. The least you could've done was make an effort. Pero pues, ni modo."

Karina followed her down a hallway, passing a glass case displaying a ball gown wedding dress. She stopped to stare at it. "You're showing off your wedding dress?" It shouldn't surprise her. This was Cordelia, after all. She lived for drama.

"It's a work of art. It deserves to be admired, not stored in a closet." Cordelia continued on, leading her into an open kitchen of white countertops and, of course, red decor, down to the red-and-white polka-dot toaster and rug on the floor.

Natalie and Marisa stood at the breakfast bar, cutting up tomatoes and lettuce for a salad. They were both wearing dresses, even Natalie, who was usually in yoga pants. A big pan of lasagna and a tray of garlic bread baked in the oven, sending yummy smells all over the space.

"Ian's not coming," Cordelia announced. "He wasn't feeling well, according to Karina." She turned on the stove, where a red pan full of oil already stood. Next to it, on the counter, was a plate stacked with slices of ripe plantains. Fried amarillos. Yum.

"Aw, too bad," Marisa said. "I was looking forward to getting to know him better."

Natalie gave Karina a knowing look and said in a flat tone, "Yeah. Too bad." She put the knife down and grabbed Karina by the arm. "Come meet Greg." Under her breath, she asked, "What did you do?"

"Nothing," Karina whispered. "And don't say anything."

"I won't. But now you owe me."

The guys were in the adjacent living room, watching a basketball game, sitting on the red-and-white polka-dot sofa. Greg turned out to be Natalie's usual type: tall and clean-cut, ready to take home to meet the parents. She'd left early to meet him for drinks and proof test him for tonight. Guess he'd passed the test.

He stood to shake Karina's hand. Jaime, with his buzz cut and golden chains around his neck, remained seated, eyes glued to the TV, not making the slightest move to acknowledge her presence. Good. The less contact, the better.

Charlie, Cordelia's husband, stood to hug her. He was lanky, with blond hair. He also looked sharp, wearing black pants and a blue button-down that enhanced his blue eyes. "It's been a while. Cordi told me you'd bring someone, but I see you came alone?"

"Yup. Just me. Hope I'm enough."

"Did you try the punch?" He raised a red Solo cup half filled with what looked like orange juice. "It's Cordi's own creation. You must try it. She's a genius."

Back in the kitchen, Karina filled herself a cup from a large red punch bowl on the counter. It tasted like orange juice and pineapple, with the fizziness of 7UP and a bite of rum. "Need any help?"

"No, we're set," Cordelia said. "And you'd make a mess."

With that, Karina sat on a stool by the breakfast bar.

"How are things going with Ian?" Marisa asked. "You don't talk about him as much anymore."

"With good reason."

"At least tell us you're serious about him," Cordelia said. "After a month and a half, you must be."

"The only reason we're still together is that I'm not tired of him yet. Emphasis on the *yet*."

"So you still expect it to end?" Cordelia asked.

"Every relationship ends."

Cordelia rolled her eyes. "You're not replacing him with Dwight, are you?"

"What? Gross."

"You're spending all your nights with him."

"Scanning and filing papers."

"What does Ian say?" Marisa asked. "Is he okay with it?"

"I need to ask his permission to do my job?"

The plantain slices sizzled as Cordelia dropped them into the hot oil. "En verdad, Karina, it's not normal that you don't want a serious relationship. I would get it if you'd been hurt before, but you've never given a guy half a chance."

If only they knew about Jason and how he'd called her a slut when she'd asked him to make their relationship public. But then they'd pity her. "I like my independence. Not having anyone to answer to."

"Not having anyone to take care of you," Cordelia said.

"I can take care of myself."

Cordelia chortled. "Ay, por favor. You beg me for leftovers every day."

"I could eat out if I wanted. The food wouldn't be as good, but I'd survive."

"What about all those favors you want from me lately?" Natalie asked with a raised eyebrow as she put the last of the chopped tomatoes into a salad bowl.

Karina scowled. "You know those are exceptions. I never ask you for anything."

"Face it, Karina." Cordelia turned over the plantains on the pan. "Everyone needs help. Even you."

"I have you guys for that."

"Friends can't do everything," Cordelia said. "I have a husband to take care of. And soon kids, so there's no room for you too."

Marisa stopped tossing the salad. "Are you—"

"No, not yet." Cordelia lowered her voice. "But we're trying." She grinned.

Both Marisa and Natalie squealed. Karina squeezed the cup in her hand so hard it cracked. Punch dripped down her hand and onto the counter. She traveled back to that moment when her mom told her she was pregnant and remembered how her whole world had changed afterward.

"What was *that*?" Cordelia handed her a paper towel.

Karina took it and wiped the countertop. "Dunno." She drank the rest of the punch. Cordelia's hosting a party again had given her hope, but this news . . . maybe this would be the last time they'd be together like this.

"Hope it happens soon," Natalie told Cordelia.

"Aw, we get to be aunties," Marisa said.

Karina got a new cup, refilled it, and sat back down. She noticed they were staring at her expectantly, waiting for her to say something.

Karina shrugged. "Good for you, I guess." She gulped down half the drink. Cordelia's life was already all about Charlie. A baby meant she'd probably quit Singular to be a full-time mom. That's what Karina's mom had done, and Cordelia was just like her.

Natalie sat on the stool beside Karina. "Cordelia's right. You can't rely only on your friends. What happens when we get married?"

They would abandon her too. Karina's hand shook as she finished her drink.

"And a friend can't pamper you like a man can," Cordelia said. "He's someone to cuddle with. All those things that make a relationship special." She scooped out the amarillos and placed them on a plate covered with paper towels.

Marisa sat on the other side of Karina, cup in hand. "Sometimes I get home and Jaime has the apartment squeaky-clean." She smiled. "He massages my feet. Those are the best days." She sighed, a faraway look in her eyes.

"Does that make up for when he's out drinking late with his buddies?" Karina said. "Or when he spends the little money he has on beer?"

Marisa pressed her lips into a thin line. "Don't start," she whispered. "I don't want a scene tonight. I told Jaime to behave, and he's holding up his end. Why can't you?"

Karina glanced at Jaime. His eyes were glued to the game. Either he hadn't heard her—even though she'd spoken loud enough—or he really was behaving, ignoring her for the sake of Marisa.

Karina's cheeks burned. "I'll try, but . . . you know me. See?" She swiveled and poked out her chest, gesturing at her T-shirt.

Marisa read the slogan. *"I speak my mind because there's only so much eye-rolling I can do."* With a sigh, she said, "Just . . . try."

The dining table, covered in a red-and-white polka-dot tablecloth, was set for eight. Karina sat next to the empty chair meant for

Ian, trying not to stare at the card with his name. On the other side of Karina sat Natalie, and directly across—Jaime.

They glared at each other. Marisa squeezed Jaime's hand, taking his side, like always. Karina would need a lot more punch to make it through the night.

After a quick prayer, they dug in. Melted cheese, tomato sauce, crispy bread, garlicky butter, and sweet amarillos overpowered Karina's taste buds.

"I still don't get why you don't open your own restaurant," Karina said between bites. "Or a food truck. Do you know how much money you'd make parked outside Singular?"

"We've been over this," Cordelia said. "I don't know how to run a business."

"And I keep telling you to talk to Lacey. Why stay stuck being a packer when you have this talent?"

"I'm with Karina on this," Marisa said, covering her mouth while she swallowed. "With your flair, you'd be the bomb."

"I enjoy my job," Cordelia said. "It's low stress, and I can dedicate my free time to my hubby." She threw Charlie a kiss.

Charlie caught it. "You know I'd support you no matter what you chose, sweet pea."

Karina gulped down punch. How could Cordelia jeopardize her dream? She was just like her mother, wasting her potential. And worst of all—neither of them thought they had a problem.

"Mami." Jaime nudged Marisa on the arm. "Get me a beer, will ya?"

Instead of telling him to get it himself, Marisa stood and went to the fridge. He hadn't even said *please*. He expected her to do as he commanded. There was no *thank you* either when she returned with it; he didn't even acknowledge her, just continued eating while she popped it open for him and placed it in front of his plate.

Karina stuck a piece of bread in her mouth. She wasn't supposed to make a scene or provoke him, but who was keeping him from provoking *her*? Marisa should've poured that beer all over him.

"Karina." Charlie pulled her from her murderous thoughts. "Cordelia told me you and Natalie went to Miami for a weekend.

Are you planning another trip? I think it would be great for Cordi to get out of the house and spend time with you girls. I'm always telling her to go out, but she prefers to stay home cooking and making the house look nice."

"What a wonderful idea!" Karina's tone was infused with glee and sarcasm as she beamed at Cordelia. "What do you say, 'Cordi'?"

Cordelia narrowed her eyes at Karina before looking at Charlie. "But honey, you know I'd rather go with you. It's more fun that way."

"We can do separate things now and then."

"But not an entire weekend," Cordelia said. "That would be too much time away from my hubby."

"How horrible that would be," Karina mumbled under her breath. "Charlie, what do you do to her in bed that she can't keep away?"

Cordelia gasped, and Charlie laughed.

Jaime burped. "I wouldn't want Mari to go unless I come too." He said this directly to Karina, daring her to say something. Taunting her.

She took the bait. "You can come if you pay your own way."

"You're calling me a moocher again?" He stood, rocking his chair back and leaning forward, fists on the table. "I can pay, bitch."

Silence fell over the room with only Greg's coughs breaking it.

"Like you've been paying for rent ever since you moved in with Mari?"

He slammed his fists into the table, his utensils clattering against his plate. "Marisa knows I'll pay her back. Tell her, mami."

"Claro que sí, papi." Marisa scowled at Karina. "You can come with us to Miami. Don't worry."

"I better." Jaime sat back down and gulped down his beer. How many had he drunk already?

Cordelia sat like a statue, hand on her chest, mouth agape. Charlie continued eating as if nothing had happened.

"You have to ignore him," Natalie whispered into her ear.

"I can't, all right?" Karina whispered back. "You know I can't keep my mouth shut around that asshole." Poor Greg was staring at Natalie with wide eyes. "I hope I didn't mess things up with you and Greg."

"It's okay. It's not meant to be. No spark."

"Ah." Karina stuck a piece of lasagna in her mouth. Cordelia criticized Karina for not giving guys half a chance, but Karina spent more time with the guys she dated than Natalie did. It was mostly because Karina had sex with them, but at least she got to be happy with a man for a few days. What did Natalie get?

After they cleared the table, Cordelia appeared with a huge white-frosted cake, a single lighted candle on top, and placed it in front of Marisa.

They sang "Happy Birthday" in both English and Spanish. Marisa teared up, and when the song ended, she closed her eyes for a moment, then blew out the candle. Everyone cheered.

Marisa threw her arms around Cordelia. "This is the most beautiful cake I've ever seen. Thank you so much. I hope it wasn't too difficult to make."

"It wasn't, don't worry." Cordelia wiped the corner of her eyes.

Marisa did the honors of cutting, while Cordelia served. Karina savored the vanilla cake, which was layered with sweetened cream cheese and guava paste. Ian would've loved it. Karina's chest ached as she gazed around at the smiling couples, settling on the place setting with his name. Ian would've enjoyed being here. He would've helped Cordelia with the food, maybe gotten the recipe for the lasagna so he could make it for Karina. And he would've been so proud of her for standing up to Jaime. This cake would've been the topper, a sweet treat to remind him of his homeland. But because of Karina, he'd probably spent the night alone instead of with a fellow expat. He didn't have any friends here. Maybe she'd take him a piece of cake on her way home.

Finally, it was time to open the presents. Marisa unwrapped Natalie's gift first, a copy of *Eat, Pray, Love*. Natalie had told Karina she hoped it would help Marisa put herself first and find the strength to leave Jaime.

Karina handed her gift next. Marisa's eyes lit up at the white cotton fabric and indigo tie-dye kit. "Aw." She jumped to hug Karina. "Thank you so much."

Karina leaned into the hug. She'd hoped this gift would score her some much-needed points. And it had. "So you can keep making cool new fabric designs." Karina raised an eyebrow at Jaime. Because of him and his debts, Marisa had stopped buying supplies for her hobby. "I'm sure you'll make an awesome dress out of it, and then we can take it to Miami together."

Jaime stood and threw his arm around Marisa. "My present beat all these, verdad, mami? Did you show 'em?"

"Of course I did, baby. I couldn't stop bragging about it." She threaded her finger on the golden heart-shaped necklace around her neck.

Marisa had been so proud when she showed it to them yesterday in the locker room. According to her, Jaime had gone all out for her actual birthday on Thursday, paying for dinner and giving her jewelry.

Karina inspected the necklace. It looked expensive, but it was probably some cheap thing he'd gotten at Whole-Mart. Or maybe he'd stolen it. She wouldn't put it past him.

"And?" Jaime asked Karina. "Still think I'm a moocher?"

His smirk only made her want to punch him in the face. She balled her fists.

Marisa stroked his cheek, stepping between them. "You did good, baby. This is the best present I ever got." She kissed him.

Jaime kept his eyes on Karina, that stupid smirk still on his lips. Karina spun away. Ugh. Why couldn't he stay a loser permanently? Every time she exposed him as an asshole, he came around and did something nice, like coming up with extra money or cleaning Mari's apartment. If he kept it up, she'd never be able to convince Marisa to dump him.

Karina joined her friends in the kitchen to clean up. Marisa and Jaime disappeared down the hallway, and the girls exchanged glances. Jaime had a kink for sex in public places. It made Marisa uncomfortable, but according to her, "There's no stopping him when he gets frisky" and "In a relationship, you have to make compromises." Double ugh.

Cordelia asked Charlie to put on music. Minutes later, the sounds of salsa couldn't compete with Jaime's grunts, moans, and whatever he was yelling out in Spanish. The girls joined the guys in the living room.

"This is happening in our bathroom?" Charlie asked.

"I'll do some deep cleaning after everyone leaves." Cordelia pulled Charlie up from the couch, and they swung their hips to the beat.

Jaime yelled out, "Me vengo, puñeta," followed by a long bleat.

"Good luck with that," Karina said. She'd never go into that bathroom again.

Seconds later the door to the bathroom opened, and everyone in the living room raised their voices, raving about the food and Charlie's dancing ability. Marisa avoided everyone's gaze, but Jaime smirked as he opened a can of beer, dropped to one armchair, and soon passed out. When his snores got so loud no one could keep track of their conversation, Marisa called it a night.

Charlie and Greg dragged an unconscious Jaime to the car while Marisa stayed to say good-bye.

"Thank you so much for this party." Marisa hugged Cordelia. "It's been the best birthday ever."

"Anything for you," Cordelia said.

"I guess that means even married women can take care of their friends," Karina said.

"Yeah, yeah," Cordelia said. "But it's not the same as the love of a man which would be only yours."

"And Ian loves you," Natalie said.

Karina's heart almost galloped out of her chest. Cordelia and Marisa gasped.

"Did he tell you that?" Cordelia asked.

"Oh my God," Marisa said.

"What are you talking about?" Karina asked.

"Come on, it's so obvious," Natalie said. "The way he looks at you, how he talks to you . . . he shows all the signs. And I've overheard how you snap at him, and yet he still wants to be with you. If that's not love, I don't know what is."

Karina stared at Natalie. Ian in love with her? Her heart raced.

"It's the truth," Natalie said.

"You're just projecting what you *wish* were true," Karina said. "Men don't fall in love that fast."

"Some do," Cordelia said in her annoying singsong voice.

"Whatever. I'm going home. Pack me some cake, will you?"

As soon as she was safely in her car, she took a deep breath. *Calm down, Heart. Natalie's wrong. Ian's not in love with me. Don't get your hopes up. Love is out of the question.*

It was two in the morning. Ian was most likely asleep, and he wouldn't eat cake at this hour anyway. She drove home.

CHAPTER TWENTY-ONE

Karina woke up to terrible cramps. Her period was making an appearance after months of absence. It was so irregular she never kept track of it.

She took an ibuprofen and settled on the sofa to watch *Brooklyn Nine-Nine* while she munched on Perkys, a heating pad across her pelvis to ease the pain. Natalie had left early for her usual morning hike, so she had the house to herself.

The doorbell rang. It was eight thirty AM, too early for visitors. Karina peeked out between the blinds.

Ian.

Why was he here? She told him she'd text him. Why did he need to know her every move? Couldn't they see each other whenever?

He barged in as soon as she opened the door. "Where's your phone? You ignoring me?"

"It's in my room." She slammed the door closed. "Are you mad at me because I didn't answer your texts?"

"No. I'm mad at you because you lied to me." He crossed his arms and glared at her.

Karina tried to keep her face from giving anything away. "I don't know what you're talking about."

"I ran into Maya last night at a bar. You know, the same Maya who works with Natalie in the lab?"

Uh-oh.

Her thoughts must've reflected on her face, because he said, "Yes. That one. She didn't understand why I wasn't at the birthday party. When I told her it was girls only, she told me Natalie was taking a date. So what's going on? I don't see you all week, and then you don't invite me to this party. Did you take someone else? Dwight?"

"Dwight? Why—"

"You sleeping with him?"

"Ew, no."

"Then who?"

"No one. I just wanted to go alone to the party. Is that so bad? I don't have to be glued to you every hour of every day."

He expelled a breath and lowered his head. "Why do you make it so difficult to be with you?"

Karina swallowed. "I don't want to be difficult."

"But you are. We were almost living together, and then I'm spending the nights alone and you don't miss me, and now you lie to me about this party. Why?"

"I think *living together* is a strong phrase. More like *crashing at your place*—"

"You like being with me?"

"Yeah."

"You want to keep being with me?"

"I . . ." She wiped her hands on her pajama pants. "I guess."

"Then I need you to be honest with me." He made her look into his eyes. "Is there really no one else?"

"No."

"Then why didn't you invite me to the party?"

She looked away. "It's just that . . . I'm not ready to be official. You being there would've been official."

"Okay. Now we're getting somewhere." He rubbed his face and paced around the room. The episode she'd been watching ended, the theme song for the next one filling the space between them. "Sabes, when you said it could get messy, I didn't believe you."

"You said you liked messy."

"Clearly, I didn't know what I was talking about."

"And now?"

He sighed. "I don't know what to do with you. You can be so infuriating. But you're also my K. And she's worth the effort."

His K, his sweet girl, a girl who didn't exist to anyone but him. Was she real or a figment of his imagination?

He smoothed down her hair. "You . . ." He laughed. "I like how you freak out over the silliest things, like a basic compliment, and how a kiss from me calms you." He took a deep breath. "But there's a limit, Karina. A man can take only so much. I know I said I could do casual, but . . . that's not who I am. I've tried not to put too much pressure on you, but I need to know if you're serious about us. Because I am. If you're only going to play games, I'm out."

There it was, the elephant in the room, the one she'd been trying not to look at, the one she'd hoped would go away but was now forced to face. It should be an easy answer for her. *No, I don't want anything serious.* But his earnest expression made her question why she didn't.

Be honest with him, Heart said. *He'll understand. If you keep pushing him away, we'll lose him.*

But what if he didn't understand? A serious relationship required a person to always be there and not want time apart because she felt suffocated. He'd think she was a freak for not wanting to spend every waking moment with him like any other woman would. Or worse—hurt that she'd feel like that when all he wanted was to be with her.

A cramp hit her, and she groaned.

"What's wrong?" he asked.

"My period." Her legs shook. "I need to lie down." She took her heating pad and curled up on the sofa.

"You need anything else? Pain medication, tampons, anything?"

It was weird that he cared so much about her period, but also kind of cute. Most guys would've been disgusted. "I already took a pill, but it still hurts. Sometimes pills aren't enough."

"Ay, bendito." He sat next to her and rubbed her belly. "Is this the first time you're having your period since we're dating? That can't be right."

"My period's crazy, and it comes and goes whenever it feels like it. There's no controlling it." Was she really discussing her menstrual cycle with a man?

"What about the pill? That makes it more regular."

"What are you, a gynecologist?"

"I have two sisters."

"And you talk to them about their periods?"

"I also dated women who have periods. Sorry if it's weird for you."

"It's not that. I've just never had this conversation with a guy."

"I want to know everything about you. So why don't you take the pill?"

"You'd like that, wouldn't you? Then you wouldn't have to wear a condom."

"I'm only asking, Karina."

Don't bite his head off because he wants to know you. She sighed. "I tried different brands, but I was always bloated and didn't feel like having sex, so I stopped. There's nothing else wrong with me, so why bother?"

"Okay. Good to know."

Now they were venturing into the topic of birth control. What was next, having kids?

"You know," he said, "my ex-girlfriend liked to have sex during her period. She said the orgasms made her feel better. Want to try?"

"You want to have sex now? It doesn't gross you out?"

"No. It's no problem. Unless it grosses you out."

"I've never had period sex."

"Then let's try it. I only want to make you feel better."

They did try it, and it did make her feel better. But that was the problem with Ian. Everything about him made her feel better about herself.

They cuddled in their underwear among her nest of cushions. How had she gotten here, being so intimate with a man, not just sexually but emotionally? She was supposed to have it all figured out.

Her mom had warned her. "Don't fall in love," she'd said. "It will only make you weak and dependent. You can do everything on your own. You don't need anyone else."

When she'd found out Karina was sexually active at age fifteen, she'd handed her an article about masturbation. "You don't need to be with a boy to make you feel good. Those feelings come from inside you. Stop wasting your time with him."

Karina had laughed it off. Being with Jason was not a waste of time, and it didn't make her weak; it made her invincible. That is, until she showed her true feelings during one of their afternoon trysts and asked him to take her to prom.

Jason stood abruptly and started getting dressed. It was only six thirty. They still had an hour to fool around before her elderly neighbor checked in on her.

"I already asked Tammy Ryan to go with me," he said, averting his gaze.

Tammy Ryan? Sure, she was pretty and got good grades, but she didn't put out. Karina had seen them together in the halls, but she'd never gotten the sense that he liked Tammy more than her.

"Why? I'm your girlfriend, so you have to take me."

"Who said you're my girlfriend?"

"We have sex almost every day."

He sat and looked at her like Mom did whenever she told Karina something obvious that Karina couldn't get. "Tammy's my girlfriend. You're just the girl I'm screwing."

A tightness in her chest made it hard to breathe.

"You didn't know?" he asked. "Why do you think I don't take you to the movies or out to eat? I do those things with Tammy. I don't want people to see me with the school slut."

Her head jerked back. "I'm not a slut." A slut was a girl who had sex with many boys, but she'd had sex with only one.

"You opened your legs the minute I kissed you. And you can't get enough of it."

"But you like me."

"I have to get it somewhere if my girlfriend won't put out. That's what sluts are for."

"I've only had sex with you."

"Could've fooled me." He circled her nipple with his thumb. "That means you're a natural slut. Even better."

What did that even mean? And why was he acting this way? "So you don't want to be with me anymore?"

"Not if you want to be my girlfriend, no. As long as you know your place, I'll keep coming back. You seem to need it."

She did need him. She needed him so much. Did that make her weak?

After he left, she thought about what he'd said. Why did liking sex make her a slut? And why would he want to be with a girl who didn't give him what he wanted? It made no sense.

The next day at school, Jason stood by Tammy's locker, laughing with her. He noticed Karina watching and gave Tammy a quick peck on the lips. Why couldn't he look at Karina the way he looked at Tammy? Why couldn't it be Karina he took to prom? And why did it matter to her so much that he wouldn't? She'd never liked dances. Had sex weakened her? No, sex wasn't the problem. She could have sex by herself. It was her feelings for Jason that made her want to be with him always, that made her sad when he wasn't there.

Karina couldn't let Jason have power over her. She couldn't need him. She'd quench her desires on her own or, better yet, find another boy to take his place.

Tammy left, and Jason gestured for Karina to come to him, as if he owned her. Instead, Karina walked over to Chad Anderson, who was getting books from his locker. She'd had a crush on him since junior high, and it was about time she acted on it. She stroked his arm and asked him to come by her house after school. Then she shrugged at Jason and headed to class.

Chad was even better in bed than Jason, but before he got too attached, Karina broke things off. With time, the pain Jason had caused her subsided and it became easier to separate her emotions from the act of sex. Men became a plaything, something to use and discard when she grew tired of it. She had the power to decide who to sleep with and when to end it. She was in control, and feelings of love would never get in the way.

Now, with Ian, there were so many feelings. Too many. Feelings she didn't want to name. Was she ready for something serious? Ian made her happy, not that hormonal happiness she'd felt with Jason. Karina was not her mom, and Ian was not Bob. She wouldn't have to change for him. He wasn't asking that of her. Maybe it could work.

Karina massaged Ian's scalp. He closed his eyes and smiled.

"I can try serious."

He opened his eyes, beaming.

"But no moving in together, okay? I need time."

"You can have all the time you want." He kissed her.

He'd said his kisses calmed her, but it wasn't only his kiss; it was his whole presence, his nearness, his smell, the feel of his arms around her. Why was that? Karina hadn't been raised to depend on a man—on anyone—for anything. But Ian made her feel safe. At peace, like when she lay on the sand on a warm sunny day, listening to the waves crashing around her.

"I saved you some birthday cake," she said.

He widened his grin. "You were thinking of me?"

She shrugged. "I'll go get it." Karina ran to the kitchen and retrieved the paper plate with the cake from the fridge, removing the aluminum foil and grabbing a fork.

"All that is for me?" he asked when she returned.

"I ate two pieces last night, so you have to eat at least half." She dug out a piece with the fork.

He sat up. "Hit me." He opened his mouth, and she put the fork in. "Diablo, está riquísimo. Delicious. Like back home."

"I know." She gave him some more.

"Where did she buy the guava paste?" His mouth was still full.

"Her mom mailed it to her."

"I have to tell my mom to send me some." He ate another bite. "I'm going to have to do an extra jog later. Or two."

"Maybe it should be three. You know how many calories this must have?" She kept stuffing his mouth with cake until he finished the whole thing. The look on his face was even better than she'd imagined.

"Oh my God, I feel like I'm going to explode." He dove back into the cushions and rubbed his abdomen. "Thank you for thinking of me." He squeezed her hand.

Her heart fluttered. "You should've been there."

"I should've."

"I got into a fight with Jaime."

He laughed. "Tell me." When she finished, he said, "I'm proud of you."

CHAPTER TWENTY-TWO

Still in Whole-Mart? Ian texted her.
  Yup. Just finishing up.
  Need hair gel. And dish soap.
  👍

The last two weeks, Karina had seen Ian most nights, whenever she didn't work too late. Sometimes she still felt suffocated, but after a day without seeing him, she could handle being with him again. It seemed like she'd struck the right balance.

She got the things Ian had asked for, then eyed a rug in different tones of brown that would look perfect in front of his couch. It was on sale, twenty-five percent off, and there were matching cushions on sale as well. She threw four cushions and the rolled-up rug into her cart.

As she was in line to pay, Karina stared at the items in her cart. They were mostly for Ian. The only thing for her was a pair of shorts. Her breathing shortened. She was shopping for him, like her mom did for Bob. She let go of the cart as if electrocuted and jumped back, bumping into the cart behind her.

Sweat accumulated on the back of her neck, and she wiped it off. Why was it so hot? She needed to get out of there. Suddenly, it was her turn to pay, and the person behind her nudged her with the cart. Karina couldn't buy this stuff. A rug and cushions for his house—what was she thinking?

"Lady, are you gonna pay?" the man behind her yelled. "Some of us have other things to do."

Karina's hands shook as she unloaded the cart. She wanted to scream, tell the cashier she wasn't going to buy anything, but her voice didn't work. So she paid and dashed out of the store. She leaned against her car, catching her breath. Ian didn't need to know about the rug or the cushions. She could come back tomorrow and return them.

She drove in a daze, and before she noticed where she was going, she'd arrived at Ian's house. Was she programmed to consider this home already?

Ian stepped out of the house and waved, opening the door for her. "That was fast." He reached into the car and popped open the trunk.

Karina remained still until Ian asked, "What's this?" and she jumped out.

He was holding the rug. "This for me?"

Karina still couldn't speak, and she nodded without thinking.

"Nice." He peered inside the trunk. "And cushions?"

"They were on sale." Her voice came out strained.

"Let's see how they look." He bounded inside and quickly went to work, moving the coffee table and placing the rug in front of the couch. He put an arm around her. "Looks great; exactly what was missing. You have an eye for these things."

Everything looked perfect, as if the new things belonged there, as if they'd been lying around waiting for the right girl to pick them up. Waiting for Karina.

"Thank you." He kissed her. "I'm happy you see this as your home."

"Home?" she stuttered, pulling at the collar of her T-shirt.

He bit her earlobe. "Why don't we break it in?"

"No!" She jumped away from his grasp and bumped into the coffee table. "I mean, I need to go. Maybe later?"

He frowned. "You okay? What's wrong?"

"Nothing. I just stopped to give you your stuff. I have more errands to run." She tripped on the way out the door.

As soon as she was safe in her car, driving away, she could breathe. She wasn't cut out to be anyone's girlfriend. In less than two months, she was unrecognizable to herself. Sure, she'd been happy, more relaxed, less moody. But who would she turn into after a year of this? Five years, ten? Because that was what a serious relationship meant: staying for the long haul. It had to end. No more Ian.

Karina burst into tears. She was crying? Over a guy? *No, no, no, stop it, Heart. It's no use. I don't care how much pain you cause me; I have to do it.* Bile rose in her throat and she swerved toward the emergency lane, cars honking behind her. She parked, then flew out of the car and vomited. *You weak, stupid body.* She wiped her mouth, got back in the car, and drove off. *I don't care what you throw at me. I've made up my mind. Stop screaming that I'm in love with Ian, Heart. I will not lose myself.*

*　*　*

Karina drove to the beach and turned off her phone. She sat in her favorite spot, taking off her shoes and digging her toes into the sand. She closed her eyes, focusing on the sun on her face, the sounds of the waves, the rough sand on her skin, but all she could feel was the echo of Ian's arms around her and his kiss warming her heart.

She wrapped her arms around her legs and sobbed into her knees. How long had she been in love with him? She should've never considered anything serious with him. Stupid.

The last time she'd cried like this was when her mom threw her out of the house. She'd been a kid then, and there'd been no warning it would end like that. This time, she'd prepared herself, took precautions. But her heart had turned out to be stronger than she'd anticipated. Roy was right: love was a sickness. It took over and changed you into someone else, someone who'd buy a rug and cushions for a guy's house when before you couldn't even buy his favorite cookies.

It's over, Heart. You lost.

It can't be over. We love him.

"But I can't stay with him. Better to end it now than to hurt him in the long run." *Or end up hurt when he finds out I'm no good for him.* She'd numbed the pain before, and she would again.

Karina stayed at the beach until the sun set, then went to a bar she'd never been to and had a few beers. It was Saturday night, so Natalie was probably out on a date. But Karina couldn't risk going back home in case Ian went looking for her. It was safer to wait.

At around midnight she made it home. Before going to bed, she turned on her phone. There were five texts from Ian and a bunch of missed calls.

7:34 PM: *You still coming over? Thought we were going to the movies.*
9:13 PM: *Went to your house and you weren't there. Where are you?*
10:05 PM: *I'm worried. Please, let me know you're okay.*
11:22 PM: *Why are you pulling this shit on me again? Don't freeze me out.*
12:08 AM: *I'm this close to calling the cops, Karina! CALL ME!!!*

Not only was he stalking her, he was about to call the cops. This was the problem with serious relationships. You needed to answer to someone else, had no freedom. It was too much pressure. Now she felt guilty for worrying him when she shouldn't feel guilty at all.

She texted him back—*I'm fine*—then turned off the phone and went to sleep.

* * *

The next morning, her head throbbed. As she headed into the living room, Natalie walked in the front door, grinning from ear to ear.

"Good, you finally got laid," Karina said.

"It was unbelievable." Natalie fell on the couch. "His name's Peter and he's an architect, and there's so much spark between us you could light an entire city."

A white pickup truck pulled into the driveway. Ian.

"Tell him I'm not here." Karina ran into the hallway.

"Who?"

The doorbell rang as Karina ducked into her room, leaving the door ajar so she could listen in.

"Is Karina here?" Ian asked, sounding pissed.

"Um, no," Natalie said.

"Her car's here."

"Oh, um, she left with someone."

"A guy?"

"Uh, um, I don't know. I just got in. Do you want me to tell her you came by?"

"Yes, yes. Tell her that." The door shut.

Natalie barged into the bedroom. "What on earth is going on?"

"I don't want to see him."

"Did you guys fight?"

"No. I want out. It's too much. I bought him a rug." Karina dropped to the bed.

Natalie leaned over her, hands on hips. "A rug."

"I'm becoming attached, and it's suffocating me."

"I take it he didn't get the memo. You need to talk to him."

"And tell him what? That he's too perfect? He's the type of guy you marry and make babies with." She pressed a cushion to her chest. "You know that's not what I want."

"Then tell him that."

"He won't understand. He'll make me change my mind. He's good at that."

"Then make something up. Tell him his feet stink, that you don't like the noises he makes, something."

"There is nothing. He doesn't stink, and I like the noises he makes; that's the problem. I like everything about him." Karina ducked under the covers.

Natalie sat beside her. "I think these are your intimacy issues popping up. You can't let this fear win. A great guy like Ian doesn't come along every day, and you're going to end up hurting him."

Karina sat up straight. "I am not afraid! In fact, this is me being brave, doing what needs to be done. Trust me. It's for his own good."

* * *

Karina kept her phone off the whole day. That was what she usually did in these situations—disappear until the guy got the message, which eventually he would. But this wasn't the usual. She still had to deal with Ian at work.

The next day, she got to the company early and looked over her shoulder all morning, expecting to see him at every turn. Surely, he wouldn't make a scene at work. But no, he waltzed in and spotted her before she ran off to hide in the bathroom.

Later, when it was time for their lunch break, Karina stopped her friends in the hallway. "If Ian comes looking for me, tell him I went out for lunch."

"Why? What happened?" Cordelia asked.

"I'm avoiding him. It's over between us."

Marisa palmed her cheeks. "Oh no. You're tired of him already?"

"More like she's freaking out about it getting too serious," Natalie said.

"The reason doesn't matter," Karina said, glaring at Natalie. "It had to end sooner or later. I told you guys from the beginning."

"But why are you avoiding him?" Marisa asked. "Why not talk to him?"

"That's what I said," Natalie said.

"It's not my style," Karina said. "Anyway, I better go."

At the end of her shift, she went to Dwight's office, and there was Ian. She stopped short and was about to backtrack when Dwight motioned for her to come in.

Karina sat at the small table set up for her in the corner of the room, shuffling papers around, waiting for Ian to finish talking about his production audit and leave.

Please, don't make a scene here.

But as soon as Dwight dismissed him, Ian asked, "Hey, Karina, can I talk to you outside for a moment?"

"I have work to do," she told the desk.

"Don't worry," Dwight said. "You can talk in here. I'll be in Lacey's office if you need me."

Damn it. Couldn't Dwight see she was trying to avoid Ian? The door shut.

"What the hell's happening?" Ian said. "You don't answer my texts or call me back. I was worried about you, and then I go to your house and find out you left with someone. Where were you?"

"I don't want to talk about this here," she said through gritted teeth.

"Then where? When? I have the right to know what's happening."

She raised her eyebrows. "The right? You don't own me."

He rubbed his forehead. "I told you there was a limit. Did you spend the night with someone else?"

Karina glanced toward the door, hoping no one had heard. She looked back at Ian. This was her way out. If she said yes, then Ian would stop chasing after her. But she couldn't do it. She didn't want to hurt him more than she needed to.

"No."

"You telling me the truth?"

She looked right into his eyes. "Yes."

"Then where were you?"

"Out with Marisa."

He frowned. "What about our plans? And why was your phone off? Why couldn't you let me know where you were?"

Karina went around the table to stand in front of him. "Listen, I can go out with my friends whenever I want. I don't owe you any explanations."

"You're being difficult again. I thought we were past this."

"Maybe difficult is what I am; have you thought about that? You haven't known me for that long."

"I know you pretty well. We've been together two months. In fact, today's our monthiversary."

"Oh God, please, no. I can't take this anymore."

"What are you talking about?"

"This. Us."

"What? Where's this coming from? On Saturday you bought me a rug, and now you want to break up?"

"Stop with the questions, all right?"

He grabbed her by the shoulders. "Talk to me, K. I can't fix it if I don't know what's wrong." His eyes moved back and forth between hers, searching, pleading.

Tell him the truth, Heart called out. *Tell him you love him and you don't know how to handle these feelings. He'll know what to do.*

Yes. With those three little words, he'd wrap her in his arms, assure her everything would be okay, that they'd figure it out together. His scent and touch would reassure her, calm her long enough to make her listen to his words. And then . . .

And then what? She'd slowly turn into her mother, into Cordelia; become a housewife and live only for him; lose her self-sufficiency and strength and give it all away? That would not be her life. She had to be stronger than her heart.

Karina broke free from his grasp. "There's nothing to talk about. It's over."

"But—"

"Just go, okay? I need to work." She turned her back to him, arranging papers until his footsteps retreated and the door shut behind him.

She dropped into her chair, resting her head on her hands. *This is a good thing. You're not meant to be in a relationship, and the sooner he gets that, the sooner he can move on.*

But what about me? Heart asked. *How do I move on?*

What you need to do, Heart, is go back into hibernation. Take these feelings with you and never come out.

CHAPTER TWENTY-THREE

The office door opened, startling Karina. She quickly wiped her face and looked up. Her heart settled when she didn't see Ian but Dwight.

"Is everything okay?" he asked.

Karina grabbed a binder. "Yup."

"Are you sure? You can go home early if you—"

"No." Her chest ached and the desire to cry wouldn't go away, but she couldn't leave. That would be the ultimate show of weakness. "I'm here to work, and that's what I'm going to do."

The old Karina would never mope over a guy. Once she was done, she was done. No second thoughts. Even if she loved Ian, her reaction to this breakup should be the same as to all the others—relief. Finally, she had the freedom to do whatever she wanted; no need to explain or report what she was doing, or answer stupid texts, or feel guilty over anything.

She opened the binder. In the past two weeks, Dwight had upgraded her from scanning and filing to helping him with the raw materials specifications, making sure they had all the documentation for each ingredient, packaging material, and cleaning and mainte-nance product they used. She was organizing everything into bind-ers, and whenever anything was missing, she contacted the supplier or looked up the specs online. It was an easy enough job, but it required a lot of time, since they had so many materials.

They worked in silence, the only sounds the tapping of the keyboard and the shuffling of papers. Their relationship had remained professional. While Lacey had hardly spoken or even looked at Karina since their confrontation, Dwight gave no hint he even knew they'd fought about him.

"I didn't know there was so much paperwork involved," Karina said. "It seems no matter how much we do, there's still so much left."

"I know. That's why I'm glad you're here to help me. Seriously, with all the procedures I need to write, I'd never find the time to organize everything."

Karina smiled. It was nice to feel needed, to help, even if it had started as an excuse. Lacey's comment about how Karina was putting the company at risk with her behavior still stung, especially when she'd only wanted to save it.

The work wasn't that bad. She'd learned so much about what went on behind the scenes, everything that needed to be in place for them to make the cookies. She'd known part of it from Leonard, but Lacey had been right when she'd said he'd left some holes. But Karina still wasn't convinced all the changes were necessary, even if Dwight kept repeating it was the minimum needed to comply with the code and pass the inspection in three months.

"Do you enjoy this kind of work?"

"Hmm?" She looked up from her desk. "Oh, it's okay. It's different from what I'm used to."

"I've been fixing to ask you something." He adjusted his glasses. "How would you like to continue working in QA?"

"Doing what, filing?"

He chuckled. "I was thinking you could be the company's auditor. You'd do all the internal auditing and be the point person for all external audits. Does that sound like something you'd be interested in?"

"Yeah, right. I'm not college educated like you."

"There are multiple trainings we can send you to. Inspectors don't care about college degrees—they want someone who's been trained and knows what they're doing. You fit the bill."

"Seriously? No college degree—are you sure? I thought . . ." Her lack of education had held her back for so long she had no idea what to think. "Me? An auditor?"

"Why not? You already successfully completed the warehouse audit, making the brilliant suggestion of adding an item to the checklist to ensure Scott enters the lot into the system. You even incorporated Sofia into the process to make her responsible for the certificates of analysis. What more proof do you want that you'd be the perfect person for this job? You're more capable than you think."

Had he gotten that from Lacey? Her chest tightened and her desire to cry returned. This was the type of opportunity she'd yearned for back when they'd moved to this plant, a chance to play a part behind the scenes. But now . . .

"Does Lacey approve?" she asked.

"I wanted to get your thoughts before I told her. I don't think she'd have a problem with it."

Karina shook off the images of her working side by side with Lacey and Dwight and came back to reality. "I doubt it. Too much time with me working closely with her man. Didn't she tell you I tried to sabotage your relationship with her?"

Dwight's eyes widened, but he quickly recovered. He cleared his throat. "You were only looking out for your friend. You don't know me."

"Lacey's my boss, not my friend."

"She considers you a friend. More than that. A sister."

Her chest ached. Had Lacey told him that, or was he just guessing?

That one time nine years ago, when they'd worked in the commercial kitchen, a deliveryman had confused them for sisters. They'd been in the middle of making a batch of Mellow Cookies when the man came in to bring them their weekly supply of oats. After handing Lacey the invoice for her to sign, he said, "I tried one of those Perky Cookies the other day. They're really good. You and your sister should be proud of what you're building here."

Karina stopped stirring the dough and lifted her chin. She *was* proud of working with such a strong woman as Lacey. Being confused with her sister was just icing on the cake.

Lacey also paused and asked in a shocked voice, "You think we're sisters?"

Karina's breath caught in her throat. What had she expected? Of course Lacey would be offended by anyone thinking lowly Karina was her sister.

"Us? Sisters?" Karina scoffed, pounding the wooden spoon against the dough. "We couldn't be more different. First, I'm Hispanic, and Lacey's as white as they come. And she's rich. Do you know how much money I have?"

Lacey stared at Karina, her expression unreadable.

The man took the clipboard from Lacey and said, "Sorry for the confusion. You two look alike, and I just assumed. Good day!" He bowed his head and left.

"He's right." Lacey returned to stand next to Karina behind the counter. "Now that he mentions it, I do see a resemblance." She added the almond milk to the bowl and stirred it into the dough.

Sure, they had the same straight, dark-brown hair and eyes, but the rest? That silk blouse Lacey wore must've cost more than Karina's rent.

"I guess," Karina replied. "But we have nothing else in common."

"We both love these cookies." Lacey pointed at the last batch they'd made, the Perkys individually wrapped and ready to go, lying on the table beside them. "And we enjoy working with them, together. Isn't that a start?"

"A start for a business, not a family."

Lacey frowned. "Even people from different backgrounds can share a strong bond."

Karina had dismissed Lacey's words, like always. She'd seen through the act. When you were paid to be part of someone else's life, you were an employee, not a family member.

But what if she had been wrong back then and Lacey did see her as a sister?

"Lacey believes in your potential, and so do I," Dwight said now. "But you should decide on your own if this is something you'd like to do."

It didn't matter if she'd been wrong about Lacey. Their relationship was ruined, and there was no going back. And her being an auditor was ridiculous. Karina wasn't cut out for so much responsibility. Just like she wasn't cut out for a serious relationship. Her heart ached.

"I don't know," Karina said. "Sounds like too much pressure."

"Look, it was only an idea. Don't stress out about it. You can keep doing what you're doing for now. I only wanted you to know you don't have to stay stuck in the same area. We can find something better for you."

There was a knock on the door, and Lacey popped in. "I finished reading your product development report and would like to discuss a few things," she told Dwight. "Do you have time?"

"Sure."

Lacey walked in and sat across from him, her back to Karina. "I found your idea of adding anise interesting, but don't you think it would be too overpowering?"

Were they talking about the licorice cookie? Lacey wanted Dwight's help, but not Karina's? If there ever was a sign that their time as a team was over, it was this.

"We'd need to test it," Dwight said, "but you need something else to take it to the next level, and the anise increases the functionality, so there's that."

"Then let's try it." She clapped and stood. "I'm excited about this. Can you find a supplier to send us a sample? I want to get on this as soon as possible."

"I'll look into it." From the glint in Dwight's eyes, it was obvious their relationship was going strong. Before Lacey could leave, Dwight added, "Can we discuss something with you? I was telling Karina she could be our new auditor, someone to take care of the internal auditing and be in charge of the external ones. What do you think?"

"I doubt that's of any interest to Karina." Lacey gazed directly at Karina. "Too much responsibility, isn't that right?"

Now Lacey was mocking her? *I'll show her.* Karina shrugged. "I already did one audit, and it wasn't so difficult."

Lacey blinked. "Is that something you need, Dwight?"

"Well, we're going to have to do a lot of internal audits in the future. It would be nice to have someone I could delegate that to. And she could keep helping out with my other duties. You know I need the help."

When Lacey's gaze returned to Karina, her expression had softened. "If Karina agrees, we can make it happen. Now, I should get back to work. Will I see you later?" she asked Dwight.

Dwight cleared his throat. "You bet." As soon as Lacey left, Dwight turned to Karina. "Did you hear that? We can make it happen. The decision is up to you."

* * *

Karina returned to an empty house. Natalie was probably with Mr. Sparks. She plopped down on the sofa, took out her phone, and stared at it. No texts from Ian. What did she expect, that he would pester her for an answer or ask for another chance? He knew her well enough to keep his distance. And she'd been adamant. He'd be a fool to reach out. She dropped the phone beside her.

There was a hollowness inside her, as if she'd lost a part of herself, as if she hadn't broken only a relationship but her own body in half. There wouldn't be any more texts from Ian, no plans to meet for dinner or the next day, or ever again. Only lonely nights for the foreseeable future, with no one to kiss her or hold her or make her feel safe.

Why did it affect her so much? She enjoyed being alone. Maybe she'd grown too dependent on him. If that was the case, then this breakup had come just at the right time, before love caused more damage.

The phone beeped, and she rushed to grab it. Not a message from Ian but from her mom. A *Toy Story* meme making fun of how Andy's mom's toys were also called Woody and Buzz.

She cracked up, then burst into tears. "Ugh." She wiped her face. "Get it together." The tears kept falling.

Not hungry, she collapsed into bed, finding no solace in her heap of cushions or Woody, with only the crack of her breaking heart keeping her company as she cried herself to sleep.

CHAPTER TWENTY-FOUR

"Yo, Karina, I thought you were cool, but what you are is cold-hearted," Tyler said on Wednesday morning.

Great, they all knew. When no one said anything yesterday, Karina had hoped they wouldn't find out, or if they did, that it wouldn't be the whole story or they wouldn't care either way. Now she was being called coldhearted to her face. If only it were true and her heart was cold as ice. Then she wouldn't feel like bursting into tears every five minutes.

Yesterday she'd had the cover of ignorance to get her through the day and alcohol to numb the pain at night, but today's hangover and what promised to be a full shift of insults made her wish she'd called in sick.

"Good morning to you too," Karina said.

"What you did to Ian?" Tyler continued as he started the mixer for a new batch of Mellow Cookie dough. "Dumping him without an explanation? I mean, *damn*, woman. I'm glad I'm done dating, 'cause there are women like you all over the place, only wanting to break a poor brother's heart."

Roy slapped his clipboard. "That's enough. Karina's private life is her business. If she wanted to break up, she must've had a good reason."

Yes, she did. At least someone was on her side. She smiled at Roy, and he winked at her.

"Mm-hmm," Tyler said, not looking convinced. He and the rest of the guys gave her dirty looks.

In the packaging area, she didn't fare much better, as she was greeted with head shakes and scowls.

"What's everyone's problem?" Karina asked Cordelia and Marisa. "I broke up with Ian. So what?"

"You were our celebrity couple." Marisa stuffed twelve-packs into a box. "We're sad you two broke up."

"Does it look like people are sad?" Karina asked. "They're mad at me, as if I attacked them."

Cordelia taped a box shut. "If you'd been more of an adult about it, then Ian wouldn't be so hurt that he has to vent to Rosa. It's your own fault."

Her cheeks burned. "Whatever. I have work to do."

Two hours later, a mixer broke down, and she called maintenance. Her heart sped up at the possibility of seeing Ian, but it was another mechanic, Brody, who showed up.

"Were you expecting Ian?" Brody *tsk*ed. "We're not letting him see you. It's bad for him. He's on work order duty from now on."

Was it written on her face how much she'd wanted to see Ian? Of course, now that the new production line was almost finished, they could spare him, keep him in the shop, away from her. This should be great news—less opportunity to see him. Wasn't that what she wanted? But her heart wouldn't let any joy in.

Karina masked her expression with what she hoped was indifference. "Why don't you do your job and keep your opinions to yourself?"

He pursed his lips. "You may be good-looking, but you're not worth the trouble. Ian should've listened to Rosa. She warned him. We all did." He turned his back on her to inspect the mixer.

Karina's shoulders slumped. Yes, Ian should've listened. "I'm going to do my rounds now," she said in a monotone voice. "Let me know when you're done." She hurried into the oven room, shut her eyes, and swallowed the sob stuck in her throat.

* * *

"Are you doing okay?" Marisa asked Karina at lunch. "You look pale. Have you been sleeping well?"

Act normal. The arroz mamposteao and pork chop in her bowl were still half uneaten. She stuck a forkful of stewed beans and rice into her mouth. "Yeah. Why wouldn't I?"

"So you're okay about the breakup?"

Karina shrugged and made eye contact with each of them. "I told you guys." She picked up the pork chop and bit into it.

"Wow." Marisa froze with her can of Diet Coke midair. "You're so strong. I can't imagine breaking up with someone as great as Ian."

You can't even imagine breaking up with someone as bad as Jaime. Karina sucked on the bone.

"I don't think she's strong at all," Natalie said. "Afraid of falling in love is more like it."

Karina scoffed. "Me? In love? How many times have we gone over this? I will never fall in love." More forkfuls of rice.

Cordelia looked down at her, trying to figure out the puzzle that was Karina. "Pues parece que no. If it wasn't Ian, then I don't know who it could be."

Karina finished her food, struggling to swallow past the lump in her throat. If only she could tell them how she really felt, but then they'd never stop hounding her to get back with Ian. It was better if they thought she was heartless.

Cordelia's chair scraped the floor as she stood to take her bowl to the sink. "Natalie, please give us some good news. Are you bringing your architect to Rosa's party on Saturday?"

Rosa's party was already this weekend? She threw a huge birthday bash every year, complete with loads of traditional Mexican food and tequila and a mariachi band to close out the night. It was the event of the year. Karina never missed it. Ian would probably be there, but that shouldn't keep her from going.

"Ooh, are you?" Marisa clapped. "I can't wait to meet him."

Natalie finished munching the last of her salad before replying. "Yes." She beamed. "He agreed to meet my friends already. Isn't that wonderful?"

"He agreed, or you forced him?" Karina asked.

Natalie's face fell. "I told him about the party and that my friends would be there, and he wants to come. Satisfied?"

Karina shrugged. She should let it go. Peter had kept Natalie out of the house the past two nights, away from Karina, not there to witness her meltdown. And now the focus was on her. This couldn't be better timing.

Karina rose to clean her bowl but dropped back to the chair when Natalie said, "Guys, I think he's the one."

"You've only known him for five days," Karina said.

"It doesn't take that long to know. Unlike some people." She gave Karina a pointed look.

"That's what you said about the last guy," Karina said at the same time Cordelia said, "Try not to get your hopes up too fast."

At least they agreed on something. Karina pointed to Cordelia and raised her eyebrows at Natalie as if to say, *See, she gets it.*

"But the way he looks at me—"

"Did he say something?" Karina asked. "Is he looking for something serious?"

"I, uh, I don't know."

"Don't assume all people are looking for 'the one,'" Karina said. "He may only want a fling. You need to ask these things up front. Isn't that what you told me, Cordelia?"

Cordelia grimaced. "I have to agree with Karina on this."

"Ask Peter what he wants so you don't end up scaring him away like you did the last guy."

"What if I scare him away by asking?"

"At least you'll know before you go in too deep. And you'll be sure."

Natalie turned to Marisa. "Do you also think I should?"

Marisa nodded.

"I don't know." Natalie packed her bowls and water bottle into her cool bag. "Being so up front about it takes away the romance. I want to be swept off my feet, not have every detail spelled out."

"You told me to be honest with Ian. Wasn't that your advice?"

"Yes, but—"

"Sometimes you have to force the truth out. You won't know until you ask him."

Natalie still looked unsure.

"Doesn't feel so great when you're on the other end of the psychoanalysis, does it?"

* * *

As soon as she finished lunch, Karina locked herself in a bathroom stall and took deep breaths. The HACCP team meeting would start in a few minutes. Time to face Ian.

On her way to Dwight's office, there was Rosa, mopping the hallway.

"Some people don't know when they find something good," Rosa said.

Karina kept walking.

"Are you coming to my party?"

That stopped her. "You're not banning me, are you?"

Rosa took on a pensive look, as if she was considering it, but Karina would not beg to go.

"I want to keep you away from Marcos, but I think it will be good for you to come. I'm going to present Ian to my niece. She's a nice, decent girl, not like you. Maybe seeing him with someone else will make you more . . . what's the word? Humble?"

"If you say so." Now she'd have to see Ian again in a few days with another girl? *Don't cry, don't cry, don't cry.*

Karina pressed her lips together and kept her eyes forward. She couldn't let on how much she missed Ian, how much she yearned to see him, to be near him. It was better to be hated for being cold than pitied for being weak and pathetic.

When Karina got to the meeting, everyone turned to stare at her, even Scott, who usually only stared at his phone. Dwight frowned in concern, and Ian . . . Ian had by far the worst expression of all. He smiled. A sad, tentative smile, but still. A smile. How could he smile at her after what she'd done to him? Why couldn't he hate her like everyone else?

The seat next to Ian was vacant, waiting for her. Thankfully, Lacey was late, so Karina took her seat, the one farthest away from Ian. She kept her head held high, eyes to the front, only turning to look at Lacey when she came in.

"So sorry I'm late." Lacey stopped short when she noticed Karina in her seat. She walked over to the seat next to Ian, placing her hand on his shoulder as she sat.

Karina should've known Lacey would take his side. So much for sisterhood.

While Dwight talked about the latest revisions to the HACCP plan, Karina sneaked glances at Ian. Every time their eyes met, her heart ached, and she turned away. When would this meeting end?

Roy walked in and leaned against the wall next to the door. What was he doing here?

Dwight nodded, acknowledging Roy's presence. "We still have a few minutes left, and I would like to update you on how far we are in the preparations for the inspection."

More talking? Karina already knew this. She would've left if it weren't because she really wanted to know why Roy was here.

"So far," Dwight continued, "I've written every procedure that was missing, and Karina has been helping me with the internal audits and organizing other paperwork. Since we finished revising the HACCP plan, we only need to tackle the employee training."

So that was it. They were trying to convince Roy to agree to their hour-long training meetings. She'd been out of the loop since her confession to Lacey. Karina hoped Roy knew what he was in for.

"Currently," Dwight said, "we train employees whenever a procedure changes and only those who are affected, but the code recommends a more regular schedule where we cover relevant topics for everyone. For example, Ian has been working here for two months, and he's only had the initial training on his first day. If it weren't for these meetings, he wouldn't know about the food safety certification program. An important requirement is for employees to be familiar with it and what it stands for. Ian performed an internal audit of the production area on Friday. Please, tell us what you found."

Ian stood. He was also part of this?

"I, uh, I interviewed some employees and asked them about HACCP and the certification program." He rubbed the back of his neck. "No one knew what it is. Most don't know there's an inspection."

"I don't believe that," Roy said. "You can't keep anything quiet around here."

"Perdón." He rubbed his neck again. "They know there's an inspection but not what it's about or that it's important or that it involves them."

Dwight also stood, looking at everyone in turn. "Every employee needs to be part of this inspection. Our contract with Whole-Mart is dependent on us passing. We need everyone to pitch in. That's why I'm suggesting we do a monthly group training, where we can discuss food safety terms and keep everyone up to date about any issues we may have. They can be shorter than an hour, if you'd prefer, but we must implement them."

Lacey turned on her chair to speak directly to Roy. "We could do it after the shift ends. That way the production process wouldn't be affected. What do you say, Uncle?"

Roy stared at Lacey a moment before replying, "If everyone else thinks it's a good idea, then we can try it. I think it would work better before the shift starts. I can concede to starting production half an hour late, but only half an hour, you hear? You can offer breakfast. Sweeten the deal."

Lacey clapped and stood to hug Roy. He was really giving up the fight and letting Dwight take over?

"It's a fantastic suggestion, Roy. Thank you." Dwight adjourned the meeting and walked over to shake Roy's hand. Now, all of a sudden, they were friends? What was happening?

Ian blocked her view. "Hi."

187

Karina stood and kept her gaze directed at the chatty group of Roy, Dwight, and Lacey.

"You have time later, after work?" Ian asked. "I think we should talk."

Karina stepped back, away from him. He was too close. She held on to the chair to keep from throwing herself into his arms. "I already said everything I needed to say."

"I think there are some things we still need to clear up."

"What do you need to know?" Her voice came out strained. "It's over. We're not getting back together."

He stroked her arm. "Please, K, talk to me."

Her heart leaped at his touch. She risked looking into his eyes. There was so much pain there. *You did this*, Heart said. *You hurt him. Why can't you just tell him the truth so he can fix it? I'll leave you alone if you do.*

Tempting but doubtful. *There's no future for him and me, Heart. The sooner he gets that, the better. I can't let him guilt me into changing my mind.*

Karina pulled back. "Every relationship has to end. Ours reached that point. That's it. That's all there is to it."

"There has to be more than that."

Roy finished his conversation and turned to leave.

"I have to go." Karina almost tripped over the chair in her haste, but she hurried out into the hallway and caught up to Roy. "What are you doing? I thought you were against these training meetings. What happened to us against Dwight?"

Roy raised his hands in defense. "I know, I know. But Lacey convinced me to keep an open mind. They have a good plan, and I don't see what I can object to."

"So, that's it? You're giving in to Dwight's changes?"

"Not necessarily, but I don't want to be against Lacey anymore. She's been coming over for dinner, and we've cleared things up. She needs my support, and I'm going to give it to her."

Aha.

Blood is thicker than water. How could she have thought he'd choose her over Lacey?

When Roy's wife died, Karina had refused to go to the funeral. It was meant for family only, and she didn't want to intrude.

"How can you say that?" Roy had said when she told him. "You're family, you hear? Never forget that."

She'd been right not to go, to move out a few weeks afterward. But she should've cut contact completely, never continued working for him and Lacey. Sure, working at Singular was an awesome opportunity for a high school dropout like Karina, but at what cost—caring for people who were not her family and never would be?

CHAPTER TWENTY-FIVE

Karina elbowed her way through the throng packed inside Rosa's living room, leading Marisa by the hand. They spilled out into the kitchen, where trays of taquitos, chips and salsa, and tamales lay on the counter.

Karina filled up a paper plate and grabbed a beer from the ice-box on the floor next to them. After the week she'd had, she needed this. No Roy, Dwight, or Lacey to worry about, since Rosa never invited the bosses. Like Karina, she believed in keeping boundaries, and having any bosses present would sour the mood.

Mexican banda music assaulted her senses, with its mix of saxophones, trumpets, and drums. She gulped down the beer, looking around the dancing crowd for Ian.

"Are you done?" Marisa yelled into her ear. "Let's go find Rosa."

Karina gobbled up her last taquito. Her stomach wasn't full yet, but that would have to do for now. They needed to stick together. Marisa was her driver and her protector in case Karina bumped into Ian and was too inebriated to rein in her heart.

They squeezed themselves between bodies, down the hallway, and out into the backyard. A large piñata in the shape of a star hung high from a tree, and children of all ages ran around, Rosa among them. Marisa hugged her and gave her a pouch she'd made herself out of striped purple fabric. Rosa thanked her, then turned to Karina expectantly. Karina shrugged. Why was Rosa expecting a gift when she'd specifically told everyone not to bring her anything?

Back inside, they found Natalie and Peter. He wasn't her usual type: a few inches shorter than her, with a beard and a glint in his blue eyes. They wore nearly identical outfits: T-shirts, jogging pants, and sneakers.

"This is some party!" Peter yelled.

"Wait till the mariachi get here," Karina said.

"And this woman throws a party this big every year?" Peter asked Natalie. When she nodded, he said, "I need to live more."

Natalie and Marisa laughed.

"Natalie told us you're an architect," Karina said. "What's that like?"

"A lot of sketching and negotiating with the client to get them what they want. Actually, you know what? I don't want to talk about work. What I really want to know is, what's up with that gigantic cake?" He pointed at the table behind him, on which sat the huge tres leches cake Rosa always ordered for her birthday parties. "Let's go see." He led Natalie away, maneuvering her around two large purple helium balloons, both shaped like the number five, that stood beside the table.

"So much for getting to know us," Karina said.

"You heard him; he's never been to a big party like this," Marisa said. "He wants to spend time alone with Natalie. What's wrong with that?" She checked her phone.

Rosa's daughter passed by with a pitcher of margaritas and plastic cups. Karina poured two cups and handed one to Marisa.

"Cordelia's not coming." Marisa dropped the phone into her purse. "Charlie's sick, and she has to take care of him."

"Please. He's a grown man; he can take care of himself."

"When Jaime's sick, he acts like a baby. It's so cute. Maybe Charlie's like that. I also wouldn't leave his side if I was Cordelia."

"Whatever." Her friends—always sacrificing everything for their men. Karina took a big gulp of margarita. It was the classic variation, with no ice and way too much tequila. The perfect drink for tonight.

"Look, there's Ian." Marisa pointed behind Karina. "Who's he talking to?"

Karina turned, and her heart skipped a beat. Ian looked amazing in jeans and a short-sleeved button-down, nursing a beer. He was deep in conversation with a curvy girl in a short, flowy pink dress who had to be Rosa's niece. From how close she was standing to him, touching his arm so she could speak into his ear, she looked anything but decent. Sinful Cookie—a calorie bomb that would satisfy you but leave you guilty afterward.

And Ian seemed ready to dig in. Maybe this girl would help him get over Karina.

Her heart ached. She turned back to Marisa. "Who knows?" She took a long sip from her drink.

"They look really into each other."

"He can date whoever he wants."

"And it really doesn't bother you? It's been less than a week."

"Nope." Another big gulp.

"Ooh, he's looking this way." Marisa gasped. "He's checking you out. Oh my God, it's like he wants to make love to you right here. Even that girl noticed, and she's not too happy about it."

Karina suppressed a smirk but couldn't resist turning toward them. Indeed, the girl was scowling. Karina locked eyes with Ian. There was longing there, desire, sadness, everything Karina felt but couldn't show. Marisa had used the words *make love*, which Karina had always found lame. For Karina, sex was dirty and fun, a way to give and receive pleasure. But Marisa was right. If Karina and Ian were together again, it wouldn't be sex or fucking, it would be making love, because Karina was in love with him, and presumably, so was Ian with her. How would that feel, to exchange not only pleasure but love? Maybe it would feel the same as always—sex with Ian had been a unique experience from the start. But she hadn't been conscious about being in love; she hadn't let him see her heart and everything that hid there. Would it be rawer, more powerful, if she exposed herself completely to him?

Sinful Cookie put Ian's hand to her waist and swayed to the music. He grinned and swung her around. Karina finished her drink and looked away, then noticed a guy staring at Marisa.

"Speaking of being checked out." Karina nudged her. "That guy over there is totally into you." She gestured with her chin.

"I doubt it." Marisa turned her head, and the guy glanced at the floor. "He was probably looking at you."

"Why do you say that? You're the prettiest girl here."

Marisa looked amazing in her indigo tie-dyed dress, made with the supplies Karina had gifted her. The fitted top and full skirt enhanced her curves. "No, I'm not. Besides, I have a boyfriend."

"You could do so much better than him, Mari."

Marisa chuckled and shook her head. "I'm not so sure about that." She jumped and dug into her purse for her phone. "Jaime's texting me. Hold on."

He couldn't leave her alone for even a few hours. Typical. Why couldn't Marisa ignore him? She read and typed into her phone. Ian still danced and laughed, as if there was nowhere else he'd rather be.

"I'm sorry, but I have to go," Marisa said.

"What? You can't leave. It's too early, plus you're my ride."

"I need to pick up Jaime. His friends left, and he doesn't have money for a cab. Are you okay staying here by yourself, or do you want to leave with me?"

Karina looked back at Sinful Cookie and Ian as they laughed and swayed to the beat. She'd looked forward to the party, but this . . . her heart wouldn't be able to take much of it.

"You'd be picking up Jaime first, right?"

Marisa made a face and nodded.

If Karina saw Jaime in this state, she'd definitely punch his face. "I'll hang out with Natalie and Peter. Don't worry." Now she only needed to find them.

With a fresh margarita in hand, she searched the house, but there was no trace of them. Maybe they were in a closet having sex? That wasn't Natalie's style, but where the fuck was she, then? Had she left without saying good-bye? Karina gulped down half the drink. Her friends were supposed to protect her from herself. They didn't know that, of course, since Karina hadn't told them she was in need of protecting. She'd always been proud of not needing anyone's help, but right now, she wished there were someone to lean on.

Karina finished her drink and went back for another. She bumped into someone and was about to yell at him to move when she noticed it was Ian.

The empty cup fell from her hand. Both she and Ian bent to get it and bumped their heads together.

"Let me," he said, rescuing the cup before it was stepped on. He handed it to her, and she indulged in the feel of his fingers as she took it from him. Her buzz was strong enough to make her want to kiss him and leave with him but not enough for her to forget why it would be a mistake. She craned her neck in search of Rosa's daughter and the margaritas, but it was impossible to find her among the throng of people.

Ian leaned to speak into her ear, and she jerked back at his closeness. He put his hands up in apology and yelled, "Saw that Marisa left. Something happen?"

"Just a Jaime emergency. Nothing important."

He smiled, then turned serious. "What happened, K?"

Her chest tightened. She could hear the longing in his voice, even through the racket. It resonated all over his body. His eyes told her she was still his sweet girl.

"Think we can talk for a moment?" he asked.

"Ian—"

"Let's go outside. It's more quiet—"

"There you are." Sinful Cookie actually had the nerve to put her arms around his waist. "They're going to start with the piñata now."

He nodded. "Oh, here. Karina, this is Maribel, Rosa's niece."

Karina raised her chin in acknowledgment.

Maribel pursed her lips and playfully shoved him toward the backyard. "You're going to miss it."

"Okay." He turned to Karina. "Maybe later?"

When Karina didn't respond, he walked away.

Maribel stayed put.

"I know who you are," she said. "Tía Rosa told me about you. You better stay away from him."

"Or what?" Karina stuck her chest out. "You don't stand a chance against me, sweetie. I can have him back with one word."

Maribel looked her up and down, lingering on Karina's T-shirt slogan: *I may be a bitch but at least I'm pretty.* Her nose wrinkled. "There are putas like you on every corner. He'll forget you soon enough." With a flip of her hair, she left.

If that girl thought she could have Ian, she was delusional. But Karina couldn't blame her. If she were in Maribel's place, she'd do the same. Ian was too hot to be alone for long.

It was time to call it a night. This party had turned into a disaster.

Someone tapped her on the shoulder. *That bitch better leave me alone.* She turned to find Marcos.

"Hello, stranger." Rosa's nephew was stocky, his dark-brown hair kept in a messy man bun. Karina had met him at one of these parties, and they'd hooked up last year—following much insistence on his part. He'd actually been great in bed, but his clinginess had gotten old really fast. "I was hoping to run into you tonight. You look great."

Ugh. "I was actually about to leave."

"What? The party's just getting started. Did you eat? Mi vieja just set up the taquiza."

Her stomach growled at the word. The taquizas at these parties were legendary. And now she wouldn't have to be alone anymore. "Eating sounds good." The margaritas were making her dizzy.

Karina could have as many flour tortillas as she could fill with different types of stewed and grilled meats, plus all sorts of toppings. She loaded her plate, filled a cup with horchata to have a pause from the tequila, and followed Marcos to the backyard. String lights sparkled above them; the busted piñata now lay in a corner. They sat under a tree. Loudspeakers carried the music from inside, although not as loudly.

"Why didn't you ever return my texts?" Marcos asked. "If it wasn't for my aunt, I'd have thought you disappeared off the face of the earth."

"Marcos, not now. I'm eating." She stuffed a taco in her mouth and washed it down with rice water. "What's done is done."

"But Karina, what we had . . . I've never had sex like that with anyone. And I've had sex con un chorro de chicas, let me tell you. But you're something else."

Karina laughed and instinctively looked around for Ian. He'd also said that about her once, that she was "something else." She found him staring right at her, or more like glaring at them. So what if she was talking to another guy? She could talk to whoever she wanted, just like he could dance with Maribel all night. Karina could even fuck Marcos if she wanted, and why not? He was willing, and she could use the sex to exorcise this love right out of her.

Karina scarfed down the rest of her food. "You know what?" She moved closer to him. "You're right. What we had *was* special."

He grinned. "I knew it."

She put aside his plate so she could straddle him, tugging at his hair.

He groaned. "Órale, mamita. You make me so hard."

"I know, papi." She kissed him.

He grabbed her ass and pulled her against him, sticking his tongue into her mouth. Karina had forgotten what it was like for a kiss to be just a kiss, a way to get turned on, nothing more. She'd never get lost in this kiss, could stay in control. She deepened the kiss. Marcos's hand went up to her breast.

"Puta descarada," a woman's voice shouted, followed by a yank to Karina's hair.

Karina fell backward to the ground, then quickly jumped to her feet. "What the fuck?"

Rosa slapped her hard across the face. Gasps spread through the people gathered outside. Inside the house, Karina could still hear laughter and voices chattering. She touched her cheek. It stung like hell. Her vision blurred.

"Get out of my house!" Rosa yelled.

Karina blinked, and her eyesight returned to normal. Around her, people gaped. Her eyes locked with Ian's worried ones.

"Que te vayas te dije." Rosa shoved her. "Didn't you hear me? I said go."

Ian stepped between them. "Rosa, cálmate."

"Didn't you see what she did? She's a whore, and I don't want her in my house."

"I'll take her out."

"¿Y tú, pendejo?" Rosa slapped Marcos on the back of the head. "What are you doing still sniffing around her ass? Don't you have any dignity?"

Ian held Karina's hand as he led her through the crowd toward the side gate. As the shock wore off, she noticed her stooped posture and straightened. Making out with a man in public was nothing to be ashamed of, but she knew Rosa was only protecting two men she cared about. Still, that didn't mean she had the right to hit Karina. Only her mom had ever slapped her, and Rosa wasn't her mother.

If Karina hadn't been so startled, she would've fought back. In the end, the only person who had the right to be hurt by what she'd done was escorting her out, had even stood up for her. What would it take for him to hate her? Did Karina really want to find out?

He stopped when they reached the sidewalk. "You okay? Let me see." He stroked her cheek.

"Ow."

"Your lip's bleeding. Let me get some ice."

Karina dabbed at her lip. A few drops of blood stuck to her fingers. She wiped them on her jeans. "I'm going home." She reached into her fanny pack for her car keys, but no, she'd gotten a ride from Marisa. "Crap. I don't have my car."

"I'll drive you."

"Absolutely not. I'll call an Uber."

"Please, let me help you. Rosa wouldn't have slapped you if it wasn't for me."

"This had nothing to do with you." She crossed her arms. "Plus I deserved it."

"No, you didn't."

Karina cocked her head. How could he still defend her? "Ian . . . you know I did."

He hesitated. "Yes. You did."

At least he wasn't a complete martyr. "Go back to the party. Have fun with Maribel. I'll be fine." She turned to leave.

He grabbed her arm. "Karina—"

"Let me go." She pulled herself free and turned to face him. "When will you get it? We're over." Her voice cracked, and she cleared her throat. "You said there was a limit, so where is it? I just made out with another guy right in front of your face, and you're still hanging on. Listen to me: I won't change my mind. You're you and I'm me, and we don't mix. We're like oil and water, and I don't want to be forced into mixing. You get it now? Is that what you want to hear?" Tears blurred her vision.

He wrapped his arms around her.

She pushed him away. "No, stop it." She wiped her face. "Stop being so fucking nice. I want you to hate me like everyone else."

"I can't. I—"

"Why would you want to be with me, anyway? I'm a fucking mess."

"You must know, K. I—"

"Forget it, Ian. Good-bye." She turned her back on him and forced her legs to move as fast as they could, her sandals pounding on the pavement, putting as much distance between them as possible. Her heart wouldn't bear if he told her it was because he loved her.

*   *   *

When she couldn't hear the music anymore, she stopped to catch her breath. She hated to run, didn't have the stamina. *Weak.* She pulled out her phone to call an Uber. There was one text from Marcos.

Sorry about my aunt. I don't know what came over her. I hope this doesn't ruin our night. Where did you go?

Karina shouldn't have told him what they had was special. That was fodder for clingy guys like him.

She looked around to orient herself, reading the street signs. Her heart still ached over her fight with Ian, and she was sick and tired of feeling this way. It was time to take extreme measures. She texted Marcos her location.

Be there in five.

*   *   *

When she got into his car, he turned on the light and grimaced. "My aunt shouldn't have done that. I'm sorry."

198

Karina inspected her face in the mirror. Her cheek bore the red imprint of Rosa's whole hand, and her lip was swollen. That fucking crone, always sticking her nose in everybody else's business. Karina would deal with her on Monday. Right now, she had more important things to do. She flipped the visor closed, grabbed Marcos's face, and kissed him. *Ow.* She winced but didn't break the kiss. A little pain wouldn't keep her from doing what needed to be done.

"Make me forget this whole night," she said.

He took her back to his apartment. They began having sex in the living room, moved to the kitchen, and ended in the bedroom, trying out new positions along the way. Afterward, Marcos rolled over to his side and fell asleep, and Karina got dressed and called an Uber. No strings, no fuss, just in, out, and good-bye. Back to normal.

But as soon as she returned home and collapsed into her bed, she burst into tears.

Are you serious, Heart? There's no reason for me to cry. I just had great sex. Better than great. So what if there was no slow kissing or cuddling afterward? That's not what sex is about. Sex is physical, not emotional, so leave me alone. The tears wouldn't stop falling, and she clung to her cushions. *I hate you.*

CHAPTER TWENTY-SIX

The next morning, Karina woke with a pounding headache and a sting on her cheek. The mirror showed the mark of Rosa's hand was still there—redder and covering half her face.

Coffee. She needed coffee.

As she waited for the coffee machine, she crumbled Perky Cookies into a bowl. Natalie walked into the kitchen, making her jump.

"You scared the fuck out of me," Karina said. "I thought I was alone in the house."

"Oh my gosh," Natalie said. "What happened to your face?"

Karina unwrapped another Perky, letting her nerves settle before replying. "You weren't there? Rosa slapped me for kissing her nephew."

Natalie filled the kettle for tea and placed it on the stove. "We left early. I . . . I broke up with Peter."

"Why?" Karina licked the crumbs off her fingers. "What happened?"

"You were right. He doesn't want anything serious."

"What did he say?"

"He doesn't believe in marriage. He wanted to keep seeing me, but I told him no."

"Why?" Karina poured milk into the bowl. "You can have fun with a guy you like."

"Because I'm not like you. I already have feelings for him. If I keep seeing him, he'll only break my heart. I don't want what happened to Ian to happen to me."

Karina's grip on the milk container faltered as she placed it back in the refrigerator. "You think I broke his heart? That's kinda extreme, don't you think?"

"Have you looked at him? He's miserable."

"He didn't look so miserable dancing with Rosa's niece."

"Can you blame him for wanting to have a good time?" Natalie filled her thermos with leaves, then spun around. "Wait, did Ian see you kissing Marcos?"

Karina's cheeks burned. "Yeah. He stood up for me, offered to give me a ride, but I took an Uber."

"Even after he saw you kissing another guy?"

"He's more saint than man." She took her cup of coffee and bowl to the coffee table. Today would be a lazy day of movies and naps. No more thoughts of Ian or last night. Her sleep had been a restless loop of images: Ian dancing with Maribel, him pleading for an answer, flashbacks of the two of them having sex jumbled in with Marcos's lips on her. She needed to bombard her brain with new images to forget the night.

The kettle whistled. Karina scrolled through her streaming list. A comedy? Or maybe horror? Natalie sat beside her.

"Are you sure you're okay? Do you want me to cancel my hike and stay here with you, keep you company?"

Karina punched the remote keys. "I'm fine."

"What made you kiss someone else in front of everyone? You know this will be the topic of conversation tomorrow."

She froze. Fuck, that was true. She should call in sick, but no. Rosa needed a good talking-to. "I can kiss whoever I want. I'm a free woman." She continued scrolling.

"Wow. I just broke up with someone and I feel like I'm dying, and you . . ." She shook her head. "Wait, were you jealous? Is that why you kissed Marcos?"

Karina scoffed. "No. Marcos was hitting on me, and I responded."

"Seriously?" Natalie took the remote away and forced Karina to face her. "This fear of intimacy is out of control. Tell me the truth. Are you in love with Ian? Is that why you broke up with him?"

Karina wrapped her blanket around her shoulders.

"You are, aren't you?"

"I don't want to be in love."

"But you are. Admit it."

Karina scowled.

"I knew it."

"It doesn't matter. I won't change my mind. It's better for him not to be with me."

"But is it better for you? I know you like being single, but it's one thing to say it in the abstract and another once you fall in love. If it were a Marisa-Jaime case, I would agree with a breakup, but Ian's great. He respects you and supports you. What's so bad about giving up your single life for him?"

Karina closed her eyes and slumped back against the couch. Did she really want to get into this? Maybe it would help Natalie finally stop nagging her. "You know I don't get along with my mom."

"Childhood trauma. Mm-hmm. Go on."

"Ugh. It's not trauma. More like a lesson." She took a deep breath. "My mom taught me not to depend on anyone for anything. She taught me that people always let you down. I looked up to her. She worked a full-time job and studied part-time to become a paralegal. She said that once she had a better job, we'd spend more time together, because she wouldn't have to work nights anymore. And then she married Bob, one of her professors. She had another daughter and forgot I existed." Karina pressed her lips to stop them from trembling.

The day of their last fight, ten years ago, her mom had picked her up from school; a rare occasion, since Karina always took the bus. The principal had called her mom in to tell her Karina was flunking out.

"You're not going to say anything?" her mom asked on the drive home. "I had to cancel Lily's playgroup to come here, and now I have to rush to make dinner."

"How tragic." Was that really all that worried her, making it home to cook dinner for Bob?

"Karina, this is serious! What is going on with you?"

"You actually care now?"

"What does that mean?"

"Nothing. Just that you haven't been interested in my grades all this time."

"Well, I'm busy, and you're almost eighteen, old enough to know what you have to do."

Karina sank into the seat. "Good. Because I've decided school's a waste of time." She kept her eyes on the road, but her mom's glare was palpable on her skin.

A howl emerged from the back seat.

Mom hit the steering wheel. "Carajo, I forgot to pack a bottle. See? I can't be running around fixing your problems. I have enough on my plate."

As soon as they got home, Mom grabbed the wailing Lily and rushed inside, settled the baby on her high chair, and then prepared a bottle. Karina threw her backpack on the couch. This was all her mom cared about: her new baby, her new family. She walked toward her room.

"¿Para dónde crees que vas?" Mom asked without looking up. "You will stay here in the living room and do your homework."

Karina crossed her arms. "Or what?"

Mom slammed the bottle on the counter and walked straight to Karina. "Are you seriously talking back to me? I am your mother, and you will do what I say."

Karina got in her face. "Some mother you are. You haven't cared about anything that happens to me since Lily was born. You think you get a say in what happens to me now?"

Mom slapped her.

Karina touched her stinging cheek. Her eyes watered. Her mom had never slapped her before.

"I will not tolerate you talking to me like this. If you live here, you will do as I say."

"Then maybe I shouldn't live here anymore."

Her mom froze. Lily's howling got louder.

Ha! You didn't think I'd call your bluff, did you?

But instead of backing down, her mom had said, "Maybe you shouldn't."

After recounting the whole story, Karina opened her eyes and let the memory fade away. "Her life now is dedicated to taking care of them. She stopped studying and is happy as a housewife, completely dependent on her husband. That's what love does to you. It makes you do things you never imagined you'd do. It changes you. Look at Cordelia. She's slowly turning into my mom. Once she has a kid, she'll stop working, and we'll never see her again."

Natalie squeezed her hand. "I'm so sorry that happened to you. And it explains a lot, let me tell you. But these are extreme cases. Not everyone reacts like that. I think it's more about your own choices rather than love being the cause."

Karina shook her head. "When love takes over, you have no control. I liked being with Ian, but he was turning me into that. I felt guilty for wanting time away from him. He always needed to know where I was and what I was doing. I couldn't disappear for one night without him almost calling the cops. That's too much pressure to put on one person."

"But if you would've been honest with him—"

"He probably would've broken up with me just as fast as you dumped Peter. Face it, there's no middle ground with relationships. You're either all in or you're not worth the time." Karina took the remote again. Bombarding her brain with images probably wouldn't work anymore to make her forget the night and this conversation. Now she'd need a complete memory swipe to make it through the day. But TV was all she had at her disposal.

Natalie slumped back into the couch and sighed. "It's not that Peter wasn't worth my time, but more that I have to stay true to myself and what I want. All I've wanted since I was a little girl is to get married. For you, your mom and Cordelia are pathetic, but that's what I want—someone to share my life with."

Karina dropped the remote. "But why do you want to get married so much? There has to be more you want out of life. It can't be just that. What if he never comes along? Is your life a failure?"

"It's not about that. I don't want to grow old alone. It's important." Before Karina could retort, she continued, "And no, friends are not enough. Having a life partner runs much deeper than that." Karina's bewilderment must have shown on her face, because Natalie continued. "My grandparents didn't have the perfect marriage—they slept in separate rooms and fought constantly—but they stayed together until my grandmother's death. My grandma was always grateful she got married and had a family, that she wasn't alone." Her voice cracked, and she cleared her throat. "But what I realized last night is that I need to be more practical; I have to stop living in this fairy-tale world and get real. The spark can only take me so far. As you've always said, I should give guys more of a break. Maybe the spark appears over time; who knows? But I won't make it a deciding factor anymore."

Karina's jaw dropped. She'd been a good influence? "Wow. It's like you're a completely different person right now. At least this will finally make you stop looking through wedding photos. I think you have enough material for five weddings." She laughed.

Natalie frowned. "I don't know. It's fun to look at the pictures and visualize myself there. Getting married is my goal, so why shouldn't I plan for the big day? It doesn't hurt anyone."

Karina's smile faded. Why did she have to be so hard on everyone?

Natalie patted her knee, then stood. "Why don't you join me on my hike? It'll help you organize your thoughts."

"What thoughts do I need to organize?"

Natalie put her hands on her hips. "Are you sure you don't want to get back with Ian? I can't imagine voluntarily keeping myself away from the one I love. Even you are not that strong."

Karina raised her chin and met her gaze. "I have to be. All I want is to go back to normal and not feel guilty all the time. I want to be free of him."

CHAPTER TWENTY-SEVEN

Karina walked into work on Monday armed with a T-shirt that announced, *This is my "don't even try me" shirt*, ready to cuss out anyone if they so much as looked at her wrong. Rosa's hand imprint was still visible on her face, which would be obvious to everyone, since makeup wasn't allowed inside the production area.

People greeted her with wide eyes and open mouths, even some snickers here and there, but for the most part nobody said anything. Cordelia was more upset over missing the action than about the fact that Karina had gotten slapped.

"Rosa really messed you up," Cordelia said. "But that's what you get for provoking the wrong person."

"You're saying I deserved this? I was attacked. If it had been the other way around, everyone would pat him on the back for being a player."

"I feel so bad for leaving early," Marisa said. "If I'd been there, I wouldn't have let you do it." She took a full box to the pallet.

Midmorning, Karina took a break and went on the hunt for Rosa. It was unprofessional, but she couldn't let the slap slide. As she passed the offices, she heard murmurs of "Rosa has good aim" and "I wish it was me who slapped her." How was Rosa the hero in all this?

Karina shouldn't have gone to that party. The longer she kept giving them something to talk about, the longer it would take to get back to normal. Why had she gotten involved with Ian in the first place? It had been a bad idea from the start.

She found Rosa in the cafeteria wiping down the tables. Karina walked up to her, took the cloth Rosa was using, and threw it on the floor. "You caught me off guard at the party, but if you ever touch me again, know that I'll hit back."

After a brief glance, Rosa picked up the cloth and continued wiping. "Oh, Karina, you look very nice this morning. Pink looks good on you."

Karina gritted her teeth, then took a deep breath. *Play it cool.* "You know what? I think I'll call Marcos and tell him to fuck me in your bed."

That got a reaction. Rosa raised her hand, palm open.

"Try it." Karina stepped closer. "I dare you. What's more worth it to you: your job or shutting me up?"

Rosa slowly lowered her arm. "Maybe si tu mamá had slapped you more, you wouldn't have turned out this way."

Her mom had slapped her once, but that was none of Rosa's business. *Stay calm.* "You mean I'd be more like your little niece? She was ready to drop her panties for Ian. Decent, my ass."

Rosa wiped another table. "She must've done something right when he asked her out."

Karina stiffened. "What?"

"You thought you could keep him on a chain like Marcos? Guess you were wrong." Rosa moved on to the microwave.

Karina gripped the back of a chair. She shouldn't be surprised. Ian had asked her for another chance, and she'd turned him down. He wasn't more saint than man after all. When a pretty girl threw herself at him, he was tempted, just like any other man.

"Karina," Lacey said from the doorway, startling her. "Why are you not in production?"

"Uh . . ."

"I heard about what happened," Lacey said. "I hope the two of you can leave your differences outside the workplace. Or do I have to write a report?" She sighed. "Which reminds me, I have to look into hiring an HR person." She tapped into her phone, then looked up at them expectantly.

"No, that won't be necessary." Rosa glanced sideways at Karina. "We're fine, right, Karina?"

"Yup," Karina said. "Totally fine."

"Good. If you need me, I'll be working with Dwight in the test bakery the rest of the day."

*　*　*

When Karina and her friends arrived for lunch an hour later, they could see Lacey and Dwight through the two Plexiglas windows, laughing and chatting as they worked.

Karina forced her gaze away. She hoped the cookie turned out horrible. Lacey getting help from Dwight would be her downfall.

"Do you think Lacey and Dwight would make a good couple?" Natalie asked between bites of lettuce.

"She's the boss," Cordelia said. "That would be scandalous."

"I think they look cute together," Marisa said. "What do you think, Karina?"

Karina knew she should change the subject. If Lacey overheard them talking, she'd assume Karina had blabbed and fire her on the spot. "Rosa told me Ian asked out her niece."

Her friends stared at her with pity. *Great job, Karina.* She stuck a forkful of stewed rice with corn into her mouth.

Thankfully, the side door opened, and Lacey walked in, carrying a tray of cookies. "Hello, ladies. I think this is the one."

"We added ginger, anise, and ground almonds," Dwight said. "Try them."

Her friends each took tentative bites.

"What do you think?" Lacey asked.

"It tastes like candy," Marisa said. "But not too sweet." She took another bite. "I love the crunchiness."

Natalie nodded. "It's very mild. I like it."

Cordelia licked off the last crumbs from her fingers. "I think this may be your best one yet," she told Lacey. "What will you name it?"

"I'm thinking Quirky Cookie. Because it's different."

"She's a genius, isn't she?" Dwight gazed at Lacey. Karina could swear sparks were flying between them. This was the true face of love. Did Ian and Karina look like this to other people? Was that why everyone was mad she'd dumped him?

"Aren't you going to try one, Karina?" Lacey asked her.

"It's heavenly," Natalie said.

"You're never shy around food," Cordelia said. "Dig in."

Karina picked one up, pressed her eyes shut, and bit into the cookie. As she chewed, she could detect the sweet hint of licorice, but not like at the first trial. No, this was more subtle. It was more anise than anything, and the crunchiness of the almonds gave it a nice bite.

"And?" Lacey said expectantly.

Karina opened her eyes. "It's all right, I guess."

Lacey's face fell. "Some people have finer taste buds than others." She moved on to Tyler and Nicholas, who dug in without a fuss.

"What was that about?" Natalie whispered. "Did you have a fight with Lacey?"

Karina watched as Lacey returned the empty tray to the test bakery, followed by Dwight. They started cleaning up, chatting and laughing, celebrating their triumph, more united than ever. Karina inwardly groaned. Lacey had been right about this cookie. She'd won. With Dwight's help, not Karina's.

Her friends were waiting for an answer, so she said, "No fight, just . . . she's mad at me because I won't take this new job Dwight offered."

"What job?" Cordelia asked.

"He says I could be the company's internal auditor, but I don't want to deal with all the crap that goes on here. My job is hectic, but Roy has all the responsibility, so it's not as stressful."

"Would you need to go back to school?" Marisa chewed on her sandwich.

"No, apparently I can go through training and get certified."

"It sounds like a great opportunity," Cordelia said. "You should take it. Aren't you always telling me to stop wasting my talent and start my own business?"

"That's different. I'm not talented."

"Dwight wouldn't offer it if he didn't think you could do it," Marisa said.

"She's right," Natalie said. "You know, I think I finally figured out what your problem is."

Karina frowned. "My problem?"

"Do tell." Cordelia leaned forward, hands under her chin.

"In addition to your fear of intimacy—which we all know you have—you fear change. You couldn't handle being in a relationship, and now you're willing to throw away this chance. It fits."

"Ooh, I think she's onto something." Cordelia wiggled her fingers. "That psychology degree has its uses."

"I always thought of Karina as fearless," Marisa said, "but Natalie makes a good point."

Karina dropped her fork into the empty bowl. "Didn't we already have this conversation? I tried to make it work with Ian, but I couldn't. That's not me being scared, that's me being sensible. Responsible, even. I'm happy being floor supervisor. I don't need the hassle of more work."

"If you'd had a serious conversation with Ian, you could've worked it out," Natalie said. "Instead, when things got difficult, you ran. The same thing you're doing now. You don't think you can handle the responsibility, and you're quitting before even trying."

Lacey and Dwight returned with a new batch of cookies, and this time they all reached eagerly for one. Dwight couldn't stop making love to Lacey with his eyes, and Karina expected her friends to comment on him and Lacey again, but they were more interested in discussing Quirky Cookie. It was so obvious; how could they not see it? Not even love-obsessed Cordelia could sniff it out.

Karina gobbled up the cookie. It wasn't a disaster but a triumph. As much as she hated to admit it to herself, Lacey had been right to trust Dwight. He was the Practical Cookie to her Dreamer, helping her turn her ideas into reality. Had love done this? Not making Lacey weaker but stronger?

And what was Ian to Karina? Her heart jumped. *He's the Calm to your Chaos*, it yelled. Karina blinked the tears away. He complemented her. Just like the almonds complemented the licorice root, and Dwight complemented Lacey.

But it couldn't be that simple. If she were to crumble up two cookies, say the Flirty and the Mellow, and mix them together to create a whole new cookie, she'd get a big mess. Just because the main ingredients complemented each other didn't mean the rest would. Cookies were more complex than that. And so were people. Just because love worked for Lacey and Dwight didn't mean it would work for Karina and Ian. It didn't work for her friends or her mom, even if they were too blind to see it. And who said it was really working for Lacey? Maybe she was faking it.

Karina brushed off the Quirky crumbs. Why was she trying to find meaning in a stupid cookie, anyway?

CHAPTER TWENTY-EIGHT

On Thursday morning, Karina reviewed her warehouse audit notes as the cafeteria filled up for the first official monthly training.

Dwight wanted her to talk about her experience doing the audit. As if anyone would care. He'd prepared a long PowerPoint presentation about the food certification program, what it stood for, and the elements the inspector would look out for. Karina had told him it was too much, but he'd insisted it was information everyone needed to know.

Karina sipped her coffee. She'd helped Dwight move the tables to the side and place the chairs facing the south wall, where he could project the presentation. As he stood beside Karina, fiddling with his laptop, her coworkers served themselves coffee or tea, piled their plates with an assortment of the fruits, yogurts, and Singular Cookies Lacey had arranged on a platter, and sat to chat while they waited. They seemed way too cheerful. They'd complained to her privately about the training and Karina had hoped for a revolt, but no, it was something different to do, and they got paid, so who cared? And food! Roy and his great ideas.

Roy and Lacey stood near the entrance, admiring the crowd, looking proud. Roy stood out in his smock and hairnet, always needing to be ready to pop into the processing area at a moment's notice. *I hope this blows up in your face.* Ian walked in and made a beeline for Dwight. Karina snapped her eyes back to her notes.

"Do you really need me to talk about the audit?" Ian asked Dwight. "Can't you do it?"

Karina sneaked a peek at him. He was tugging at his sleeves. Was he nervous? He was supposed to talk about his audit of the production area. It was the first time she'd seen him so close since their fight on Saturday. She had the urge to wrap him in her arms and kiss the jitters away.

"It's an informal talk," Dwight said.

"You have a presentation prepared," Ian said, pointing at the laptop. "How is that not formal?"

"Geez, relax," Karina said. "I didn't know you were such a scaredy-cat. You know all these people. It's not a big deal."

Ian didn't look convinced.

"Maybe Karina can give you some pointers?" Dwight said, before going over to check on the projector.

Karina glared at his back. Didn't he know she was dying inside? *No, of course he doesn't, since you're so good at pretending.*

"You want to share some secrets?" Ian stood way too close, hands in his pockets, invading her personal space. One of his dimples appeared.

Karina took a step back. "Picture everyone naked?"

Both dimples flashed. "That should be easy." His gaze ran across her body.

What was he doing? Flirting with her?

"Okay, settle down, everyone," Lacey yelled out. "Dwight has prepared an informative presentation for us, and I want everyone to pay close attention." She sat in the front row and gestured for Dwight to begin.

"Thank you, Lacey. As most of you know, our contract with Whole-Mart is contingent on passing a food safety inspection, which is due in three months, on July eleventh. One of the requirements for this inspection is a proper training schedule, and I thought it would be good to have a meeting every month to go over food safety terms and to give you updates on what goes on in the plant."

As Dwight talked, Ian stood beside Karina, his hands shaking just as hard as her heart beat against her ribs. How could he keep acting as if nothing had happened, as if they were still together? Didn't it kill him to be near her? His hand knocked against hers. She wanted so much to grab it, squeeze it, let him know she was there for him.

She moved to stand on the other side of Dwight.

When it was Ian's turn, his voice trembled, and he stumbled a couple of times, but overall, he did a great job. People smiled at his adorableness and encouraged him with their nods to keep going. As he turned away from them, Karina gave him a thumbs-up. She couldn't help it.

Then it was her turn. She read her notes, droning on with unnecessary details, hoping to bore everyone to death, but when she looked up, they were alert and engaged. What the fuck?

They even took part in the Q and A session at the end. Some had doubts about going ahead with the inspection even though it was voluntary, but once Lacey reiterated what was at stake for the company, they seemed satisfied.

As soon as the meeting adjourned, Ian went to her. "You were right. It wasn't that bad."

"You were shaking."

He laughed. "Okay, maybe it was a little bad." His features softened. "K, why can't we talk and clear everything up?"

Karina sobered. "Stop. Let it go." They couldn't even have a casual conversation about work without it turning personal. When would it end?

"I can't. I told you."

"That didn't stop you from asking out Maribel."

He frowned. Why had she brought it up? This conversation was veering out of control. "I have to talk to Dwight." She turned on her heels.

Dwight was huddled with Lacey and Roy as they all congratulated themselves on a job well done. One happy family. Roy even slapped Dwight on the back.

Ian blocked her path. "I don't know what you heard, but I'm not—"

"Do you see that?" She pointed at the cheery trio. "Roy didn't want this stupid training, and now it's like the best thing ever."

"The training worked," Ian said. "Everyone knows more about the program, and we'll do well in the inspection. Isn't that what matters?"

The inspection *was* what mattered. When had she forgotten that? Everyone was happy with the training, so why couldn't she be?

Lacey put her head on Roy's shoulder while he and Dwight shook hands. It had all worked out. Lacey had gotten Roy to accept Dwight, Dwight had gained a new ally, and Roy felt included again. Everything they'd hoped for, achieved without Karina's help. Was she even an important part of the team anymore?

Lacey and Roy had made their choice, and it wasn't Karina. It was Dwight. Just like her mom, they'd chosen someone else over her. And why not? She'd sabotaged them and mixed work with personal, going against her own beliefs.

"You okay?" Ian asked.

Ten years ago, she'd yelled at her mom, "Maybe I shouldn't live here anymore," and her mom had come back with, "Maybe you shouldn't."

Maybe I shouldn't.

"Please, talk to me," Ian said. "Let me fix it."

She gazed up at him, her eyes brimming with tears. A hug from him would ease the tension inside, help her breathe. This must've been what Leonard felt, seeing Karina every day, unable to reach out, pretending everything was normal when it was anything but.

He'd been right to leave.

Karina blinked the tears away. "It's too late." She stepped around him, toward Lacey. "I need to talk to you."

It was clear from Lacey's concerned expression that she understood it was urgent. "Let's go to my office."

Maybe she was proving her friends right and she was a coward, but it was only a matter of time before Lacey fired her. Why wait? There was no place for her at Singular anymore. Only pain lingered here, her own failures lashing out at her.

As soon as the door shut behind them, Karina spit out the words. "I quit."

Lacey's shock gave way to sadness as she led Karina to the sofa and sat beside her. "I know you've been going through a hard time, with the breakup and everyone saying mean things about you. I should organize a training on harassment—"

"It's not just that. I don't think I fit in here anymore."

"Why would you say that? You're an integral part of this company."

"You asked me to help with the inspection, and I betrayed you. You were right—I put the company at risk by not telling you right away that Roy thought you were trying to push him out." Karina dropped her chin to her chest.

Lacey sighed and rubbed her back. "Yes, you were wrong to do that, but ultimately, it was because of you I found out how he felt and was able to reassure him."

"That's not all." Karina wiped a shaky hand down her jeans. "Leonard left because of me. I slept with him and he wanted more, but I couldn't give in to him, and then he didn't want to be around me anymore. It hurt him too much."

"Does it hurt you to be around Ian? Is that why you want to quit?"

Her heart ached. It was weakness to admit such a thing, but it was the truth. "A little."

"If Leonard hadn't left, I would've never met Dwight, and I think he's better for this company. Don't you agree?"

"He *is* more thorough than Leonard. And more detail oriented. I'll give him that."

"See?" Lacey squeezed Karina's shoulder. "Everything turned out for the better. Dwight tells me you've grown into the job, that you ask significant questions, and you always improve on his instructions. He sees great potential in you; otherwise he wouldn't have offered you the position of internal auditor. Why would you give that up? You can do so much more—I've always told you that. Why can't you believe it?"

"Wait." Karina raised her head and stared at Lacey. "You want me to stay even after what I just told you?"

Lacey smiled and looked at her as if to say, *Duh*. "I suspected about you and Leonard, but he left on his own volition. I'm glad you're owning up to your mistakes. It means you trust me, and I need you to trust me now when I say you should take this opportunity. Don't hold yourself back because of fear."

Was she afraid? She'd been ready to leave the best job she'd ever had to avoid facing Ian, so what did that say about her? She'd sworn she wouldn't change for a man, and here she was, about to do exactly what her mom had done when she met Bob.

"You say I'd be great as an auditor, but you didn't think I was talented enough to create the cookies with you when we moved into the plant."

Lacey's eyebrows shot up. "I've never thought you're not talented. Where did you get that from?"

"You threw me away into production, and you replaced me with Leonard—"

Lacey gasped. "I didn't throw you away into production, Karina. Is that what you think? Because what I know is that I put my most trusted and experienced employee in charge of the most critical job, which is overseeing the production of the cookies." She pressed a hand to her chest. "I was rewarding you, not punishing you. How could you think that?"

Karina lowered her head. "I . . ."

"I thought you loved making the cookies."

"I did. With you."

Lacey sighed. "Why didn't you say something?"

Karina shrugged. "I didn't know how to bring it up. I was still grateful to have a job; it seemed silly to complain. But then you decided to discontinue the Flirty and started making another cookie without me . . . it got to be too much."

"I see." Lacey fidgeted with her watch. "I didn't know the Flirty meant so much to you."

"Of course it does. It's *my* cookie."

"You didn't seem to care . . ." Lacey stood. "In any case, that's a conversation for another time. For now, I want you to trust me when I say that you can do anything you set your mind to. I've seen how you rise to the challenge when you're pushed. You know, it scared me to start this business. I didn't know what to expect. But my uncle believed in me, believed in the product, and he pushed me to go for it, and here we are. Let me be that person for you."

Karina had first tasted Perky Cookie one night after dinner with Roy and Lacey. Roy was enthusiastic about the business potential; he'd been positive it would be a success. And he'd been right. Lacey had followed his advice. Even when they'd disagreed, she'd always fallen back on his expertise. Because she trusted him. Was that also a part of love? Trusting someone unconditionally, discovering you were capable of more than you thought?

"Why?" Karina asked. "Why do you want to be that person for me?"

"Because I care about you. I've always cared." She smiled. "You're family."

Those words had never rung true, but as Karina stared into Lacey's eyes, not a hint of pity in them, she yearned to believe.

CHAPTER TWENTY-NINE

"Let's go to Friday Fest," Karina announced as she walked into Natalie's room.

In the last two weeks she'd focused on her new job prospect, reading the code for the certification program and familiarizing herself with the plant's policies and procedures. Roy was supportive of her decision, and Tyler would replace Karina as the new floor supervisor. She was now spending the mornings with him and the afternoons working with Dwight, leaving her nights with too much free time. But this new dynamic kept her contact with Ian to a minimum, preventing her from breaking apart. He was officially dating Maribel; Rosa wouldn't shut up about it. Karina caught glimpses of him in the hallway now and then, but she steered clear of him to keep her heart safe.

She hadn't risked hooking up with anyone after Marcos. He'd texted her multiple times, until Karina had taken pity on him and texted back, *Forget about me. Find someone else.* It was her most mature breakup yet.

Everyone had moved on from attacking her, and even her friends believed Ian was in the past. Karina hoped time would kill the love in her heart, so all she could do now was return to her old life. Friday Fest was symbolic in that way.

Natalie sat at her desk, tapping on her laptop. "I can't. I'm fixing my résumé." She turned around. "I'm finally going to put my degree to use and find a new job."

"Oh. Wow." Karina dropped to the bed. Now that they'd become closer, she was leaving?

Natalie sat beside her and bumped her shoulder against hers. "After our talk, I realized I've lost sight of my career goals. Singular was always meant to be temporary. It's time."

"No, I get it." Karina faked a smile. "That's exciting."

Natalie returned to the desk. "Are you okay going alone to the fest? I'm in the zone right now, and if I stop, I'm afraid I'll never get it done."

"Yeah. No biggie. I'll go by myself."

*　*　*

As soon as she got to Marina Square, she felt like her old self again: free like a bird, her heart going along with what she wanted and not demanding the impossible. She went straight to the barbecue food truck, already salivating from the smell of her favorite ribs.

A familiar-looking man turned from the truck, his order of ribs in hand. Their eyes met, and her breath caught in her throat.

Ian.

He stopped short. "Hi."

"What are you doing here?" Even this sacred place, he'd invaded. She looked around for Maribel but didn't see her. He was holding only one carton of ribs, but maybe he was getting them for her?

"The ribs, same as you. Oh, they're running out. Here, take mine. I'll get something else." He handed her the carton, then took her place in line.

So they weren't for Maribel. Karina stared at the ribs. "You can't give this to me."

"I know that's what you want. Eat it. It's no problem."

Karina didn't need to be told twice. She peeled one off and bit into it, relishing the spicy-sweet sauce and the perfectly seasoned meat. By the time Ian ordered, the carton was empty.

"They haven't run out yet," Ian said. "Want more?"

Karina nodded, and Ian asked for two orders. He handed the cartons to her and left to buy sodas. Meanwhile, Karina settled on a bench overlooking the Indian River, the sun low on the horizon, almost touching the water. When Ian returned, it was like they'd traveled three months back to their first date.

The beginning chords of "Sexual Healing" traveled across the palm trees toward them. Great. Karina tried to keep her eyes on the setting sun, but they only wanted to stare at Ian. She hadn't seen him in normal clothes since Rosa's party, and his bare biceps were making her salivate more than the ribs. Why was he here? He was supposed to be over her and she was supposed to be starting fresh.

"I missed seeing you eat like you haven't seen food in a week," he said.

Karina laughed and choked. Ian tapped her back. Her skin tingled. She continued coughing longer than necessary.

"Sorry," he said. "Should've waited until you stopped eating."

Karina wiped her eyes. "You miss seeing me eat like a pig? That's a weird thing to miss."

"You don't eat like a pig." He paused. "A little, maybe."

They both laughed and gazed at each other. *Oh, Ian. Why do you torture me like this?* Her heart would never let go of him if he made it do somersaults with only a look.

"You want anything else? Ice cream?" He pointed at her T-shirt, which said *I'm not responsible for my actions when I'm hungry.* "I don't know how you could still be hungry, but better safe than sorry."

I'm hungry for your kiss, for your touch, for you . . . "Nah, I'm good. I should get going." She stood.

"Wait." He grabbed her hand. "I confess I came here to see you. Since you avoid me at work, I thought we could talk."

"What? I don't—" It took all her strength to pull her hand away. "Aren't you dating Maribel?"

He made a face. "I know everyone's talking about it, but we've only gone out a couple of times as friends."

Heart banged against her chest. *There's still a chance! Let go of your fears and tell him the truth. Look how well it went with Lacey.*

Lacey has known me longer, and our relationship is mostly professional. Ian is different. It's not that easy.

Karina looked over his shoulder, and there, a few feet away, were Rosa and her husband. "Shit." She ran behind a food truck, hiding from view.

Ian ran behind her. "What is it?"

"Rosa's here. I don't want her to see us together."

"Let's go to Crabby's. I'll buy you a beer."

"Ian. I can't—"

"Let's just hang out as friends. I won't mention the breakup, I promise."

His eyes were pleading. Why say no? She could feed some of her hunger, stare openly at him, hear his voice, surround herself with his calming presence, if only for an hour.

"I guess one beer won't hurt."

Karina insisted on paying, and they settled on a table overlooking the water, like last time. She hadn't been back at this bar since their first date.

"Why didn't you want Rosa to see us?" Ian asked.

"Are you kidding me? She'll broadcast it first thing Monday morning."

"And you don't want anyone to know you were with me?"

She cocked an eyebrow. "Do you work in the same place I do? Everyone hates me because of what happened with us. I don't want them to think we're back together; then they'll speculate, and when they find out we're not, they'll blame me. I don't want to go through that again. Work and personal should be separate, remember?"

"Is that why you don't talk to me anymore?"

"I do talk to you."

"Almost never. Should be the other way around, no?"

"Then why isn't it? Why do you want to talk to me after what I did to you?"

He took a swig of his beer. "I miss you."

Her heart fluttered. "You shouldn't."

"You don't miss me?"

So much. She took a sip of her beer. "You said you wouldn't bring up the breakup."

"You're right. Let's talk about something else." He thought about it. "I haven't congratulated you on your promotion. How's that going?"

Karina relaxed into the chair. "Well, I have to take all these trainings. Dwight's organizing a HACCP one for the plant, and then I'll fly to Virginia next month for a training on the certification program and another for internal auditing. I still have to take some tests, and I'm not great with tests, so let's see if I even pass."

"I'm sure you will."

"But what if I don't? For Dwight, it's a done deal. Lacey ordered a new desk and chair for me, and Roy and I are training Tyler to take my place. On Tuesday, I'm doing a walk-through of the plant to help us get ready for the inspection. It's all happening too fast."

"I think you'll make a great auditor," Ian said.

"Really?"

"You're responsible and careful. You're also not afraid to tell anyone they're doing something wrong. Isn't that what an auditor should do?"

"They should also find positive things and give constructive criticism. I don't know if I'm so good at that."

"You're capable of more than you think."

She smiled. "That's what Lacey and Dwight say."

"They're right." He paused. "I'm happy for you."

They gazed at each other. How could she not love him? It was his laid-back nature, how he could see the good in anything—even in her, who'd hurt him so much.

"What happened to us?" he asked, his voice a whisper.

Karina swallowed and looked out toward the marina. Multiple answers popped to the tip of her tongue: *I got scared; it got too intense; you were changing me and I don't want to change; I'm no good and it wouldn't have taken you long to realize it; I pushed you away before you could hurt me . . .*

"K?" He took her hand. "Talk to me."

She stared at his fingers on hers, her skin burning at his touch.

Just say the words, Heart yelled.

"I . . ." She cleared her throat. It was getting hard to breathe. *Why is he doing this to me? This was my night to be free.*

Their feet met underneath the table, and she shivered. He licked his lips and took a sip of his beer.

"Let's go back to your place and have sex," she said.

He spit into the bottle. "Sorry?"

What are you doing? Heart asked.

My body's in control now, not you. This is what I know, what I can handle. Stay out of it.

She cocked her head and said in a flirty tone, "You don't want to?"

"That wasn't my plan. I only wanted to spend time with you."

She stroked his arm. "We can spend time together that way too."

"You're serious."

"What's the big deal? I'm still attracted to you. I assume you're still attracted to me?"

His mouth fell open. Did she really want to do this? *Fuck yeah.*

"We'd have to set some ground rules, of course," she said. "First, it would only be tonight. We're not getting back together."

Now his brow furrowed. Before he could say anything, she continued, "And second, no romanticism. Just good old-fashioned sex. In, out, and done."

"No kissing?"

"Some kissing is okay. But no cuddling afterward."

"Oh, come on. There has to be some cuddling."

"Fine." She paused. "Do we have a deal?"

He considered it. He probably hoped she'd change her mind about them. That's why she needed to keep pretending it wouldn't mean anything to her. If he believed they had a chance, it would only break his heart again when she rejected him, which she would. No matter how amazing the sex was, she'd have to.

Plus she couldn't put in danger her newfound drive to become the internal auditor. What had happened to her mom wouldn't happen to her. But even if she risked her own heart breaking, she needed to be with him one last time for some "sexual healing" of her own. She was counting on him to do all the romantics in the world like he used to. There was no way he'd adhere to "just sex." It wasn't in his nature. And then Karina could stop wondering how it felt to make love.

"Okay," he said.

"Great." She chugged her beer. "Let's go."

CHAPTER THIRTY

Ian waited for Karina outside while she parked in his driveway. As soon as the front door shut behind them, she kissed him.

He wrapped his arms around her waist, and they stumbled back against the door. *Oh my God, did he always kiss like this?* She'd thought her yearning had turned him into a myth, but nope, he was actually better than she remembered.

"Come here." He pulled her toward the couch. When she noticed the cushions and the rug she'd bought him, she froze.

"Let's go to your room." She tugged on his hand.

"You know I like taking it slow."

"I said no romanticism." She dragged him to the bedroom.

"Dios." He turned on the lamp and rummaged through his underwear drawer. "I only have one condom."

"One is enough." That way she wouldn't be tempted to go for round two. She took off her T-shirt.

He stared at her a moment before doing the same. Damn, he looked airbrushed. There should be a law against looking that good.

When they finished undressing, they stood facing each other. The longing in his eyes, the desire, the love, awakened every suppressed emotion in her heart. Maybe this was a mistake. What if this damaged her and she could never look at another man again? But then he kissed her, and there was no backing out.

They fell onto the bed. Ian bit her lips and her jaw, his nails scraping her skin as he kissed down her body. This wasn't her Mellow Cookie but a maniac desperate to devour her, much as she'd devoured those barbecue ribs earlier. Funny that tonight, when she yearned for sex to last, he was rushing to get started. Before she knew it, he'd rolled on the condom with shaky hands and was inside her.

They moaned. Ian lay on top of her but didn't move. He dug his hands into her hair and kissed her, savoring her. His breathing evened and he stopped shaking. His heart beat steadily, in sync with her own. She wrapped herself around him, and the tension that had accumulated since she'd left him loosened.

He thrust, and Karina's heart expanded, transporting the love inside it to every cell in her body. She'd been afraid a relationship would turn her into someone else, and here she was, changed forever. Her love for him embedded itself into her core. The damage was irreversible.

They weren't making love; the love had already been inside them. They were multiplying it, spreading it, transmitting it to each other through their skin and their breath. They were a part of each other now, and when the connection broke, Karina would always be incomplete, a broken half roaming the earth.

Fuck, did Ian feel her love for him? Her eyes shot open. He was gazing at her. Could he see? He kissed her, and she got lost in him until it became too much and she told him to go doggy-style.

They changed positions. Shortly after thrusting into her again, he stopped. "Coño. The condom broke."

"What?" Her voice came out strained. She was so close.

"The condom broke, and I only had one." He threw it on the floor.

"You can come outside. Just keep going."

He pushed inside her again, and within moments she came with such force her legs gave out, her body dropping to the bed. Ian kept hold of her hips and orgasmed onto her lower back.

Karina pressed her face into the mattress, breathing hard. Why had she come here? So much for being in control of her heart. Now she was ruined and had to find the strength from somewhere within herself to leave him again. Love or no love, changed or unchanged, broken or not, she couldn't budge.

You can't walk away after this, Heart said. *It will haunt you forever. I'll make sure of it.*

He wiped her back with a towel and lay beside her. She opened her eyes. He was glowing.

"You look beautiful." He rolled her onto her side, spooning her. His fingers traced around her belly, and she sighed, sinking into him. "My K."

He still saw her as his sweet girl, even after everything that had happened. Could he truly see a hidden part of her she couldn't recognize, or was he just delusional?

He kissed her neck. "I love you."

"What?" She turned to face him.

He stroked her cheek. "I love you, K." He pressed his lips to hers.

Her heart gave in until her brain caught up to what was happening, and she pulled back. "I think that's enough cuddling." She shot out of the bed and searched for her clothes.

"Karina, I tell you I love you, and this is how you react?"

She put on her underwear. "You agreed to my terms. No romanticism. And then you tell me you love me. What am I supposed to do with that? I came here for sex, and we had sex, so there's no need for me to stay any longer."

Ian remained in bed, lying on his back, his hands over his face. "Dios. Eres tan frustrante. You're so . . . maddening." He got up. "I don't get you."

"There's nothing to get. This is me, how I am. Deal with it."

"At least talk to me. You don't need to run away like I'm going to kidnap you."

"There's nothing to talk about. I already said everything I needed to say." She buttoned up her jeans.

"And hearing me tell you I love you doesn't change anything?"

"Why would it? I already told you—we're not right for each other."

"Why not? We were happy together. You can't deny that."

She finished dressing and put her hands to her hips. "Were you really happy with me? Even when I didn't want to sleep over or return your texts or had plans with my friends?"

"You always changed your mind."

"Because I felt guilty. I didn't want to feel guilty for being who I am."

"That is how I made you feel—guilty?" He shook his head, still completely naked, threatening her resolve. "I don't believe it. You were happy with me too. I know it."

"If you don't want to believe me, that's your choice. I had my fun, and now I'm leaving." She didn't move. He looked so hurt. *How can you leave him like this?* Heart demanded. She gazed up and down his body, freezing him in time. His muscles were more defined, as if he'd lost weight. "Are you eating well?"

He looked down at himself and rubbed his abdomen. "There's no one to cook for anymore."

Karina swallowed the lump in her throat. "You should try again with Maribel. Maybe it'll work out this time."

It was a few moments before he replied. "Is that what you want?"

"I want you to be happy."

"What if I'm only happy with you?"

"Then you have bigger problems than I thought." She pressed her eyes shut to keep from crying. Then he grabbed her arms, and she met his gaze. "Don't," she said, but didn't pull away.

"I know there's something you're not telling me. You act like you don't care, but I know you do. It's how you've always been. Please, tell me what's going on. Let me fix it."

Tell him you love him too, that it hurts you to be away from him, Heart yelled out. *Save us both from this pain.*

Karina pulled free from his grasp. "There's nothing to tell. It's over." She wrapped her fanny pack around her waist. "Thanks for the sex. It was great."

He pushed his fingers through his hair. "Why are you like this?"

"Like what?"

"I know this wasn't just sex for you. Why can't you admit it?" He sat on the bed, shoulders slumped. "I thought . . . when you asked to come over that . . . we were making up."

Karina covered her face with her hands to hide the tears on the brink of spilling out. Why did she keep hurting this man? He deserved so much better.

She knelt in front of him. "Listen to me, really listen this time. I'm not good for you."

"No. You're not." He laughed. "But that's up to me to decide. And I can't help how I feel." He gazed at her. "Everyone around me keeps saying I should let you go, including you. But that look you gave me after the party told me this breakup is just as hard for you as it is for me." He took her hands in his. "Did someone hurt you? You can tell me. I'm here. Let me love you."

How could he know, how could he see her so clearly? "Love me how?"

He smiled. "With all my heart and soul. Forever."

His words took her back to her mom's wedding, to the vows Mom had read aloud to everyone when she tied herself to Bob. Ian didn't see Karina at all. He saw only an illusion, a girl who wanted the fairy-tale happily-ever-after, a man to rescue her. He needed to see that was not her. He needed to see who everyone else saw or he'd never let go.

Karina stood on trembling legs and turned her back to him. "I don't know what you saw that night, but you're wrong." She swallowed. "I don't regret breaking up. I was bored with you, so I fucked someone else. That's why I dumped you. So I could be with him."

He sucked in a breath. "Dwight?"

"No!"

"Then who?" He swung her around to face him, desperation in his eyes. "Rosa's nephew—was it him?"

She turned her gaze to the floor. "No one you know, just a fling. It didn't last. The point is, I'm not cut out to be in a serious relationship. If we get back together, I'll cheat on you again. It's who I am."

Prove you really see me. Tell me I'm lying, that you don't believe I'd do that. Then there'd be no excuses left.

His silence and stillness choked her. She looked out the window, toward the street, to her car, her escape.

He cleared his throat, startling her. "I see." His voice broke. "At least now I know. I won't bother you again." He stepped into the bathroom and shut the door.

Karina gasped for breath and ran out of the house. Once safe in her car, she burst into tears. This was it. The end. Ian would never forgive her after this, even if she begged him. He'd never trust her. He'd move on and forget about her.

Karina was relieved.

Heart was devastated.

CHAPTER THIRTY-ONE

Karina lay awake in bed hours later, images of the night replaying over and over in her head, the echo of Ian's broken voice at the end consuming her.

The phone rang. Ian? She grabbed it. Marisa. Calling at three in the morning. This could not be good.

"What's wrong?" Karina asked.

"Jaime had an accident."

Karina sat up and wiped her face. "Is he okay?"

"Yeah." She paused. "He was drunk."

"Oh, Mari, how many times—"

"Please, not now. They're bringing the car. The cop said it's really banged up. Can you come over?"

"I'll be there in ten."

"Thanks."

Karina changed clothes. When would Marisa learn? She hoped Jaime wasn't hurt too badly. If he was, Marisa would dedicate her free time—and her hard-earned money—to nursing him back to health, and she'd never get rid of him.

Karina had to convince Marisa to dump him tonight. If Karina had the strength to break up with a wonderful, loving man like Ian for his own good, then Marisa could find the strength to dump a loser drunk who used her for *her* own good. All Karina needed was to help Marisa find that strength. The only question was how. Karina had been trying for months without success. Would tonight be any different?

* * *

Marisa was sitting by the curb next to her empty parking spot when Karina arrived.

"Did they arrest him?" Karina asked.

Marisa nodded. "I need to post bail."

Karina put her hands on her hips and leaned over her. "The hell you are. Leave him there. He deserves it."

"He was in an accident. He's probably hurt and in pain."

Karina sat beside her. "Looks to me like you're the one who's hurt."

Marisa hugged her knees to her chest. "Don't start."

"Then why call me? Why not your BFF, Cordelia? You knew this was coming."

"I know." She pressed her forehead to her knees. "But you're good under pressure, and that's what I need—a friend to help me with this situation, not to make it worse."

"I'm here, aren't I?" Karina sighed. "But I can't stay quiet. I tried, but . . . I'm afraid if you don't dump him now, you never will."

"It was an accident; it could happen to anyone."

Was Marisa delusional? "He was driving drunk. In your car. That he doesn't pay a penny for."

"I let him take it. I knew he was going to drink, but nothing bad ever happened before. He always knew when to call it quits."

"You know that's not true. Remember your birthday party, how the guys had to carry him out?"

Marisa turned her head away. "You don't understand. I have to stick with him through the good times and the bad. Jaime's going through a rough patch since he lost his job."

"That was a year ago, and he hasn't tried to get a job since. He's too happy living off you."

"He tries. He just can't catch a break."

"Ugh, Marisa, wake up." Karina grabbed her by the shoulders. "You can't seriously buy this. Why would he get a job when he can hang out all day at home and let you worry about the money? He's a loser, he's always been a loser, and he's taking advantage of you. Why do you keep choosing him?"

"I know for you he's a loser, but for me . . . he's the best boyfriend I've ever had. You don't know what's out there, how men really are. Either they use you for sex or they cheat on you, lie to your face, call you fat and stupid . . ." She wiped her eyes.

Karina's jaw slackened. Poor Mari. No wonder she kept holding on. She was so thirsty for love she was satisfied with the few drops Jaime threw at her. Karina wrapped an arm around her. "He doesn't deserve you. Don't sell yourself short."

A tow truck came into view. And atop it, an impossibly bent and twisted black car.

"Oh my God," Karina said. The car was destroyed. Good thing Jaime had survived, because she was going to kill him.

Marisa stood dazed. It wasn't until the driver got out and called out her name that she reacted. She had to pay $250 for the tow truck, money she'd never get back.

After the driver left, they both examined the car. The windshield was smashed, and both air bags had been deployed. Most of the damage was on the passenger side. If Marisa had been with him, she would've died.

Karina took out her phone. "We should take some photos."

Marisa remained where she was, holding her purse to her chest. After a few moments, she sobbed, "I shouldn't have let him take it."

"It's not your fault. It's his." Karina stroked her back. "I know I've been hard on you, but you have to let him go. Just because he's better than your other boyfriends doesn't mean he's what's best for *you*. I mean, look at your car." Karina waved her hand toward the jumbled mess of metal. "Would someone who loves you do this to your car? He doesn't respect you."

"But I love him. I can't—" Marisa sobbed harder.

Karina knew how difficult it was to let go of someone you loved, but she couldn't let Marisa off the hook. What Marisa felt wasn't love, not the real thing. Not when she believed this was the best she could get.

Marisa's phone rang. It was Jaime. Damn it. Just one "I'm sorry" from him and Karina would lose. But from what Karina could make out, it seemed Jaime only wanted to make sure Marisa would post bail. The nerve of him. At least Marisa wasn't being as accommodating as always. Could this finally be it?

Marisa dropped the phone back into her purse and remained still. Karina held her breath. After a few minutes, Marisa said, "Okay."

"Okay?"

"Let's pack up his things. Now, before I lose my nerve."

They went up to the apartment. Karina tackled the closet, throwing Jaime's clothes into a trash bag. How she wished they were actually throwing it in the trash where it belonged. She moved fast, worried that at any moment Marisa would stop her.

Marisa gathered his stuff around the apartment, and Karina helped her empty the refrigerator of his beer and junk food, stuff Marisa didn't eat. They finished in less than thirty minutes.

They placed the bags by the door, and Marisa gazed around. The small apartment looked so much better without his junk. Marisa's handmade indigo tie-dyed curtains and cushions popped.

"How does it feel?" Karina asked.

"Like I'm the one who got out of jail?"

Karina let out a breath and chuckled. "You're not out yet." She paused. "How do you want to do it? You want to take him directly to his mom's?"

"She'll be so worried."

"That's her problem, not yours. Let's go."

They stopped at an ATM before driving to the station. Marisa chewed on her nails, and Karina worried she'd change her mind as soon as she saw Jaime. But Karina had said enough for one night. Now it was up to Marisa.

"You want a cookie?" Karina asked. "Your choice." She stopped at a red light and opened the glove compartment. "I carry all sorts now. Maybe a Perky for energy or an Active for strength?" She grabbed one of each as she talked and handed them to Marisa. "Or a Mellow to relax? A Flirty to be bold?" The light turned green and she drove on.

Marisa stared at the cookies in her lap. "Uh . . . I think I need to be like you tonight. I'll take the Flirty." She stashed the other cookies back in the glove compartment and unwrapped the Flirty, biting into it. "You know, I'd never tried this one before. It's good."

"Of course it's good. It's inspired by me." Karina smirked.

When Marisa finished eating, she asked, "Do you really think I can do better? I mean, look at me. I'm out of shape, almost thirty, with all this relationship baggage hanging around my neck. Who's going to want me?"

"Lots of guys."

"You say that 'cause you can get anyone. But I'm not like you. I'm not as confident or as strong."

Oh, if only she knew how broken Karina was inside. But that would depress her. Marisa needed fearless Karina now. "Then be more like me. Stay single for a while; don't even think about a relationship. When we met you, you said you'd just ended a relationship with a controlling bastard, and not a few weeks later, you were hooking up with Jaime. Have you ever been single?"

"I can't be alone."

"I didn't say alone; I said single. It's not the same thing."

"What about sex?"

"You can get any guy to have sex with you. Sex has nothing to do with being single."

"Don't you feel lonely sometimes?"

So much. "I have you, Cordelia, and Natalie. Plus work. There's no time to feel lonely."

Before Marisa stepped out to go into the station, Karina held her hand. "You can do this." Marisa nodded and went inside.

A few minutes later, she appeared with Jaime in tow. He only had a bandage on his forehead. Lucky bastard. When he saw Karina at the wheel, he frowned but said nothing. He lay down in the back seat and closed his eyes. They drove to his mother's house with only his snores breaking the silence. Karina couldn't wait to see his face when he realized what was happening.

Marisa pointed out the house, and Karina parked in front. She opened the trunk and took out his trash while Marisa shook him awake.

"Why are we here?" Jaime said. "Did you tell my mom what happened? You know how worried she gets."

"She doesn't know."

"Then why—" He noticed the trash bags Karina had unloaded onto the curb. He ran to them and peered inside. "Is this a joke?"

"I'm laughing," Karina mumbled.

His nostrils flared. "Did she put you up to this?" he asked Marisa.

"I didn't put her up to anything." Karina stepped between them, right up in his face. "She finally got the balls to dump your ass."

Jaime balled his hands into fists.

Marisa pulled her back. "Wait in the car. I'll take it from here."

"You sure?"

Marisa nodded, and Karina returned to the car. She cracked open the window so she could listen in.

"What did that bitch say?" Jaime asked. "You know she hates me."

"She didn't have to say anything. You said enough with what you did to my car."

Go, Mari, you can do it.

"Okay, yeah, I messed up, but you know I'll make it up to you."

"How? With what? You got your license suspended; you don't have a job—"

"I'll figure something out."

"Like you've been figuring it out for a year now?"

YES! Keep going!

"What do you want me to do?" he asked. "You know I keep waiting on Marcelo to hook me up."

"Marcelo, Marcelo. You always blame your problems on someone else. Do you enjoy living off your girlfriend?"

He pinched the bridge of his nose. "I can't believe you're bringing up all this tonight. I almost died."

Oh, please.

"Nobody asked you to drink and drive, especially not with my car. I didn't give you permission for that." Marisa's voice broke. "You know how much that car meant to me."

"I know, mami, I'm sorry." He knelt in front of her. "I promise I won't drink anymore. That was my last beer."

"How many times have I heard that before?"

"This time I'm serious." He took hold of her hands. "I swear to God, Mari." He kissed his thumb and forefinger. "Last night scared the living shit out of me. I'm ready to get my life in order."

Marisa looked at him with pity. *Please, don't listen to him. Come back to the car.* Karina was tempted to honk the horn to break the spell, but Marisa needed to do this on her own.

After what seemed like forever, Marisa pulled her hands away and stepped back. "I hope so. But I need to look after me now."

He lowered his head and stood up. "I'm going to make something of myself, you'll see. Then I'll pay you back."

"You don't owe me anything."

"You sure?"

"I'm sure you'll never pay me back."

"Yeah, I get it. You and your friends think I'm a big loser. You all make fun of me behind my back, don't think I'll ever own a garage, but you'll see. I'll show you. I'll show everyone."

"Take care of yourself." Marisa wiped her face and got into the car.

Karina grinned and put the car in gear. "You were awesome. I wish I'd taped it so you could see how strong you are."

"Yeah?"

"Oh yeah."

Marisa laughed and grabbed her hand. "Thank you. You were exactly what I needed tonight."

Karina smiled. It was nice to feel needed. "I'm glad I could help."

"You'll be there for me, right? I'll need my friends now."

"Of course. You won't be alone." *And neither will I.*

CHAPTER THIRTY-TWO

On Tuesday, Cordelia brought no leftovers for lunch, and Karina went to the drive-through and got burgers and fries for the two of them. As Karina ripped open the bag with her burger and took a huge bite, Cordelia picked at her fries. She wasn't sharing the latest gossip or prying into their lives. Something was wrong. Karina gave a questioning look to her friends, who both shrugged.

Marisa had spent the rest of the weekend at Karina's house, commiserating with Natalie over their respective breakups. They had invited Cordelia, but she'd preferred to stay with her hubby, as usual.

"Are you sick, Cordelia?" Karina asked.

Her head shot up. "Hmm? Oh, I didn't sleep well."

Karina could relate. Ever since The Night When All Hope Ended, Ian's voice telling her "I love you" had echoed in her head, making sleep impossible. But her skin didn't look as pale or her eyes as sunken as Cordelia's.

"I baked a cake last night," Cordelia said. "You girls want to come over after work and share it with me?"

Karina raised an eyebrow. "What about your hubby?"

"He's, um . . . he's on a business trip until Thursday."

"Is that why you couldn't sleep?" Karina asked.

Cordelia rolled her eyes. "Will you come or not? I know I didn't come to your little sleepover, but maybe we can do another one at my house. I don't want to spend the night alone. I'll cook something for us. What do you say?" She bit her lip and looked at them expectantly.

Wow. Was this what marriage did, turn a normally confident woman into a blubbering mess? Cordelia was acting as if she'd missed her last fix because she couldn't find her dealer.

"That's so nice of you," Marisa said. "Of course we'll come."

"Yeah," Natalie said.

"You know if there's food, I'm there," Karina said.

Cordelia whimpered and reached for their hands. "Ay, gracias, mil gracias!"

*   *   *

After lunch, Karina did a walk-through of the plant inside and out, similar to what the auditor would do during the plant inspection.

As Karina walked the outside perimeter of the plant, she turned the knob on the door near the mechanics' break room. It opened. All doors were supposed to be locked from the outside to prevent anyone from wandering in. She saw Brody passing by and called him.

When he stepped outside, she asked, "Why is this door unlocked?"

"So we can smoke in peace." He took out a pack of cigarettes and a lighter from his pocket and lit one up right in front of her, blowing smoke into her face.

She wouldn't back down. This wasn't a joke. Too much was at stake. "You have a key."

"It's more convenient like this. Chill."

She stepped closer, invading his personal space. "You think the inspector will chill?" She pointed at the cigarette butts on the ground. "Look at this dump. It's unacceptable. We need to do this right, Brody, or we'll fail."

He raised his hands in surrender. "Okay, calm down. I was just messing with you." He threw the butt onto the ground and stomped on it. "I'll clean this up, don't worry. And I'll talk to the guys. We can build a trash can with an integrated ashtray—how about that? Would that help?"

Karina exhaled. "Yes, that would be very helpful. I need to document this and speak to George, but when I do my next walk-through, the door better be locked, is that clear?"

"Sure thing. I'll go get a trash bag." He went back inside.

Karina fixed the doorknob so that it would lock automatically when it shut, documented everything, and continued on. In the production area, she stood in a corner to watch as the guys weighed the quinoa powder and the peanut butter for the Active, then poured both into the mixer. It was amazing how many times they fiddled with their hairnets or touched their faces without rewashing their hands and changing their gloves. She made a note to retrain on personnel hygiene. When she'd supervised them, she'd focused on only the tasks themselves, making sure they were measuring correctly or writing things down. Now she saw what Dwight always complained about. They needed to get their act together in the next two months or they'd never pass the inspection.

The packaging area was littered with boxes on the floor instead of on pallets, which Cordelia promptly fixed. There were more deviations in the warehouse: a box of expired cookies and an open container of cookie batter, left for rework in the freezer, that was supposed to be closed tight. She notified Scott, and he threw away the cookies and covered the batter. Karina also found a forklift with a cracked mirror and a malfunctioning drop-down door in the warehouse.

The cafeteria, in contrast, was squeaky clean, not a deviation in sight. The bathrooms as well. Damn it. It was hard to admit, but the nosy hag was good at her job.

As if Karina had conjured her, Rosa was kneeling next to the lockers, wiping them down as Karina passed through.

"Did you find anything?" Rosa asked without looking up.

"No. Truth is, you're one of the few who know what they're doing."

Rosa chuckled. "As if I didn't already know." She glanced at Karina, looking almost friendly, and Karina left before it got too weird.

She walked into her last stop—the maintenance shop. Ian was the only one there, sitting on a roll stool by a small desk with a computer. He gave her a cursory glance and returned to his work. No smile, nothing. Her heart ached. Only four days ago, he'd told her he loved her. Now he couldn't even look at her.

Good job, Karina, you found his limit, Heart said. *Are you happy now?*

I thought you were gone. Why are you still active? After so much pain, you should be in ashes by now. Leave me the fuck alone.

She took a deep breath. This job was her life now. Nothing left to do but keep going.

The shop consisted of some desks, stools, and various pieces of equipment and parts for repairs. The shelf for tools was tidy enough, but the lubricant closet wasn't locked. Karina made a few notes. Audit done. She glanced at the clock. Already three. She'd spent three hours on this audit, and it was probably nowhere near as thorough as the real one would be, but it was a start.

She read through the list of nonconformities she'd found, sneaking glances at Ian in between. Aside from the retraining on hygiene rules, which was Roy's responsibility, corrective actions belonged to George, the maintenance manager. The repairs for the forklift mirror and the drop-down door should get started right away. For that, she needed a work order. And Ian was in charge of that. Great. She braced herself as she approached him.

"Ian? I need two work orders."

He gripped the desk before turning to face her. "What for?"

Karina flinched at his impersonal tone but quickly composed herself and read the items aloud for him.

He jotted them down on a notepad beside his monitor. "Anything else?"

"No, that's it for now."

He turned back to the computer.

Karina clutched the clipboard, rooted to the ground. "Ian—"

"What?"

The anger in his eyes made her take two steps back. "I . . . I hope we can still work together."

"Don't worry. I know how it goes. Work and personal don't mix. If that's all . . ." He gestured at the computer. Now Karina was a nuisance to him.

"Yeah. That's all." She turned on her heel and hurried to Dwight's office.

Don't cry, don't cry, don't cry. You got what you wanted. Now you can focus on your promotion. Nothing else should matter.

As she turned to exit, Dwight walked in. "Is George in?" He glanced toward George's office.

"No," Karina said. "Here. I finished the walk-through." She handed him the checklist.

He read through it. "A cracked mirror on the forklift? Did you ask Scott how long it has been like that?"

"He didn't know."

Dwight sighed and shook his head. "Good that we thought to do this."

"Maybe we should do it monthly. In addition to the other programs. What do you think?"

"I don't see why not. And it's your call, Miss Internal Auditor," he teased.

Karina beamed. She glanced at Ian. He was scowling at them. Her smile faded.

"How long has this been going on?" Ian asked.

"I'm sorry?" Dwight said.

"Ian." Karina gave him a warning look.

"No, seriously, I want to know." He jumped off his stool and got in Dwight's face. "How long have you been sleeping with her?"

Dwight paled. "Uh . . ."

"Ian, stop it." She pulled at his arm. "Don't disrespect him like that."

He spun toward her. "Disrespect? Are you serious? Did you show me any respect when you cheated on me with him?"

Dwight's eyes bulged. "What?"

"How many times am I going to tell you it wasn't him?"

"And you expect me to believe you? Tell me, Dwight, how long have you been sleeping with Karina? Was it since before I came to work here?"

Dwight held up his hands. "Listen . . . Ian—"

"Dwight is with Lacey." Karina slid between them. "He's with Lacey. Tell him, Dwight."

"It's true. Lacey and I are a couple. I have no interest in Karina other than as a colleague and a friend."

Ian blinked and took a step back.

"See?" Karina said. "You know I'd never hurt Lacey."

"But you would hurt *me?*"

Karina swallowed and looked down at her safety shoes. His eyes full of anger, pain, and disappointment made her feel like a murderer. She'd killed the tenderness and compassion that used to be there, that calmed her, that made her heart leap. His love for her was dead because of her lies.

Ian rubbed his face. "Sorry, Dwight, but Karina has messed with my head so much it's hard to know when she's telling the truth. I hope this doesn't affect our working relationship."

"Not at all." Dwight pulled at his collar. "Already forgotten."

"Thank you." Ian shook his head at Karina and stormed out of the shop.

Dwight let out a huge breath.

"I'm so sorry, Dwight. I told him it wasn't you, but he kept insisting—"

"It's okay. I'm glad we could straighten it out."

But they hadn't straightened it out. It was a curlicued chaos. In trying to avoid hurting Ian, she'd caused him even more harm. What was wrong with her?

CHAPTER THIRTY-THREE

The earthy smell of green bananas and pigeon peas carried Karina into Cordelia's kitchen.

Natalie and Marisa sat on the stools by the breakfast bar, drinking wine, while Cordelia bent over a large pot on the stove.

Karina dropped onto the remaining stool. *Ian hates me. What have I done?* She poured herself a glass of wine, gulped it down, then emptied the bottle into her glass.

He should hate you, Heart said. *You don't deserve his love.*

No, I don't. I never did. She swallowed a sob with wine.

"I hope these bollitos turn out well," Cordelia said. "It's my first time making them."

"I'm sure they will," Marisa said. "Everything you make always tastes so good."

"It's not necessarily about the taste, but the texture. If the green banana mass is too soft, the bollitos will crumble. If it's too tough, they'll be hard to eat. My mom talked me through it, and I followed her instructions to the letter, but you never know." She peeked into the pot, then grabbed her glass of wine and turned to them. "So what's new with everyone? How's your job hunt, Nat?"

"The postings I find require either a graduate degree or years of experience. But I'm not ready to give up yet."

Cordelia took a sip. "And you, Mari? How's life without Jaime?"

"It's fine." Marisa ran a finger along the rim of the glass.

"But?" Cordelia asked.

"I know you guys probably think I should enjoy my new freedom, but I'm lonely, and it sucks."

Cordelia took her hand. "I get that. I'm so lonely without Charlie around. It's hard."

"You can stay with us for as long as you need," Natalie said. "Right, Karina?"

Wrong. All wrong. More wine.

"Oh, can I?" Marisa said. "I'd love that. I've never had roommates. I went from living with my parents to getting married—"

"You were married?" Natalie asked.

"Yeah. I was eighteen; he was twenty-five. He cheated on me."

"I'm so sorry."

"I'm over it. After getting divorced, I lived with a series of guys, and . . . maybe I should get a roommate?"

Natalie put her glass down. "Or we could find a bigger place and move in together. What do you think, Karina?"

"I think I made a mistake." Karina burst into tears. She wiped her face to keep her friends from seeing her like this, but all the pain she'd kept trapped for weeks was finally pouring out, and there was no stopping it.

Arms surrounded her, patting her back. Natalie whispered, "It's okay," giving her permission to let it all go. A wail erupted out of her.

Cordelia's shocked voice asked, "What is happening?"

After a few minutes, the sobs subsided and Karina straightened. Her friends were staring at her with worry. Marisa handed her a tissue.

"Better?" Natalie smiled and squeezed her shoulders.

Karina nodded and took a deep breath.

"What was that about?" Cordelia asked. "I almost died of fright."

Karina sniffled. "Ian. He hates me, and I . . ." Her lip trembled. "It hurts."

"But I thought you were over Ian," Marisa said gently.

"I'm not." Karina wiped her nose. "I love him."

Marisa palmed her cheeks. Natalie squeezed Karina's hand.

Cordelia spilled her wine all over her apron. When the others stood to help her, she raised her hands to stop them and dabbed herself with a napkin. "Pérate, pérate, are you telling us you broke up with Ian even though you're in love with him? Why would you do that?"

"I don't know. I think there's something wrong with me." More tears.

The lid of the pot with the stew rattled. "Ay, mis bollitos!" Cordelia rushed to check on them, dipping a spoon and biting into a dumpling. "They're done! Quick, let's serve them before they get too soft. One of you, grab the rice." She took the pot to the dining table.

Marisa served a spoonful of rice into each plate, and Cordelia followed with a ladle of stew on top.

"Sit, all of you," Cordelia said. "Karina, this will make you feel better, you'll see."

Karina stuck a forkful in her mouth. The dumplings were soft without dissolving completely, and the earthy taste of the pigeon beans blended perfectly with the green taste of the bananas and the starchy rice. Not only tasty but . . . nourishing. She choked on a sob, but she swallowed it and continued eating, taking small bites, savoring the meal.

"They're incredible," Marisa said.

"Divine," Natalie agreed.

Cordelia had her palm pressed to her chest, eyes closed. When she opened them, they were brimming with tears. "Ay, Dios mío. This reminds me so much of my mom. They're not exactly like hers, but almost." She chewed and moaned. "It was my favorite meal growing up. I've never tried making it because Charlie doesn't like it."

"But if it's your favorite meal, why wouldn't you make it?" Marisa asked.

"That's what I'm trying to figure out." She took another bite. "So Karina, what happened? Why have you been pretending not to feel anything for Ian?"

"Yes, why?" Marisa asked. "We could've been there for you, like you were there for me on Saturday."

"I just . . . didn't want you guys to think I was weak."

"For loving a man?" Cordelia scoffed. "Then we're all weaklings."

"But that's what I see when I look at all of you. Marisa was willing to stay with someone who didn't deserve her. Natalie was obsessed with finding 'the one.' And you can't stop living for your husband, to the point where you won't make your favorite meal because he doesn't like it."

Cordelia's mouth fell open. She took a sip of wine. "Maybe I overdo it. I always put Charlie first, even if he doesn't ask me to. My mom is like that. She does everything for my dad, and that's how she raised me to be. 'A good wife puts her husband's interest over her own.'" She air-quoted, then moved her fork around her plate. "Charlie's probably already spoiled. If I claim my independence now, our relationship will suffer."

"Not if you talk to him about it," Karina said. "Isn't that what you're always telling me?"

"You're right. Maybe I should. Pero this conversation started because you said you made a mistake. Do you want to get back with Ian?"

Karina sighed. "I don't know. When I broke up with him, I was so sure I was making the right decision, but now . . . Everything's messed up, and it hurts so much to be around him. I didn't know love could hurt like this. Pretend for a moment he dumped me, okay? How do I get over him?"

They burst into laughter.

Natalie wiped the corners of her eyes. "If we knew the answer to that, we wouldn't complain about relationships. You know how I feel about Peter, even though we were only together for one week."

"And believe it or not," Marisa said, "I miss Jaime. I even miss my previous boyfriend, and he was a creep. I have no idea how you can get over someone who didn't hurt you at all."

"The only way to get over someone," Cordelia said, "is to meet someone else. Before I met Charlie, I was still pining for my ex who'd left me two years before. I was always wishing he'd call me and ask me to come back, but of course he never did. But once I met Charlie, I couldn't remember what I saw in him. In your case, I think your only hope would be for Ian to get married. That way you'd know it's over for real."

"So I'll stay like this forever, with this feeling in my heart?"

They nodded.

"But you have something we didn't have," Cordelia said. "A chance to go back."

"Plus you two will probably work together for years," Natalie added. "If it kills you to be with him now, how will it feel when he meets someone else?"

"Isn't he dating Rosa's niece?" Marisa asked.

Karina was about to say they were only friends when she remembered how she'd encouraged Ian to try again. Maribel was probably consoling him right this second. Sourness filled her mouth, and she stuffed in a forkful of food to mask it.

"That's just a fling," Cordelia said. "Does it bother you to hear about her, Karina?"

"Duh."

"Then imagine how it would feel when the rumor is he's engaged. Because it would happen eventually."

If her stomach was already churning from picturing him in bed with another girl, then knowing he'd forever be with someone else would probably completely incapacitate her. Was this what she had to look forward to?

"Tell Ian you love him, that you're having second thoughts," Natalie said. "If Peter called me and told me he'd changed his mind, I would take him back like that." She snapped her fingers. "It's not too late."

"That's the thing. I think it *is* too late," Karina said. "You guys don't know the whole story." She recounted how she'd run into Ian at Friday Fest—omitting the part where they'd had sex—how he'd told her he loved her, how she'd lied to him, and about his confrontation with Dwight earlier that afternoon.

After a few moments of stunned silence, Marisa spoke. "But it's all a misunderstanding. You can still clear it up."

Karina shook her head. "I've hurt him too much. Face it, guys, I'm not good for him. I think I'm damaged somehow. He deserves someone better."

"You're being too hard on yourself," Cordelia said.

"Am I? I tried to be serious with Ian. I really did, and I felt trapped. Suffocated. My mom . . . she's just like you, Cordelia. She can only think about her husband and not herself. She says she's happy, but how can she be if she puts her identity to the side? I don't want to be like you or her. I want to be free to do whatever and not be a slave to love."

Cordelia held up her hands. "Un momento, mamita, I'm not a slave. Yes, I clean the house and cook for Charlie, but he takes care of the garden and the trash. He fixes anything that breaks down and takes care of the finances. He fixes me baths, cracks jokes when I'm sad, dances with me even when he's not in the mood." She grinned. "A relationship is hard work, but if you love each other, you'll get through it."

"Why don't you see a therapist?" Natalie asked. "They'd help you resolve your intimacy issues and childhood trauma."

Karina grimaced.

"What about your mom?" Marisa asked. "Why don't you talk to her?"

"We don't really talk."

"See, that's your problem." Cordelia pointed her fork at her. "You don't talk. Or you talk too much, but not about what matters. You should work on that."

"You're all loving this, aren't you?" Karina said. "Being the ones hassling me instead of the other way around?"

"Pues, claro," Cordelia said. "It's good to finally see your heart. You've been hiding it for too long." She patted Karina's hand. "Now, let's eat some cake. Tonight, we escape reality."

Cordelia had spent last night shredding coconut to make a four-layer coconut cake with egg-white icing. Karina almost had an orgasm when she tasted it. It was insane. A fleeting memory of feeding Ian cake flashed in her mind. She'd been so happy then. Why did she have to ruin it? Something was definitely wrong with her.

They devoured the cake and watched *Girls Trip*. She smiled at her friends gathered around her, feeling closer to them than ever before.

"Let's go away to Miami one of these weekends," Karina said.

"Ooh, great idea," Marisa said. "Jaime's not there anymore to sabotage me."

"I'm in," Natalie said.

"What about you?" Karina asked Cordelia. "You think you can handle a few more days without your husband?"

"With you guys"—she reached for their hands—"I can handle anything."

CHAPTER THIRTY-FOUR

On Sunday, Mother's Day, Karina went inside a McDonald's for the first time since living with her mom. She ordered the Big Breakfast with Hotcakes with extra packs of butter and sat at a booth. Her mom used to love the hotcakes, would always come here to celebrate Mother's Day. It was their special treat, their tradition. Then Bob came along, and McDonald's wasn't good enough anymore, replaced with brunch at whatever restaurant was trendy.

Karina took a huge bite of hotcake drenched in syrup and butter. She followed up with a bite of sausage. The sweet and salty tastes blended in her mouth. Yum. It had been too long. Did her mom miss this? Did she secretly still eat here or did she consider this food beneath her now, a calorie bomb best avoided? Karina bit into the biscuit.

Karina looked around. A few families with young children, some old couples, no one eating alone except for her. Natalie and Marisa had gone away to spend the weekend with their families. Cordelia and Charlie would celebrate with their church group. Everyone had plans and people to share them with. What did she have? A lump formed in her throat, and she swallowed it down with coffee. Sometimes it did get lonely. Having someone to lean on wasn't so bad.

Lacey and Roy had invited her to their family's Mother's Day celebration, but no matter how welcoming they'd be, she didn't belong there. She didn't belong anywhere but here.

* * *

She finished eating and gazed at her phone. Eleven twenty. Her mom would probably be at brunch. Though they were estranged, Karina always called her mom on holidays and for her birthday, even though she didn't deserve the courtesy. She usually called right after breakfast to get it over with, but she had no energy for pretenses today. Her friends' advice echoed in her head. Should she confide in her mom, maybe receive some wisdom that could help her?

After a movie and a nap, cocooned in her nest of cushions, Karina finally called at six. As soon as her mom picked up, Karina said, "Happy Mother's Day."

"Ah, finally. I was worried you wouldn't call."

"Since you're always doing something fun with Bob and Lily, I didn't want to interrupt."

"I can always make time for my oldest daughter. Especially when we haven't spoken since your birthday."

"You can call me if you want to know how I am."

"You never answer your phone."

This was pointless. "How was your day?"

"Lily and Bob cooked for me, and then we went to . . ."

Karina stopped listening. It made her cringe to hear about all the fun things her mom did with her new family.

"I'm getting a promotion at work." Karina cut her off.

"Even with only a GED?"

"I just need two trainings and to pass two tests."

"You were never good with tests. Is there somebody helping you?"

"Yes." *Since you're not there anymore.* "They told me they're not that difficult. We'll see. The trainings are next month."

"Good luck."

Karina grasped a cushion, wiping her hand. She should hang up now. They'd already talked enough.

"Have you met anyone new?" her mom asked.

Karina's usual answer was no, but this was where she needed to be honest. "I dated this guy for two months, but we broke up."

"What happened?"

"I . . . It was getting too serious, so I broke things off."

"Why would you do that? For the love of God, Karina, you want to end up an old maid?"

"Nobody cares about that anymore. There are women who never marry."

"Those women are stupid. You don't want to end up without a man. Who'd take care of you? I won't be around much longer."

Hearing her mom talk like that still shocked her, even after so long. "I thought I was supposed to take care of myself. It's not like you take care of me that much anyway."

"If I don't take care of you, it's because you don't let me. When was the last time I saw you? You live only two hours away and you never come visit."

"You can come visit too, you know. Doesn't seem like you miss me that much."

"You've never invited me. And I have your sister to deal with. You don't even care about her enough to come see her."

"I have a life of my own, and I don't do well with kids."

"Much of a life you have, all alone, pushing away eligible men."

"I'm not alone. I have friends."

"And what happens when your friends get married and have kids? You're going to hang around like a weird old aunt? They won't be there for you as much. Believe me, I should know. I had no one when I was raising you. No one. You know how hard that was for me?"

You had me. We were supposed to be a team, but now it seems I was a burden. Karina gripped the phone. "And yet you managed. You were even studying. What happened with that?"

"I found a good man. I didn't need to struggle anymore. I could focus on taking care of my daughters."

"Daughter, you mean."

"Ay, Karina, por favor. I tried with you, but all you did was fight me."

"So it's my fault my own mother chose her new family over me?"

"What did you expect me to do? All I got from you were tantrums and rebellions. I didn't have the time or the patience. I went where I was needed."

Karina wiped her face. "Like *I* didn't need you?"

"You sure acted like you didn't." After a long moment of silence, her mom added in a softer voice, "When you're a single mother with no one to help you and you find a good man, you do everything you can to hold on to him. You were grown and on your way out. Lily needed me more than you. That's how life works sometimes."

This was the wisdom Karina had been waiting for? *Life's unfair; deal with it*? She should've known.

"I have to go now," Karina said. "Talk to you on your birthday. Bye." She threw the phone on the bed and spooned her cushions.

She'd been stupid to think her mom could have any answers. The mom she used to know was gone, replaced by this Stepford wife. If someone as independent as her mom could change so much because of a man, why wouldn't the same happen to Karina? They shared the same genes, after all. She loved Ian, but she loved the life she'd built more. It was better to quit him now than resent him later. She had a promotion to strive for. Unlike her mom, she'd make something of herself without a man.

CHAPTER THIRTY-FIVE

Karina marched into reception with a confidence she didn't have, heading to the display of Singular Cookies. Today was the day she'd been preparing for over the last two months. Either she'd pass the tests and become the plant's internal auditor or she'd go back to production or worse—prove that she didn't belong here at all and go back to being a maid.

Bright Cookie stared at her accusingly. It was the only one she hadn't tried. The carrots had kept her away, but maybe it would make her smart, morph her into the type of person who would beat those tests.

Armed with a couple of cookies, she headed toward Dwight's office. It was empty. Dwight was probably in Lacey's office, as was his routine most mornings.

Karina sat at her desk and unwrapped the cookie. Her stomach rumbled. With all the nerves, she'd been queasy since she woke up, and she'd missed breakfast. She bit into it. The carrots weren't that noticeable. It tasted more like cinnamon. And of course, it all came together with the walnuts and dates. Lacey knew how to make a cookie.

Lacey and Dwight walked in, both wearing expectant smiles.

"And?" Lacey asked. "Are you ready?"

Karina lifted the cookie. "Trying to be."

"You'll do great, you'll see," Dwight said. "How were the trainings?"

She'd flown to Virginia to be trained in person, which had taken three days. At first, she'd felt out of place, but the trainer and the other attendants—all men, experts in their field—had assured her she had nothing to worry about. The tests were multiple choice. She had three tries. But that didn't take the pressure off.

"They were okay," Karina replied. "I got along with the guys, and the trainer gave me his business card in case I had questions. I spent the weekend poring over the materials and the code, but I'm scared that everything's jumbled in my head now."

Dwight and Lacey exchanged worried glances. They probably also thought she couldn't pass and were just trying to sound encouraging to keep her from freaking out.

"I think you're stressing too much about this," Lacey said. "Why don't you let Dwight guide you through them?"

Karina slammed her hands against the desk. "Absolutely not. I don't want to cheat. If I'm going to do this job, I need to know what I'm talking about. And that means I should know the answers to the test. Otherwise, why am I doing this?"

"I didn't mean cheat," Lacey said. "Dwight can prepare a mock test. Isn't that right, Dwight?"

He nodded. "Of course."

"No thanks. I should be able to do it by myself."

"There's no shame in asking for help," Lacey said.

"Not with this." Karina pouted and finished her cookie. After swallowing the last bite, she felt nauseous again. These tests were going to kill her. "And now please leave me alone, so I can focus."

*   *   *

Congratulations. You passed.

Karina stared at the monitor. She'd passed the internal auditing test on her first try. Not one wrong answer. And she hadn't consulted her notes; she'd remembered most of it. It seemed like when learning

257

was fun, it was no trouble. She still had to tackle the test for the certification program, and that one was surely more difficult.

It turned out she was wrong. She finished in less than half an hour with only three answers wrong. It was like everyone had said: a confirmation that she'd paid attention. Karina leaned back in the chair and brushed her hand across the top of the desk. Her desk. It had arrived a few weeks ago, but now she'd earned the right to call it that. For the first time she felt like Dwight's equal, not his subordinate but someone with equal say in matters that affected the company.

"Dwight, I passed."

He clapped. "See? I knew you could do it. And now we can make it official." He came over to shake her hand. "Congratulations on becoming our new internal auditor."

Karina beamed. "Thanks."

"We need to celebrate your first official day. I'll get Lacey."

Karina's stomach rumbled. Once she talked to Lacey, she'd go to the cafeteria for a snack.

Lacey walked in with a bouquet. The smell of roses made Karina gag, and she covered her mouth.

Lacey rushed to her. "What's wrong?"

Karina raised her hand to keep her away. Her mouth filled with saliva. "I need to go to the bathroom." She took two steps, then bent over and threw up onto the floor.

Lacey moved the hair out of Karina's face. "Dwight, go get Rosa." She helped Karina to a chair. "Was it something you ate?"

"I just ate the one cookie. I was too nervous. I've been nauseous all morning."

"You should go to the doctor," Lacey said. "Why don't I drive you?"

Karina wiped her forehead. "I'm fine. It's over." But her stomach was like crashing waves inside her. She rested her head on her hands.

"You should get checked out. It could be stomach flu or food poisoning or . . ." She looked at Karina funny before talking to someone on the phone.

The smell of vomit was making Karina nauseous again. She pinched her nostrils closed. Dwight arrived with Rosa, and she grabbed paper towels to soak up the mess Karina had made.

"Let's go." Lacey held out a hand to help her stand, but Karina didn't take it. It was bad enough Rosa knew about her vomiting. Karina didn't need everyone else to witness her being escorted out like an invalid.

As they passed by the test bakery, Lacey gestured for her to wait while she went inside. She came out with a bag full of cookies.

"Eat one." Lacey took one out of the bag and offered it to her. "The Quirky has ginger. It's good for nausea."

Karina's stomach grumbled, and not in a good way. "I don't think another cookie will help. Let's just go to the doctor." If she wasn't in the mood for a cookie, then there was definitely something wrong with her.

* * *

After Karina waited half an hour for blood results, a nurse escorted her into a small office.

The doctor, a young redheaded woman, came in and sat on the desk in front of her. "It turns out you're not sick, Miss Cortés. You're pregnant."

Karina's stomach dropped, and she gripped the sides of the chair to keep from tumbling off it. She stared at the doctor, her mouth agape. This had to be a fucking joke. She hadn't had sex since . . . Ian. When she told him to keep going after the condom broke.

The doctor waited patiently for her to digest the news. She must've gotten this reaction all the time from unsuspecting women blindsided by two words that changed everything. Karina swallowed. "Um." She cleared her throat. "How, uh, how long?"

"Do you know when the first day of your last period was?"

"Uh, my period's pretty irregular. I skip months sometimes, and I don't keep track of it."

"Well, with the onset of the nausea, I'd say around six to eight weeks? You should go to the health clinic to verify."

Karina did the math in her head. Rosa's party was over two months ago, so it couldn't be from Marcos. And they'd had no issues with the condom, unlike with Ian. But . . . why did it have to be Ian? Why not anyone else?

259

"Miss Cortés?"

"Hmm?"

"I have to see other patients, but I'll prescribe you something for the nausea." She typed into her computer.

"Can you write me a note for work? But don't mention the pregnancy, only that I have a stomach flu or something? I don't want to go to work tomorrow, and I don't want them to find out."

"Not a problem."

Before heading out into the waiting room to face Lacey, Karina took a deep breath. *Act normal.*

Lacey stood as soon as she saw her. "And?"

"It's a stomach flu. Here." She handed Lacey the note. "The doctor says I should stay home and rest."

Lacey read the note. "Sure, take all the time you need." She stared at Karina. "For a second, I thought you might be pregnant."

Karina laughed, hoping it didn't sound too fake. "Me, pregnant? Can you imagine?"

* * *

After stopping at the pharmacy to fill out the prescription, Lacey dropped Karina back at the company so she could get her car. After reassuring Lacey that she'd be okay and taking the nausea pill, Karina drove to the beach.

When she arrived, it was desolate, dark clouds hovering in the horizon. As she stepped out of the car, strong winds messed up her hair. Karina sat in her usual spot, arms wrapped around her knees. The ocean roiled much like her stomach. She pressed her lips together to keep from vomiting again.

A baby.

Her mom had never taken her to the beach as a child, even though Karina had found pictures of her at the beach in Puerto Rico. It wasn't until Karina moved to Fort Pierce that she could finally share in the experience. She couldn't imagine being away from the ocean. It was a part of her, just like this baby inside her.

Why did this have to happen to her, especially now, when she'd gotten a promotion, found a new drive in her career? A fucking baby.

She let the wind blow the tears away. When her mom had gotten pregnant at sixteen, her parents had demanded she get an abortion, but her mom wanted a baby. She had left, cut herself off from her family and her homeland. And what a lousy mother she'd turned out to be. How would Karina fare any better when she'd never wanted a baby to begin with?

Sand stuck to her face, and her hair beat against her head. No tranquility to find here. Her warm ocean breeze was gone, calming someone else with his touch.

* * *

At home, she nestled among her cushions, hiding under the bamboo sheets she'd bought, the same brand as Ian's, with the same ocean smell from the linen spray. She breathed it in and her body relaxed. She might not have the real thing anymore, but this consolation prize was better than nothing. Karina drifted off to a world where she was not alone but cuddled in Ian's arms with nothing to worry about.

When she woke, she found her friends eating at the dining table. The scent of garlic made Karina run to the bathroom and throw up again.

Natalie knocked on the door and popped her head in. "How are you feeling? We heard you have the stomach flu. Did you eat anything? We brought you soup."

Karina shook her head. Just that small movement made her stomach roll. "I'm not hungry." She went back to bed. Her friends followed her into the bedroom.

"You look awful," Marisa said.

"If you don't want food, then you must really be sick." Cordelia pressed the back of her hand to her forehead. "No fever."

Karina stared at her friends' worried faces. They'd grown closer since that night at Cordelia's house, had bonded even more on their weekend trip to Miami last month. They'd promised to make it a monthly tradition, even if it was only a sleepover at one of their houses. Karina needed to tell someone. This was too big to keep to herself.

"I lied," Karina said. "I don't have the stomach flu." She paused. "I'm, um . . . I'm pregnant."

Wide eyes all around.

"From who?" Cordelia asked.

"Aw, this is great news," Marisa said. "Congratulations."

Karina pressed a cushion to her chest. "No, this is not great news. I don't want a baby."

"Who's the father?" Cordelia asked. "Marcos?" When Karina shook her head, she asked, "Dwight?"

"No, and for the record, I've never had sex with Dwight and never will."

"Then who?" Cordelia gasped and grasped her chest. "Ay, Dios mío! It's Ian, isn't it?"

Karina only stared, but the answer must've been written all over her face, because Cordelia clapped once. "Aha! I knew you couldn't stay away from him. When was this?"

"Why didn't you tell us?" Natalie said.

"It was just one night," Karina said. "When I ran into him at Friday Fest last month. It was easier not to tell."

"Holy shit," Natalie said. "You're having Ian's baby?"

"But why isn't this great news?" Marisa asked. "You love Ian. This could bring you together."

"Doubtful." Karina grabbed Woody and stared into his smiling face. Ever since the news, there'd been a voice inside her, a whisper that had turned into a scream with every passing hour. But now it was time to say it out loud. She hoped her friends would understand, because this was one thing she didn't know if she could handle alone. "I don't want to have a baby, even if it's his. I've been going around it in my head, and I just . . . I can't do it." She peeked at them.

Cordelia gasped and backed up a few steps, holding her stomach as if she'd been punched. Marisa looked confused. Natalie asked, "You mean . . . ?"

Karina returned her gaze to Woody and nodded.

"Dios mío, Karina, an abortion?" Cordelia said. "You'd kill your baby?"

Her angry tone made Karina recoil, but she wouldn't be shamed. "I want it out of me."

"No puedo creer esto," Cordelia said. "I can't believe I'm hearing this." She shuffled to the doorway. "I've been trying for months, and you have unprotected sex one time and you get pregnant? And then you want to get rid of it? How is that fair?"

"It's not my fault you can't get pregnant. I'd take back that stupid night if it meant I could avoid making this decision."

"Cordelia, calm down," Marisa said. "Just because it's not the choice you'd make doesn't mean it's not the right choice for Karina." She sat next to Karina and took her hand. "I'll support you no matter what you decide."

Karina's vision blurred with tears. It meant so much not to be judged.

"Are you sure about this?" Natalie asked. "Because you can't take it back if you change your mind later."

"No, but I'm sure I don't want a baby. Not now. Maybe ten years from now, but definitely not now."

"What about Ian?" Cordelia was leaning against the doorway, arms crossed. "Doesn't he get a say?"

She'd completely forgotten about Ian's role in all this. If he didn't hate her already, when he learned she wanted to get an abortion, he'd hate her forever. Did she want to lose the last thread of goodwill he might still have toward her?

"I can't tell him."

"It's his baby," Cordelia said. "He has a right to know."

"What do you guys think?" Karina asked the others. "Should I talk to him?"

They nodded.

"But what if he's against it?" Karina ducked farther under the covers. "He can't force me to have it, right?"

"Ian would never do that," Natalie said. "He's a good guy. He'd want you to be happy."

"You shouldn't keep something like this a secret," Marisa said. "I don't know, but I think he'll support your choice if he really loves you."

"Talk to him," Natalie said. "You can figure it out together."

"I'll think about it," Karina said. "I'm going to the clinic tomorrow to check on the pregnancy and talk about my options . . ."

"You're making a mistake," Cordelia said. "We could help you raise the baby. You wouldn't have to do it alone."

"I couldn't handle a relationship. You think I can handle being a mother? Even if I have help, the responsibility would always be mine, and I don't want it."

Cordelia ran toward the bed, leaning over her. "Do you think Ian's going to forgive you having an abortion? If you do this, you'll never get him back."

"Even if I did want him back, if he doesn't respect my decision, he's not the right man for me." As soon as the words were out of her mouth, Karina burst into tears. She'd been resigned to losing him, but it seemed a small piece of her heart still held on to hope.

Cordelia knelt in front of Karina. "I'm sorry, but this is wrong. I love you, but I will never agree with this."

"I don't need you to agree with me." Karina sniffed. "I need you to respect my decision."

"I can do that. I accept it's your choice to make, not mine." She gripped Karina's hands, then let them go. "That's all I can do for now."

Karina wiped her face. "Will you stop being my friend if I go through with it?"

Cordelia closed her eyes and took a deep breath. "I don't know. I only ask you to think about it. A baby is a miracle. You'll never know what you're capable of until you try."

CHAPTER THIRTY-SIX

The next day, Karina parked outside Ian's house.

His truck was in his driveway. There were no other cars, so he was alone. She wiped her clammy hands on her jeans and waited. Did she really want to tell him? At the clinic earlier, the doctor had confirmed she was between six to eight weeks pregnant, based on the size of the fetus.

Even though she wanted to please Cordelia and keep her friend-ship, there was nothing left to think about. Karina had scheduled the abortion for Friday. The doctor at the clinic had reassured her she wouldn't feel anything during the procedure and that she'd have, at most, bad cramps afterward. It seemed simple enough. A few min-utes of discomfort, some pain, and in two days this whole pregnancy would be a distant memory.

Now the only thing left to do was tell Ian. She'd obeyed today's T-shirt slogan—*When all else fails, I say fuck it and go to sleep*— spending the day napping and watching movies in between, trying not to think, waiting until Ian got out of work. But now that she was here, she couldn't move. What if he hated her? She took out the last Quirky from the bag. Maybe it was the ginger or the combination with the licorice, but they'd helped her feel better today. Karina licked off the crumbs and clambered out of the car.

When Ian answered the door, her breath caught in her throat. He wore shorts and a T-shirt, his hair slicked back, not a curl out of place. Her hand itched to rumple it like she'd done countless times.

His brow furrowed. "What are you doing here?"

"I need to tell you something. Can I come in?"

"I thought you already said everything you needed to say."

"Not this. It's something new. Something that concerns both of us."

"I don't—"

"Please, Ian? It's really important. You know I don't beg."

"No, you don't." He sighed and let her in.

She sat on the couch and hugged one of the cushions she'd bought. It smelled like him.

"Why did you keep this?" she asked.

"They look good."

"But don't they remind you of me? Does Maribel know I got them for you?"

He hesitated. "Maribel and I are not together anymore."

"Oh?" She forced herself not to smile. Her heart sped up. *Stop it, Heart. Who cares if he broke up with Maribel? After he hears what we have to say, he'll probably sigh in relief that he's not with us anymore.*

"I heard you were sick. How are you doing?"

This was her opening. Karina had run different scenarios through her head about the best way to approach the topic but hadn't come up with anything good. "I'm not sick. I'm pregnant." She paused. "And it's yours."

He hovered above the armchair across from her, then dropped into it. "Sorry?"

"I know I shouldn't have blurted it out like that, but there was no other way to tell you."

He gaped at her, hands on his knees. She lowered her gaze to his handmade crate coffee table, his *Men's Health* magazines lying next to a row of white candles. So romantic and manly, so Ian. How had he ever gotten messed up with her?

The sound of his voice startled her. "You sure it's mine?"

It should hurt that he'd ask that first, but she'd earned it. "Positive."

"But . . . we used protection—"

"The condom broke."

"True." He paused. "I must've pulled out too late."

"I'm not here to blame you. It is what it is."

He scrubbed his face. "A baby. Wow."

"I don't want to keep it."

"You don't . . . What?"

He didn't seem angry, only shocked. She let out a long breath. "It's for the best. I'm not ready for a baby right now. Or maybe ever."

He frowned. "Okay, so . . . you're saying . . . you want to get rid of it?"

Karina nodded, her gaze back on the table. She should've done this over the phone. Her stomach heaved, and she sucked a ginger candy.

"Why are you telling me this?"

"I thought you should know."

"But you already decided."

"Yeah."

"Then why tell me? You could've done it, and I would never know."

"*I* would know. It seemed wrong to keep it from you."

Ian stood and stared out the window. Karina's head swam, and she stretched out on the couch, the worn leather caressing her skin.

"I need some air." Ian grabbed his keys and walked out the door.

Time to leave. But she was so tired. She closed her eyes and dozed off.

When she woke, the sun had set, and the room glowed in the candlelight. Ian sat in the armchair, watching her. She sat up straight.

"Are you sure?" His voice came out strained and worn out. He didn't want her to go through with the abortion. It was written all over his face. She couldn't let him try to change her mind.

"Do you want to have a baby in nine months?"

"I don't know. It would be ours."

Her hand went to her stomach. Their baby. Would she make a different choice if they were still together?

He sat beside her, resting his hand atop hers. "We can start over. You, me, and this baby. You wouldn't have to do it alone. My feelings for you . . . haven't changed."

Her heart fluttered and she gazed into his eyes, full of love once more. There was still a chance to be together. But only if she kept the baby. Images of Ian holding a baby boy flashed in her mind: him beaming at Karina, tears and adoration in his eyes, the love bursting out of him. But other images seeped through: Karina carrying a wailing baby, trying and failing to get it to sleep; the baby pulling at her nipples to breastfeed; the pressure of being responsible for someone else's life. She shook her head to snap out of it and moved his hand away.

"Do you really want me to get back together with you because of a baby I don't want?"

He leaned on his elbows, resting his head on his hands. "No."

"Then this is the only way."

He jumped to his feet. "Carajo, Karina, you don't make things easy for me. I have to be okay with this even if I don't want to?"

"You don't know what this is like." Her voice broke. "Being pregnant is no joke. I'm nauseous all the time, I keep throwing up, I'm tired. I don't like feeling like I'm not in control of my body. It's like I've been invaded. And the inspection's next month, and I . . . can't . . . work like this." She cried into her hands.

"It's okay, it's okay." He put his arm around her and pulled her to him. "I'm sorry. You're right. I have no idea. What do you need from me?"

"Nothing." She sniffled. "I just wanted to tell you."

He wiped the tears away. They were close enough to kiss, but it would be wrong. She settled for resting her head on his chest.

"When?" he asked.

"Friday morning. And it can't come soon enough. I don't want anyone at work to suspect." She paused. "If they haven't already."

"You need money?"

"I can handle it."

"Let me help you. It's my—I'm responsible."

"I don't want you to feel responsible. It's my decision."

"We're in this together." He smoothed out her hair. "Let me come with you. I'll take the day off."

"And give more fodder to the rumor mill? They'll put two and two together and—"

"Who cares? I want to be there for you." He held her hand. "You shouldn't be alone."

Karina gazed at her hand in his. He still loved her, even now. But after . . . "You really think you can handle being there?"

"No, but I know I need to be there. For you."

CHAPTER THIRTY-SEVEN

Ian drove Karina to the health clinic on Friday and held her hand as they walked past the protesters to the front door.

He held her hand while they were in the waiting room and throughout the procedure. They gave her local anesthesia, and she felt only a mild discomfort, but she kept her eyes closed, taking comfort in Ian's touch.

After, Ian took Karina back to her house and helped her to bed. She went to sleep, and when she woke, he was still there, watching her from the plush chair beside the bed.

"How long did I sleep?" she asked.

"About two hours. It's almost two. You hungry?"

"Not really."

He leaned on his elbows. "How do you feel? Does it hurt?"

"A bit." She pressed her hand against her abdomen. There was the dull pain she associated with her period. She'd expected worse, since she'd also opted for an IUD, but no, it wasn't so bad. And the nausea was gone. "Where are the pills?"

He handed her the bottle they'd picked up on their way back. "I'll get you some water." He left and came back a few minutes later with a full glass and her heating pad.

Karina took the pills and lay back down, pressing the pad to her stomach. "You don't have to stay here. I'm fine. Really."

"I want to stay until Natalie comes back from work. In case you need anything."

"You've already done enough. It's okay."

He pushed a hand through his hair. "Why is it so hard for you to accept help? Or is it only with me?"

"I—"

"Maybe *I'm* the one who needs comfort right now." He emphasized his words by pointing at his chest.

"You said you were okay with it."

"And what if I'm not?"

Her stomach cramped, and she winced, rolling onto her side. "Don't you fucking make me feel guilty about this. I won't let you shame me for having an abortion."

"It's not that." He sighed and pushed aside a couple of cushions so he could sit on the bed. "I respect your choice. It's your body, and I can't put myself in your position. But I can't stop thinking maybe . . ."

"Maybe what?"

He sighed. "Maybe the baby was a sign we should be together."

"Oh, please, Ian. We had unprotected sex, and that was the result. It happens."

"Yes, but why did it happen to us? You break up with me, then months later we have sex—when I thought I'd never be with you again—and we make a baby. What are the odds?"

"You want me to Google it for you?"

He closed his eyes and pressed his hands to his lips. "Be serious for a moment." He stared at her. "We made a baby. For a few weeks, you had a part of me inside you. It connected us." He exhaled. "Did you . . . get rid of it because you didn't want to be connected to me in that way?"

"What? No. This had nothing to do with you. I'm not ready to have a baby. I don't know if I'll ever be. It's as simple as that."

"And you never thought to keep it?"

She gritted her teeth. Why was it so difficult to understand? "No."

"Did you ever imagine having a future with me? Or was it all a game for you?"

She wrapped the sheet tighter around herself. "Please. I can't deal with this right now."

"Okay." He stood. "But let me tell you, I did imagine it. You living with me, you walking to the altar, you pregnant with our child, us growing old together. I imagined all of it. It wasn't a game for me. But you, you were with another man; you left me like I was nothing. You know how that made me feel?"

Her eyes blurred, and she pressed them shut.

"You won't say anything to me?"

"Do you hate me for having an abortion?" she asked in a low voice.

"No. Not for that. For everything else, yes." He walked to the door. "Take care of yourself. Get a lot of rest. See you around."

Karina cried into her cushions. What a mess she'd created. All because she wasn't brave enough to tell the truth.

*   *   *

Natalie found her in the same position an hour later. "How are you doing?" She sat behind Karina and stroked her back.

"I don't know."

"Did you change your mind?"

"No." She paused. "It's gone."

Natalie squeezed her shoulder. "Cordelia went home to cook you something, and Marisa wanted to get you flowers. They'll be here in a little while."

Karina sat up to face her. "So Cordelia doesn't hate me?"

"She's not thrilled, but she wants to be there for you. We all do."

Karina's eyes filled with tears. They were sticking by her, even after witnessing her darkest side. "I'm so happy to hear that. I really don't want to be alone right now."

"You won't." Natalie smiled and patted her hand. "Where's Ian? I thought he'd be here."

"He wanted to stay until you came, but we had a fight, and he left."

"What happened?"

She groaned. "Oh, Nat, I'm so stupid. I never should've let him go. He loves me."

"You already knew that."

"But I mean like real love, the kind that holds your hand while you get rid of his baby kind of love."

Natalie clutched her chest. "Ugh, you're making my heart hurt."

"He said he thought the baby was a sign we should be together."

"Now you're making me cry." She fanned her eyes.

"What should I do?"

"What you should've done from the beginning—tell him the truth. Let him make up his own mind."

"You're right, you're right. Ugh." Karina covered her face with a cushion. "He would've understood. I was just so . . . scared. But after today, I owe him the respect he showed me."

* * *

Can you come over? Karina texted Ian the next day. *I want to explain.*

After a few minutes, he replied. *OK.*

They sat on her couch. Karina offered Ian water and filled one glass for each of them.

"Feeling better?" he asked.

"It's not as bad as yesterday, but it still hurts a little."

He tapped his fingers on his thigh. She hugged a cushion against her chest, staring at the plants along the wall.

"Thank you for yesterday," she said. "It meant a lot."

"No problem."

"Do you wish I hadn't done it?"

He sighed. "If we were still together, I would've wanted you to keep it, but you didn't want a baby, and you don't want to be with me, and I have to accept that. I only wish things weren't so complicated between us."

"I know. It got messy."

He chuckled. "Yes. Messy." He paused. "And you? You regret it?"

"I feel relieved, actually. My body belongs to me again—no more nausea, no more worrying about people finding out. Now I can move forward, focus on the inspection."

"Good. I'm happy if you're happy."

Why did he have to say things like that?

"You said you wanted to explain?" he asked.

"Give me a moment." She closed her eyes and loosened her grip on her heart, letting it speak for her. "It wasn't a game for me." When he didn't respond, she added, "It got too serious too fast, and I didn't know how to handle it." She paused. "I'm sorry."

"Is that why you cheated on me?"

She risked a peek at him. "I didn't cheat. I told you that so you'd get over me."

He frowned. "So . . . there was no one else?"

"No. I was always your K. I was just afraid to let her out."

"But . . ." He scrubbed his face. "I don't understand. Why didn't you tell me the truth?"

"It's hard to explain." She straightened. It was easier now to face him. "Okay, so everything was fine, and then you wanted to celebrate our monthiversary. I freaked out; you were right. I started making up all these excuses so I could have more space from you. Like the trip to Miami. That was a lie."

"But you texted me photos."

"I ended up going, but there was no plan. And there was no stalker. I made that up so I wouldn't have to sleep at your place. And Natalie *loves* you. She's definitely not a virgin, and she doesn't care if I have guys over."

His eyebrows stretched to his hairline. "This is crazy. I can't believe you lied to me about all that."

"Those are not the only things, believe me."

"So . . . you were happy? You lied about that too?"

"Yeah. At least in the beginning, before my feelings got too confusing and . . . and scared me."

"Wow." He let out a breath. "Why didn't you talk to me?"

"You wanted the happily-ever-after, and I wanted to have fun. Would you have stayed with me if I told you that?"

"I don't know. But it would've been better than what you did. You lied to me, you avoided me, you ended up breaking up with me, and for what? Why was it so hard to trust me? If I would've known, I would've taken it slower and put less pressure on you."

"I don't think it would've changed things. We're too different."

"We could've worked something out. I tried to give you space, but it felt like you'd rather be alone than with me."

"That's exactly what I mean. I wanted to be alone and not feel guilty about it. But you made me feel like wanting that was wrong."

"When did I make you feel that? When I asked you to come over after not seeing you for a week? Why was it wrong to want to spend time with you?"

"Ian, you were everywhere. At work, at my place, on my phone. Everywhere. You were suffocating me."

"Then why couldn't you say that? I would've understood."

"Yeah, right."

"No, Karina, that's where you're wrong. I would've done anything to make it work. All you needed to do was set the rules, and I would've followed them. But you made me figure out the rules on my own, and it only confused me."

"Why set rules when it would've ended sooner or later?"

"So you *didn't* want it to work out. You told me you'd try serious."

"That was later. By then I thought I had a good handle on things."

Ian shook his head. "I had a girlfriend that was like you. She pulled away whenever things got too deep. But she talked to me. Her ex had cheated on her, and she was afraid of getting hurt. I gave her the space she needed, and in time, she trusted me. We were together for a year. That could've been us, if you'd only been honest with me."

Karina's lip trembled. So much time wasted because of fear. Would they have lasted that long?

"It doesn't matter anymore. What's done is done."

"Is it?"

There was hope in his eyes. After everything. Her heart beat against her ribs. "Would you really want to be with me again after everything that's happened? Because I'm still me. Maybe I wouldn't lie anymore, but I'd still need space."

"At least I'd know what I was getting myself into."

"And you'd really put yourself through that?"

He held her hand. "This—what you just told me—I feel like I finally get you. There's still a lot I don't know, but that only makes me want to know more." He smoothed her hair. "You're a revelation, K. I'm so relieved to know I wasn't wrong about you. Whenever you'd let your guard down, I could see the tender, vulnerable side not everyone gets to see. It made me feel powerful to peel off your layers." He gazed into her eyes. "I want to keep discovering you."

Her body went numb. "Even after yesterday?"

He smiled. "Yesterday, you were brave and strong. And today you're here, talking to me face-to-face and telling me the truth. You say you haven't changed, but you have. You've changed a lot."

Tears fell down her face. He wiped them away. Here it was, everything she'd hoped to hear. Her heart jumped for joy, but underneath there was another feeling. A knot in her stomach.

"I want to be with you." He stroked her face. "No matter how hard it is."

Her hands shook. She needed to be alone. She jumped up to stand. "I can't do this right now."

"Wait." He grabbed her shoulders. "Don't be scared. Talk to me."

She took a deep breath. "I had no plans of getting back together. I just wanted to tell you the truth. I owed you."

"So you don't want to be with me?"

"Yeah, but . . . this is happening way too fast. It's a lot of pressure." She pressed her hand to her forehead. "I need time to think. There are all these feelings I need to sort through. It's too much."

"Okay." He hugged her. "I'll be here when you're ready."

Karina wrapped her arms around him and relaxed. When would her brain and her heart finally make peace?

CHAPTER THIRTY-EIGHT

At two in the morning, Karina rolled around in bed, unable to sleep.

What vital information was she missing? Love shouldn't be this complicated. Ian accepted her for who she was; he'd proven it multiple times. And now he was willing to forgive her and start over. She should be jumping at the chance, not cowering in fear. Why was it so hard for her to be in love?

The answer came immediately: *Because your mom taught you love was a weakness, and you witnessed firsthand what it turned her into.* Was love worth the risks? She picked up her phone from the nightstand and called her mom.

As soon as she answered, Karina blurted, "Are you really happy with Bob?"

"It's late, Karina," her mom whispered. "Why are you calling me at this hour?"

"Answer the question."

"Of course I am."

"But you never wanted to get married. You went from studying to be a paralegal to being a housewife and stay-at-home mom. How does that happen? Why would you give that up for a man after you warned me so many times not to fall in love, not to depend on others? Don't you miss who you used to be?"

Her mom sucked in a breath. Karina's heart pounded in her chest.

"Hold on a moment," her mom said.

There was a shuffling sound, then a door shutting and then, nothing. Karina glanced at her phone to make sure her mom hadn't hung up. They were still connected. She pressed the phone back to her ear and waited.

Her mom sighed. "I was a bitter, lonely woman when I told you those things. I wanted you to grow up to not need anyone, so you wouldn't be disappointed when no one came to help you. But it was never how I felt."

Karina rubbed her forehead. "What do you mean? You lied to me?"

"Not intentionally. I wanted to believe those things, to be okay being a single mother and a modern woman, but I always wished deep down for a good man to come along and take the burden off."

"Okay, so . . . what you're saying is that you *wanted* to get married and be a housewife? What about being a paralegal?"

"Válgame, mija, tonight you're full of questions. What happened? Why did you call?"

"This man I told you about—he makes me feel weak when I'm supposed to be strong. Or maybe it's the other way around; I don't know. I believed all the stuff you fed me, and now you're telling me it's a lie. What am I supposed to do with that, huh? I'm supposed to forget everything you taught me?"

"Is that why you broke up with him, because of what I said?"

"Yes, Mom! You really messed with my head. Tell me the truth."

"It's not that easy. I did some things I'm ashamed of—"

"And you think I haven't? I lied to this man, to get him to forget me. And now he's willing to give me a second chance, and I don't know if I'm strong enough to be with him. Tell me, what am I supposed to do?"

"Do you love him?"

"Yes! So much. And it scares me."

Her mom blew a breath. "If you want to be with this man, then be with him. There's nothing wrong with that."

"How could you tell me this now after you programmed me for years to be my own person, to not depend on anyone but myself?"

"You can still be that. A man won't change you unless you let him. And you are so strong. Stronger than me."

"Okay, now you're freaking me out. This isn't my mother I'm talking to. This is some alien creature. It's all backwards. I need to know what's going on."

"Oh, Karina. I'm so sorry." Her mom started sobbing, and it was a few moments before she could talk. "The truth is . . . the truth . . ." She took a deep breath. "I always wanted to be a wife and a mother, ever since I was little. Your father came along, and I wanted to marry him, so I got pregnant to force his hand, but he didn't believe you were his. Then my parents threw me out, and I had no one. Well, no, that's not true. I had some help, but everyone turned their back on me when I became too inconvenient. And the thing of being a paralegal . . ." She sniffed and took a deep breath. "I needed to give you some stability. You were flunking out, wasting your time with boys. A friend of mine became a paralegal and married a lawyer. I thought I'd give it a try." She paused. "And it worked."

Karina dropped the phone. This was the great Debbie Cortés, the independent, strong woman she'd always looked up to? No wonder Karina had turned out so messed up. Pushing everyone away because of the way her mom made her.

Like her first friend, Luisa, back in kindergarten. It was at her fifth birthday party that Karina first realized her family wasn't the norm. As soon as her mom picked her up from the party and they were inside the car, Karina blurted, "Where's my dad?"

Her mom froze. "Why are you asking that?"

"Luisa says everyone has a dad, so where is he?"

Her mom looked toward the house, alarmed. Karina thought she would yell at everyone inside, but she put the car in gear and drove away.

"He's back in Puerto Rico," her mom said.

Good, she knew where he was. "Can we call him later and tell him to come? That way I can show him to Luisa."

Her mom gripped the steering wheel. "No."

"Why not?"

"I shouldn't have let you go to that party. What did they tell you?"

"Luisa's dad said some kids don't have dads, but they were sad for me and gave me hugs." Her face crumpled. "Is it bad that I don't have a dad?"

"Maldita sea esa gente entrometía." Her mom slapped the steering wheel.

Uh-oh. Her mom spoke Spanish only when she was really mad. Had Karina said something wrong?

"I didn't think I'd have to tell you this so soon," her mom said, "but it's better for you to know. Your dad wants nothing to do with us. He's a coward. Some men are like that. Don't worry about it. You don't need a dad. In fact, you don't need anyone."

Karina bit her lip. "I don't?"

"What have I always taught you? Learn to do things on your own, because Mommy won't always be there to help you. Isn't that what we've always talked about?"

Karina nodded. Her mom was always saying that whenever she asked for help. But Karina wished her mom would help her, or at least teach her. It was sometimes hard to know what to do.

"So my dad won't come?"

"No."

Her shoulders drooped. "Is he angry with me?"

"It has nothing to do with you. He doesn't want to be a dad, so just pretend he doesn't exist."

But he did exist. He just didn't want to meet her. "That's why everyone looked so sad."

"You shouldn't care about what other people think. Not having a dad is nothing to feel sad about. It means you have a strong mom who does the job of two people. That's what you say if anyone asks: 'My mom doesn't need my dad, and neither do I.'"

Her mom *was* strong. She could win a fight with anyone.

"What about abuelos? Luisa has two abuelas and two abuelos. Do I have any?"

"Mierda." She pulled at her hair. "No, Karina, you don't have any grandparents or any other family but me. They're bad people, and I don't want you to ask about them ever again."

Karina wanted to know more but stayed quiet. If her mom said they were bad, then they were bad. Karina didn't need them. She had her mom, and that should be enough. But then why did she feel like crying?

"Luisa's dad said not everyone was lucky enough to have a big family."

"Ay, por favor. Having a big family isn't as great as he makes it. There are always fights and too many people to please. Being alone is better. You don't have to worry about anyone else or end up disappointed. Other people will always let you down. Believe me, I should know. They want their money back or something in return. In life, you have to learn to stand up on your own two feet and be strong."

"Then I should learn to make a piñata. Luisa's dad made her one. It was so cool; there was so much candy!"

"Why waste time making one when you can buy one? Or even better, give the kids as much candy as they want. Piñatas are a dumb tradition anyway."

"Can we buy a flan? Luisa's abuela said she'd make me one."

"Esta gente." Mom shook her head. "Tell you what. We'll go to the store right now and buy a flan. You don't need anyone else to make you one."

Mom liked the flan, but Karina didn't. This was Luisa's favorite dessert? Ice cream was so much better.

When Karina got to school on Monday, Luisa had told everyone Karina didn't have a dad. Some kids looked at her with pity, while others made fun of her. Karina told them what her mom had said, that they were strong and didn't need a dad.

"And piñatas are not that special," Karina said to Luisa. "I can buy one or hand out candy. I don't need a dad for that."

Luisa pouted. "Why do you have to be so mean? I told my dad to make you one, and he said he would."

That's nice. But the way he'd looked at her . . .

"Aren't you listening? I don't need your dad or anyone else. I'll prove it. I'll bring a piñata tomorrow, and we'll all have candy."

She did, and the other kids loved it. But Luisa had never invited her to her house again.

"Karina?" Her mom's voice through the phone brought her back to the present. "Are you still there?"

Karina wiped her face and pressed the phone to her ear. "Why didn't you tell me this before? How could you let me leave when you knew . . . ?"

"You were too young and . . . I thought you'd hate me. You were always so angry."

"How could I not be angry? You became someone else right in front of my eyes. I thought Bob was controlling you. Turns out it was you controlling *him*."

"Don't say that. I may have manipulated the process, but I've grown to love him. He's a good man."

"Does he know?"

"No. And don't you dare tell him any of this."

Karina shook her head. "I guess I know where the liar in me comes from. Great job of raising me, Debbie."

"I did the best I could. You don't know—"

"How hard it was. Yeah, yeah. I do. You've told me my entire life."

"Can I give you some advice?" Mom asked.

"Why would I take any more advice from you? You ruined me. There are people in my life who treated me like family, and all I did was keep my distance because who needs family anyway? This is what you did to me. And Ian—"

"Is that his name?"

"He loves me. I have no idea why, but he does. And these ideas you put in my head—they're too much a part of me to switch off just because all of a sudden it turns out they're all a bunch of bullshit."

"I'm so sorry, Karina. Will you ever forgive me?"

"I don't know. I need time to process everything. Thanks for . . . thanks for telling me the truth."

CHAPTER THIRTY-NINE

Can you come over today? Lacey texted the next morning. *I need help with a new cookie.*

Karina gripped her phone as she read the message. The conversation with her mom had left her with a lack of sleep and a hole in her heart, but here was a reminder that someone cared, that she was needed. She threw on a pair of jeans and a T-shirt and drove to Lacey's condo, gorging on Perky Cookies on the way. The last time she'd been there, they'd worked at the commercial kitchen.

She walked up to the penthouse. Lacey was still in her pajamas, light-pink silk ones with a white bathrobe loose around her. "I didn't expect you so early." She gave Karina a once-over. "Did something happen?"

Karina threw herself into her arms and wept. Without another word, Lacey pulled her into the apartment, shut the door, and held her while she cried. The remaining pregnancy hormones in Karina's system were wreaking havoc on her emotions, but maybe it was time to finally let them out.

When she was calm enough to speak, she asked, "Do you really see me as your sister?"

"You know I do."

"Apparently, I don't. I don't know what's real anymore."

Lacey led her in and told her to sit while she made them coffee. The first sip warmed Karina enough to say, "I'm sorry for doubting you, for pushing you away, for not letting you in, for betraying you, for not trusting you, for everything."

Lacey took her hand. "Thank you for that. My uncle and I always sensed this resistance in you, which was understandable after what you went through with your mother, but we knew deep down you cared about us. That's why we never put too much pressure on you. We were sad when you didn't come to the funeral and moved out shortly afterward, but you were always so independent . . ."

"I thought you were just being nice because you felt sorry for me."

"We did sympathize, of course, but we saw someone who was hungry for love, and we had enough to give, so we did."

Karina's chest ached. All that love, wasted. Roy had given her a job even though she was still a minor, hadn't fired her when she couldn't cook and instead had made the meals himself, had treated her like a daughter. Like Lacey. And Lacey had confided in her, through her divorce and her early struggles with the company, and made her a trusted employee in her new venture. Karina had been so blind, but she wouldn't be anymore.

"Last night," Karina said, "I learned some things I can't wrap my head around. I see how different my life would've turned out if I'd been able to see the truth staring me in the face. It's so surreal." She told Lacey every truth she'd ever hidden, from what had truly happened with her mom to the abortion to Ian wanting a second chance.

Lacey put an arm around her. "Thank you for confiding in me. It means a lot for you to trust me this way."

Karina wiped her face. "Okay, enough sadness. What's this new cookie you need help with?"

"Oh." Lacey straightened. "I don't know if now's the right time to make them."

"I need this, Lacey. Please. I want to help."

"Well . . . it's a pregnancy cookie. To help stay strong and fight morning sickness. Inspired by you, actually."

"Me? Oh. Right. You correctly suspected I was pregnant."

"But now you lost it, and I had no idea, and I don't want you to feel uncomfortable—"

"It's okay, Lacey." Karina patted her hand. "I'm fine. It was the right choice for me, and I have no regrets. Plus I'm all for helping fight morning sickness. That shit is awful. Did you know it's more of an all-day sickness?"

Lacey laughed. "Okay. Let's get to work."

Karina followed her to the kitchen, and Lacey explained her plan. She wanted to make a cookie that incorporated some of the top foods to eat while pregnant: banana for potassium, dried apricots for iron, sunflower seeds for vitamin E, and ginger for morning sickness.

"Banana and apricots?" Karina asked. "You think that goes together?"

"We won't know until we try."

They debated whether to use fresh or dried ginger and settled on dried for the first batch. As they mixed the ingredients and prepared the dough, Karina's body filled up with that warm feeling of family and belonging, and she leaned into it, letting it seep into the cold spaces she'd neglected for so long.

After the cookies baked and cooled, the kitchen smelled like cinnamon and banana bread. Karina and Lacey gazed at each other and took their first bites.

"They're better than I thought," Karina said. "You can hardly taste the apricots. And the seeds give that crunchiness that most Singular Cookies have."

Lacey chewed slowly. "I don't taste the ginger. Do you?"

Karina took another bite. "Not really."

"Perhaps the fresh ginger will make the difference." She scribbled on the recipe.

Karina finished the cookie and took another one. "You got another winner, Lacey. Pregnant people will love it. But what about us nonpregnant folks? Are we allowed to eat them too?"

"Of course. Everyone needs a mother." Lacey snapped her fingers. "Motherly—that's what we'll call it." More scribbling.

The piece of cookie stuck in her throat, and she struggled to swallow it. Karina stared at the Motherly. Her mom's words from last night came back. Her lies. Her betrayal. She put the cookie aside. "Why don't I make some more coffee?"

As she worked, she thought about her life and the choices that had led her to this moment. In this internal audit, there were three critical nonconformities:

> Ever since Luisa's birthday party in kindergarten and Karina's conversation with her mom on the way home, she'd pushed people away instead of accepting their help, afraid they were only being nice because they felt sorry for her.
> Being second best to Jason when she was fifteen had made her lock up her feelings in a box so she wouldn't be hurt again.
> Her mom choosing Bob over her had made her feel worthless and unlovable, so she'd stopped believing she'd ever find anyone who'd accept her for who she was.

Karina had implemented some corrective actions in her life by opening up her feelings, accepting help, and learning to trust. Now she needed to believe she was worthy of love. Could she do it? Maybe. But she couldn't do it alone.

When the coffee was ready, they took their mugs and the plate of cookies to the balcony and sat to enjoy the view. The palm trees swayed in the breeze, and yachts traveled across the Indian River beyond. After the emotional hurricane Karina had gone through these past two days, she was ready to rebuild, but with different materials this time. It was time for an emergency course correction, for her to finally take Natalie's psychobabble advice.

"You mentioned one time you were seeing a therapist. Did it help?"

If Lacey was surprised by the question, she didn't show it. "Yes. I still see her. After what happened with Daniel, I didn't trust myself in another relationship. I was so scared of getting hurt again. It made me see things that weren't there, like when I thought you were trying to steal Dwight away, remember?"

"I thought love was making you crazy."

Lacey laughed. "Love does make you crazy, but it also brings out the best in you, like me going to therapy so I can be a better partner for Dwight. I have a lot of baggage, and he doesn't need to carry it too. He and I went through a rough patch where I thought we wouldn't last."

"Was it because of me? I'm sorry."

Lacey dismissed her worry with a wave. "You were part of it, I won't deny it. Dwight was angry at me because I told you about us. But there were other issues. At one point, I thought his friends from church were influencing him against me. By the questions they asked, I could tell they didn't think I was a suitable match for him— me being older, divorced, not to mention his boss." She sighed. "But Dr. Brooks kept telling me to concentrate on the facts and not my wild theories. To give Dwight space to figure things out and let him come to me. And he did. Now I need to keep calm and not get ahead of myself." Lacey squeezed Karina's knee. "Are you considering therapy for yourself?"

Karina stared at her lap. "I want to make it work with Ian, but I don't know how. I'm so scared of messing up again. You think therapy would be good for me?"

"I think therapy is good for everyone."

"Is it hard?"

"You have to be honest with yourself and put in the work."

"And do you think your relationship with Dwight will last?"

"I hope so. You never know what the future holds. I only know that I love him and I want to be with him. That's enough for me."

Karina slumped her shoulders. "I wish it was the same for me."

"Try the therapy. It will help you sort out your feelings for Ian and your mom."

"Oh God. Don't get me started on her. I'm so angry." Karina raked her fingers through her hair.

"She's your mom." Lacey stroked her back. "It would be good for you to have a relationship with her. Do you want that?"

"I don't know. Maybe."

"Think about it. I can give you Dr. Brooks' card. Or would you like me to make you an appointment?"

"Will it be expensive?"

"Our company health insurance has coverage, and she also offers payment on a sliding scale, based on your income. You have nothing to lose."

* * *

On Tuesday afternoon, Karina sat in an armchair facing Dr. Brooks, a middle-aged Black woman with an easy smile and kind eyes.

Karina tucked her hands under her legs to keep them from shaking. Was she really ready to expose her flaws and dirty deeds to a stranger? Tough-girl Karina didn't think so. She wanted out. But K had been waiting for this chance since she fell in love with Ian, and fear would not get in her way anymore.

"Tell me, Karina, what brings you here?" Dr. Brooks sat comfortably, one leg crossed over the other, hands on top, ready to listen. Her welcoming smile was reassuring.

"Where do I start?" Karina expelled a breath. "My mom raised me to not depend on anyone but myself." She talked briefly about her history with her mom. "After I left home, I thought I was fine. I enjoyed being single, not having anyone to answer to. But then I fell in love and ruined things and . . . ugh." She covered her face. "He's willing to give me a second chance, but I don't know how to be with him, and it . . . it scares me."

"This is a good start. You're aware you have a problem, and you're being honest about it. Tell me, why do you think you're scared?"

"I always thought that love changes you, and it does, but not always for the worse. I see that now. But if I go back to him and try to have an actual relationship, where I talk to him about my feelings, I'd be vulnerable. Exposed. What if he gets to know the real me and hates it? What if he prefers someone else, like my"—she swallowed—"like my mom did?"

Dr. Brooks nodded. "Do you want to repair your relationship with your mother?"

"I don't know. It would be nice, but so much time has passed . . . I wouldn't even know where to start. Maybe it's too late anyway."

Dr. Brooks leaned forward. "It's never too late to heal, Karina. And you seem like a wounded person to me. You deserve to love and be loved. Will you let me help you?"

Karina stared into Dr. Brooks's kind eyes. Wounded, that's how she felt. Her soul was like cookie dough that had been battered for too long. But after a period of rest, that mass took shape, baked to transform into an end product that was worth the initial mess, that you were proud to share with the world. Before you got there, you had to continuously improve on the process, through trial and error. That was Karina: a work in progress, undefined but with potential.

You're capable of more than you think.

She'd never find out what she was capable of until she tried.

CHAPTER FORTY

A week later, Karina stood in Roy's foyer. He and Lacey had invited her to celebrate the Fourth of July with them and the rest of their family.

She hadn't been to his house since she'd moved out nine years ago. Everything looked exactly as she'd left it. Even Anne's room on the first floor was intact. It brought tears to her eyes as she and Roy passed it on the way to the backyard. He noticed and put his arm around her.

"She's still with us, you know," he said.

She stopped walking and faced him. "I'm sorry for not being there for you. I couldn't handle death. I didn't know why her passing affected me so much when I'd known her only a few months. As with all emotions that scare me—because that's what it was, a huge case of fear—I ran when I should've stayed. Do you forgive me?"

"There's nothing to forgive, kiddo. You're here now; that's what's important. Come outside."

The backyard teemed with kids of all ages and some adults playing football. Karina could make out Roy's three brothers with their wives, children, and grandchildren. One big happy family. Small groups clustered on picnic blankets, watching the game or chatting, drinking beers and soaking in the sun.

Lacey's parents—who Karina knew only from afar—wrapped her in hugs, followed by Lacey. Karina might not be related, but they sure were making her feel welcomed.

After handing Roy the packages of hot dogs and buns she'd brought, she grabbed a beer from the icebox inside the covered deck and filled up a plate with some of the patriotic goodies set up at the buffet table—a taco salad flag and red-white-and-blue potato and fruit salads. One item stood out—a tray of Motherly Cookies. Lacey had probably brought a batch to get her family's opinion. Karina added one to her plate, then joined Lacey at the picnic table.

"How's the therapy going?" Lacey asked.

"I've only had two sessions, but it's going well. She's helping me categorize my emotions, things like that. I knew I was a mess, but not like this." Karina laughed. "It's—"

Lacey's mom, Elizabeth, joined them. Karina clamped up, not wanting to share more in front of someone who was practically a stranger, but Lacey waited for her to continue. If they were going to treat each other like sisters, Karina could speak openly in front of Lacey's mom. That was what families usually did.

"Um, it's going to take time to sort through everything. We'll see. But I've found the therapy useful, at least."

"Be patient," Lacey said. "You're in excellent hands."

"Are you also seeing Dr. Brooks?" Elizabeth asked. When Lacey nodded, Elizabeth added, "She's brilliant. Dr. Brooks helped me with a bout of depression I suffered while going through early meno-pause." She slapped Lacey's hand. "Do you remember how horrible that time was for me?"

"She had frequent mood swings," Lacey told Karina, tipping her head to her mom. "It was scary, but we worked through it together, didn't we?" She gazed at her mom and squeezed her hand. "The three of us attended a few sessions to help her cope. I am *not* looking for-ward to when it happens to me."

The two of them laughed, both looking so comfortable with each other; no strain in their conversation, no awkward silences. It seemed like they could tell each other everything, without shame. Was a rela-tionship like this possible for Karina and her own mom?

The doorbell rang. "That must be Dwight." Lacey rushed inside and appeared a few minutes later with him, holding hands.

It was disconcerting to see him outside of work. He wore a polo shirt and shorts on top of skinny, hairy legs. Too much for Karina to see of her boss. Lacey's mom greeted him warmly, as if she already considered him part of the family.

After saying hi to Roy and Lacey's dad outside by the grill, he sat with them, telling them about the traffic jam he'd suffered through on his way here. He kept hold of Lacey's hand and his shoulders relaxed, an easy smile on his lips. It was like being in front of a different person. Nice to know he could unwind now and then.

Karina finished everything on her plate except for the Motherly. She wanted to savor it. The ginger was more prominent this time, but that maternal feeling of comfort was still there, more so today than last week, now that she was here surrounded by family. "Have you tried Lacey's newest creation, Dwight?" She held the cookie up for him.

"Not yet. But she told me all about it." He went over to the buffet table and grabbed one, taking a bite. "Mmm. Delicious."

"They're fabulous," Elizabeth said. "Maybe Lacey should've studied food science instead. She's so creative with recipes."

"Well . . ." Dwight finished chewing. "Food science is more than just creating a tasty recipe. We have to design something functional that can withstand processing and has a stable shelf life. That'll be the next stage in the development of this particular cookie in order to add it to our product line."

Elizabeth nodded, though she seemed confused. Lacey asked her to help her with a salad, and they both went inside.

Dwight shook his head. "I hate it when people think my profession is like being a chef."

Karina laughed. "If you only bake cookies at home, it's hard to know what it takes to get them into a supermarket. Lacey didn't know at the beginning either."

"But she learned, and look where she's at now. And you too."

"Yeah." Karina finished the cookie. "I was wrong about you."

Dwight frowned.

"When you started working at Singular, I thought you were so arrogant, criticizing everyone else's job, acting as if you knew better, but now I know you only want to make everything the best it can be. And you make me want to be like that too. Thank you for seeing potential in me. I hope I don't let you down."

Dwight seemed taken aback but smiled. "You won't. I'm glad you changed your mind about me. I think we work well together, and I'm excited to have you as my partner in crime in QA."

They feasted on burgers, hot dogs, steaks, and an assortment of side salads. Karina hadn't celebrated this holiday properly since she lived with her mom. She'd gone alone downtown to the festival held every year; her friends were always away with their families. But today she was surrounded by love and laughter, comfort food and people to share it with. She pictured herself joining her mom, Bob, and Lily. Would it feel as good as this? And what about Ian—could she see him there too? It was a fuzzy image, full of resentment and fear of opening up her present to her past.

Karina ate more than she should, which was an accomplishment for her. She almost declined dessert, but who could say no to ice cream?

At around five, they drove downtown to the festival, where more food, music, and arts and crafts awaited them. Karina kept on the lookout for Ian. How had he celebrated today? Had he spent the day alone at his house, or at the beach, or maybe with another mechanic or even Rosa? Karina hadn't seen him at work, what with being stuck in the office all day with Dwight, making the last preparations for the inspection next week. Her heart longed to see him, but her brain wasn't ready to face him yet.

At nine, the huge firework extravaganza began. As Karina gazed at the sky, her phone vibrated in her pocket. It was a text from her mom—a photo of another fireworks display, Cinderella's Castle in the foreground. Karina's eyes watered. As a child, her mom had taken her every year to Magic Kingdom on this date. She must've continued the tradition with Lily. Under the photo she'd written, *Wish you were here. Happy 4th of July!* ♥ *Mom.*

Maybe that fuzzy image could one day become reality. Karina took a photo of the sparkly display above and sent it to her mom.

* * *

Two days later, Karina and her friends were having their first-ever monthly sleepover at their new house, which they had moved into last weekend. Marisa was officially their roommate.

There were still boxes left to unpack around the dining table, where they sat eating takeout from a local Puerto Rican restaurant. After eating so many of Cordelia's leftovers, Karina had wanted to give her friends a treat. And since she still couldn't cook, this was the best she could do. The move last week had left them exhausted, so they wanted to celebrate properly and fill their new living space with friends, food, and laughter.

Karina piled rice, red beans, fried pork, and tostones on her plate. She bit into the fried green plantain, relishing it. Meanwhile, Marisa spooned white rice into a measuring cup. This was her new ritual since joining Weight Watchers to lose those last five pounds, and if it made her happy, who was Karina to judge?

"I have news." Natalie put her fork down and smiled. "I am now the new human resources manager for Singular Cookies, Inc."

"What?" Karina emptied her mouth. "Since when?"

"Since today. You know how Lacey was always mentioning she needed to hire someone? Well, I did some research and found out that most people in human resources have a psychology degree, and it was like a completely new world opened up. So we better pass this inspection and start the expansion, because I'll be in charge of the new hires."

"Let's drink to that." They clinked glasses of rum and Coke.

"I'm opening an Etsy shop." Marisa slapped her hand over her mouth.

"You are?" Karina asked.

"I've been thinking about it, but after listening to Natalie, I've decided." She hit the tabletop. "I'm doing it. Now that I have a back-yard, I can get more professional with my shibori dyeing."

More clinking of glasses.

Karina stared at Cordelia. "And you? Are you finally taking those business classes?"

"I . . ." She shifted in her seat. "Okay, I know you're all going to hate me, but I'm not doing it." Cordelia raised her hand to stop their retorts. "I know, I know, but hear me out." She took a deep breath. "I've realized I don't want to be a professional chef anymore. I want to start a family and dedicate myself full-time to my children."

"So you'll quit Singular?" Karina asked.

Cordelia nodded. "Eventually. But that won't change anything. We'll still have our sleepovers and parties at my house."

Karina's first thought was, *What a waste of potential*, but if this was what Cordelia really wanted, she needed to respect that. "I'm sorry I was so judgmental of you guys. I shouldn't have held you to this impossible standard when I'm a worse mess-up than anybody. Thank you for sticking by me all these years."

Her friends exchanged glances.

"Thank you for that," Cordelia said, "but this new Karina is hard to get used to, sorry."

Marisa reached across the table for Karina's hand. "We knew you were looking out for us. Even if it was annoying at times."

"Super annoying," Natalie said. "But it looks like the therapy is helping."

"It is." Karina tipped her face to the ceiling. "I still can't believe I'm going to therapy. Me of all people. But I still don't know what to do about Ian." Karina sighed. "On my last session, Dr. Brooks brought up couple's counseling, but I don't know if he'll go for that. It seems like way too much work."

"He won't mind," Marisa said. "He loves you. He said he'd wait until you were ready."

"What if I'm never ready?"

"You're overthinking it," Natalie said. "Just—"

"Don't think about it, I know." Karina said. "This didn't work out for me too well the last time."

"Or maybe it was exactly what you needed. If it weren't for me, you would've never given Ian a chance. So listen to me now: stop looking for reasons why it may not work and focus on the positive. What is the worst that can happen if you don't get back with him?"

Her heart screamed out the answer. "I'll never know real love?"

"And which is the worst-case scenario—being with him or not being with him?"

Karina rubbed her sweaty palms on her jeans. It was getting hard to breathe. Therapy had helped her realize she always panicked when she had to face her emotions. She closed her eyes and took deep breaths. "I honestly don't know. Both are scary."

"Stop worrying so much, Karina," Cordelia said. "The important thing is that you love each other, and love conquers all."

"In fairy tales, maybe. In the real world, there are many ways for me to screw this up." Karina sighed. "Wow. Look at me. Now who's the one who can't shut up about a man?"

They laughed.

"But . . . if it doesn't work out with him, I can count on all of you, right?"

"Claro, nena," Cordelia said. "Chicks before dicks, always." She winced. "Well, except for Charlie's. Sorry."

CHAPTER FORTY-ONE

On Tuesday morning, Karina performed another walk-through to ensure everything was set for the inspection tomorrow. She found the fucking door near the mechanics' break room unlocked, again. Damn it. Hadn't she gone through this last month?

Last month. Did she do the walk-through in June? A sinking feeling settled in her stomach. June had been full of drama, with the abortion and her mom's bombshell and beginning therapy. She'd done their monthly program audit following Dwight's schedule, but she was pretty sure she'd only done the one walk-through.

Was this bad? It had been her idea to do it monthly from now on. Knowing Dwight, he'd probably added that detail to their procedure. But if she didn't find anything critical, maybe they could get away with it. She'd be extra thorough to make sure she caught everything.

In production, the guys were still fussing with their hairnets occasionally, but that was a continual problem. She gave them a quick reminder and moved on. No issues in the packaging area, cafeteria, or bathrooms. Next stop, the warehouse.

As she closed in on the storage area for the oatmeal, she noticed some oats on the floor toward the back. She knelt to inspect the bags. One of them had a tear. How long had it been like that? She moved it and inspected the others. Two more had tears. Fuck. This was bad. If they'd been using broken bags for the cookies, they could be contaminated. She ran to Scott's office and found him at his computer.

"Did you notice some oatmeal bags are broken?" she asked.

"Huh?" he said, without looking up.

She tugged at his arm. "Come with me." She led him to the area and showed him the bags. "How long have these been here?"

"A month?"

"Did you check them when you received them?"

His face turned serious, as if she'd offended him. "I always check them."

"But did you document it?"

At this, he looked doubtful. Karina didn't have time for his incompetence. "Show me the receiving checklist."

They went back to his office and looked at the checklist for that specific oatmeal lot. Everything was documented fully, and there were no observations that the bags were affected. At least he had done some things right. But that meant they had a bigger problem.

"Could there be rats?" she asked. "Please tell me there are no rats."

"I'm sure there aren't any."

"Call Dwight. And Lacey. Roy too." She pushed her fingers through her hair. "Fuck. I messed up big-time." She dropped down into Scott's chair. So much for being able to handle this promotion. She knew she wasn't cut out for this.

When they arrived, Karina explained the situation. "I don't know how long they've been like this. I . . ." She swallowed. "I forgot to do the walk-through last month." She dropped her head. "I'm sorry."

Dwight cleared his throat. "Okay. Let's not panic. Only three bags are broken, right? Roy, do we have documentation that shows that the guys checked the bags before use?"

"No. But we do check them and wouldn't have used them if they'd been like this."

"Darn it. Without documentation, there's no proof. This could cost us the inspection."

He looked the angriest she had ever seen him. He'd worked so hard to get them here, only for her to mess it up.

Lacey took him by the arm. "What can we do? There has to be a way to fix this."

"We can investigate and write a report, but I don't know if it will be enough. It all depends on the inspector."

Karina wiped her hand against her leg. "I'm so sorry, Dwight. This is all my fault. I let my personal life interfere with my work. Some internal auditor I am, missing an audit. I literally had *one* job."

"No, Karina." Lacey squeezed her shoulder. "Don't blame yourself. This is my fault. I shouldn't have rushed to schedule this inspection. Dwight was right. If we lose the company because of my mistake . . ."

"I'm the quality assurance manager," Dwight said. "If there's anyone to blame, it's me. The inspection is my responsibility. And I had to be so meticulous that I had to add this monthly walk-through to the procedure when it wasn't necessary. I could've just written we do it regularly."

"Don't be so hard on yourself," Roy said. "We should've been documenting the checking of the ingredients. That's on me."

"And what about me?" Scott said. "I'm the warehouse manager. I know you all think I suck at my job, but I take it seriously and do the best I can."

He looked so miserable. For the first time, Karina saw him as a human being and not an incompetent fool. "It's okay, Scott." She sighed. "All this work just to fail in the end. If we don't pass, I swear I'll go back to being a maid. No sense in pretending to be something I'm not."

Roy clapped, startling them. "Now wait just a minute. No one is abandoning ship. We came this far, and we'll face the consequences together. The last few months, I have seen team work and productivity improve thanks to those monthly trainings I was so opposed to. We are stronger together. Whatever happens, we'll get through it."

Lacey rolled her shoulders. "My uncle is right. We're a team. A family. And families stick together."

* * *

They came up with a game plan.

Karina finished the walk-through and documented the nonconformities and corrective actions. Scott threw away the torn bags, cleaned up the area, and removed the bags from inventory. He and Karina checked the area for rat droppings or any other sign of an infestation. They found none.

Dwight and Roy were in charge of interviewing the dough preparers, revising the checklist to add their observations on the ingredient packaging, and retraining them.

Lacey contacted the oatmeal vendor to report the damage. She also contacted the pest control company to send a representative to come do an urgent check of the traps and see if there was any rodent activity.

Karina helped Dwight collect all the paperwork for the oatmeal and the production logs that had used that particular lot. Then it was up to Dwight to write a report detailing all of their actions and their plan moving forward to prevent this sort of thing from happening again.

The guys at her training had said that the most important thing was to document everything, that as long as they had a logical justification, they'd be fine. Karina hoped that was true.

* * *

By the end of the day, she was exhausted. Dwight was with the pest control inspector and Karina was at her desk, finalizing her audit report. She'd asked George to call a meeting of the maintenance team to make it clear why it was so important to keep that door locked.

"Please, guys, I beg you, leave the lock on," she'd said. "I know it's easier to leave it unlocked, but it's a security risk. Anyone could come in and put poison on the cookies; who knows? I know it sounds unlikely, but these are the type of things that could make us fail. Okay?"

They'd nodded and promised, but Karina was sure it had been for nothing. The only saving grace had been Ian's reassuring gaze, but one mechanic on board wouldn't make a difference.

A knock on the door made her jump. The sight of Ian again caused her heart to continue on its own.

"Is Dwight around?" he asked.

"He's out with the pest control guy. What's up?"

"I wanted to give him this maintenance report he asked for."

"You can leave it on his desk."

Ian did, then he stuffed his hands into his pockets and stared at her. "Anything else?"

"Actually, that was only an excuse." He rubbed his neck. "I didn't have a chance to talk to you earlier. How are you?"

"Busy." She shuffled papers. "There's huge chaos. We have a deviation, and we can only write a report. We're hoping the inspector's not too strict or we're screwed."

"Diablo."

"I know. Dwight's on the verge of a nervous breakdown."

Ian nodded. "When I asked how you were, I wasn't talking about work."

It seemed the time for this conversation had arrived, whether or not she was ready. He pulled up a chair. "Did you decide yet?"

"You were supposed to give me time to think."

"It's been almost three weeks."

"I know, I know." She ran a hand through her hair. "With the inspection, I hardly have time."

He slowly shook his head. "My family thinks I should move on, that you are an obsession for me."

"You didn't tell them about—"

"No, of course not." He paused. "I need to know what's going through your head. Talk to me."

She took a deep breath. "I started going to a therapist. Can you believe it?"

"You have? That's great. I'm proud of you."

Her heart fluttered. She wasn't damaged goods to him, at least. Not yet. "She's been helping me figure things out, but . . . there's still a lot for me to work through."

He frowned. "And you want to keep waiting?"

"Look, Ian." She leaned forward, elbows on the desk, hands clasped to her chin. "There's a lot of stuff you don't know, about my mom and how I was raised. It's going to take a lot of time for me to process it all and undo the damage. I don't know if I should be in a romantic relationship right now. Do you understand?"

"I understand you still don't trust me. Why can't I be there for you and help you through this?"

She wanted help, especially his, a calm harbor from the ravaging storm inside her. "We may have to go to couple's counseling. Would you be willing to do that?"

"Why do you ask me that? Of course I would." He moved to the edge of the chair and placed his hands on the desk. "Don't you get it yet, K? I love you."

"You said you pictured us being married and having kids. What if I never want that? Do you really want a relationship without that kind of future?"

He sighed. "I know that on paper we don't make sense, but who can predict the future? I was with someone I was sure—*sure*—was the one, and then *poof.*" He blew on his fingers. "My feelings changed. I want to live in the now, be a rebel, be wild. Isn't that what you taught me?"

Who was this man? He was supposed to be the sensible one.

"All I know is that I was happy with you, and without you, I'm not," he said. "I want to be happy again."

"It wasn't all good."

"But when it was good, it was great. The fact that you're going to therapy means we'll have more good than bad. What's holding you back?"

"I'm scared, Ian. Scared it won't work out, scared it will, scared you won't love the real me. I'm a big glob of fear."

He opened his palm, inviting her to take it. She accepted. "I'm scared, too. But I love you, and that's all that matters to me. We'll never know what will happen if we don't try."

Karina stared at their entwined hands. She yearned to try, to find out if she could make him happy. But what if she messed up and broke his heart again? She didn't have the best track record. This chaos because of her negligence was proof.

"Remember when we talked about Marisa and you said some people like the drama?" she asked. "Is it really love, or are you addicted to the drama, like your sister?"

He scowled and removed his hand. "You think I want to be with you only because of the drama?"

"It's just a question."

"Do you love me?"

YES! "I, uh, I . . . care about you."

"You can't even say it."

"I'm better at showing it."

"¿En serio? Are you showing me love by rejecting me again when all I want is to love you?" He scratched his head. "¿Sabes qué?" The chair scraped against the floor as he stood. "I'm tired, Karina. I don't know how else to reassure you. If you want a relationship with me, it's up to you. I won't try to convince you anymore." With one last look, he turned to leave.

Her breath caught in her throat. She opened her mouth to yell for him to stop, to tell him she didn't want to lose him, but nothing came out. Ian stepped into the hallway and stopped short. "Sorry, Rosa. Didn't see you there."

Great. Rosa must've been snooping by the door. Sure enough, in she came with her bucket and mop a few seconds later.

Karina kept her gaze on her monitor while Rosa mopped. Rosa clicked her tongue.

"If you have something to say, say it," Karina said through clenched teeth.

"Stop giving that boy false hope and leave him alone. Now I see why he stopped being with Maribel."

She was about to say, *Maybe she doesn't like giving blow jobs,* but stopped short and sighed. "You're right, I should leave him alone. Problem is, my heart won't let me."

Rosa frowned, surprised, but then smiled and wagged her finger. "Ah, I was wrong about you. You're just a scared little girl in love." She gave her a quizzical look. "Want some advice? Listen to your heart and not your head. The heart is always right."

* * *

Karina went home, ducked under the covers, and tried not to think about the look on Ian's face or Rosa's words. The decision should be simple. Her heart wanted to be with Ian, so she should be with Ian. But the rest of her still couldn't let go of her fears.

303

Now she had not only the fear of not being able to make it work with Ian, but also the fear of losing him forever if she didn't make a decision. He was pressuring her, but maybe she needed some pressure to get rid of this fear once and for all. Or was it already too late?

Her heart ached.

It's okay, Heart. If it's not Ian, it'll be someone else. We're not alone. We have our friends, Roy, Lacey, and our job. We'll be okay.

Heart wasn't having it.

Karina grabbed the new cushion her mom had sent her. After their exchange on the Fourth of July, they'd continued texting. Karina had sent her a few photos of the new house, including her bedroom. Her mom hadn't known she still collected cushions, so she'd sent her this one. It had a photo of the two of them, back when Karina was around eight, posing with Woody on one of their trips to Disney's Hollywood Studios. There was no Bob or Lily in sight, no boys on the horizon, just Karina and her mom. Her heart fluttered.

Is this what you really want? Will calling her get you to calm down and leave me in peace? She picked up her phone and tapped her mom's number.

"My love, I'm so happy you called. How are you?"

"I'm okay." Karina paused. "I've been going to therapy."

"Is it helping?"

"Yeah." She gulped. "Thank you for the cushion. It's nice."

"It was the least I could do after . . . after everything." Her mom grunted. "What happened with Ian? Are you back together with him?"

"No. He . . . maybe he's not for me. I love him but . . . I should focus on my healing now. I'll only end up hurting him."

"Do you want my advice?"

"Okay."

Her mom sighed. Karina could picture her smiling. "Don't make the same mistakes I did. Don't lie to yourself about what you want. I spent so much time pretending to be someone I wasn't, ashamed of wanting an old-fashioned life in a modern world, and look where it got me. If I'd been honest, you would've been happy for me when I met Bob, because you would've known all along how I felt."

"Yeah." What would that have looked like? Having a father figure, playing with her sister, staying close to her mom. So much lost because of lies. She was tired of lying, of hiding her true feelings. It was time to let the whole truth come out.

Karina expelled a breath. "You broke my heart when you married Bob. I felt like you chose him over me, that he was more important . . ." Her voice broke. "I was rebellious to get your attention, and when I finally did, you let me leave. I felt so abandoned." Karina sobbed. "You abandoned me, Mom."

"I'm so sorry." Her mom was also crying. "I was so focused on holding on to Bob that I . . . I did neglect you. Having a baby takes all of your attention, and whenever I tried to reach out, you pushed me away. I didn't have the energy to deal with you. I'm sorry. I was your mother, and I failed you."

It had all been a misunderstanding, a lack of communication. Like Dr. Brooks always said, *Communication is key.*

"You're my daughter, and I love you. I've missed you so much. Will you ever forgive me?"

Her mom *did* love her. She hadn't chosen Bob and Lily over her; she'd gone down the path of least resistance because Karina had made it hard for her. It had been Karina's own stubbornness that had led to this pain.

"Yes, Mom. You messed up, but so did I."

Her mom's sobs made Karina lose it again. When she recovered, she continued, "Knowing you miss me is enough. You made the choices that made you happy, and I have to respect them, the same way other people respected the choices I've made."

"Oh, Karina, you don't know what it means to hear you say all these things." She sniffled. "I thought I lost you. I kept trying to reach you, but you—"

"I know."

"But now there's a path forward, yes?"

"It's going to take some time, Mom. But . . . I'm willing to try."

Light shone in the darkest corners of her being. It had been buried under all the anger and the hate, but now K was free, to love and trust again.

CHAPTER FORTY-TWO

After a good night's sleep, the best in a long time, Karina was ready to face what lay ahead: the inspection. She arrived early and headed to the bathroom for one last look in the mirror.

Her hair was gathered in a ponytail, for once perfectly styled and not wild around her head. Her outfit was a Marisa original—black dress pants and a sleeveless button-up blouse in a junk food pattern. This was more professional but still Karina: irreverent, unique, fun. And it gave her curves! Her feet were comfy in black ballerina slippers instead of her usual sneakers. Maybe it was time to move on from her slogan T-shirts.

The inspector's name was William Clemens, and with his bald head and walrus mustache, he looked like a sergeant ready for battle. Not a good omen. He set up his laptop on Dwight's desk, next to the binders with the procedures to audit.

"Here's how I work," the inspector told her and Dwight in a clipped tone. "I'll start with the walk-through to get familiar with your process and your people. Later, I'll go through the written procedures and finish the day by looking at the end-of-production cleaning and sanitation. Sound good?" He grabbed a notebook without waiting for an answer.

Karina and Dwight exchanged worried glances before leading the inspector into the production area, where Roy and Tyler joined them. The inspector asked them about the process and then headed into the mixing room.

They stood in a corner while William observed the guys weighing coffee powder, preparing a batch of the Perkys.

Keep your hands away from your face, keep your hands away from your face.

He asked each of the guys, "What are you doing there?" waiting for them to elaborate about every detail of their work. Then he asked them questions about hygiene, such as, "Do you know why it's important to wash your hands frequently?"

Karina wiped her own hands on her smock. Each of the three guys answered surprisingly well. To her ears, at least. The inspector's face was inscrutable. And they didn't touch their faces! She gave Tyler a thumbs-up. He'd done a great job replacing her.

In the packaging room, the sergeant asked Cordelia, "What is HACCP?"

Her eyes widened and she glanced at Karina. Karina tried to mouth the answer, but the inspector glanced sideways at her and she stopped.

Cordelia swallowed. "I don't know exactly what it stands for, but I know it's a written plan to help us determine safety risks and the best ways to control them."

Yes! Karina smiled at Dwight, then back at Cordelia. The inspector didn't look impressed and moved on to another packer, asking her to go through the metal detector checks.

As they moved through the plant, William commented here and there on things they could do differently. The suggestions were good, but would the fact that they weren't being carried out already count against them?

In the cafeteria, William interviewed Rosa about her job duties, and she went into minute detail, even sharing unwelcome information about how difficult it was to keep everything clean because some people didn't know how to throw their trash away. This elicited a small smile from William. As they continued on, Karina whispered, "Thank you," and Rosa beamed at her.

William insisted on visiting the offices, asking everyone about their job duties, even though some of the employees, like the accountant, didn't work directly with the cookies. But William still asked him about the certification program, and surprisingly, he knew the answer. Dwight had been so right about the training. If he hadn't been so adamant, they would've failed big-time.

Next stop: the maintenance shop. William had a lot of questions for George about how he managed work orders. As they walked around the shop, Karina caught Ian's eye and mock grimaced. He smiled and her heart leapt.

William stopped in front of Ian, leaning forward to read his name on his overalls. "Ian. Can you tell me what steps you take when you have to do a repair inside the processing area?"

Ian stuttered, but after taking a deep breath, he went through all the steps. Karina could've kissed him. She gave him two thumbs-up and he smiled, sending another bolt of joy to her heart.

They walked the perimeter outside the plant. William approached the exit door near the mechanics' break room.

Please be locked. Had her pleas worked?

William turned the knob, and Karina held her breath. The doorknob stopped rotating and there was a clicking sound.

He couldn't open it! Karina squeezed Dwight's arm, and he patted her hand. *She* had done this. It had been her audit and her suggestions that had made the others aware of what they'd been doing wrong, and they'd corrected themselves. Her hard work and dedication had paid off. Smart-ass Karina, who'd quit school because she found it a waste of time and never thought she'd amount to anything, had come a long way.

But she shouldn't celebrate just yet.

After lunch, William went through the written procedures, asking for records as he went. Karina kept a copy of the code in front of her, keeping track of their progress. Two procedures in, he found a section missing. Another procedure needed rewording. Some procedures needed more clarity; others were not thorough enough. How much would this cost them?

"Let me have the last three internal audit reports," William asked.

Dwight expelled a breath and handed them to him. "We had an issue with the last audit and the warehouse. I wrote a report about it."

William frowned and took the report without a word. Karina's leg shook.

"Hmm," was all he said after five minutes. Then, "So you missed one audit from your schedule. That will cost you. 'Say what you do and do as you say,' as we call it. But there's no guarantee you would've caught it on the previous audit, especially if the bags were hard to see." William tapped the paper. "You made a thorough investigation and found no real reason for concern." He finished reading and put the report aside. "I think you've handled everything as well as can be expected."

Dwight visibly relaxed, and Karina could breathe again. As long as they hadn't missed something huge, they should be okay.

Once William got through the procedures specifically for the certification program, the audit ran more smoothly. The rest of the procedures had been implemented since the start of operations and verified thoroughly during previous audits.

After he observed the final cleaning and sanitation in the production area, Roy, Dwight, and Karina took William to Lacey's office to hear the results of the inspection.

"First off," he said, "I'd like to commend you on all the effort you put into this. It shows. Small plants like yours struggle to manage the tasks required for certification. I still have to finish the report, but I think you're in good shape."

Dwight gasped. Karina felt all her muscles unclench. Roy slapped Dwight's back. Lacey said, "That's wonderful." She gifted the inspector an assortment of Singular Cookies as a thank-you for his work.

As soon as the auditor left, Dwight threw his arms around Lacey. "I can't believe we survived."

"You were so right, Dwight," Karina said. "The way that inspector went through everything was insane. Even with all the changes you made, he kept finding stuff to add."

"Yeah, Doc," Roy said. "I thought you were exaggerating, but the changes were necessary. I'm sorry I was too stubborn to see it earlier."

Dwight smiled at them. "This was a group effort. *We* did this." He gazed at Lacey. "Now who wants to celebrate?"

*   *   *

"Everybody, settle down," Lacey told the group assembled at the cafeteria the next morning. "I would like to announce that we passed the inspection!" She jumped up and down.

Everyone clapped. They already knew, of course—rumors flew around here—but it was still a thrill to officially hear it. They'd passed!

Lacey had arranged for a catering company to set up a breakfast buffet stocked with scrambled eggs, sausages, hash browns, even a waffle station, and not to be outdone, their own Singular breakfast cookies. By now, the food was mostly gone. They'd been eating and chatting for about an hour before Lacey stood and called them to order.

"Now that we've fulfilled Whole-Mart's requirements and our new production line is ready for use—thanks to our maintenance team; give it up for them—"

Lacey paused for the applause. The mechanics whooped and pounded the tables they'd joined so they could sit together

"—we can start hiring new employees. In charge of that will be our new human resources manager, Natalie Camacho."

Natalie waved her arms in the air to the applause.

"We'll start selling to every Whole-Mart in the state, with a new addition to our product line—the Quirky—and more coming on the pipeline. If that goes well, and I'm sure it will, the next phase will be to add a night shift so we can sell nationwide." She clapped, and everyone followed.

Lacey had done it. How could Karina ever doubt her? Lacey had proven time and time again that anything was possible. It was amazing to witness her dreams coming true.

"And," Lacey said. "I know there've been rumors that we were discontinuing the Flirty." She stared at Karina. "But the Flirty is not going anywhere. She's an important part of our family and our origins."

Karina choked up. Not only had Lacey fulfilled her dreams, but she'd included Karina in them. They would always be tied to each other and this company.

"Thank you all for your hard work these past months," Lacey continued. "You are what makes Singular, Singular. Each of you is an important part of this company, and it's because of your hard work that we've made it this far."

Karina cheered, looking around the room at the smiling faces. Tyler sat with the other dough preparers, whistling through his fingers. Rosa prayed to the heavens. Scott seemed oblivious, tapping on his phone. Others fist-bumped or high-fived each other. These people . . . they were her family. They meddled in her life and got mad at her when she messed up, but they also listened to her suggestions and cared about her well-being. All that time she'd been thinking she didn't need a family, she'd already had one. Singular was her home. This was where she belonged.

Her gaze found Ian, who was listening to whatever Brody was whispering in his ear. Maybe it was already too late, but she had nothing to lose and nothing to fear. The T-shirt she'd selected today read, *This hot mess is ready for her cleanup*, and it was so right. Her subconscious had known before she did. Ian met her gaze.

I'm capable of more than I think.

She stood up on a chair. "I'd like to say something." The crowd settled down, all eyes on her. "I know I can be a bitch sometimes, that I don't make it easy for people to like me, but you"—she gestured toward Ian—"you love me for some reason."

The room went silent. Ian raised his eyebrows. She took a deep breath.

"I know I said I wanted to keep work and personal separate, but this is my family, and I want them to know . . . I love you." Some gasps. "Yeah, that's right, I love him. I'm not as coldhearted as you think." She glared at Tyler. "I've been fighting my heart for so long, but I'm so tired. Some of you may think I'm weak and pathetic, but I don't care. I'm going for what I want, and what I want"—she gazed at Ian again—"is you."

Karina's heart had known since the moment she saw Ian, had tried to tell her all along, that Ian was "the one," her "soul mate," and every romantic cliché she didn't believe in. Or maybe she did. Love made you crazy. It changed you. And Karina had changed, but for the better.

Rosa muttered something in Spanish that sounded like approval. Brody slapped Ian's back. Ian's eyes shone with tears.

Karina wiped her face. "I'll do everything in my power for us to work. But it'll be hard. And messy. You still like messy, Ian?" She braced herself.

"I do." He grinned, both dimples on display. "I've missed messy." He stood, and Karina ran into his arms, kissing him. The room erupted in a cacophony of cheers, whoops, and applause, but it hardly registered. She was immersed in the calm ocean of Ian's embrace, safe once again.

Cookies were like people, not because they had a personality of their own but because they consisted of multiple ingredients that created a singular flavor profile. And someone could know when they'd found "the one" not because of a spark, but because that person accepted the cookie as it was and didn't want to change the recipe. That was Ian for Karina. There was no need to be afraid or lie to herself anymore. She did deserve him.

She deserved love.

AUTHOR'S NOTE

The idea for this book originated with a dream I had back in 2017 while I was pregnant with my first (and only) child. In it, a woman told a man she was pregnant, that she was going to keep it, and that he didn't have to be involved. From the dream I knew two more things:

1. The man and the woman worked together. They were standing outside the company I used to work at. Because of that company's process, I knew the man was a mechanic and the woman worked in production. They weren't college educated.
2. The man and the woman had been in a relationship but weren't together anymore.

That day, I wrote the scene where Karina gets pregnant accidentally (her name was always Karina). I thought this would be the first scene in the book and the story would be about him wanting to be involved despite her insistence that he not be, and how they would get back together because of the baby. To be honest, I thought this plotline was boring and overdone, but since I'm a believer in "telling the truth," as Stephen King mentions in his book *On Writing: A Memoir of the Craft*, I was willing to follow the story wherever it led.

From this scene, I knew Karina was the one who'd broken up the relationship. Then I wrote the scene of their first date and the first time they had sex. As I wrote, it became clearer that Karina didn't want a serious relationship and that was why she'd broken up with the man. It got me thinking: *If she doesn't want a serious relationship, why would she want to have a baby?*

That's when I knew she wouldn't keep it, so I was stuck with either adoption or abortion. But why would a woman like Karina subject herself to a pregnancy at all? That left only one choice: abortion. But I thought, if she had the abortion, the man would hate her forever and he wouldn't go back to her. I felt stuck.

You see, up to that point, my main exposure to abortion had been the story line in *Grey's Anatomy* where Cristina wanted an abortion but her husband didn't, and it created this huge conflict between them. Her getting the abortion destroyed their marriage, so I didn't know how to reconcile those two things. I put the story aside.

While being pregnant, it was hard for me to write. I couldn't sit for long periods, and I spent most of my time lying around. So it wasn't until my daughter was born that I began writing again. I had another novel I wanted to rewrite, but Karina's story remained in the back of my mind. And then one day I was mopping the floor when the thought came to me: What if instead of breaking them apart, the abortion was the thing that brought them together? I *knew* I had something.

I did some research. I was sure there were probably many stories that included abortion but was surprised to find they were in the minority. One article (Tripler, 2015) mentioned how a character having an abortion makes them unlikable, even though there are characters who are murderers or worse who are celebrated. Another article (Gueren, 2017) compiled anonymous stories of people who'd gotten abortions for all sorts of different reasons. In some of the stories, the woman had an abortion and ended up marrying their partner and having children with them later on. These were eye-opening. An abortion didn't have to be the end of a relationship. I'd always perceived abortion as this life-changing event, a decision that a person struggled with and ended up regretting. Though this can be true for some people, it's not true for all. For some, it's an easy decision and they don't regret it. I knew this would be the case for Karina, and I wanted to be true to her character.

Once I made the decision, everything clicked into place, and the story flowed. Some early critiques mentioned how they felt the abortion plotline was unnecessary or that I would lose half my readership, but I was determined to keep it. I fixed the story so that the abortion became essential to the resolution so that no one could force me to take it out. And I'm grateful no one did.

I was raised Catholic and always believed abortion was a sin. But I've also always lived under the teaching that you shouldn't judge other people, since you never know what's it like to be in their shoes. I'd always wanted a child, but in reality, I hated being pregnant and looked forward to when the baby would be out of me and I could finally have my body back. Having a child is full of challenges, and I wouldn't wish it on anyone who doesn't choose it.

This experience and my research helped me empathize with Karina and people like her in order to write the book. I hope those of you who have read can agree with me that this was the right choice for Karina, as it is for many other people. In the end, the lesson I want to emphasize is that everyone has the right to make the choices that are right for them and their situations, and the rest of us need to respect those choices and try to understand them.

While writing Karina's story, I sought other books and media that feature abortion in a respectful way. Here are some recommendations:

The Mothers by Brit Bennett
Red Clocks by Leni Zumas
Truth and Other Lies by Maggie Smith
Crazy Ex-Girlfriend, Season 2, Episode 4, "Why Won't Josh and His Friend Leave Me Alone?"
Jane the Virgin, Season 3, Episode 2, "Chapter Forty-Six."

References

Gueren, Casey. "Here's What It's Really Like to Have an Abortion." BuzzFeed. January 21, 2017. https://www.buzzfeed.com /caseygueren/heres-what-44-women-want-you-to-know-about -their-abortions

Tripler, Jessica. "Why We Need More Abortion Stories in Our Fiction." Book Riot. September 22, 2015. https://bookriot.com /need-abortion-stories-fiction/

DISCUSSION QUESTIONS

1. Bake a batch of each Singular Cookie to taste at your book club meeting. Which one is your favorite? Now go to www.singularcookies.com and take the quiz. Do the results match your choice?

2. Karina describes people as cookies. If you could choose any cookie to describe your personality, which one would you choose and why?

3. Karina also notices what everyone around her eats and the speed at which they eat their meal. What and how do you eat—mostly processed foods like Karina, home-cooked meals like Cordelia, raw food/vegetarian like Natalie, low calorie like Marisa, low carb like Ian, or somewhere in between?

4. Karina begins the story very judgmental about her friends' choices, then slowly becomes more tolerant as she learns more about their inner lives. Have you ever misjudged someone at first glance, then later changed your mind about them as you learned more? How have people misjudged you?

5. How did your opinion of Karina change throughout the book?

6. Karina's haven is the beach. What is yours?

7. The back of the book describes Karina as a Latina Fleabag. If you have watched the show, do you agree with this comparison? How are Karina and Fleabag similar? How are they different?
8. Karina gets accidentally pregnant and decides to have an abortion. Did this choice make sense for her? Do you think Ian's reaction was realistic?
9. The story is set at a fictional cookie manufacturing plant. Were you surprised by how cookies are produced at an industrial level? Were you expecting more of a bakery, like Ian says in the book?
10. Most of the characters are of Puerto Rican descent. Have you ever visited Puerto Rico? Would you like to? Which of the dishes mentioned in the book would you most like to try?
11. Do you think Karina and Ian's relationship will last? Why or why not?

RECIPES

SINGULAR COOKIES

Here are all the recipes for the Singular Cookies. I designed these cookies with the food industry in mind. They each feature a functional ingredient to increase their nutritional value, but feel free to add or replace ingredients. Mix and match if you want. The point is to have fun and express your own personality. Some cookies, like Bright and Active, were designed to be vegan, but you can make them all vegan (except Mellow) by using a flax egg instead. I used wheat flour and almond milk but use whatever fits your tastes and dietary needs. I can't wait to see your own creations!

Bright Cookie

2½ cups (224 g) old-fashioned oats
¾ cups (122 g) flour
¼ cup (35 g) coconut sugar
1 tsp baking powder
⅛ tsp salt
1 tsp ground cinnamon
¼ tsp ground nutmeg
¼ tsp ground cloves
½ cup (42 g) chopped walnuts
¼ cup (35 g) chopped dates
1 cup (93 g) grated carrots
½ cup + 1 tbsp (100 ml) milk
⅛ cup (66 g) maple syrup
1 flax egg

Mellow Cookie

2½ cups (224 g) old fashioned oats
¾ cups (122 g) flour
¼ cup (35 g) coconut sugar
1 tsp baking powder
1/8 tsp salt
½ tsp cinnamon
4 tbsp ground chamomile
1 ½ tsp lemon zest (approximately 1 large lemon)
2 tsp lemon juice
¾ cup (150 ml) milk
¼ cup (100 g) honey
1 egg

Perky Cookie

2½ cups (224 g) old-fashioned oats
¾ cups (122 g) flour
¼ cup (35 g) coconut sugar
1 tsp baking powder
⅛ tsp salt
½ tsp cinnamon
1 tbsp chia seeds
¼ cup (27 g) unsweetened cocoa powder
3 tbsp instant espresso powder
½ cup + 1 tbsp (100 ml) milk
¼ cup (66 g) maple syrup
1 egg

Flirty Cookie

2½ cups (224 g) old-fashioned oats
¾ cups (122 g) flour
¼ cup (35 g) coconut sugar
1 tsp baking powder
⅛ tsp salt
½ tsp cinnamon
3 tbsp maca root powder
½ cup (90 g) dark chocolate chips
½ cup (50 g) dried cherries
½ cup + 1 tbsp (100 ml) milk
¼ cup (66 g) maple syrup
1 egg

Active Cookie

2½ cups (224 g) old-fashioned oats
¼ cup (35 g) flour
½ cup (68 g) quinoa flour
¼ cup (35 g) coconut sugar
1 tsp baking powder
⅛ tsp salt
½ tsp cinnamon
2 tbsp whey powder
½ cup (145 g) peanut butter
½ cup (100 ml) milk
¼ cup (66 g) maple syrup
1 flax egg

Quirky Cookie

2½ cups (224 g) old-fashioned oats
¾ cups (122 g) flour
¼ cup (35 g) coconut sugar
1 tsp baking powder
⅛ tsp salt
½ tsp cinnamon
1 tbsp ground ginger
2 tbsp licorice root powder
½ cup (65 g) chopped almonds
½ cup (100 ml) milk
⅛ cup (30 g) maple syrup
1 egg

Motherly Cookie

2½ (224 g) cups old-fashioned oats
¾ cups (122 g) flour
¼ cup (35 g) coconut sugar
1 tsp baking powder
⅛ tsp salt
½ tsp cinnamon
2 tsp fresh ginger, grated
½ cup (70 g) dried apricots, chopped
½ cup (60 g) sunflower seeds
1 ripe banana, mashed
¾ cup (150 ml) milk
¼ cup (66 g) maple syrup
1 egg

Instructions:

1. Preheat oven to 350°F (177°C). Line a baking sheet with parchment paper.
2. If you want to use a flax egg, mix 1 tbsp ground flaxseed with 3 tbsp water. Let mixture sit in the fridge for at least 15 minutes. It should take on a thick consistency.
3. Add dry ingredients (oats, flour, sugar, baking powder, salt, spices, nuts/seeds, dried fruits, functional powders) to a large bowl and mix.
4. Add wet ingredients (milk, syrup, egg) and mix until everything is combined.
5. Scoop out batter onto baking sheet using a ¼-cup scoop. Flatten cookies with the outside edge of the scoop. You should get 10–12 cookies per batch.
6. Bake cookies for 15–18 minutes until brown. Cool on a wire rack before eating.
7. The cookies keep well in the freezer. Just take one out, pop it into the microwave, and enjoy!

ACKNOWLEDGMENTS

First of all, I'd like to thank God, for opening a window I didn't even know existed when all doors closed. Thank you for showing me this path and helping me find my passion.

To my wonderful agent, Lindsay Guzzardo, for helping me find new layers to this book, allowing me to go deeper into Karina and her journey. Thank you for your professionalism and for keeping me steady through the ups and downs of publishing.

To Toni Kirkpatrick, for loving my book and championing it. And to the Crooked Lane/Alcove Press team: Melissa Rechter, Holly Ingraham, Matthew Martz, Rebecca Nelson, Madeline Rathle, Dulce Botello, Thai Fantauzzi Perez, Hannah Pierdolla, Rachel Keith, and cover designer Sarah Brody. Thank you for valuing my input, answering my questions, and for all the hard work you put into bringing this book out into the world.

As is true for many writers, my debut is not the first novel I ever wrote. I'd like to thank the Scribophile writing community for helping me to learn how to write, especially Sue Seabury, Maggie Penn, Jennifer Ostromecki, and Rosie Amber Dibi. Additional thanks to Ken Loomes for his help with this book and his continued support.

Acknowledgments

To the Twitter writing community for their encouragement, opinion threads, writing advice, contests, and support. Special thanks to the #RevPit team for their services, and to Sione Aeschliman, Miranda Darrow, and Michelle Rascon for offering feedback on my query and first pages.

To the Women's Fiction Writers Association for their resources, programs, support, and encouragement. It is because of this group that I was able to connect with so many writers and learn about the publishing industry. Thanks to my mentor, Ramona DeFelice Long, for helping me see I needed to do a serious rewrite; to my critique group, Mary Beasley and Dawn Wingfield, for reassuring me I was on the right track; and to the Pitch Girls, Jocelyn Goranson and Susan Gambrell Reinhardt, for helping me streamline not only my pitch but my story.

To author Kelly Siskind for her first chapter critique and awesome advice on voice, book coach Lidija Hilje for her wonderful insight into Karina's arc, Peggy Loftus Finck for her great Query Quorum, and author Kristin Rockaway for her advice on comps.

To author Y. M. Nelson for replying to a tweet from a stranger and offering a wealth of information about what it's like to work inside a cookie manufacturing plant as well as for agreeing to read an early draft of this book. Any mistakes or deviations from facts are my own.

To Lainey Cameron, Angelia Ingram-Cook, Katherine Caldwell, Eliana Megerman, Madeline Lugo, and Janine Zänger for beta reading and offering me helpful feedback.

To Rebecca J. Sanford, thank you so much for sticking by me and for loving Karina and this story. Your words of encouragement and support have kept me going. I'm so happy we get to go on this journey together.

To Lyn Liao Butler for reading multiple drafts of this book, offering honest feedback, and just "getting" me and my book. Thank you for loving all my crazy ideas (the conversations with heart, the company ad) and for adding some of your own (the catfight). I'm so glad we connected and hope we can continue working together in the future.

Acknowledgments

To my grandmother (RIP), who shared with me her love of tele-novelas; my dad, for teaching me to love reading; and my mom, for showing me to love movies. These three building blocks have made me the writer I am today. Also, thank you to my daughter for helping me discover a new side of myself and loving me unconditionally.

Last but not least, thank you to my wonderful husband, Michael Müller, for your support, encouragement, and awesome drawing skills. It's because of you I even considered writing. Thank you for giving me the time, resources, and space to follow this new path and for always believing in me. Thank you for reading even though you mostly read fantasy books. The fact that you got emotional at the end meant the world to me. I love you and I'm so lucky to have you.